The Best Things in Life

Vanessa Walters was born in Barnet in 1977, and continues to live in North London. She was educated at Queen's College, Harley Street, and now attends University College London where she is reading Law.

Vanessa's first novel *Rude Girls* was published as a Pan paperback original in 1996. *Rude Girls* was a WH Smith Fresh Talent title. *The Best Things in Life* is Vanessa's second novel.

Also by Vanessa Walters in Pan Books

Rude Girls

Vanessa Walters

The Best Things in Life

PAN BOOKS

First published 1999 by Pan Books

an imprint of Macmillan Publishers Ltd
25 Eccleston Place, London SW1W 9NF
Basingstoke and Oxford
Associated companies throughout the world
www.macmillan.co.uk

ISBN 0 330 37565 2

9 8 7 6 5 4 3 2 1

A CIP catalogue record for this book is available from
the British Library.

Typeset by SetSystems Ltd, Saffron Walden, Essex
Printed and bound in Great Britain by
Mackays of Chatham plc, Chatham, Kent

In memory of James Nsabi.
A great man who watches over me in death
as he watched over me in life.

chapter
one

Sian turned to Deris and groaned.

'Don't distress yourself. By my Tag-Heuer I make it twenty minutes to closing time.'

Sian smiled. 'Tag-Heuer? Last month it was your Rolex. Before that you had, was it Omega? I can't remember. Anyway, what's with the fakes man? When you gonna buy a real watch?'

'On this pay? Let's try 3001.'

'I'll buy you one when I'm a famous singer.'

'Gee, thanks, but I won't hold my breath eh, Skinny?'

Sian gave a small laugh. 'Can you stop calling me that. I'm willowy.'

'Yeah, willowy like my golf club.'

'Oh, forget you, man. It's Friday and I've never felt so glad to get away from this shithole.'

'Thanks again.'

'No, you're safe, Deris, it just gets so hectic here sometimes. If it wasn't for you, I don't think I'd last till lunch. Every day you manage to come in smiling and cheering everyone up but don't you sometimes feel like a slave?'

'On these wages, I don't even think I'd get slave status.' Deris gave his watch another glance. 'I think we can start tidying up now.'

'Better not start facing up the shop just yet, Deris. There are still people in here and Alan gets annoyed if we start tidying before the customers have left.'

'Who cares? It's the weekend. When six o'clock gets here I'm out of those doors like a flash, customers or no customers. Sian, pass me one of them rubbish bags next to you so I can start cleaning up this space.'

Two middle-aged men in anoraks were comparing different types of hiking boots. Three giggly girls were holding up basketball shirts. In between, a tall, dark-haired young man wearing faded blue jeans and a black sweater had taken a Timberland jacket off its hanger and was trying it on. A shop assistant walked over to offer help. She received a curt rebuff so swept off indignantly towards the till point.

'Marianne, did I see you get blown out back there?' asked Sian, moving from behind her till to lean on the counter top opposite Marianne. Marianne pushed back her thick blonde curls.

'He doesn't know what he's missing,' she said, scowling.

'C'mon, girl. Don't take it personal. Besides, I thought you had a man.'

'So? Doesn't mean I can't pull. He has cute slanted eyes. See for yourself. What do you think, half Asian or half Oriental?' The two girls watched the young man replace the jacket, circle the clothing rail and take another jacket off its hanger.

'Not what I'd call kriss but if you like the "can't afford a jacket or a decent pair of jeans" look, then he'll do. Looks like he's gonna be there all night. Maybe you can try again later.'

Marianne rejected Sian's suggestion by turning her back on the object of their attention.

A tall woman in a swirling beige raincoat marched across the shop floor and dumped a shoe box on the counter.

'How m—'

'I bought these trainers here yesterday around mid-day for my son, but they don't fit. I want a refund, please.'

Sian opened the box, took the trainers out and checked the soles.

'That's no problem, madam. Can I see your receipt?'

'I'm afraid I don't have it on me.' The woman drummed her polished nails on the counter top.

'Well, I'm sorry—'

'Listen, I was in here yesterday. I was told that if they didn't fit I could have my money back. They don't fit, so what do you want a receipt for?'

'I believe you, madam, but I can't refund a purchase without a receipt.'

'It's the shop's own brand for heaven's sakes, girl, can't you read?'

Sian looked at Deris meaningfully and then at Marianne who was tidying a shelf of baseball caps and struggling not to laugh. Deris assumed a placatory expression.

'You know something, madam, there is a sticker on the till.' Deris stretched over and pointed to it. 'You see, no refund or exchange without proof of purchase.'

'I don't care about any stickers and I want a refund on these trainers, now!'

'There's nothing I can do but maybe you'd like to speak to the shop manager?' Sian suggested wearily.

'I'd better do that. Thanks.' The woman replaced the lid on the shoe box.

'I'll get him, he's in the stockroom,' said Marianne.

A few moments later, a small, balding man in his early thirties emerged from the stockroom. He smiled warily as he approached the till point.

'I'm Alan Richardson, the manager. Now, what is the problem?'

Sian briefly explained the situation.

'No, that's not quite right! I was told that I could return the trainers if they didn't fit. And they don't fit.'

'Who told you this?'

'I don't know. One of your staff. Possibly that blonde girl.'

'I'm afraid Marianne wasn't working yesterday,' said Alan Richardson, his hands drawing his tie tighter.

'I don't know. They all look the same in their tracksuits, don't they?'

'I'm sorry, madam, but there will be no refund until we see a receipt and that is the end of the matter. I don't make the regulations and there is nothing I can do without a receipt.'

'The customer is always right. Isn't that one of your bloody regulations?'

'That sort of language is not welcomed in this shop,' Alan Richardson replied curtly.

'Oh, damn your shop. Sportsworld? Doltsworld would be more appropriate,' the woman said as she picked up the shoe box, turned and walked out of the shop.

'What's a "dolt" anyway?' asked Marianne as Alan Richardson headed back towards the stockroom. He grunted in reply and disappeared.

'Tell me that I'm rich and famous and the last twenty years of my life have just been a very long nightmare.'

'Sorry, Sian. I'd really like to. But I'd be lying and that ain't my steelo.' Deris gave Sian a rueful grin. 'Anyway, it's Friday, man,' he continued briskly. 'Time to cool out and pop Moet down at Swingers.'

'Can I afford to go to Swingers, never mind pop Moet?' asked Sian, with raised eyebrows. 'Since you're obviously loaded what are you doing this weekend?'

'Oh, I'll probably take my woman out. Cinema, restaurant, you know my flex.'

'Which one is it this time?'

'Ayeisha and she's the beautifulest thing in this world.'

'Not like your usual hood rats then.' Sian dodged a punch. 'Only joking!'

'We're going to watch that new Spike Lee film then maybe hit a bar, buy a couple of drinks.'

'Lucky for some.'

'Why don't you come along?' asked Deris.

'On my jays? Thanks, but the idea of playing goose-berry to you two doesn't exactly thrill.'

'I'll bring a friend along. We'll double date.'

'Hey, don't make me sound like some charity case, I get men, OK. I'm just waiting for Mr Right.'

'You're just still crazy about Stephan,' said Deris, shaking his head. 'Why don't you admit it?'

'I was crazy to have that boy in my life,' said Sian with a sigh. 'I don't know why I don't just go out with you, Deris. I mean, even if you are short, fat and ugly, we'd manage.'

'With you being so lanky, dry-head and pop-eyed, I'm sure we'd do just fine.'

'OK, OK.' They both laughed.

'So, you ready for the singing competition then?' asked Deris.

'Yeah, I guess there's not much more I can do. I've practised the song enough times.'

'It's the song you wrote yourself, isn't it? You had one deejay guy mix up some music for you?'

'Yeah. The tune is my own though, I didn't buy that keyboard for nothing. This is an important night for me so I'm not gonna go out singing some other singer's tune. I'm gonna sing my own music.'

'When you win, ha ha, you could buy me a real watch, innit?'

'If I come first, I'll get studio time and some dough. If I come second the prize is three hundred and fifty pounds. Third prize, well, there's just one hundred pounds' worth of HMV gift vouchers.'

'Second place sounds good, then you could really buy me a Rolex and still have change.'

'The way my life's going right now, it'll be a surprise if I win anything. If I come first, I'll go to a studio, make a demo tape nobody's gonna give a second glance to and then I'll be back to square one. I'll try my best, but at the end of the day I'm not counting on anything.'

'So, if you come second, you're gonna spend it all on bills? No designer garms, a Mosh skirt or D&G bag?'

'I'll take Buelah somewhere nice, buy Lisa these shoes she's wanted for time and I'll get a bag for myself and maybe a dress or something. But I'm not inna that designer craze, man, it's just eating people up and – I don't believe this, oi, stop! Deris!' Sian ran out from behind the till point.

The young man glanced back over his shoulder as he ran towards the shop front; he was wearing a Timberland jacket. The alarm went as he streaked out of the door. Deris pushed past Sian and sped after him. By the time Deris reached the pavement the thief had faded into the evening rush.

'I swear he jumped on that seventy-three bus going down there,' said Deris, angrily clenching a fist as he came back into the shop.

'He's long gone. Might as well face it. You did your best.' Sian patted Deris on the shoulder. Alan Richardson was waiting for them at the till point.

'Marianne tells me that we have just lost a Timberland jacket. Sian, in my office now and Deris too. Marianne, take over Sian's till,' he snapped before walking away.

7

'You two are gonna get it,' said Marianne shaking her head. 'Deadly sin, that. Letting people steal the stuff.'

'Alan's always brewing about something. I think it's his one joy in life.'

Deris laughed uncertainly at this as they made their way towards Alan's office, past the ski accessories, golf clubs and tennis racquets.

'Look how knock-kneed he is,' continued Sian. 'Looks as though he needs a good meal and always fiddling with that tie of his. One day he's going to strangle himself.' She demonstrated. 'Oh, come on, Deris, you know I'm funny.'

'Yeah, Sian. Too funny. But I just wanna keep my job, you get me?'

Alan Richardson's office door was open.

'Come in,' he said, sitting back in his swivel chair. He rested his chin on his clasped hands and regarded Sian and Deris.

'Before you leave this evening, I will need a written description of what happened and what the man looked like for the police and our insurance company. But first, Deris, explain to me how this unfortunate incident occurred. No.' He raised a hand to silence Sian who had opened her mouth to reply.

'I don't know, y'know. It's just one of them things, innit? It's bad and that, it being a yout' an' that but it's the climate we live. Young people don't wanna work, they're confused.' Deris' voice trailed off.

'This is the fourth time this month. It's ridiculous. We're not talking socks or sweatbands here. That jacket was a hundred pounder.'

'It's yout's these days,' repeated Deris.

'It's you two and all your bloody talking! It's all you do. Chit-chat all day. You ignore the customers, you allow thieves to escape.'

'Well, that's not our job, to stop thieves, is it?' interrupted Sian indignantly. 'You should hire security for a shop like this with all the customers we get. You're lucky that man didn't turn round and give one of us a kick on the way out. Deris could've been knifed. In fact you're lucky, 'cos then he would be suing you. Deris is a hero.'

'Well, er, I . . .' Deris grinned sheepishly.

'Also,' Sian continued, 'how were we to know that the guy was a damn thief? He looked all right. Not like the usuals. You were on the shop floor and you didn't say anything.'

'I was sorting out an incident you had created with a customer.'

'Yeah, right.'

'Deris, you are over six foot, quite athletic. With those long legs of yours I'm sure if you had been alert, you would have managed to catch the culprit. I suppose you also refuse to accept responsibility too?'

'Well, mmm—'

'Deris, don't back down. It ain't our fault.'

'No.' Alan Richardson leaned forward. 'It never is, is it, Sian? You are consistently rude and idle. You arrive late and leave early. Whenever an incident occurs, however, it is never your fault. You always have some excuse. I'd be interested to know how you think you earn your salary because I'm baffled.'

'Yo, I work as hard as anyone else here.'

'Maybe it's the singing. Yes, I know, one day you'll be a famous pop star and you'll tell me where to stick the job. But, until then, you'll earn every penny the hard way.'

Sian shook off Deris' restraining arm. 'I'm telling you where you can stick your job now!'

'Sian, calm down,' said Deris, looking concerned.

'No, Deris, I quit. Alan can't push me around and treat me like I'm some school kid. I'm not having it.'

'Sian, I'm sure you remember that there's a two-week notice period. But I accept your resignation two weeks from now. Perhaps, when you're gone, I could give your wages to a security guard. Then we'd all be happy, wouldn't we?'

'Whatever,' Sian snapped, as she turned and strode out of the office.

chapter
two

As the tube rattled towards Walthamstow, Sian caught sight of her reflection in the dusty window. She didn't really look like star material. Her hair was neither brown nor properly black, neither long nor short and there was nothing about her face that was striking. She wasn't unattractive but at the same time there was nothing in her appearance that was going to stop traffic. She chewed on her pen. She wanted to get the song done before she got home. For Sian, song writing was a spontaneous but often frustrating process. Now she was trying to remember a line that had come to her earlier that afternoon. After a while she yawned and stopped writing. Her head lolled towards her shoulder and she drifted off into a dream where she was on stage with a vast sea of faces before her. *Sian*, they roared as she stepped forward. Then she took the microphone off its stand and her lilting voice silenced the crowd . . .

At the entrance of Walthamstow tube station, Sian slowed, allowing the scrum of other passengers to rush past her. After the sweaty, crowded tube train, she found the chilly mid-November twilight exhilarating. She crossed the busy road and hurried towards the bus depot. She clambered onto a waiting bus, bought a ticket and found a seat upstairs. Another stressful day had taken its toll and Sian sat, leaning against the window, watching the world go by as the bus slowly ground its way along Hoe Street towards Leyton.

Twenty minutes later, after a drive punctuated by the honking of frustrated horns and the grating of brakes, the bus turned a corner and the bluish-white lights of the Leyton Rise Estate finally came into view. Sian brought up the rear as half the bus emptied onto the pavement.

An unusual stillness lurked in the shadows around the poorly lit tenement blocks as the bus passengers made their way up the sloping drive towards the housing estate. It was too dark for playing out but too early for making trouble. Apart from the distant blare of a police siren it was quiet. Sian slowed as she reached the first of the four worn-out blocks. She looked up at the twelve-storey block to her left. It was impossible to tell if Lisa was home. Then she remembered the lift wasn't working in Lisa's block and decided she couldn't face the stairs. Instead she turned towards the rundown block of flats on her right, where she lived. A harsh floodlight chased away the shadows. The smell of cheap industrial-strength bleach masked less pleasant odours. The steel lift opened its scratched and rusty doors revealing 'Thugs iz uz' in iridescent blue spray-paint on the back wall.

Sian got into the lift and punched a button. The doors grated closed and the rusty machinery squealed into action. At the eighth floor she stepped out and walked along the landing to the family flat, looking out as she did so at the other brooding blocks of the estate. From the balcony she could just make out the building site along the back of the estate. The five rows of houses being built were the first of the new homes for the residents of Leyton Rise Estate, which would eventually be pulled down. Before she reached her front door, it opened and Buelah stood barring her way, a halo of fuzz around her untidy plaits.

'What are you trying to do, Buelah? Scare people?'

'That was exactly fifty seconds slower than your usual sprint, Sian. I'm ashamed of you.'

'Well, I'm tired and you should have better things to do than time people. Now move.'

'Move, transport, transfer, shift, relocate, even budge. Next time, use your imagination,' retorted Buelah, cracking her gum as Sian barged past.

'Give me some, please.' Sian held out a hand as her younger sister followed her into the kitchen.

'Sorry, it's my last one.'

'All right, be like that, but don't expect to come to my room this evening then.'

'OK, OK. God, you're so mean,' complained Buelah with a rueful grin as she produced another stick of gum from the pocket of her faded jeans.

'Where's Mum?' asked Sian, putting the gum into her mouth.

'In the living room, with Mrs Dega,' whispered Buelah.

'Great,' groaned Sian as she opened the refrigerator. 'They'll be in there all night.'

She took out a carton of apple juice and poured some into a glass. 'What's the problem this time?'

'Mr Dega,' said Buelah with a cautious glance at the doorway. 'He's been at the betting shop again.'

'Dat Keaton. Me nuh kno' what fe' do with dat husban' of mine,' mimicked Sian.

Buelah giggled. She perched on the kitchen table. 'Lately she's been having loads of problems with Mr Dega and Ceelie. Especially since Ceelie's had the baby.'

'I know Mrs Dega's Mum's best friend but I don't know how much more of this I can take. She's always here!' Sian walked over to the stove. 'What's for dinner?' she asked, looking in the various pots. 'There's no food left and I haven't eaten since morning.'

'Well, there won't be any dinner until that Mrs Dega's gone. Maybe we'll get Chinese,' said Buelah hopefully.

Sian sank into one of the white plastic chairs by the kitchen table and yawned.

'Ooh, hard day?' asked Buelah in a fake honeyed tone.

'So what did you do at your school today then, Boffin, that's made you so feisty?'

'We had the netball try-outs.'

'And I suppose you were well in there.'

'Yeah, actually. I scored nuff. But I like football better, netball's too girly. Football's a real game.'

'Is it so wrong to be a girl, Buelah?'

Buelah snorted in derision. 'Like you? All you and Lisa ever do is talk about boys and clothes and parties.'

'You don't have any friends to talk to, geek. When you're my age and you have biceps and a 'tache, don't come crying to me.' Sian stood up. She drained her glass and set it down by the sink. 'So who's washing this lot up?' She pointed to the pile of plates in the sink.

Buelah shrugged.

'Get to it, Buelah.'

'I'm not doing it!' Buelah protested. 'You know it's your turn to wash up.'

'Me? Do you know how many hours I worked today?'

'Yes, but Mum was at the hospital and I was at school.'

'Well, it better stay there then, 'cos I sure as hell ain't doing it.'

Sian left the kitchen, crossed the linoleum in the narrow hallway and, deliberately avoiding the living room, ran up the stairs. Buelah followed.

'Aren't you even going to say good-evening to Mrs Dega?' Buelah asked between cracks of gum.

'Nah, I'm too tired. I've had a crazy day today. I quit my job.' Sian entered her room and eased off her trainers. She threw herself full-length on the bed.

'Oh man, how exciting. What happened?'

'I'm tired, B. All my friends have found proper jobs or gone back to university. I'm stuck in a dead-end job. I'm tired of being shouted at, tired of dealing with idiot customers, tired of being made to look stupid when people come in and steal stuff 'cos the manager's too mean to hire security staff.'

'Someone stole something?'

'Yeah, some guy ran out with a Timbo jacket and they started trying to pin blame on me and Deris.'

'Did he hurt you?'

'Nah, he was trying the jacket on one minute and the next he had dashed out with it on.'

'That was stupid. It's gonna have a tag, right?'

Sian shrugged. 'They just melt those things off. Anyway, I'm always getting blamed for something in that shop. They don't even pay us decent money, so I said, "Hey, I don't have to put up with this. I quit!"'

'Lord 'ave mercy,' said Buelah, melodramatically clapping a hand to her head. She giggled with Sian. 'That's just how Mum's gonna say it. Lord 'ave mercy upon my soul.'

Sian rolled her eyes then sat up.

'Bet you're sorry now.'

'Hell, yeah. I got Mercury bills, credit card bills, overdraft bills. Plus it's Mum's birthday in two weeks then it's Christmas. If I don't come first or second in Sunday's competition, I'll be screwed up like Mrs Dega's jheri-curl.'

Buelah stifled her giggles.

'It's true, y'know, Sian. It's all nasty and dripping with grease. I saw the inside of her hat after church on Sunday and it was black and soggy around the rim.'

'Forget her, man. What am I gonna tell Mum? It's Friday so you know she's gonna be asking me for money for the rent.'

Buelah scratched her head.

'Well, she might be OK, 'cos it's not a church night.'

'So what?'

'Mum's more moany on a church night, she keeps talking about what's wrong with the world and how she has to live right and all that.'

'Hmm. I'll tell her after the competition,' Sian said, taking her phone out of her bag. 'Damn, my battery ran out, no wonder I didn't get any calls.' She got off the bed and bent down to plug her charger into the socket. She rested the charger on her desk, slotted the phone into it and checked her voicemail.

'What the hell is Tiffany on now?' Sian exclaimed. 'She's left five messages.'

'Oh, she rang twice since I got back from school.'

'Did she say what it was about?'

'Nah. She wouldn't tell me, she treats me like I'm three, not eleven,' said Buelah in disgust.

'Yeah, well, Tiffany has a mental age of about six, and it's much worse to be twenty-one and act six than it is to be eleven and act three, trust me.'

Buelah nodded and they laughed as Sian dialled Tiffany's number.

'Hi, Sian!' Tiffany exclaimed. 'Where have you been? I've left x amount of messages on your damn phone. I've got so much drama to tell you.'

'OK, hold up, one minute.' Sian stacked the pillows behind her. She mimed a yawn then raised her eyebrows at Buelah. 'Yeah, I'm ready.'

'I miss him.' Tiffany sniffed exaggeratedly.

'And that was your drama? Girlfriend, we've been over this. The guy isn't worth all this stress. He only went out with you in the first place because you're blonde and a model. Plus he's too damn moody. Remember that time when you and him were driving home from Samantha's and he got so angry because he thought you had been looking at some guy that he crashed the car.'

'He was just driving too fast. It had nothing to do with our argument.'

'That makes it all right I suppose? Anyway, he's been giving you backhanders and don't you dare deny it.'

'What gave you that idea?'

'We all know, Tiffany. Slick told me. He's Leon's bre and he's my cousin, of course he's gonna tell me. As soon as the man got what he wanted he started cheating on you, slapping you and now he's had his kicks he's dumped you for this "mystery woman". I told you not to get involved with any Leyton bres long before you moved out of Leyton Rise, but you wasn't responding to no one so now take the shame and move on.'

'Leon is not what I'd call a Leyton bre. Leyton bres sit on the wall behind the estate and smoke weed and wear Mosch caps with the labels hanging out. Leon doesn't even *live* in Leyton.'

'Stratford. Big deal. It's still our manor.'

'Besides, when he's not moody, Leon is the most tender and protective guy in the whole world. No one else comes close, he can be your best friend—'

'And I can be Pastor Matthews.'

'Very funny. Sian, he says things that make your toes curl up.'

'Until he gets what he wants.'

'Well, all the girls in this area are after him. Even Lisa.'

'That's 'cos she's just as superficial as you are. OK, the brother is kriss, but I just don't think someone who calls you his bitch is that nice a person. Call me stupid but maybe I think you just like him because he has dollars in his pockets and is going to be some famous footballer any day now. He's like a trophy and he knows it.'

'Well, looks are sixty per cent and money is thirty per cent so I didn't do too badly. Anyway, I love him. I must really love him otherwise I wouldn't care. I meet plenty of guys that's driving sports cars and playing football and they don't phase me. Why do you hate him, anyway? What did he ever do to you?'

'Well, for one thing, about three weeks ago, when we were all at Buzz bar he told me I would be quite pretty if I were a few shades lighter. Don't laugh, Tiffany. I didn't think it was very funny.'

'Oh, come on, it must have been a joke.'

'Then he told Lisa that when he had finished with you she was next on his list.'

'Why didn't you tell me?'

'Oh, come on, Tiffany. I'm sure it was just a joke,' said Sian in a honeyed tone.

'You're so mean. When Stephan dumped you, wasn't I there offering my shoulder?'

'Thanks for the memory but actually all I remember is you telling me about how you met Four-Play at some party and how one of them made moves on you.'

'Anyway, I don't care about the bad things he's done. I just want him back.'

'If you've got time that needs wasting, go ahead,' retorted Sian.

There was a pause.

'So, um, anything else been, er, happening?' Tiffany asked.

'Well, I suppose the highlight of the week is that

Lisa got the Dolce and Gabbana dress she was looking at for weeks, to wear for her mystery date.'

'Oh? Which one?'

'I don't know. She's been seeing him for around one, two weeks now and she calls him the best kept secret.'

'Not the guy, idiot, the dress. Who gives a damn what guy Lisa is seeing? She's always got about ten on the go at once. What dress did she buy?'

'Oh no, I'm not falling for that one again, Tiffany. The last time I told you what dress Lisa bought you went and got the same one and I never heard the end of it.'

'Forget you. I'll find out from Vanya.'

'Whatever, I'll leave the designer-label war to you and Lisa.' Sian yawned. 'I don't have money to waste now that I'm practically unemployed.'

'Hmmm.'

'Yeah, it's true, I lost my job.'

'Sssh, listen, I've just got the wickedest idea to get Leon back. All I've got to do is invent some mystery man, someone rich, good-looking and averagely famous. But not mega, that would be too obvious.'

'Why bother? It just makes you look desperate.'

Tiffany sighed and her tone was defensive. 'I've been hurt before and then I just walked away and cried alone. This time I'm gonna fight. I don't care who this girl is, it could be Naomi Campbell, but that man is mine!'

'Well, it's not likely to be Naomi Campbell since I've never seen Leon with a girl darker than a milky-bar.'

'I better get off the phone, there's this model's party on Saturday night and I've got to tidy up my place tonight.'

'Anything good?'

'Well yeah, I think it's going to be a really flashy affair, lots of stars and journalists, beautiful clothes and all the prettiest models are going to be there. I know that sort of thing intimidates you so I, er, asked Lisa to come with me instead.'

'Oh.'

'Anyway, I'm taking my camera so I'll show you all my pictures. Jeez! Is that the time? Well, I'm glad to hear everything's fine with you, I'll speak to you tomorrow. Bye.'

'Bye.'

Sian stretched. She studied the small room, her keyboard on its stand beside the mahogany wardrobe, the desk piled high with clutter and the old black and white television at the foot of the bed. She didn't want to go to any of Tiffany's parties anyway. She didn't have long hair, 38DD breasts or know her Exté from her Gaultier so she didn't really see the point. And although she sometimes felt like 21 going on 52, if being like Tiffany meant allowing men like Leon to walk all over you, she was better off out of it.

Buelah turned away from the television. 'What did Tiffany want?'

'That girl is crazy. I'm worn out with her foolishness. She just can't let go.'

'Can't let go, huh? Are you talking about yourself?' Buelah enquired innocently.

'Har, har, feistly lickle wretch. What I wanna know

is why a celebrity party would intimidate me but not Lisa or Tiffany.'

'Maybe because Lisa and Tiffany are fun and know lots of boys and you don't.'

'What do you mean fun?'

'Well, Lisa's always buying new clothes and going out with guys and you don't go anywhere. You don't like any of Lisa's boyfriends and you never do anything good with your hair.'

'So you think I'd be better off if I went out all the time and had boys calling me twenty-four-seven?'

'Well, they are both really pretty, and they always make me laugh when they talk about themselves but I think you're better than them, Sian. You're smarter than them and they're always getting into trouble and crying and you don't. At least you can sing and make music on your keyboard. I bet they wish they could.'

Buelah stood up and stepped across to the window. She opened it and looked out.

'Lisa's coming,' she said. 'She's just leaving her block. She'll be here in about –' Buelah checked her watch '– five minutes.'

'How long were you spying through that window before I came, B?' asked Sian sarcastically from her star-shaped position on the bed.

'Ever since that stupid Mrs Dega came.'

'She's not that bad.'

'I hate her. Mummy tells her all my problems and that woman just loves to stick her nose in. "Bernie, you too sof'. My pick'ny now, dem get one slap you see and whatever dem was doing, dey jus' stop it quicktime."'

'True.'

22

'And I don't think she can read properly because she's always asking Mum to explain letters to her and stuff.'

'Not everyone is like you. Teacher's pet.'

'Yeah, I know.'

Buelah walked across to the door.

'The doorbell hasn't rung yet, where are you going?' asked Sian, sitting up as Buelah opened the bedroom door and slipped out.

'I know,' Buelah called back, as she thundered down the stairs. 'But I like to time people.'

chapter
three

Buelah followed Lisa back into Sian's bedroom and sat on the floor next to the door.

'Hi, Skinny,' said Lisa, walking over to the bed and hugging her friend. 'Buelah's been telling me what happened. What are you going to do?'

'I think Deris was more worried for me than I was. He nearly cried. Anyway, how are you, Miss D and G?' asked Sian, smiling back.

Lisa smoothed down her neon pink denim dress. 'It's Versace actually and it looks da bomb, nah true?'

Sian nodded. Lisa walked over to Sian's over-flowing desk and surveyed the panorama of photos tacked up above. Buelah as a baby, cousin Slick in his younger days, Sian's grandparents, Lisa and Sian as toddlers, the whole crew on a girls' night out and a faded one of Sian's father and mother on their wedding day.

'That one of Slick is new.'

'Yeah, last time I was over at Aunt Cherry's house I raided their photos and took it.'

'Sian, this room is a shithole. I thought you were going to do something.'

'I tried.'

'You just changed the pictures around. More pictures of Stephan—'

'Nah, it's the same number.'

'Don't take me for fool, Sian. I can see, y'know. Look, Stephan at home, Stephan at the Equinox, Stephan at work, why don't you just dedicate your whole wall to the creep?'

'He just liked to take pictures. So what?'

'An' why put up that one of me in the off-key gold suit at the carnival? It looks so dated. That was back in the ragga days, when I didn't know any better.'

'I wanted a change. I can't have the same ones all the time.'

'Sian. I know I keep saying this but I hate this room. This room is so poky and everything is so brown.'

'It isn't. The wallpaper is beige and the wardrobe is mahogany.'

'The carpet is definitely brown and all them other colours you mentioned sound brown to me. Anyway, you know what I mean. How you ever gonna keep a man with a room like this? Don't you realize people can tell a lot about you from your room.'

'Yeah?'

'When you go in Tiffany's new flat, you see Versace and Mosch in her wardrobe. She has lovely pine floorboards, pretty white net curtains and a top-dollar sound system.'

'Yes, I've been there too.'

'When you go in my room, you see the D and G in

25

effect, and a colour scheme, pink and white, nice dressing table with all my make-up neatly on top. Top of the range stereo, top of the range television. When people go into Tiffany's room, they'll say, "Rah, this girl's goin' places, spends her wong wisely, her room is kriss and so is she, maybe I'll stick around." Any man can look at my room and he'll see that everything in there is name-brand. Clothes, stereo, television and he'll know I'm a designer broad also. But when they see *your* room, Sian, with brown this and brown that and that rubbish TV, guess what they're gonna think of you!'

'Well, the money isn't there. You gonna pay for it?'

'Great! No man and now no money either. Sian, are you crazy? OK, you know I'm here for you, but lately you've been doing a lot of off-key things.' Lisa walked over to the desk and knelt down to pick up some loose papers that had fallen onto the floor. 'Anyway, it doesn't take money to keep your desk tidy.'

'For real,' said Sian, sighing. 'Most of the paper is Buelah's. She never clears up.'

'You always blame everything on me,' complained Buelah.

'You two are as bad as each other,' said Lisa. 'Anyway, I see Mrs Dega was here. Her and your mum were going out as I came in. What's Mrs Dega been saying about my mum this time? I know she's always got something to say. "Dat white woman yam black man like I yam rice 'n peas." "Tek' dat white woman pick'ny, Lisa. How come everytime I see her she wid a different man."'

Sian and Lisa laughed.

'Your mum looks as though she's lost a little weight,' Lisa continued.

'Are you sure? She looks just as fat to me.'

'Your mum's not really *fat* fat. It's just breasts and hips.'

'And thighs and stomach and arms, eh, Buelah.' Sian grinned over at Buelah. 'She's been on my case too much lately. Still trying to get me to go back to church.'

'Is there any point? You haven't been to church for about a year now apart from the odd convention. Anyway you're tainted goods now, like me.'

'Listen, if I'm tainted goods, then you have a government health warning on you.'

'Very funny. Anyway, I've got major biz to tell you,' said Lisa, sitting down on the bed next to Sian.

'What is it about me that everyone has to tell *me* their drama? Why not Tiffany or Vanya or Ebela?'

'Ebela's studying all the time, Vanya is practically married so she's not interested in mentalk, Tiffany, well, telling her your drama is like broadcasting it to the nation on the BBC. You're the only one left with any sense.'

'Goodbye, Buelah,' said Sian. 'Don't act like I can't see you there beside the door, just splurt.'

'Oh, please. I'm not gonna tell anybody Lisa's drama.'

'No, go and do your homework or watch telly. There's no one downstairs now.'

Buelah got up slowly then with her hand on the door handle she turned around. 'I hate you and I'm never giving you any of my gum again,' she said as she swept out of the room slamming the door behind her.

'And don't eavesdrop with that cup thing either,' Sian called out.

'What cup thing?' asked Lisa.

'Miss Boffin made one of those phone things with two plastic cups and a piece of string and she hid one of the cups over there by the door and last time Stephan was here she listened to the other end in her room. Thank Jesus we were just talking,' Sian said, chuckling. 'Don't get me wrong. I rate my sister. She's bright, but I have to show her who's in control here.'

'You're so dark to her,' said Lisa, laughing.

'You say that every day. She brings it on herself. She's only eleven and yet she's all up in people's business. She's too clever for her age, man. When I was eleven I was so innocent and quiet. I think it's good for kids to be a bit dumb. You wouldn't believe we were sisters.' Sian took out her chewing gum and threw it in the small bin next to the bed.

'Well, you look exactly the same. Both long and skinny as rakes and even though you're quite light compared to Buelah, you both have the same features.'

'What do you mean? I look like my dad, long face, slanty eyes. Buelah looks like my mum, round face, little nose and big eyes.'

'I guess you're right. I think I mean the way you cuss, you both have the same ways.'

'That's 'cos Buelah copies my steelo.'

'The way you walk, the way you laugh, the way you both do this snake recoil thing with your neck when you're pissed off.'

'You do that too.'

'That's 'cos I picked it up from you when we were

about Buelah's age. Man, we were so dumb. Buelah's reading books and is really mature, we were still singing "My Name is".'

'What are you on about now?'

'Come on, Sian, you remember.' Lisa stood up. 'First we'd clap and sing, "My name's Elizabeth Taylor, I'm a movie star. I got a cute, cute figure and a sexy bra." Then we'd gyrate our hips and chant "Elizabeth, Elizabeth, ooh ahh, Elizabeth, Elizabeth, ooh ahh". The other one was Marilyn. "My name is Marilyn Monroe and I know how to sing. I got ruby red lips and a diamond ring. Marilyn, Marilyn, oh no. Marilyn, Marilyn, oh no." Then we'd do our own names. "My name is Lisa Peters, I'm a pretty girl. When I grow older, gonna rule the world. Lisa, Lisa, oh no. Lisa, Lisa, oh no."'

'Refresh my memory, what did I used to say?' asked Sian with a smile.

'"My name's Sian Wallace, I sing heavenly. Gonna be a star like Mariah Carey."'

'Mariah Carey wasn't out then,' Sian pointed out drily.

'Who cares?' Lisa said settling back down on the bed. 'I've got bigger news.'

'The best kept secret?'

'Yeah.'

'This time, you're gonna give me a name, right?'

'Well, he's asked me out officially so I guess I can. It's Leon.'

'You lie!'

Lisa got up and danced around the bed laughing.

'Not Tiffany's meltdown-good-looks Leon?'

Lisa held out her hand on which a little gold bracelet jangled.

'Lisa, sit down. How can you be so dark to Tiffany? She is crazy in love with Leon. All this time, *you're* the one who's been seeing her man?'

'Not her man any more.'

'She's one of us, Lisa. She's been a Rise girl from day one same as Vanya or Ebela.'

'She'll get over it. It's no biggie. Tiffany's always flirted with the guys I've been out with. So call it payback time.'

Sian stood up and put her hands on her hips.

'Payback time? Listen up. The girl was crying eye-water down the phone not fifteen minutes ago, like she gonna slit her wrists or something. She's telling me, Oh I want him so bad, I love him, I can't live without him, and you're talking about *payback time*. That's fucked up, Lisa.'

'Yeah, but I know what I'm doing, I'm not a little girl any more,' said Lisa defensively. 'Besides, Sian, you're acting high and mighty but I bet if Leon asked you out instead of me you would've been tempted.'

'I doubt it. Everything about him spells trouble, but even if I was tempted I wouldn't go out with him if he was dealing with one of my best friends. I'm thinking differently of you now, Lisa. If you can do this to Tiffany, you could do it to me too.'

'Tiffany's a whiney bitch who'll get over it. You're my bonafide. It's not the same. Furthermore, she couldn't feel the way I do about him.'

'The two of you only want him because he has kriss

wheels and money and will soon be a famous footballer. Do you even know him? He beat Tiffany up couple times and he'll start on you once he gets what he wants.'

Lisa gave a sheepish giggle at which Sian put her hand to her head and fell back onto the bed.

'You have *no* respect for his relationship with Tiffany.'

'If he doesn't respect his relationship with Tiffany, why should I?'

'Because Tiffany's your friend and he's just another egg in your basket. You can call it competition but you knew she loved him. Ain't no excuse on this earth can change that. You knew.'

There was silence. Lisa gloomily eyed her gold-painted fingernails.

'So, what was it like then?'

'Oh, after all that, now you want to know what it was like sleeping with him?'

Sian looked embarrassed. 'I'm just curious. I mean, both you and Tiffany are crazy about him and he's a creep so I want to know what he has going for him. If you and Tiffany are going to be comparing notes any-way, what's the problem?'

'Well, let me put it like this. The brother is fine with his clothes off and ain't nuthin' wrong wit' tha' bump-n-grind,' said Lisa, putting on an American accent. Sian held out her palm and Lisa slapped it, the girls looked at each other and collapsed into giggles because the world was good but the oneness they shared was better.

'But don't tell a soul. I don't know how Tiffany's gonna take it. Leon's mine but you're right, Tiffany *is* a

Rise girl and I don't wanna screw up our friendship, so I'm just gonna keep it on the downlow until she gets used to being without him.'

'You should have thought of that before causing all this trouble for a guy who isn't even worth it. When are you and Tiffany gonna realize that the best things in life do not come driving a red Lotus.'

'Forget you,' said Lisa with a dismissive snort. 'What drama's been happenin' in your life then, girl? Apart from losing your job.'

'Nothing too tough. I've been practising for the competition.'

'Where's the boyfriend?'

'What do you mean by that?'

'Exactly what I just said. You've been boyfriend-less for months now. Why don't you get yourself a man?'

'I'm not like you, out with a different man every week, I'm waiting for Mr Right,' said Sian.

'Run that past me again? Sian, don't talk cack. You don't rave any more. You never hang out in the manor. When guys try talking to you you act stoosh and scare them away. If you was trying to find Mr Right you'd be out there, looking. What's wrong with Casey? He's fine and he drives a Beamer.'

'The local dealer. No thanks.'

'Or there's Shankar. Shankar ain't all that but he drives a convertible and he wears designers.'

'The Shankar with a couple of kids on this very estate?'

'OK then, how about Andre? He's stone broke but he's really smart, at university and he's sweet.'

'Andre's no fun. Anyway, he's from my church so that's an instant no.'

'I can't win, can I? Who were you expecting anyway? Devonia from Four-Play? This is Leyton Rise, Sian. You need to get with the programme.'

'I just want to be single right now. Why are you and Deris on my case? Is there anything wrong with cooling out for a bit?'

Lisa wagged a finger. 'Yeah, but I just know this has somethin' to do with Stephan. Why can't you give up the ghost, Skinny? I know for a fact that he's chasin' other girls right this minute and doesn't give a damn about you.'

'I know that. But I loved Stephan and even though he made me hate him, I still love him. I love him with a passion. One day with him was worth more than a week with any other guy.'

'He was kriss but you're just gonna have to forget him, baby,' said Lisa softly, putting her hand on Sian's shoulder.

'Well, I've tried to forget him but I can't. You wouldn't understand, you're always being chased by men and you've never been dumped either.'

'Just because some guy pops your cherry, that doesn't mean you have to marry him and live happily ever after.'

'Sssh, Buelah might be listening. Anyway Stephan has nothing to do with me not wanting to date guys. Let's change the subject. Let's talk about the competition that's going to launch me into the bright lights.'

'Sian, you know you're gonna win already, so why

don't you just relax, sit back and let it move you?' Lisa giggled.

'It's not funny any more. Lately I've been realizing how much I want to get out of here. When I was a kid I thought Leyton Rise was the place to be. I knew everyone and you were just in the opposite block. All the boys hung out on the wall around the back and if one of them spoke to me I thought I was blessed. But then I woke up and saw it for what it really was: a blind alley for all the losers and problem families God put on this earth.'

'What, this palace?' exclaimed Lisa. 'Girlfriend, how can you be so ungrateful? How many homes do you know what have their own lift? Why would you wanna give up a view that goes all the way to Leyton railway station and don't forget the in-house entertainment. It's not everywhere that you can listen to your neighbour's drum and bass CD for free.' Lisa gave Sian a high-five and they laughed.

'You know where I'm coming from, Lisa. There must be more to life than the Stephans and Andres and Leons of this world. And just looking at trainers and tennis racquets every day of the bloody week at "Sports-world" is starting to make me feel sick.'

'I thought you liked your job.'

'They don't pay me enough to like it. I just about bear it. I wish I could do hair like you.'

'Don't watch that. The pay isn't any better and the hours are long and hot. The women cuss you behind your back in patois they know you can't follow and the men leer at you when they come in to have their hair cut.'

'That should suit you-ow!' Sian rubbed her arm and then grinned unapologetically. 'So, I hear you're going with Tiffany to this party tomorrow night. Too upmarket for the likes of ugly old me, huh?'

Lisa clapped a hand over her mouth.

'Damn, I completely forgot! I'm going out with Leon tomorrow. Tiffany's gonna kill me.'

'Yep, she was really excited about it.'

'Anyway, she only asked me today when she popped into Cutting Edge and I was rushed off my feet and with Tiffany being white, people always wonder what she's doing in there, so I just agreed. How come you're not going?'

'She didn't invite me. Said it wasn't my scene. I don't mind, specially as it's the night before the competition and in a way she's right. You and Tiffany are both pretty and have nice clothes and know how to flirt and stuff.'

'That's cack. Tiffany's pretty but she's so false, especially when she's talking to some rich guy or something. It just puts people off her. Plus she's boring, always going on and on about her shoots and who she knows. That said, Tiffany probably didn't mean it like how it sounded. She doesn't think deep enough to come up with a put-down like that.'

'Forget her. Where are you off to tonight?'

'Leon's takin' me out. He said it's a surprise but the champers will be in effect. Must be a party of some kind.'

'What are you doing tomorrow?'

'I'm workin' tomorrow, how 'bout you?'

'I'm not working but I promised I'd baby-sit Buelah

for Mum in the afternoon 'cos she's doing something for the church. In the morning I'll probably practise my song.'

'When you're turnin' down Michael Jackson for duets, you'd better remember your bestest friend, y'know,' warned Lisa, getting up.

'Don't you mean "if?"'

'Whatever. I'm goin' now to call my best kept secret. See ya.'

'Yeah, call me tomorrow to tell me how it went.'

'Are you sure you can handle the details?'

Sian picked up a pillow and hurled it at Lisa. 'Go home, you freak.'

chapter
four

Sian changed into an old jean skirt and T-shirt and went downstairs. Buelah was curled up on the sofa in front of the television.

'Mum still not back?'

'She went to get dinner. I think she couldn't afford Chinese, so we're having something from The Carib,' Buelah said without looking up.

'What's this film about?'

'Why don't you watch it and see, you punk?'

Sian kissed her teeth and bent down to pick up the phone.

'When Mummy catches you on the phone, she's gonna beat you,' said Buelah smugly. 'Last month the bill was full of mobile calls.'

'Did anyone ring for me?'

'Andre phoned twice. I told him you'd gone away for the weekend.'

'Good girl. Anyone else?'

'No, Stephan didn't ring. Unlike Andre he has a life.'

'Don't be a brat,' said Sian heatedly. She sat down in the armchair next to the phone, dragged the phone up onto her lap and dialled Stephan's number.

'Sexy speaking,' said the deep male voice at the other end.

'Hi, Stephan, it's Sian.'

'Oh, what's up?'

'Nothing, I just called to say hello. Sounds busy, who's there?'

'Just a couple of friends. The usual, Peter, Femi.'

'Say hello from me.'

'Sian says hello.'

There were distant grunts of acknowledgement.

'So how come I haven't heard from you for so long, Stephan?'

'I've been busy. You know how it is, places to go and people to see.'

'Are you raving tonight?'

'Yeah. You know I always go to SW1 on Fridays. How about you an' your double?'

Sian giggled. 'Lisa's out with her man but I'm staying in.'

'Why?'

'I'm waiting for you to ask me out.'

'What was that?'

'You heard.'

'You should take me out.'

'That's the man's job.'

'This is the Nineties! Women's lib an' that.'

'Are you going out with someone yet?'

'What's it to you? Don't tell me you're still crazy about me?'

'I miss you, anything wrong with that?'

'Really? What's brought this on?'

'You don't really care.'

'Girls come and girls go. We had fun but now it's over. Should I care?'

Sian imagined him sitting in his living room making eyes at his friends. She could smell his aftershave and feel the scratchy stubble on his jaw.

'Sian, are you still there? Why phone if you have nothing to say?'

'I have plenty to say but I wouldn't waste it on a creep like you.'

There was a click, then a snort from Buelah.

'Don't you have any pride?' she asked disdainfully. 'My own sister can't take no for an answer.'

'What would you know, you little mistake?' Sian put the telephone back onto the floor beside the armchair and left the room. In the kitchen she wiped away her sudden tears.

The front door opened and Bernadette walked in carrying a white plastic bag. Buelah jumped up from the sofa and hurried into the hall. 'I'll take the food, Mum,' she said, taking the bag from her mother and carrying it into the kitchen. She put the bag on the kitchen table and began taking the containers out. 'What did you get?' Buelah asked, as Bernadette entered the kitchen. She removed a cardboard lid and inhaled the spicy aroma. 'I'm sooo hungry.'

'Dere's jerk chicken and rice 'n peas. Sian, I got you those saltfish dumplings you like and enough plaintain for everybody. See it dere, next to de rice an' peas. Lord, de Carib getting quite expensive. Nearly ten pound I spend.'

Bernadette Wilson was a heavy woman with ebony skin and delicate features. Her face was a picture of faded beauty, its brilliance dulled by hardship and heart-break. They sat down at the table and Bernadette said grace. Then they began to eat.

'So, Mum, how was the hospital today?' Sian asked.

'Yeah, anybody die?'

'Buelah! What a thing to ask. Work was just same as usual, but as I mop up in one of de bathrooms one patient, an old man, had a heart attack.'

'And he died!'

'Buelah! No, he didn't die. De doctors made him better but it was a bit scary. It's like so much t'ings happen in dat place, I t'ank God for my own health.'

'Any gossip – anyone we know been in?'

'Sian, I don't go work to spy on people.'

'Oh, please,' begged Buelah. 'There must be *something*.'

'OK, but don't tell no one 'cos I'll lose me job.' Bernadette leaned towards the centre of the table and lowered her voice. 'You know Mr Singh who owns de shop?'

The girls nodded.

'Well, I see him and his wife in hospital today. Gynaecology Department.'

'What does that mean?' asked Buelah.

'It means babies, doesn't it?' said Sian. 'They're having *another* one?'

'But they have four children already!' Buelah exclaimed with a giggle. 'Where are they all gonna sleep?'

'Is what I said to Hortense. Their flat same size as

ours so already it look like some sleeping in de bathroom.'

'Ha, so you tell us not to say anything but you go blabbing to Mrs Dega,' Sian said teasingly.

'She won't tell anyone. Hortense is a good woman.' Bernadette chuckled. 'You know she was talking so much I nearly fell asleep. Hortense tell me her sister went back to Jamaica recently and visit my parents. She write to Hortense and mention it, for she knows how we is close.'

'Oh, how's Granny? Still being ruled by Grandad?'

'Or is it de other way round?' asked Bernadette. They all laughed. 'Yes. Hortense was telling me how it nice down dere and how she planning to get her piece of land. She say to me, "Bernie, land out dere is just eating up so fast. You haffe move now or forever hold your peace."' They all laughed again.

'Sian, I wish I had some money, I would jus' be dere now, choosing my plot of land in Negril, or Montego Bay, and talking to builders 'bout a white house with a red roof and a verandah, and a first-floor balcony where I can sit and watch de sun set over de Caribbean and an orchid.' Bernadette exhaled wistfully.

'You mean "orchard", Mum.'

'Yes, Buelah. I mean an orchard. I always had a thing for apple trees.'

'It's nice to dream,' said Sian.

'Sure is, honey. You should go dere anyhow, for you never been and you's a big girl now.'

'Yeah, I want to go. I need a holiday, and of course I miss Granny and Grandad, even though Grandad always looked at me like I was doing wrong.'

'Dat's jus' his way. For real, you should start saving up your money and go.'

'That's a little difficult.'

'Why is dat?'

'Sian got sacked today,' Buelah blurted out.

'Is dat true, Sian?'

'I, er, quit,' said Sian glaring at Buelah.

Bernadette tutted.

'Lord have mercy! I keep my job now for how long?' Bernadette did some laborious adding up on her fingers. 'Ever since your father gone. Eight years and I don't let nobody upset me to de point where I leave. And jobs not easy to find like before.'

'But I'm so tired of—'

'Just shut up! Every day you tired of this, you tired of dat and it becoming a real problem.'

'Relax, Mum, I'm a big girl. I'm here and I'm OK and I'll find another job.'

'But what happened to cause you to quit?'

'Someone stole from the shop and Sian got the blame.'

'Buelah, I can speak for myself. This man ran out of the shop with a jacket. The shop has no security so Deris had to run after the thief, but he escaped. Me and Deris got blamed.'

'Are you all right?'

'Yeah, we didn't get hurt although Deris could have if the guy had tried to fight him instead of running away.'

'So why de manager blame you?'

Sian kissed her teeth. 'He said we weren't paying attention and that I have an attitude problem, but if you ask me, it's 'cos we're black. There were other staff in the shop but he didn't say jack to them.'

'This is what happens when you leave de church. Things start to go wrong, fall apart. De devil drag you in another direction. Sian, why don't you come back to church? You know how everybody miss you. Pastor Matthews ask after you. Brother Johnson, now in charge of de choir ask after you. Isabelle now leading de choir. Him say she not as good as you and wish you would come back. De other children in de choir say they wish you would come back too. Hortense say you going down de same road as Ceelie, her bad chile.'

'Do you see me with a kid?'

'No, but—'

'Well then.'

'"The girl with golden voice," they say. "She sings so well."' Bernadette sighed.

'Well, when I win the competition and become famous, then they'll understand.'

'Sounds to me like this singing competition gotta solve a whole lot of problems. At dis uncertain time in your life, Sian, you need guidance. You need to go to church.'

'Come on, Mum. I haven't been for about a year now.'

'Pastor Matthews sit me down just last Sunday and say to me to tell you dat it doesn't matter if you miss a few months of church or you have doubts, long as you come back in de end. You were much happier when you were in church. Since you leave, look what happen. You upset over this Stephan bwoy, you don't know where you life goin'. You get sacked from you job.'

'I was not sa—'

'Quit, sacked, you still don't have no job! At least if you were coming to service you would feel better inside. I do, it strengthens me for de coming week.'

'I just don't believe in all that tambourine-bashing, spirit-getting stuff any more. I mean, everyone dresses up, jumps around and gets emotional but it's all a front. You can't prove that there really is a God out there, so how do you know?'

' "Faith is de evidence of things not seen",' quoted Buelah.

'See, Buelah knows,' Bernadette pointed out with a proud chuckle. 'Well, I give up. Buelah, how was school?'

'We had netball try-outs. I'm sure I made the team, I was bad – scored nuff goals. But English was the best, I got an A for my story!'

'Dat lovely. Is good to see dat *someone* in this family is smart and know what they about. Me wan' you do well at school, Buelah. Den you can get a good job and buy you mum me dream house by de sea.'

'Oh, Buelah's just into books, including the Bible. She'll read anything. Anyway, she's probably only into church because the people there won't tell her to her face that she's weird.'

Buelah sniffed. 'Mum, you're wasting your breath on Sian. She's so stupid, if her head wasn't attached to her neck, it would float away.'

'C'mon, girls. Buelah, jus' leave her because one day somthin's gonna happen to make this girl know dat dere's a God out dere.'

'Most women only go to church to find husbands

anyway,' remarked Sian. 'Not that that's a bad idea, but good men are like miracles: non-existent.'

'Mum can find a good man, Sian, she is just being picky.'

'I wish I was, honey. Unfortunately, good men don't seem too interested in good women who already have good children.' Neither Sian nor Buelah knew how to respond to this. Bernadette smiled at her children. 'Now what happened, de food taste so good it strike you dumb?'

chapter
five

Lisa stood in front of the mirror and smirked as she tucked her black Aquarius T-shirt into her black jeans. She turned and admired her side profile. She picked up a big scrunchie with her left hand as she used her right hand to twist her hair up into a high ponytail. Her forehead puckered into a doubtful frown as she tried to decide at which angle to attach the scrunchie.

'Oh, don't *I* look nice!' A voice brimming with laughter broke Lisa's concentration.

She turned to see her mother, standing in the doorway watching her. June entered the room and stood behind Lisa. She mimicked Lisa's actions, twisting this way and that, then pulling her blonde permed hair this way and that. Lisa laughed.

'So what if I *do* look nice?' Lisa had inherited June's blue eyes but aside from that, it was hard to see the resemblance. Lisa had thick dark hair and generous curves while June looked in need of a suntan and a slap-up meal. 'Being kriss, for me, is a way of life.'

June stooped over Lisa's dressing table, examining

the neatly arranged lipsticks and bottles of neon-coloured nail varnish.

'So where was Miss Kriss last night that she's so late for work?'

Lisa turned away. 'Out,' she said airily. Lisa picked up her mobile, made sure it was switched on and put it in her DKNY shoulder bag. She grabbed her leather jacket and went downstairs to the kitchen. Her brother Liam sat at the kitchen table in his Batman pyjamas, legs not quite reaching the floor as he ate his Coco-Pops. Lisa ruffled his curly hair.

'So how come you're not getting ready for football club, little man?' she asked, planting a kiss on his soft cheek.

'I'm not well,' he explained. 'Mum said I could stay at home wiv' her.'

'All right for some.' Lisa walked across to the sink. She parted the frilly net curtains and looked out of the window. 'Rah, why didn't someone tell me it was chucking it down outside?'

June came into the kitchen with her arms full of washing. She dumped it on top of the washing-machine. 'You came home late enough, you must have known it was raining.'

'It was dark and I was dropped home.'

'Dark? Are you sure? At five in the morning?'

Lisa shook her head with a little smile.

'I went on a date, OK. You know, with wine and a little dancing and a kriss guy on my arm.'

June finished loading the washing-machine and closed the door.

'So who was the lucky guy?' she asked as she opened the powder drawer.

Lisa yawned and leaned back against the sink. She smiled at no one in particular, then chuckled.

'I had a wicked night, Mum. I went to this house and garage rave up west. The place was packed. Everyone there was dressed really smartly. Bare Moschino, bare Dolce and Gabbana. It was an older crowd *and* we were on the guest list. I think I drank too much Moet.'

'Yeah, so,' prompted June as she peered at the wash program. 'Who was the guy?'

'He's just a nice guy I've known for a while but never like, you know, taken it any further.'

'Nice, is he? I take that to mean that he's driving.'

'Fast and red and private-plated.'

June laughed. 'Does a job come with the car or is it all about the wheels?' She nudged Liam who giggled without knowing why.

'Football player.'

'Wow! Which team does he play for?' asked Liam enthusiastically.

'Is he a friend of Tiffany's boyfriend?' said June.

'Something like that.' Lisa stopped smiling and turned abruptly to the cupboard on her right. She took out a packet of biscuits, opened it and began to eat one.

'I'm thinking of replacing those net curtains with blinds,' said June, pointing towards the sink. 'I'm going up Walthamstow to have a look at some today. What do you think?'

'I think that whatever you get it will be pink and white and frilly like everything else in this place. Anyway, I can't discuss it now. I'm late!' Lisa stuffed another biscuit in her mouth and made her way out of the kitchen.

'I know how you like it,' June called after her. 'All champagne and red sheets and smelling like a boudoir of sin.'

'Whatever. I'll be going out tonight.'

'Oh yeah, what's new? You're out so much, I wonder you even know your own address.'

Lisa stuck her tongue out as she turned to go, leaving June and Liam to their laughter.

On the bus heading up to Walthamstow, Lisa's mobile rang. 'Leon' came up on the small illuminated screen. Lisa pressed the 'OK' button.

'So, what's up, hon? Missing me already?' she asked softly.

'You know I am. Last night was like, damn. I wanted you to be here when I woke up so we could do it all over again.'

'Yeah, well, I had work.'

'Fuck work. I'm more important than that.'

'I'll see you tonight. Oh, shit. I can't. I've got something to do.'

'That's right. Me.'

Lisa giggled.

'No, seriously, I have to sort out my room. I've hardly been in it. Even if I wasn't doing that, I've been invited to a party.'

'Hey, Lisa. I don't ask twice,' Leon growled softly.

'Good, 'cos I don't like arguing.'

'Why are you acting like this? When we go out, we have fun, right?'

'Yeah. That's true, but everyone needs time apart. You don't want me to get bored of you, do you?'

'You're getting bored of me?'

'Well, not yet and I wanna keep it that way. So let's just leave it for tonight, huh? Look, I can't talk right now, I'm on the bus.'

'Well, don't expect me to call back, if this is the way I'm gonna be treated.'

'Good, and furthermore, if you have a problem with me having a life, you can go back to Tiffany and put *her* under manners. I'm not gonna come running when you snap your fingers.'

'Wanna bet?'

'I'm tired of this conversation.' Lisa switched off her phone, not waiting to hear Leon's reply and yawned. The day hadn't started yet but already she felt knackered. She needed about eight hours more sleep. Damn was how she would have described last night too, although she would never tell Leon that. She could have handled the raving or she could have handled the sex but one straight after the other was a bad combination.

Lisa smiled wryly as she recalled the summer. On her feet all day, sweeping up and running too many errands. The atmosphere all steamy from the hairdryers and the sinks and flat irons cooking in the burners. She'd nearly quit, like with her jobs at Next and Debenhams, but even Lisa knew when she had run out of cards to play. Besides, she liked working with blackheads. The jokes, the cussin', the informal way the salon did business, although sometimes she felt they wondered if a girl who was half white could really do negro hair properly.

Her phone rang. Her lips curved into a smile when she saw Leon's name come up again. Treat 'em mean, keep 'em keen. Worked like a charm, every time.

'So, Leon? Are you gonna be sweet?'

'You lil' bitch. I just called to say it's Saturday night. I know you, Lisa. There's no way you would be having a quiet night at home and if you think I'm letting you go out with Tiffany to catch men, think again. Tidy up your room but call me afterwards and then I'll come pick you up.'

'How do you know about that party?'

''Cos I just called her.'

'I might be tired. I didn't get much sleep last night.'

'Don't push me, babes. I know your game.'

'I know you do. You've used it yourself too many times.'

'Oh yeah? Just call me when you hit home.'

'I'll think about it.'

'No, don't think, just call me.'

'All right.'

'Right. Tonight then. Till then, behave yourself.'

'I will, and Leon?'

'Yeah.'

'Last night was, uh, good.'

Lisa looked out at a world that now seemed a fraction brighter. Leon was hers. She didn't care what anyone else might say. Men were simple creatures and she had things locked down on this one.

Cutting Edge was a successful, family-run hairdressers in Finsbury Park. Its bright, modern interior, decorated in grey and yellow, attracted a steady stream of customers from the local West Indian community. Several of the stylists had won awards but prices were still reasonable.

'I'm really sorry, Mr Nelson,' said Lisa apologetically. She had to raise her voice above the old ska tune blaring out of the hi-fi speakers fixed to the wall behind the reception desk. 'I can see it's a madhouse in here.'

A row of long-faced customers were giving Mr Nelson the evil eye and glancing at their watches meaningfully. He smiled for their benefit and then hissed at Lisa across the reception desk, 'Dis woan do, Lisa. You've let me down before dis an' I cyan keep lettin' you off.'

Lisa took off her leather jacket and hung it over her arm. 'I'm really, really sorry, Mr Nelson. It won't happen again, serious.'

Mr Nelson sighed and held his hands up in resignation. 'Well, me too old and you too pretty for argument. Go on.'

Lisa grinned, then turned and walked past the waiting customers.

'Hi, Denise, you OK?' Lisa stopped by a small light-skinned woman with cropped brown hair who was setting a customer's hair in rollers.

'I dunno, Lees. Looks like I'm the only one gets here on time,' she said, smiling. Lisa looked past Denise into one of the large yellow-framed mirrors. She smoothed her hair down.

'That's because you're the only one with no social life, darling. Is it Sesame Street in here or what?'

'You know what Saturdays are like. Kids all over the place and there's more waiting for you downstairs.'

'Well, I suppose I better get to it. I'll talk to you later once I'm sorted.'

Lisa made her way towards the stairs at the back of the spacious salon.

'Hey, my girl got bags under eyes. Lisa, wha' gwaan. I thought you was saving yourself for Junior here.'

A couple of customers tittered as Lisa turned around to see Melanie who was by the sinks. Lisa smiled at Junior who was standing beside Melanie washing a young girl's long afro hair. Junior tilted his dread-locked head towards Melanie and raised his eyebrows as if to pooh-pooh the idea.

'Melanie, you're just jealous 'cos you want Junior for yourself,' retorted Lisa.

Melanie laughed loudly. 'Junior couldn't handle a big woman like me. I would kill him.'

'Hey, I might surprise you,' said Junior indignantly.

'You better eat some spinach first, then,' Melanie said, prodding him in the shoulder with a wet finger, ''cos you ain't no Pop-Eye as far as I can see.'

Lisa stepped to one side as a fat lady padded past, her hair swathed in a grey towel, drops of water trickling down her neck.

Lisa hurried downstairs to the basement which was divided into a barber's and an extension of the hairdressing going on upstairs.

'Mornin', Paul.' Lisa smiled at the old man who had been at Cutting Edge so long he was part of the furniture. The barber twirled his clippers and smiled in reply. The men waiting to have their hair cut watched Lisa as she went into the staff room. She hung her jacket on a hook then slipped a yellow and grey striped apron over her T-shirt and jeans.

'Evenin', Lisa,' said the supervisor scathingly but with a grin as Lisa shut the door of the staff room behind her.

'Hi, Myrtle. Sorry I'm late. Where do you want me?'

Myrtle glanced across to where two women were having their hair plaited and three children were quietly colouring on the floor.

'I'll send down the next customer waiting to have her hair plaited. Just wash and blow-dry it. We've got a big backlog,' she said, putting a hand to her head. 'Look, I just hotcombed my hair this morning and it's frizzing out already. The fans aren't doing much.' She gestured to the big electric fans at each end of the basement.

'Well, it's cooler than upstairs. It's like a sauna up there with all those hairdryers at full blast.'

A young woman walked down the stairs into the basement. 'I'm looking for a Lisa?' she said to the two women.

'That'll be me,' said Lisa, smiling. 'Right this way.'

Lisa guided the customer to a seat at the sinks. While the woman removed the clip from her hair and ran her fingers through it, Lisa wrapped a towel around the woman's neck.

With an assembly line of heads to wash, set and blow-dry the day passed relatively quickly. As the last customer was leaving the basement, Lisa sat down in a swivel chair beside the hot irons and let her hair down. She picked up the hairdryer first and blow-dried her hair straight, then she took up the large barrelled curling iron and began curling the ends under.

'Your hair looks real pretty. What's the big occasion?' asked Denise as she crossed the basement floor, sat down in a neighbouring chair and began easing her feet out of her sandals.

'Well, my man is taking me out so I thought I'd make an effort.'

'Anywhere special?'

'Nope. I can't be out too late. My friend, Sian, is in a singing competition tomorrow so I can't afford to sleep all day.'

'Sian is that girl who always comes in here looking for you?'

'We're real close.'

'I didn't know she could sing.'

'She's got a beautiful voice. Mariah Carey, move over.' Lisa picked up a hand mirror and looked at the back of her head. 'Help me with this please, Denise. I'm trying to curl up the back but I can't reach and the curls are going the wrong way.'

'OK, but you owe me, man. I'm whacked.' Denise stood up slowly. She took the curling iron from Lisa and began curling the back of her hair.

'What's this about a singing competition?' asked Melanie loudly, staggering across the basement with a basket of dirty towels for the washing machine.

'Oh, Lisa's friend's gonna be in a singing competition tomorrow.'

'Is it the one that was advertised in *The Voice*? The TalentSearch singing competition?'

'Yeah, that's the one. The final is tomorrow.'

'I know someone who entered that,' mused Melanie. 'Got slung out after the first heat though. Anyway, Lisa, I don't wanna know about that, I wanna hear about this guy.'

A slow smile lit up Lisa's face.

'Let's just say that he's all ice.'

'All ice? Is he cold?' Melanie asked.

'All ice. Pure diamonds,' Denise explained.

Melanie looked blank for a moment then her face creased up in good-natured laughter.

'Damn, I'm getting too old for this. All ice? You hear that, Paul? Paul, come in here.'

Paul came out of the staff room, jacket on and bag of clippers slung over one shoulder.

'What are you girls on about now?'

'Paul, Lisa says her new man is "all ice". Did you ever hear that expression?'

Paul shook his head.

'No, me neither. I said it must be age. We're too old for the game.'

'Only in your case, Mel. Only in your case,' Paul said, slapping Melanie on the shoulder. Melanie was silent for a moment, then her familiar laughter reverberated around the basement once more.

chapter
six

'Hey, leave me alone, B,' muttered Sian in protest after being woken up by Buelah, bursting into her bedroom and bouncing up and down on the bed. She lifted her scarf-wrapped head and observed her sister through half-closed eyes. 'Aren't you going to church?'

'We've been and now we're back, bighead. It's nearly two o'clock.'

'What?' Sian sat up and stretched her arms into the air. 'I didn't sleep too good last night. I kept waking up. I was worrying about the competition. How was church?'

Buelah undid the toggles on her navy-blue duffle coat and shook it off.

'Well, Mrs Dega got the spirit as usual and kicked my ankle, because of course she came and sat next to us.' Buelah raised a leg and peeled back an ankle sock so Sian could see the bruise. 'She didn't even say sorry.'

Sian laughed. 'Why is it so cold in here anyway?' she asked.

'I don't know, maybe the central heating's broken again. There wasn't much hot water this morning.'

Buelah sifted though the magazines, bills and photographs that were testimony to Sian's chaotic existence. She picked up a photograph of a light-skinned young man perched on the back slats of a park bench with a summer sky behind him. The tilt of his chin was deliberate and the look in his hazel eyes was insolent but he had a pretty smile. Buelah turned the photo over. 'To Sian, forever, love Stephan'. Buelah shook her head as she slotted it into the middle of a pile of papers.

'Oh for God's sake, Buelah, leave my things alone.'

Buelah climbed on to the bed, leaning against the wall beside her sister.

'Are you getting nervous?' she asked as she pulled the duvet to cover her legs.

'What do you think?'

'What time are you leaving?'

'Well, it's gone two now. The competition starts at seven. At about three, Lisa's coming over to do my hair.'

'I can't wait! Mum told everyone at church.'

'Oh, why did she have to say anything?' Sian kissed her teeth.

'Well, she asked if they would pray for you. Oh Sian, I think you're so brave, going to sing in front of hundreds of people. Suppose you win?'

'I don't even know if I want to win really. Take your foot off my leg, it's not a radiator.'

'Sorry, but I don't have any room!'

Sian shifted over slightly. 'Yeah, like I was saying, I'm really hoping for second prize. That's three hundred and fifty pounds in cash. Almost two weeks' wages. That would just wipe out so many of my problems. First prize is fifteen hours recording time in a private studio and two hundred pounds. That's a great prize but it wouldn't really solve my money problems. Third prize, well, that's just record vouchers. I can't even believe I'm doing this anyway. The first heat was bad enough.'

'Well, if you have a gift, better use it.'

'True.'

'Then, when you're famous, we can get a proper house and a car and wear Versace every day.'

'When I'm famous? I have to win first. Then we'll see, you punk. Then we'll see.'

Lisa left her block shortly after three.

Sian and Lisa had become especially friendly when they realized they both lived on the eighth floor of their respective blocks and that their bedrooms were opposite each other. At nights, they communicated from their bedrooms using torches and a Morse-like code. Sian, the slender, shy church girl had taken to Lisa like a moth to a bright light. Lisa was pretty and daring and impulsive. Sian would listen to her adventures and keep her secrets. Trouble was, after all these years, Sian still felt like that moth. Sian loved singing for the same reason she loved Lisa. Her voice was the only thing about her that could be beautiful and different. Most of the time she sang to escape the hardships of the real world, to forget the father who had walked out of her life and never looked back. When she sang Sian even forgot about the good things like Buelah and Lisa; there were only the lyrics and the tune and her dreams.

'Hey, Buelah, are you videoing the entrance now, or what?' Lisa asked, as Buelah opened the front door just as Lisa was approaching it.

'You know I like to time people,' explained Buelah, looking at her watch with a sigh. 'You always take different times. Today, you were slow but usually you're fast.'

'You're one crazy person, Buelah,' said Lisa, shaking her head. 'Smart, but crazy.' She followed Buelah into the hallway. 'Mum home?'

'Yeah. She's asleep though. She was really tired after church so she went to lie down. She'll probably wake up soon.'

'Well, she'd better if you guys want to watch the competition.'

Buelah opened the door to Sian's room.

'Sian, please don't tell me you're planning on wearing that old white dress!' Lisa said as she slumped onto the bed.

'If you can wear gold and black Versace jeans then I can definitely wear white,' Sian retorted as she held the dress up to the light.

Lisa pursed her lips obstinately.

'Sian—'

'There's nothing wrong with white. It's nice and safe.'

Lisa got up and walked over to the wardrobe where she began sifting through the contents.

'There are gonna be lots of other singers, mostly black girls, competing. You need to stand out and be – I don't know – memorable or something.'

'White *is* memorable.'

'Something gold or silver or even pink would go down better. Pink is definitely in.' Lisa pulled out a pink lycra dress with sequins. 'Isn't this the dress I bought for you when I was working at Debenhams?'

'Yeah, but—'

'I've never seen you in it. Try it on. I think it would look a hell of a lot better than your tired white dress.'

Sian took the dress reluctantly and changed into it.

'Now twirl.'

Sian swivelled awkwardly. 'Lisa, there's a reason why I never wore this.'

'Mum's never gonna let Sian wear that. You can see her breasts!' Buelah exclaimed. 'And it's so short!'

'OK, so it's a little low but that's what will get everybody's attention.'

'My voice will get their attention.'

'You hope. I should know, I came third in Miss Lovely Legs at Shenola's.'

'*I'm* not wearing a G-string.'

'No one's expecting you to go that far. But you need to show a little pizazz.' Lisa rummaged in the drawer. 'Here. What about this leopard print shirt and your black flares?'

Sian and Buelah glanced at each other and laughed. Lisa looked at them.

'Where's the joke?'

'You trying to dress me is the joke, Lisa. It's like Wu-Tang Clan dressing the Queen Mother,' said Sian chuckling.

'You *look* like the bloody Queen Mother but at the same time you want to be selected as the hottest, newest voice of the year. Not smart at all, Sian.' Lisa replaced the shirt and put her hands on her hips. 'Take it off and go and get in the bath. Wear the white if you have to. At least it doesn't need ironing.'

'Watch her, Buelah,' said Sian, as she picked up a towel and headed off to the bathroom. 'Just been in my yard five minutes and already acting like she owns the place.'

When Sian returned to her room she found Lisa doing her make-up in the mirror.

'And I thought this was my competition,' said Sian.

'I just want to look my best for you, Sian,' said Lisa dryly. 'Here, try this on with your dress.'

'Your gold chain belt?'

'It'll at least sparkle up your dress. Men find chain belts so sexy and at least one of the judges has gotta be a man. Hey, it works for me.'

'Yeah but look at the kind of guys you attract.' Sian sat down on the bed. Lisa got the hairdryer and leaned underneath the desk to plug it in. She spread some grease between her hands and rubbed it on Sian's hair.

'I take that comment to mean my bwoy.'

'Some mothers do 'ave em, huh? How is Leon then? Still managing to ignore Tiffany's charms and if so for how long, huh?'

'Tiffany has nothing on me. Next to my charms, whatever Tiffany has looks like weeds. Now I'm going to do a bob, swept over to the side. Sound good?'

'You know anything you do to hair sounds good.'

'Puhleeze, tell that to my boss.' Sian laughed as Lisa started on her hair with the hairdryer.

'So, nothing fancy, eh, Lisa? No freeze gel, no pin curls, no bonding, no cutting.'

'Don't worry, Sian, I got your steelo locked down. Something smart but not extra, mature but not grannified and sexy without being too out there.'

'Rah, all that from hair. Anyway, it sounds all good. So carry on telling me about Leon. What's going on with the poser?'

'We had an argument about his speed driving. He doesn't really drink, he just drives crazy.'

'He looks the type.'

'The night he took me to that club he drove so fast I thought he was gonna kill somebody on the way home.' Lisa giggled.

'So tell him to stop, Lisa. I mean it's your fucking life.'

'Well, I did but he just laughs and says, "Oh that was nuttin', babes." Just like that. I love it when he calls me "babes".'

Sian shook her head. 'You're too damn craven, Lisa.'

'That's where you're wrong. I've never been craven about any man and I never will. I figure that way, nothing can touch you. You know I'm speaking the truth. Look at you and Stephan. You cared about him and he threw it back in your face. Right now, I'm just having fun, my way.' Lisa was smiling as she said this but it was a rueful smile.

'Treat 'em mean, keep 'em keen?'

'All right then, so you know where I'm coming from. Now, where is The Cave?'

'In Camden. It's a small night-club.'

'It must be, I've never heard of it. Will it be jam?'

'I don't know. My heat was jam and there should be even more people at the final, I guess.'

'Wow, I'm getting quite excited now!' Lisa stretched an arm out and picked up the curling tongs. She looked on the desk for the brush attachment. 'I'd better hurry up. I don't want to make you late. What did you do yesterday?'

'Just cooled out at home. Practised a little but not too much so my voice got a rest. I checked my backing tape and made sure it's rewound to the beginning and labelled.'

'Sounds good so when does your quitting take effect?'

'Hmm, well, I've been thinking about that. Alan said I have to work another two weeks anyway but not long after that it's Christmas when I'm really gonna need some wong. There should be some good overtime so unless Alan says anything I'll just keep my head down and keep working.'

'What shall I do to help?' asked Buelah.

'Wash out the bath for me, please, darling, and then get me a bowl of cornflakes.'

Buelah pouted before trundling off in the direction of the bathroom.

'I spoke to Ebela this morning,' said Lisa.

'Really? I forgot to ask what you'd done today.'

'Not much. Saturday night really took it out of me. Ebela called me this morning to say hello. Said university work is getting her down. Man, I'm glad I didn't go to university. It sounds really tough.'

'Well, *you* couldn't do it, anyway, Lisa. You're someone who just wants to work, get their money at the end of the month and find a guy with a big wallet. You're not interested in being smart.'

'Fuck off. What are you then? At least I have a trade. You just serve smelly trainers all day.'

'Yeah, I know, I do the same kind of job as you do. Calm down.'

'I am calm, but don't say I'm not interested in being smart. Everyone wants to be smart.' Lisa stood back. 'There. Finished. That looks really nice.'

Sian stood up and twisted her head right and left. She studied herself in the mirror before smiling and nodding her approval. Then she slipped into her white dress and buckled on Lisa's gold chain belt.

Buelah returned with a bowl of cereal which she gave to Sian. Sian ate hastily as Buelah fussed about like a firefly, exclaiming at how pretty the sideswept bob was, how like a model Sian looked in her long white dress and how her make-up made her eyes look so mysterious.

'I wish I could come with you now, Sian. You know Mum always takes ages to get ready,' Buelah said as Sian finished eating. 'Mum, come and look. Sian is beautiful,' she shouted.

Sian attempted to brush such praise aside, but she could not help smiling, buying into Buelah's flattery just a little.

'You think so?' She stood up and twirled slightly, and then did a graceful full turn.

'*I* certainly do.' Bernadette was standing in the doorway in her dressing-gown. 'But I hope you feel as good as you look.'

Sian crossed the room to her mother and Bernadette's plump arms unfolded and hugged Sian. Buelah joined them, burrowing under their embrace until her head emerged in the middle.

'Oh dear. I feel like if I don't win, I'll be letting you down.'

'If you don't win, it not de end of de world,' Bernadette reminded Sian.

'Yeah and no matter how hard it gets, remember you have to have been in the deepest valley to know what it means to stand on the highest mountain.'

'Oh Lordy, Buelah's been reading again. What book this time?' asked Lisa.

'Just some quote book,' Buelah admitted shyly. 'But I think it's the right one for the occasion.'

'You're right. As usual. Damn, when I'm famous, I'm gonna miss you guys.' The others laughed but Sian didn't join in. Winning the singing competition might be her ticket out of Leyton Rise and that was no laughing matter.

chapter

seven

Sian and Lisa walked slowly along Camden High Street past Camden Lock and the market. They stopped at the entrance to an old stableyard.

'Is this it?' asked Lisa doubtfully.

'Yeah, look over there in the corner,' said Sian, pointing across the yard to a sign reading 'The Cave', ringed by small red lights, hanging above an open doorway. The girls made their way towards the sign. There was a ticket office just inside the doorway. A young man sat pouring change into a till and chatting over his shoulder to a slim brunette who was perched on a wooden stool, painting her nails.

A poster for the competition was pasted onto the glass window.

TalentSearch Grand Final

Sunday 16 November

Tickets £3

The Cave 7.00 pm

'Tickets three pounds?' exclaimed Lisa. 'They'd best not ask me for money. I'm the support team, why should I have to fork out?'

Sian laughed, pulling Lisa out of the view of the ticket office.

'Calm down. You probably won't have to. It don't start till seven and it's just after six now. We are so early, I doubt there'll be anyone else here and if there is, just say that you're singing like me. They won't know no different,' Sian said quietly.

They stepped forward again.

'Hello, come for the competition already? You're too early,' said the man, pulling up his shirt sleeve to look at his watch. 'Well, not that early but the sound crew are still setting up downstairs.'

'Well, we're here now,' said Sian. 'We might as well hang around.'

'Right then, that'll be six pounds, please.'

'Er no, I'm – we're singing tonight,' Sian explained. 'Gary Wilson said we wouldn't have to pay.'

'Hold on a minute,' the young man said as he turned away. 'Carol, can you get me the list of performers, please?'

'Sorry, no can do, me nails ain't dry,' Carol said, holding up her glossy nails. 'Don't know where it is anyway.'

The young man raised his eyebrows, got up from his chair and began looking in various boxes.

'Great idea, Sian,' moaned Lisa. 'They only have a *list*.'

'We'll just have to speech it then, innit. Don't stress.' Sian nudged Lisa reassuringly.

The young man carried a pile of papers back over to the desk by the ticket window and hurriedly leafed through them.

'One moment, I know it's in here somewhere. Here's the schedule, list of judges, list of journalists, list of organizers, ah yeah, this is it. List of performers.' He lifted his head. 'Names, please.'

'Sian Wallace.'

He ran a finger down the list. 'Yup, here it is, right down the bottom. And your friend?'

Lisa cleared her throat. 'Ahem, well, I'm not a performer exactly but—'

'That'll be three pounds then. Sorry, rules are rules. No exceptions.'

Lisa flashed a brilliant smile.

'I know I'm not a performer exactly, but, er, I am Sian's personal assistant.'

'You what?'

Lisa nodded confidently.

'You know, hair, make-up, psychological support team. Without me, Sian don't roll. Without Sian, everybody loses.' Lisa stepped up close to the glass and smiled encouragingly. 'She's got the biggest voice you ever heard. She's the favourite.'

The young man digested this information and scratched his head. He looked over his shoulder for a second opinion, but the slim brunette just shrugged her shoulders.

'Let 'em through, Dave. You'll only get 'assel from whassizname if he finds out you wouldn't let one of his singers in.'

'Don't I know it. OK, anything for an easy life.' He

nodded in agreement as he passed Sian and Lisa two tickets underneath the glass. 'No witnesses anyway. If the bouncers were here, it would have been different. Just follow the stairs down.'

Sian and Lisa made their way down the narrow staircase to a small auditorium. There was a well-stocked bar to their left with the iron grille still down. The stage was at the far end. In between there were tables and chairs arranged in a semi-circle around the stage. Everything was painted black. Three men were in the process of wiring up several large speakers on the stage. They paid the girls no attention.

'Smells like a pub,' said Lisa, wrinkling her nose as she looked around.

'The smell isn't that bad, really. Anyway, smells better than the lifts at Leyton Rise.'

'Well, if you put it like that . . .'

'I could imagine that when there's people here and the music's started, cigarette smoke curling up over the heads of the audience, it could be really cool. The room completely dark, the stage a pool of white light—'

'There you go, daydreaming again. I can't imagine your mum here though. Bernie would call this a den of iniquity.'

'You know my mum. Anything without a cross on it is a den of iniquity.'

They laughed. Lisa nodded towards two more girls coming down the stairs.

'At least we're not the only ones.'

Sian shuddered. 'It's begun. I hate this time, leading up to the start. I feel like I should be gearing myself up but I just feel like running away and finding a hole to hide in.'

'Well then, you should have a drink. Ever tried Southern Comfort with Coke?'

Sian shook her head as Lisa steered her in the direction of the bar. The bartender raised the grille slightly.

'Sorry, girls, I'm not serving yet.'

'I know, but could you make an exception for us?' asked Lisa, giving the grizzly bartender one of her sexiest smiles. 'My friend's in the competition but she's real nervous. I'd be really grateful.'

The bartender hesitated, then nodded. 'OK, but don't flash the drinks around. I'm doing this just for you. I'm not supposed to open until six thirty.'

'Hey, we'll keep it quiet. Two Southern Comforts with Coke. No ice, please.'

Lisa paid for the drinks. 'Over here, Sian,' she said carrying the two drinks across to one of the tables. 'We can sit and check out the competition as it arrives.'

They sat down.

'Mmm, this is nice.' Sian sloshed her drink around and took another sip. 'I can feel it warming up my stomach.'

Lisa emptied her glass. 'Don't sip it. Drink it quickly, that's when you get the full whack.'

Sian gulped her drink then laughed. 'You're right, that wasn't a bad drink.'

'Still nervous?'

'Just a little.'

'I know you're going to wipe the floor with these

other so-called singers. I bet most of them will be more interested in their appearance than their voices. Anyway speaking of appearance, I think we should find out where the competitors are supposed to hang out. Then I can tidy up your hair. It's kinda windswept.'

After getting directions from one of the electricians on the stage, Sian and Lisa walked through some swing doors and along a whitewashed corridor. Lisa opened the first door on the right and turned on the light. They found themselves in a large room. Sian closed the door. The dirty white wall paint was peeling, the strip light gave off a harsh glare, cigarette ends and sweet papers were scattered across the stone floor. A dresser extended along the far side of the room and a smeared mirror stretched along the wall just above the dresser. A few chairs were scattered around the room. Two coat rails on wheels stood off to one side.

'Brr, it's freezing in here,' exclaimed Sian. She wiped the top of the dresser then perched on the edge as Lisa got out her make-up bag. Lisa touched up Sian's make-up, then took a brush and tidied her hair.

'OK, I think that's it. Best not to fuss with it any more, you look perfect.'

Sian slid off the dresser and turned around. She peered uncertainly into the dirty mirror.

'Are you sure?'

'Yeah, you look great. Now what about practising your song one more time?'

'I should do some scales first.'

'Yeah, don't mind me. I'll be checking my messages.'

Sian went through her breathing exercises then

several minutes of scales while Lisa checked her voicemail.

'The moment I saw you, I was lost to the world. Never did I ever hope to find someone who I'd love from the depths of my soul. That was every moment in time . . .'

'Sounds good. I like the rift when you sing "soul". It goes up very high.'

'Yeah. I'm not a proper soprano, more a mezzo soprano so I really had to practise that, in order to get it just right. I like it too. It was worth the effort.'

'God, what's *he* calling me for?'

'You have reception down here?' asked Sian.

'Yeah. You can get reception in most clubs, it's just that when the music's loud, you can't hear it ringing, so you may as well not have reception.'

'OK, so, who's *he* and what's *he* saying?'

'It's Nathan. He must have called while we were on the tube. You remember Nathan, from way back when we were at Waltham Forest Sixth Form?'

'I liked him. He was cool. You made him drop his girlfriend for you and then you dumped him after two weeks.'

'That's life, baby. Anyway, he still hasn't gotten over it. He left a message saying we should meet up. I can't believe it. That era is just over, like ra-ra skirts and Public Enemy tracks.' Lisa reached out with her palm and Sian responded with a high-five. The door opened and the two girls they had seen earlier trouped in and walked up to the dresser. They exchanged brief hellos then the two girls busied themselves with their appearance, combing and tweaking each other's hair into place.

Three more girls walked into the room. They pulled chairs into a corner, sat down and lit up.

'Those were the days, girl,' said Sian with a sigh.

'Yeah, when we used to wear lace leggings.'

'Spray gold in our hair.'

Lisa giggled. 'Yeah, we've come a long way, girl. Now we're into Versace and rouge-noir lips and men with plans, as opposed to boys with toys.'

'Hold up, which "man with a plan" are you referring to? That cheating, lying, no-good Leon?'

'Among others.'

'I'll bet you're tired of him already,' said Sian.

Lisa sashayed up and down in front of the dresser.

'Sian, watch and learn. When you go out with a guy, love doesn't come into it. There are just good vibes.'

'Oh yeah, like good clothes, good hair, good sex, good car and good places to go?'

'That's right, and those who don't know better get to know or they're going to be calling little-dick dudes like Stephan who treat them like dirt.'

Sian's neck recoiled like a snake.

'I hate to say this, Lisa, but you're a real bitch.'

'Yeah? Then I'll be the best bitch I can be.'

'You're just as bad as Stephan at the end of the day if you make guys trust you and love you and then not care.'

Lisa shrugged.

'So what if I do?'

'There's a price to pay, Lisa. There's always a price.'

'Is Stephan paying? Is your dad paying? I know my dad isn't paying.'

'Yeah, well, Leon looks like the kind of guy who doesn't give free lunches.'

'Leon can't handle girls like me. He's used to white chicks like Tiffany, who bat their eyelids, give it up on the first night and fall in love the next. He's planning to play his games with me, I know, but I've already seen his cards.'

'Sometimes you seem really, I don't know, angry at life,' said Sian softly.

'I don't get angry, Sian, I get even,' said Lisa, wearing her prettiest smile.

The door opened again as she spoke and another group of girls came in. They set their shoulder bags down on the dresser and began taking out hair lacquer and combs. The noise level rose.

'Sian, I am just dying to use the loo. You'll be all right?' asked Lisa, standing up.

Sian nodded and Lisa slipped out of the room.

'There are gonna be loads of people, aren't there?'

Sian turned to see a short black girl with afro puffs, grinning like a Cheshire cat. Sian nodded and smiled.

'What are you singing then?' asked the girl.

'Just a few words I wrote myself. And you?'

'"The Greatest Love of All". I'm a true blue Whitney fan. I think she's the best singer ever and I want to be just like her. Hey, I recognize that girl from my heat,' she said, pointing to a tall thin black girl who was brushing her hair in front of the mirror.

'Yeah, I recognize some people too,' said Sian. 'So what's your name?'

'Heather Ashton, and you?'

'Sian Wallace.'

'Where did you come in your heat?'

'First.'

'Me too and I reckon tonight's my lucky night,' Heather said enthusiastically.

Sian smiled weakly. She turned to watch as two men entered the room. The room quietened.

Gary Wilson, the organizer and promoter of the annual TalentSearch competition, turned towards the now hushed singers. 'Welcome, finalists. I hope everyone is feeling great.' There was a low groan. 'Just remember that by being here you are all winners.' He waved an empty box. 'I hope everyone is here? I need all the singers to hand in their backing tapes now.' Tapes began dropping into the box. 'Only clearly labelled tapes,' Gary Wilson warned. 'Any questions?'

'Oh, my tape isn't labelled properly,' shrieked one girl, searching among the tapes.

'Look what you're doing to the other tapes,' shouted another girl crossly. 'You're going to break one if you keep digging like that.'

'Sian, there are hundreds of people out there,' said Lisa, coming back into the room. 'Phew, it's so crowded now in here.'

'Are Mum and Buelah here yet?'

'No. At least, I didn't see them. Don't worry. They'll get here, I know it.'

'I wonder if the judges have arrived?'

'Oh, I checked that out, on my way back from the loo. They're all seated just to the right of the stage. You're gonna have to stand well forward on the stage and look in their direction a lot. Make sure to smile.'

'Did you recognize any of them?'

'Yeah, one is that radio presenter, Darius Philcott. There is a woman with blonde dreadlocks who I think is some singer from way back. The others, I dunno. Music industry people, I guess. I didn't realize there would be so many people here. There's someone walking around with a video camera too. I wonder if you'll be on MTV.'

'I don't want to be on television. Suppose I muff it up.'

'Sian, live a little. You only get one life.'

Gary Wilson, standing in the middle of the crowded dressing-room, was still being bombarded with anxious questions from other performers in their glitzy dresses and too-bright make-up.

'I don't know what that girl behind me is wearing,' whispered Lisa, thumbing behind her. 'She looks like a spaceman in that silver suit. You'd think she would make the effort to look good.'

'She looks all right, Lisa, come on, don't run her.'

'And I say free that weave. It looks like a mangled cat.'

'Leave her alone. Why is it that you've got a cuss for everyone? Hey, there's the boy who came second at my heat,' said Sian.

'The blond one in jeans and the checked shirt?'

'No, the one next to him with brown hair. I really liked his song. Don't you remember? "Redemption Song"?'

Lisa gave an uncertain nod. 'What was so special about it?'

'He's not going to win but the song was really meaningful. Most of us are singing about boyfriends and stuff that isn't really important. He made that song sound, oh I don't know, it was good. I reckon he's my biggest competition.'

'OK, everyone, that's enough questions. Let's get the show on the road. I've got the order here, it's alphabetical,' yelled Gary Wilson, waving several sheets of paper. 'Marietta Arnold is first. Where is she? No, no one's going to look for her. I need everyone backstage. Where's Heather? Heather Ashton, you're second. The judges will be in the front row on the right. Nobody goes anywhere. I'm going on stage now. Ali here will call out the name of the next performer.' Gary Wilson pointed to the young Asian man who had just walked back into the room. 'When you're called come and stand next to Ali and he will tell you when to head down the corridor to the stage to Michael. You can't miss Michael, he's large and wearing a red sweater. It's very simple. One person is on stage, one performer waits in the wings, one performer stands next to Ali. When you've finished performing you can go out into the audience and find a seat or come back and get your stuff. That's how it works. Please don't make too much noise in here, we don't want performances being messed up now, do we? Come with me, Marietta. Good luck, everyone.'

Sian put her hand over her face.

'Don't start thinking negative,' hissed Lisa, gripping Sian's arm. 'You're gonna wipe the floor with these punks.'

'I don't know if I can do this,' said Sian, looking at Lisa worriedly.

'You're a Rise girl,' said Lisa with a grin. 'Sure you can do this. Rise Girls can do anything.'

chapter
eight

Backstage, Sian was looking at one of the lists of performers. Her name was third from last.

'Oh, you're so lucky,' wailed Heather, who was hastily smoothing down her baby hairs. 'Wish me luck, everyone.'

'Good luck,' chorused some nearby singers.

'OK, Heather, down the corridor to Mike. Fat, black guy in jeans and a red sweater with headphones. Good luck,' said Ali.

The room became increasingly empty and quiet.

'Sian Wallace,' said Ali.

'I'm up,' Sian said nervously.

'It's OK, Sian,' Lisa said reassuringly. 'Just sing it how you sang it a couple of hours ago and you'll be fine.'

Lisa followed Sian down the corridor and patted her on the shoulder as Sian stopped next to Michael. 'You look good,' he said quietly.

'Thanks,' Sian muttered.

'When I say go, walk through there.' Michael

pointed past two large speakers. 'Watch out for the cables. Once on stage the mike is on a stand right in front of you. You can take the microphone off the stand if you want. Once you get on stage Gary will introduce you. When you've finished go off stage by the steps, just down here on the right.'

Applause rang out. 'Good luck,' Michael said. 'You'll do great.'

As Sian walked onto the stage she could hear Gary Wilson's introduction.

'Now, ladies and gentlemen, put your hands together for Sian Wallace from Leyton.' There was a smattering of hand-clapping. 'Sian is twenty years old and is currently working at Sportsworld. She won her heat with an excellent song, "Moments In Time". Sian wrote the lyrics and music herself. She is a very talented lady. Sian Wallace, come on up.'

As Gary Wilson's introduction faded Sian found herself staring into a sea of blurred faces. She took the microphone off its stand. She smiled nervously, inhaled deeply, then held the microphone a little away from her mouth. She began to sing and as her sweet voice hung in the air, Sian felt for the first time in her life that she was somebody. When her song ended to thunderous applause, Sian bowed to the audience, replaced the microphone and made her way towards the steps at the right of the stage. In a daze she soon found herself being hugged by Lisa.

'Was it all right, Lisa?'

'It was bloody wicked, baby.'

'Yeah, well, let's wait and see,' said Sian. 'Let's go and try and find Mum and Buelah.'

'OK, follow me,' said Lisa.

The last act was a hopeless attempt by a male group called XYZ to be the next Jackson Five. The dance routine was hampered by the small stage and the lead singer kept running out of breath before finishing his words.

Gary Wilson came onto the stage as the lukewarm applause died.

'Well, well, well, after all that jumping around, I don't know about those guys who just went off, but I definitely need a drink. I'm sure we would all like to put our hands together now and thank all the performers who took part this year.' The audience applauded loudly, some with stamping and whooping. 'I would also like to say again how pleased I am at such a big turnout. Every year the TalentSearch Competition exceeds my expectations. The performers are of a higher standard, there is more publicity and the prizes are exceptional. I believe the competition is all about providing opportunities for young people to showcase their talent and, if successful, move on to bigger and better things. Our list of past winners includes singers such as Nicola Hadaway now part of the group "Make My Day" and the actor Dean Potter who was in last year's drama series on BBC1 *The Equation*. Our winner last year was Lindsey May who is working hard at a singing career. Lindsey will sing for us now. When she has finished, don't go away. We will take a break while the judges make what is going to be a very tough decision to determine who the winners are.' Gary Wilson made a sweeping gesture indicating the judges to his right. 'While the judges discuss please feel free to go to the bar and buy a drink. We'll start again in about half an hour. Whatever you do, don't go home. I would like to say it ain't over till the fat lady sings but our winner might not appreciate that description. Now please welcome back the winner of last year's TalentSearch Competition.'

Lindsey May, a voluptuous redhead, stepped onto the stage and as the applause died away she began to sing.

Sian and Lisa walked towards the back of the crowded room looking for Bernadette and Buelah. Their progress was slow as it seemed that almost everyone they passed wanted to congratulate Sian.

'There they are,' said Lisa finally.

'At last,' said Sian. 'I was beginning to think they hadn't made it.' Buelah was chattering away but Bernadette looked depressed, her forehead creased into a frown.

'Hi, Sian.' Buelah stood up and hugged Sian. 'I thought you sang the best. It was just sooo good. I'm sure you will win. Those last boys were awful. The worst part was when the lead singer tripped on the microphone cord. I thought I was going to die laughing.'

Sian looked at her mother hunched in the chair. Bernadette smiled back reassuringly.

'Don't mind me. Me jus' so worried in case you don't win. Me jus' sitting here, hoping for everyt'ing to turn out right. You sang better than anyone, but those three girls with de hairpieces were real good, also the bwoy with his guitar. I think de judges will like him.'

'Well, I don't really need to win, I just want to come second.'

'Come second? When you can get all that free studio

time and really do something with your gift? Don't be stupid.'

'Well, I have bills and there is more cash if I come second.'

'Bills will always be there, but de chance to be somebody won't. You don't want to come second, so you can pay bills this month 'cause next month come round, money finish. You want to go on, do great things like that singer, de man was talking about.'

'Oh, you don't really believe him do you, Mum? He is always talking rubbish. That group "Make My Day" is really hopeless.'

'Well, he could say anything him want, I suppose, but Sian, you never want to be second in life, you want to be first, every time.'

'Yeah, whatever. Anyway, we're going to the bar, do you want a drink?'

Bernadette shook her head, but Buelah asked for a Coke. Lisa and Sian walked across and joined the queue. When they returned with Buelah's Coke and their own drinks, Gary Wilson was back on stage.

'Ladies and gentlemen, some silence please. The judges have reached their decisions and we are lucky to have the maestro of track making, Vince Havering of CREAM, to announce the winners.'

A stocky, bald black man in a cream suit with a gold chain dangling from his neck strode onto centre stage and shook hands with Gary Wilson who then handed him the microphone. 'Hello, everyone, I'm Vince Havering, wearing a cream suit because of course I'm here from CREAM, my own recording and music management company. Well, it's been a long and enjoyable night. We've seen a lot of class acts, and now here is the TalentSearch Trophy which the most deserving contestant will take home.' He held up a miniature bronze microphone stand. 'I think that what we were looking for as judges was originality and good presentation skills as well as voice quality since there's a lot more to being a successful performing artist than just singing. CREAM began small but is now fairly successful, even if I say so myself. It started off as a one-man operation with no reputation to trade on or money to impress artists with. What was key in CREAM's success was potential. That's why people chose CREAM in the early days and I like to think that's what we spotted tonight. It's very hot underneath these lights and it's very overwhelming. A lot of the performers were young. We weren't expecting Whitney Houston but we came close. It was a tough decision but it was finally agreed that third prize should go to the Whassup Girls who sang "Rescue Me".'

A scream arose from near the back of the auditorium and the three girls made their way to the stage. Vince Havering presented each girl with a huge bouquet. After much screaming and waving at the audience the girls made their way off stage. 'Second prize we thought should go to Ben Swift who sang "Redemption Song".' Again the audience broke into loud applause as the young white man made his way onto centre stage. Vince Havering presented Ben Swift with a cheque and a bottle of wine which he held aloft as the audience cheered. As he moved off into the wings Vince Havering walked forward again.

'And now for the moment we have all been waiting for. First prize, ladies and gentlemen, for a good stage performance, simplicity of style and sheer voice quality is awarded to Sian Wallace for her self-written song "Moments In Time". Sian Wallace is this year's winner of the TalentSearch Competition.'

Somewhere in the audience, as Sian walked towards the stage to collect her trophy and sing again, Buelah hugged Bernadette and Bernadette resigned herself to the fact that Sian would never be going back to lead the choir at City Mission Church in Leytonstone.

chapter
nine

Sian came out of Holloway tube station and walked along the busy main road. She counted the side streets as she passed them, turning right when she reached Eden Mews, a long narrow street of car repair workshops and garages. A glistening streak of oil ran into the gutter. Sian avoided the oil, only stopping when she reached a red convertible BMW parked outside a newish building sandwiched between two garages. She glanced at a brass plate that read CREAM before pressing the button on the brown intercom.

'Hello, who's there?'

'Sian Wallace here to see Vince Havering.'

'OK, come right up.'

There was a buzzing sound and Sian pushed open the white door. She walked into a small hallway and then up a narrow stairway. At the top of the stairs she found herself in a grey-carpeted reception area. A secretary wearing a green bandanna around her mousy hair sat studying a computer screen through thick spectacles. She looked up at Sian and smiled.

'Vince'll be out any minute. Take a seat,' she said, gesturing towards a black leather sofa to her left. As Sian moved towards the sofa, a door opened.

'Yo, Sian! We're over here in the studio.'

Sian turned to see Vince standing in the doorway. He was wearing baggy jeans, a denim shirt and a denim baseball cap back to front. A gold Rolex glistened on his wrist.

'Thanks, Jackie,' he said to the secretary. 'This is Sian, the girl I was telling you about.'

Jackie sat back in her chair. 'Oh yeah,' she exclaimed. 'The one who won that singing competition.'

'She's got a wicked voice. We're going to make her a really good demo tape, so you'll be seeing a lot of her.' Vince held the door open for Sian as she made her way across the reception area.

'Wow, that's great,' said Jackie, nodding enthusiastically. 'Congratulations.'

'Thanks,' said Sian.

'One-thirty, you're early,' Vince exclaimed, shutting the door behind her. 'Great.' He propelled her into the middle of a small room. 'Yo, everyone this is Sian who's gonna make one hell of a demo tape.'

Sian smiled shyly at the two men sitting in front of a computer terminal.

'Over here's Jules, my right-hand man.' A white man with a brown ponytail and preppy check shirt over a white vest offered his hand.

'Next there's Otis, my left-hand man.' Otis was ebony with dreadlocks. He was leaning back against the desk and raised his hand in greeting. 'Otis is our sound engineer. Jackie gets the mail, does our invoicing and stops nasty people from getting in, that sort of thing. Finally this is Sireeta.' Vince gestured to a light-skinned black girl reclining on a blue sofa. She was wearing a mini-skirt and black knee-high zip-up boots. She smiled briefly. 'Wicked, wicked singer just like you, Sian.

'Let me tell you guys,' Vince continued. 'The singing competition was live. There were lots of good singers in there but you know me, how I was looking for a whole package. I mean, no one's going to vote for some girl who looks like a toad. Take those three girls who came third. They gave Sian a run for her money but at the end of the day they looked bush-wacked, the lot of them. Looks and personality is important, just as important as the voice and Sian had all three. Tall, pretty and voice like a fuckin' angel. Where did you start singin', doll?'

'Pentecostal church. I led the choir for a bit.'

'You're like a soprano then?'

'The choir director said I was a mezzo soprano. I had a bit of trouble reaching the really high notes.'

'Yeah? Well, it's not a problem. Most of today's soul is driven by the bass singers. There aren't that many high notes.'

'Yes, I noticed that.'

'So then what happened?'

'I left school, stopped going to church and got a job.'

'Straight from school to job?'

'No, I tried secretarial college for a while but it wasn't really for me, way too boring. I just wanted to earn my money and start living.'

'What kind of job do you have?'

'I work at Sportsworld in Oxford Street.'

Vince giggled. 'Not much of a job is it? Rubbish pay, rubbish hours.'

Sian nodded. Vince slapped her shoulder. 'Don't worry, doll. With your voice you won't be selling trainers for much longer if you play your cards right. Needs a lot of work, don't get me wrong. It's got a lot to do with your team. But luckily, you've got the right team. Ever been in a studio before?'

'Not really, the guy who did my backup tape did it at his house. He had turntables and a keyboard.'

'Well then, let me show you around.' Vince took Sian's arm. 'Over here we have the mixing desk. Move aside, Otis.' Otis swivelled out of the way. 'See, all these grey, red and blue knobs are more confusing than they look. Basically they allow us to control how much bass and volume there is in any one recording. These meter-like things running across the top are VU meters.'

'What do they do?' asked Sian.

'They also track how much bass is in the tune, how much volume, how loud your voice is, how loud the instrumental is. All these things can be finely tuned on the mixing desk. See these two PCs at each end of the mixing desk? We store everything we record on them, every drum beat, every instrumental, everything we do is via these computers. They're wired up to all the equipment. If they crash, we all go home.'

'Tell me about it,' said Otis grimly.

'Anyway, to your right, is the voice room. It has double doors. The front one is just here,' Vince said, pointing across to a door. Peering through a large glass window Sian could see a small room. The room was empty except for a stool with a headset and a micro-phone on a stand.

'That's where you'll be spending most of your time. Trust me, by the time we've done your demo tape, you'll hate that room.'

'You got that right,' echoed Sireeta, shaking her head.

Sian smiled. 'Actually, I can't wait. I've got so many ideas. I write too, y'know.'

Vince put his hand on Sian's shoulder.

'Doll, you've just come off the streets and don't know nothing about what's gwaanin' in the music industry. Just go with the flow. I'm the producer and I'm here to make you a star. Let me take care of the writing. Trust Vince. I'm a lickle yardie.' He laughed loudly while Sireeta giggled. 'Come on. There's one place left.'

Vince strode across to a door that opened on to a room with three low sofas, a small refrigerator, a hi-tech stereo system with speakers either side and a large television. On a coffee table in the middle of the room were a large bag of crisps and two ashtrays filled with cigarette butts.

'This is the chill-out room where the rest of us will be spending most of our time,' he said with a chuckle.

Back in the studio, Vince took a sheet of paper from the breast pocket of his denim shirt.

'Here are some lyrics I whipped up earlier, doll, for your debut track,' he said, unfolding the sheet.

Sian took the piece of paper and studied it. After a few minutes she looked up. 'This doesn't make much sense.'

'C'mon, doll,' said Vince with an irritated sigh. 'This sort of lyric is the lick now. Take Four-Play, Venus Claire, Notoriety V, any one of them and you'll see this is what be boomin' now. Here, let me help you.' He snatched the sheet of paper away from Sian. 'Love me bad, I'll love you bad, love me back, I'll love. Can I see you, don't tell me who, yeah yeah. When you got one mmmmm rub your thighs against my thighs I'll go down if you don't front. Whoa yeah.' He paused and grinned at Sian.

'Yes, but what does it mean?' persisted Sian.

Vince clicked his fingers at Sireeta. 'I'm gonna need a lickle 411 over here.'

Sireeta stood up and gave Sian a supercilious glance before taking the sheet of paper from Vince and walking into the middle of the room.

The way Sireeta sang it, the song gelled together after a fashion.

'Right, there you go. We gotta get this show on the road, Sian, time is dollars so take the lyrics from Sireeta and show me what you can do.'

Sian took the lyrics, then cleared her throat. Just as she was about to start singing the buzzer went.

'Damn, who is that?' asked Vince, crossing the room and opening the door.

'Lady, says her name is Lisa,' said Jackie.

'Who's Lisa?'

'Oh, that's my friend. You don't mind if she comes up, right?' said Sian.

'No, no, let her up,' ordered Vince. 'Have a go, Sian. Just copy Sireeta's style.'

Sian attempted to sing the song but stopped as Lisa walked into the room.

'Hi, I'm Lisa, Sian's, you know, manager. Sorry to be late, I had to work this morning.'

'Yo, come in, Mona Leesahh.' Vince stepped forward and snaked his arm around Lisa's shoulders. 'Meet the posse. My, ain't she pretty? And such lovely hair too. The prettiest manager I've ever met.' Jules and Otis mumbled their hellos. Sireeta managed the ghost of a smile. Lisa looked at Sian and raised an eyebrow which was returned with a knowing look and a gesture to sit down.

'OK, silence, everybody. Go for it, Sian, without music a cappella style. This time I want lots of emotion, ad libs, let's make this real sexy, Vanessa Del Rio style.'

As Sian's last note faded out, Lisa burst into laughter. The others watched Vince. He paced the area in front of the mixing desk and scowled.

'I'm sorry, man, b'lieve, I'm just, it's just that – Sian, I know you never wrote those lyrics, rude girl,' Lisa said.

'What's wrong with the lyrics?' demanded Vince haughtily.

Lisa looked around. 'Am I the only one?' she asked. 'The singing's kriss, but the words are pure foolishness,' she said then tittered helplessly. 'Rub your thighs against my thighs, what *is* that shit?'

'OK, listen, Sian, I don't mind your manager or mate or whatever coming down. But you've only got fifteen hours of studio time and they're ticking. When we've got the song worked out, you've still gotta practise the lyrics until you know them like your own face. Then you have to put the song on tape, so tell your pal to shut the fuck up so you can get your demo tape done. I need a break.' Vince stormed out of the studio and into the chill-out room, slamming the door behind him.

Lisa stood up with her hands on her hips. 'Well, excuse me, everyone, but the way I see it, Sian can either have Vince's claptrap demo tape or she can have her own, the way we like. We grew up making songs same as any of you and she's got her own style, her own lyrics and her own tunes, songs that mean something.' Lisa looked over at Sian who nodded gratefully.

'I can work with Vince's melody and style but I can do better, much better with the lyrics if I can just get a paper and pen,' Sian said hesitantly.

'Here you go,' said Jules, passing her a pen and a pad of paper.

'Well, you'd better try 'fore Vince comes back, eh, girlfriend,' said Sireeta smirking.

Sian sat down on the sofa.

'Well, we must get rid of some of these lyrics for a start. This isn't a real song, it's just a rehash of all the songs anyone's ever heard.'

'How do you think it could be changed?' asked Otis. 'I know Vince's lyrics are out there but it sounds all right to me.'

'Well, for a start I think the lyrics I used in my song for the competition could fit in here, so the first line wouldn't go "Love me bad, I'll love you bad", it would read "Ev'ry moment loving you. Ev'ry day a dream come true".'

'It sounds good,' said Otis nodding.

'It's all right,' said Sireeta, 'but she's only done the first line.'

Sian worked her way through the song, altering parts of it to fit in with the melody Vince had hummed. She sang as she went along.

'It sounds great,' said Lisa enthusiastically.

Vince came back into the room. 'OK, what have you got for me?'

Sian sang what she had done.

Vince nodded. 'I have to admit it's sounding better than my lyrics. You're lucky.'

'Yeah, it's growing on me,' ventured Jules. 'It's the same vibe as what's out now but it's much prettier.'

Vince held up his hands. 'OK, OK, you girls done all right. Now we got to get it perfect. Go into the voice room, Sian, put the headphones on and pick up the microphone. We're going to see how it sounds coming out of the speakers.'

Sian went into the small room behind the window and took up the headphones. She sat down on the stool.

'Stand up, Sian,' Vince said talking into a microphone. 'With all your training you should know that you can't sing properly with your diaphragm folded up like that. Sing the song through again, a cappella but slowly as if you're doing a ballad.'

Sian sang the song with a gospel touch. Her voice, resonating through a speaker, filled the small studio. Vince, Lisa and the others nodded their heads to her voice.

Vince clicked open a file on the computer and selected one of the stored drum patterns. Sian could hear a drum beat through her headphones, a fast, jerky rhythm. She did not adjust her singing speed quickly enough and kept stumbling with the lyrics. She held up her hands.

'Sorry, I need to try that again. It was a bit confusing.'

'Understandable. You need to concentrate a bit more, Sian,' said Vince into the microphone.

'Yeah, I know. The a cappella was fine, but this is hard.'

'Just bear with us. Keep singing the song over and over. We're going to be playing around with different beats, instruments, you name it. We're throwing you in at the deep end 'cos you don't have much time.'

After Sian had sung the song about ten times, Vince finally stood up. 'That's enough. Sian's beginning to sound like a tired old woman.' He flicked the tape out of the cassette machine by the turntables and motioned for Sian to take the headphones off and come out through the double doors. 'That's it for today.'

'That's it?' asked Sian with a confused expression as she re-entered the room.

'Yep. In the week we'll put the melody on tape and start building the track with harmonies and drum beats. You'll have to practise some harmonies to sing in your own time. If you want to add another song, you'll also have to write it on your own 'cos you're gonna run out of studio time if we do it here. Then you should have a decent demo tape. Don't worry, you're doing very well, you just need to get used to working in a studio. I know it can be intimidating with all this equipment and people but you did fine. We're busy here on Monday and Tuesday. Could you make it on

Wednesday, say about two o'clock? We'll go late if necessary.'

'That's fine with me. I'll do a half day at Sportsworld but all I've done today is sing this song until I'm sick of it.'

Vince laughed. 'Welcome to the music business, doll.'

chapter
ten

The two girls walked slowly along Holloway Road towards the tube station. They linked arms and huddled together against the cold.

'Shit, this weather doesn't joke,' complained Lisa.

'For real. Man, I didn't think I'd spend my whole Saturday singing the same song over and over again,' Sian sighed. 'It was so boring.'

'Welcome to the music business, doll,' mimicked Lisa. 'Bloody fool.'

Sian nodded with a yawn. 'Bogus, but nice enough.'

As they approached the tube station, a red convertible BMW pulled up next to them. The driver's door opened and Vince stepped out.

'Yo, you girls going back to Leyton?' shouted Vince. 'Want a lift? I'm dropping Sireeta to Ilford, so Leyton's on my way.'

Sian looked at Lisa.

'Yeah, it's bloody freezing,' Lisa said then hesitated. Vince seemed to be arguing with Sireeta. With a long drawn-out kiss of her teeth Sireeta opened her door, swung her legs out of the front passenger seat and got out of the car. She opened the rear door and got into the back of the car. Lisa made to follow.

'No, Lees, come sit with me,' said Vince.

Lisa raised her eyebrows and glanced at Sian who shrugged her shoulders. Lisa got into the front passenger seat. Sian sat in the back with Sireeta.

The car sped off.

'So, Lees. What do you do when you aren't being Sian's manager?' Vince's hand slipped from the gearstick to her knee and lingered a second or two. He laughed when he caught Lisa's furious glare.

'I'm a hairdresser.'

'Man, you girls aren't exactly high flyers, are you? Where do you work?'

'Place called Cutting Edge.'

'That in Finsbury Park?'

'Yeah, you know it?'

'Everyone knows Cutting Edge. My mum used to take me there when I needed a hair cut. Haven't been in for years, though. Can you sing too?'

'Nah. I leave that to Sian. I stick to the management. The power behind the throne. So, how many singers are *you* producing at the moment?'

'Well, I've got a few who I'm working with right now. I'm very choosy. You can't have them too old or they're telling you what to do. You can't have them too young or they have to be home a certain time and it's hassle.'

'Have you had any hits?' asked Sian eagerly.

'I've had a few underground hits, nothing you girls would remember. But my time's coming. I've got some

98

wicked singers at the moment, Sireeta included. The voice is fine so right now we're trying to find a style for her that we know will sell. Speaking of which can't you even sing a little, Lisa? Y'know, you don't really need to sing these days, it's all about image.' Vince's sweeping gesture caused the car to swerve dangerously. 'Sian can sing, she's got a lot of talent but talent only gets you so far.'

Sian muttered an ungrateful thanks but Vince ignored her.

'Appearances are everything and, y'know, Lees, you're too damn pretty not to be a singer, I mean just look at that hair.' Vince stretched out and grabbed a fistful. 'Good skin, teeth, are those eyes contacts? You should be on videos, man. See, I've got plans for us, me an' you an' Sian too,' he called over his shoulder. 'I'm Vince, I can make you girls stars, ain't that right, Sireeta?'

'Yeah, Vince, stars just like you made me.'

All three girls tittered. Vince shrugged it off.

'Listen to this track I whipped up last week for a man I've just started working with.' Vince pushed a cassette into the car stereo and turned up the volume. 'This is gonna smash bigtime,' he said enthusiastically as the opening notes began.

'So, what do you think? Don't tell me you didn't love it,' Vince asked, smiling, as the track ended. 'Sireeta? Sian?'

'It's—' Sireeta began.

'Lees, what do you think?'

'I dunno. Sounds cool.'

'Come on. You're a manager. You can come better

than that. In your expert opinion would you say we have star potential here?'

'Hell, who knows? He can sing. I think the track could be a bit more up-to-date, the flow's a bit eighties. I can't see it rippin' up dancefloors anywhere and it's not slow enough to be a ballad. But—'

'Don't worry, Lisa. When you've been a manager for longer than five minutes you'll know where I'm coming from with this track.'

'No doubt,' said Lisa with an indifferent shrug. 'If you didn't ask me for my opinion I wouldn't have said nothing.'

'OK, point taken. Listen to this next track though. This one definitely is a ballad.'

Lisa listened and after a couple of minutes nodded.

'Yeah, see I like that one. The beat is bang up to date. The melody's kriss and the lyrics aren't too bad. Did you write it?'

'Yeah,' said Vince smiling. 'With the singer of course. He's a wicked piano player so he came up with most of the harmonies.' He peered out of the wind-screen. 'All right, this looks like Leyton. You'll have to direct me from here. I'm an Islington man so I don't know these East sides. Couldn't see myself living out here. Not really a place to park my ride, know what I mean?'

Lisa directed Vince to the Leyton Rise Estate.

The car pulled up by a pub at the back of the estate. A group of older boys appeared out of an alleyway. Seeing the red BMW they slowed.

'Rah, look at those roughnecks standing there like

they're getting ready to car-jack us or something. Are you sure you girls are gonna be OK?'

Lisa burst out laughing. 'Don't be stupid. We've known most of those guys since we was about five. The one in the baggy jeans is Sian's cousin, Slick. The little one is Johnny. The big one is Louis and the one hanging back is Carl.'

'All right, all right. They might be your friends but they look more like rude boys to me. I'll see you Wednesday at about two o'clock, Sian. Great singing, by the way. Er, Sireeta, I need to discuss something with Lisa, wanna wait outside for a minute?'

'Mutherfuckin' speng don't get the message yet,' Sian heard Sireeta mutter as she grabbed a packet of cigarettes and opened the car door. Low whistles greeted the sight of Sireeta's tight lycra miniskirt and kissy make-up but Sireeta gave stare for stare as she chafed her arms from the chill and lit up.

Inside the BMW Vince turned down the volume and looked across to the estate's rundown blocks and then at the group of boys ogling Sireeta.

'So, this is where you live. Ghetto style. I was wondering where you and Sian get your attitude from.'

'Yeah, well, bye.' Lisa unbuckled her seat belt and turned to open the car door.

'C'mon, Lees, make this easy on me.' Vince tugged at her elbow and Lisa reluctantly sat back pouting. 'So, how about a little of that 411. You knows I like you.'

'Sorry? What are you talking about?'

Vince guffawed. 'No need to go on like you haven't noticed the attraction between us.' He leaned closer.

'You could really go places with your looks and a guy like me to hook you up. I could make you a star.'

'I thought Si—'

'I know you two are friends and all that but here's the deal, Lees. A couple of dates with me and you'll see your name in lights.'

'You got the wrong girl, Vince. I don't even wanna be a singer. Plus I have a man.'

Vince sat back and watched Sian talking to the boys. 'Well, I'll be straight with you, Lees. Sian isn't gonna get her demo tape finished on the studio time she's won through the competition. Fifteen hours ticks by very fast and then it's back to Sportsworld unless you girls got some other options. Even if the tape is finished, you still gotta get people in the industry to listen and if you don't know no one you'll be banging your head against a brick wall. But as a manager you probably know that.'

Lisa did not reply.

'That's what I thought. Now it's gonna take a little generosity on my side to get Sian a tape that can take her places. All I'm looking for in return is a little generosity on yours.' Vince turned and put a hand on Lisa's shoulder.

'Hey, get off me, man, are you saying what I think you're saying?' Lisa shook her head in disbelief.

Vince smiled. 'The nicer you are to me, the further your friend will go. Being in the music industry yourself, Lisa, you'll know that you don't get something for nothing. That's the deal. Think about it.'

'Well, I've thought about it,' said Lisa heatedly. 'And you can go to hell.' She opened the door and got out of the car.

'About time too,' muttered Sireeta. She flicked her cigarette onto the pavement and walked around the back of the car to get into the front passenger seat.

'Tomorrow, Lees,' Vince called out of the window as he eased the car forward. 'Sleep on it. I'll be in touch.'

'My, my, my, Rise ladies are dealin' with high life,' observed Louis, walking into the road and staring after the BMW. 'Eh, I gotsta have that beanie's digits, y'know.' He straightened up and walked back over to Sian and Lisa, grinning as he took his mobile phone from the inside pocket of his leather jacket and prepared to enter the telephone number. 'So what is it?'

'I wouldn't give you her number, even if I had it,' said Sian. 'She was going on like she's too nice.'

'Yeah, so?' Louis shrugged. 'I'd slam it, then up, up and away.' There was more laughter. Lisa and Sian shook their heads and started walking away.

'Hey, Lisa.' Johnny sidled up to Lisa, drawing up his skinny frame to appear as tall as possible. 'You dropped something.'

The girls stopped.

'Oh yeah? What?'

'The conversation, so why don't we pick it up right here?' Johnny smiled hopefully. From the pub behind them the steady thrum of house music drifted out into the night.

Lisa tittered rudely. 'Go pick on girls your own age, little bwoy. I hear Buelah's single at the moment.'

'And she don't want you,' added Sian. 'Slick, have you seen our crew anywhere?'

'Well, Vanya, Tiffany and Ebela be parlayin' at

Singh's. Tell Tiffany to start eating proper food, she's even skinnier than you and if it gets worse I won't like her no more.'

'Well, she don't like you anyway,' Sian pointed out. 'Why should she go from a footballer with a Lotus to a broke bre who doesn't even have a ride?'

'Ain't you got anythin' better to do than standin' there distressin' your cuz? Why don't you go sing a song?'

Sian laughed. 'What's up with Carl?' she asked, changing the subject. Carl stood apart, staring down the deserted street.

'He's been smoking,' explained Johnny. 'Boy still can't handle his weed.'

'Me not red, mon,' argued Carl quietly. 'Me jus' watch the road dem, t'inking 'bout the stars and the people, how people be so different an' the worl' be so fuckup.'

'He's red,' decided Lisa and Sian together.

After joking around a while longer the girls walked up the alleyway towards Singh's off-licence and the boys drifted off along the main road. The off-licence was a part of one of the blocks. It had been there ever since Sian could remember. The shop was owned by Mr Singh, an Indian, who manned the shop with the help of his family and a large Alsatian.

'Hi, Sian, hi, Lisa,' said Vanya, glancing up from in front of the till. She was pondering two packets of crisps. 'Sorry, Mr Singh. I know I'm taking ages. I can't decide so I guess it'll have to be both. Sian, I read in *The Voice* about your singing thing. That's really good. Now where did I put my purse?' Vanya slapped her car keys down on the counter and rummaged inside her handbag. 'I know it's in here somewhere.'

'Don't worry, you owe me one.' Tiffany came over and paid for Vanya's crisps and some water.

'It's probably my Carl,' Vanya explained apologetically in her slight Bajan lilt. 'You know how he's always helping himself. Have you seen him?'

'Yeah, red as hell,' said Lisa. They all laughed.

'Oh Lord,' said Vanya, embarrassed. Ebela, a hefty girl with dyed blonde hair, patted Vanya on the back.

'Don't worry; at least you know he'll be too out of it to get into any trouble. Where are you girls coming from?'

'Sian started the studio time she won in the competition. We've been at the studio for hours. Sian's making a rough demo tape. The producer is this guy Vince Havering. He owns this production and studio hire company called CREAM.'

'CREAM, eh?' said Tiffany with a smile. 'So does he have any?'

'Well, it looks like he's *bathin'*,' continued Lisa. 'When I got there all I could see was bare equipment. Computer this, mixing desk that. I mean how much wong does a set-up like that cost?'

'Lots and lots of money,' said Vanya.

'Hey, what's this Vince guy like?' asked Tiffany again, ''cos I need a man.' She nudged Vanya and they giggled softly.

'You wouldn't want him, girl. He's quite dark at putting tracks together but other than that he's an idiot

– and ugly,' Lisa explained as they made their way out of the off-licence. Vanya tore open a bag of crisps and passed it around.

'So, how did it go at this studio?' asked Ebela.

'It felt so good to actually be doing something interesting for once,' said Sian happily. 'Vince was a bit difficult to get along with though. What was he saying to you in the car, Lisa?'

'Oh, you know, the usual rubbish lines. "Look at that hair. Are those eyes real? My, ain't she pretty?"'

The others laughed. They turned a corner and walked past the construction site at the back of the estate. Four young girls ran past them and on towards the off-licence

'Anyone wanna do something tonight?' asked Lisa.

'I've been out too much lately,' said Ebela with a sigh. 'I've got so much work to do.'

'How's university going?' asked Sian.

'The second year's harder than I thought it'd be. The work is really killing me but it has to be done.'

'Sure, I'm down to rave. I might as well. There's nothing else going on,' said Tiffany. 'S'not like I got a man telling me what to do any more.'

'I knew I could count on you to be up for a night out, Tiff. Vanya, what are you sayin'?' asked Lisa.

'No suh, jus' me an' my soca go 'roun' these days,' said Vanya. 'You guys should come with me and Ebela sometime, the atmosphere at soca raves is so happy. Everybody enjoying themselves. Not like at the usual clubs where the women think they're so kriss and go on screwface all night.'

'I just can't imagine dancing all night to soca. Sian, you coming?'

'No, I'm tired. I had today off for the studio so I've got work tomorrow. I have to be at Oxford Street at ten o'clock to open up.'

'But it's Sunday,' complained Lisa. 'No one works on Sunday.'

'Well, it's double pay so I'm not going to say no.'

The girls stopped by Vanya's block.

'Just come, Sian, you're only young once,' wheedled Lisa. 'Stephan might be there.'

'So?'

'So? Don't try it, you know you'd go to bloody Australia if Stephan was going to be there.'

'Shut up. I don't give a damn about Stephan.'

'Touchy subject,' said Tiffany aside to Ebela.

'I was only joking. Jeez, you take life so fuckin' serious,' said Lisa.

'Sorry, I forgot, everything's a joke to you, isn't it? Other people's problems or dreams, it's all one long party.'

'Sian, you'd better get some sleep, girlfriend, you sound tired,' said Lisa scathingly.

'You only care about two things. Yourself and that bloody Leon,' snapped Sian, then her hand flew to her mouth.

'Oh, so that's the secret you two have been keeping for so long. We were wondering who Lisa's mystery man was,' said Ebela, not noticing Tiffany flashing Lisa a bitter glare.

'Sian, Lisa, what the hell's going on? Is that *my* Leon, you're talking about?'

'I'm sorry, Tiffany, believe me I am but—'

'You're my friend. What are you doing with my man?'

'He's not your man any longer,' Lisa corrected her.

Tiffany stepped forward but Ebela held her back.

'You fuckin' went behind my back and took my man?' shouted Tiffany, shaking Ebela off.

'He *left* you, Tiffany. I know it's cold, girl, but your man *left* you – for me.'

Tiffany dissolved into bitter tears.

'Sian,' she appealed. 'We all of us are Rise girls. We're supposed to be tight like family. Now Lisa's stolen the one thing that meant anything to me and she can pretty it up but we all know it was just a bump 'n grind, that's Lisa all over. So I'm asking you, who's right?'

'Yeah, Sian,' said Lisa, stung, her cheeks a deep red. 'Tell us who's right? Tiffany doesn't even love Leon.'

'You *knew* I loved him,' interrupted Tiffany.

'If you can love a guy who's knocking you about then you're a stupid bitch who doesn't know the first thing about love.'

'*You* don't love him.'

'No I don't, but Leon wants *me* and I'm free. He treats me right, doesn't push me around and says the right things. What you don't get, Tiffany, is that it's got nothing to do with love and it ain't got jack to do with friendship either. I'm free so it was on him and he chose *me*. Now, Sian, where's the wrong in that?'

Both of them waited, expectant of being vindicated. Sian stared at them blankly for a few seconds then held up her hands in a sign of defeat.

'I'm gone,' she said quietly and walked away down the alleyway.

chapter
eleven

Sian opened her locker and took out her black leather jacket.

'Hey,' said Deris as he walked into the staff room carrying a brown McDonald's bag. 'You on lunch too?' Deris put the bag down on one of the four formica tables set out in the staff room and began taking off his puffa.

'No, I'm going down the studio now. I took half day.' Sian shut her locker door and put the key in her shoulder bag.

Deris hung his puffa on the back of a chair then he pulled out another chair and sat down. He lifted a yellow carton out of the bag. 'I'm surprised Alan let you off. He's still pissed about the robbery.' He opened the carton and inhaled deeply. 'Man, I'm so hungry.'

'He wasn't cool about it but there wasn't much that he could say. I've hardly taken any of my holidays this year and Marianne had already agreed to cover me. And anyway, I've finished checking all the stock in that damn stockroom. God, I hated doing that. He is giving me all the shitty jobs to do at the moment.'

'He's making a point. It'll pass.'

'Well, it better had.'

'You still leaving, Sian?'

'Not right now. That two hundred pounds I won has already gone on bills so I need to keep working as long as I can. But it's not permanent. It's just till my singing takes off.' Sian buttoned up her leather jacket. 'Is it cold out?'

'Windy. Just as I came in it started to rain as well.'

'Oh bloody hell! I've got no umbrella.'

'Then you'll get wet, genius. Here, have some fries.' He took a carton of fries out of the bag and pushed them in her direction. Sian walked over to the table, sat down and helped herself.

'Thanks.'

'So are you gonna tell me what's gwaaning at that studio of yours or is it top secret?' Deris asked between bites of his burger.

'This is only my second time. The first time, on Saturday, was like an intro, to meet everyone and share ideas and give them a feel for my voice and style. We used the song I sang in the competition with a few differences, recorded a melody using a keyboard and started trying different drum beats over the melody. I must have sung the same song about ten times. I never thought singing would be such hard work.'

'Look at you, grinning away and talking all that studio lingo. Think you're a pop star already, innit?'

Sian laughed. She took a napkin from the bag and wiped her hands.

'Look at the time, I've gotta dash, but how's about you ding me tonight when you finish work?'

'Maybe, but you're not the only one with places to go and people to see. Give Alan a kiss from me on your way out.'

Sian chuckled, stood up and headed for the door.

Otis and Jules were hunched in front of a computer terminal when Sian walked into the studio.

'Hi, it's quiet. Isn't Vince going to be here today?' Sian joked as she took off her jacket and dropped it on the blue sofa.

'He's just sorting out some business. Said he'd make it soon as he could,' explained Jules, straightening up. He smiled. 'Everything all right with you?'

'I'm fine, really looking forward to getting started. No Sireeta?' Sian asked hopefully, looking around.

'I think she only came to the studio the other day out of curiosity. Don't worry, we're quite safe. Isn't that right, Otis?'

They both laughed.

'Yeah,' said Otis, chuckling. He pushed his swivel chair back from the mixing desk and turned to face Sian. 'Right, I've just called up the melody of the track we came up with yesterday and after you've had a listen, we can all brainstorm over harmonies, beats and stuff. Have a rest,' he said, pointing to the sofa.

'Sounds good,' Sian agreed as she settled on the sofa. The melody was still playing when Vince appeared in the doorway. He was wearing a white T-shirt, loose white drawstring pants and a white baseball cap. His gold Rolex flashed in the light. He was carrying his mobile.

'Yo, I'm back, men,' he announced, crossing the

room and slapping palms with Otis and Jules. 'What's been happening?' He turned to Sian. 'Hey, Sian, you all right?' He checked his watch. 'Early again! I like a girl that can keep time.'

'Did you manage to sort out your business?' Sian asked.

'Yeah. I'm a very busy man, fingers in many pies. But the thought of you two sexy girlies at the studio just made me – where is Lees anyway? In the loo?'

'She couldn't come.'

'Why not? She's your manager right? Is she sick?' Vince demanded.

'Does she really *need* to be here?'

'As your manager she should be here, managing.'

Sian shrugged. 'She's at work.'

'Well, what's she doing after work?'

'How should I know, she may have a date or something. What's the problem Vince?'

'I really liked her input at our last session. It was very, uh, helpful.' Vince paused. 'But anyway, don't let me disturb you. I'm going to do some paperwork since Jackie's not around today. I'll be in and out.'

Sian played the melody on the keyboard as she hummed various possible harmonies. Jules experimented with drumbeats. Otis rifled through his vinyl collection, looking for some breaks.

'Run DMC?' Otis called. 'They might really spice up the track.'

'Too hard,' said Jules, shaking his head. 'Think "ballad", Otis, and we might get somewhere before midnight!'

'What's going on?' asked Sian.

'We're looking for a break, a few bars, from an old classic tune that everyone will recognize that we can insert at the beginning to get people in the mood immediately; then we'll repeat the break all through the track,' Jules explained.

'James Brown, a couple of bars from "I Feel Good"?' Otis waved the LP.

'"Moments In Time" meets James Brown? I don't feel it,' said Sian. 'Maybe on the remix,' she joked.

'"Isn't She Lovely?" Stevie Wonder. Any takers?' said Otis. 'Going once, going twice.'

Sian took the LP from him. 'You could be onto a winner with this one. Let's have a listen.'

She passed the LP to Jules who put it onto a turntable. They smiled, rocking to the music and tapping their feet. Jules set the record again. Otis called up Sian's track.

'Sian, go into the voice room and sing along with the combination. It's not fast so shouldn't be too difficult but don't worry if it takes a couple of run-throughs to get it right,' reassured Otis.

Otis gave a low whistle as the music faded. 'Those two songs are made for each other.' Jules nodded. 'We just lay one tune on top of the other and we're done.'

'It's gonna take a bit more pushing and pulling,' said Jules cautiously. 'But we're definitely heading in the right direction.'

They resumed their tasks. Sian went back to the keyboard. Jules worked at the drumpad and Otis sat on the floor studying the contents list of an LP of sample cuts.

'Does Vince have days?' Sian asked cautiously.

'Wild Thing, Prince, Diana Ross . . . what do you mean by "days"?' replied Otis, not bothering to look up.

'Like denim days, white days, orange days. All his clothes always seem to be the same colour. On Saturday he was in denim. Today he's wearing white.'

Otis grinned. 'Vince is just the extrovert staked out in all of us. He's either mad as hell or out of his mind with happiness, splashing money around, or stingy. He loves bright, pretty things, gold chains, gold Rolexs, customized BMWs with state-of-the-art alloys.'

'Nothing like the bangers we have to drive each morning, eh?' said Jules.

'So how do I get to be a famous singer then, guys?' asked Sian jokingly. 'Come on, you must have some tips.'

'She's asking *us*?' said Otis, turning to Jules in mock incredulity. 'We're the little guys, not music industry moguls like Vince.' He got up off the floor and walked over to the sofa where he sprawled out. 'We get to spend our time on the floor wiring machines to microphones, speakers, all sorts, and doing endless sample searches that leave us with fucking neck-ache!'

'First you need a demo tape,' said Jules.

'Ain't going nowhere without that demo tape,' Otis echoed.

'And it has to be zippy.'

'Zippy?' mimicked Otis. 'That's so white.'

Jules laughed in protest. 'OK, OK, it would have to be *wicked*, man, cool like my ice, throw the mutha out, know what I'm sayin'?'

Otis folded up with laughter.

'Next you need to find someone with their own label to listen to it seriously,' continued Jules.

'And where do you find this person?' asked Sian.

'Wherever and whenever. Through people, at parties, by working for a record label.'

'Why don't you ask your manager?' asked Otis, twisting up in laughter once again.

'Rah! Everyone's just shockin' out in here,' exclaimed Vince as he opened the door and strode into the studio. 'I hope you're getting some work done.'

'Yeah, we did quite a bit. Show him, Jules,' said Sian eagerly. Vince listened, his head cocked to one side.

'I'm impressed,' he said as the track ended. 'The Stevie Wonder tune laces the track up tight. But it still needs work.' Vince walked up to Sian and slung an arm across her shoulders.

'So, d'you think Lisa will have finished work by now?' he asked quietly. 'Maybe she'd come and join the party now. She'd like to see our progress.'

'I dunno—' began Sian.

''Course she would. Give me her number – not Cutting Edge, her mobile. I'd like to talk to her. She is your manager, after all.'

Vince held up his mobile and tapped in each digit as Sian reluctantly surrendered them. 'There,' he said, smiling broadly. 'Not so difficult, was it?'

Jules and Otis were quiet.

'Well, I'm gonna call her. I think managers should be at the studio in their free time.'

'But why does it matter?' Sian protested. 'We didn't need her today.'

'*I* have things I need to talk to her about. Business things,' Vince insisted. 'But hey, let me not disturb you guys any more. I'll just slip out of here and leave you to work.'

'What's his problem?' said Sian, sighing when Vince had shut the door behind him. Jules and Otis looked at each other.

'Why don't you start recording some of your harmonies?' suggested Jules. Sian nodded glumly and went into the voice room.

'Vince is on some obsessed shit with that Lisa girl,' said Otis softly, watching Sian. 'He was never this bad over Sireeta.'

'Well hey, you always want what you can't have the most.'

'But it's not right. Look how he treats Sireeta now. Gives her excuses not to come to the studio, putting her material aside 'cos he's trying to get Lisa to take her place. Someone should tell him it's wrong to play games with people's lives.'

'It's not your problem, Otis, so don't pick it up,' Jules said testily. He gave Otis a warning glance.

'Women come, women go. Vince's love life is not our business. All we care about is our *jobs*, right?'

Otis was quiet.

'*Right*, Otis?' Jules repeated. Otis nodded finally.

'Yeah, you're right, Jules. It's none of our business,' he said, sighing.

'Good man,' said Jules, relieved, as he patted Otis on the shoulder. He turned and waved to Sian. 'OK, Sian, let's go,' he said into the microphone.

An hour later Vince came back into the studio. He

walked up to Jules and talked to him briefly and quietly, without his usual braggadocio.

'I'm going now, doll,' he said, turning to Sian. 'You guys haven't got much longer in here this evening so there's no point me joining in now. Sian, you know that you only have five hours left after today, one decent session at most. Tell Lisa that. Remind her that we've got a deal.' Vince paused. 'Can you do Saturday afternoon like last weekend?' he asked Sian.

'Yes, that'd be OK. What sort of time?'

'Say about two o'clock like today, OK?'

'Yeah, cool with me.'

'Good, and tell Lisa that she'd better make it here on Saturday or nothing happens. Tell her no show, no tape. She'll know what I mean. She'll remember our deal.'

chapter
twelve

The following Saturday afternoon Sian walked out of Finsbury Park tube station and cut between the buses parked outside. She turned into Stroud Green Road. The grey tassels of the yellow Cutting Edge canopy flapped in the strong breeze. Sian stopped underneath the canopy and took a deep breath before pushing open the door. There were still people waiting at reception. Two toddlers were chasing each other around the coffee table.

'Hi, Mr Nelson.'

'One minute, Sian. That was a wash and set you jus' had so that'll be fifteen pounds. Out of twenty pounds.' Mr Nelson opened the till and gave the customer her change. 'Thank you and please call again. All right, Sian?'

'Yeah, sorry to trouble you but is Lisa around?'

'Downstairs.' Mr Nelson turned to a woman who had followed Sian into Cutting Edge and smiled. 'Good afternoon madam, how can I help you?'

Sian glanced up at the television which was showing

a music video as she walked past the row of women sitting under dryers.

'Y'all right, Sian?' boomed Melanie. 'I saw your picture in *The Voice*. Congratulations on winning.'

'Thanks. Lisa downstairs?'

'Yeah, putting overalls and t'ings in the washing-machines, last time I saw her. In the washroom next to the toilets.'

'Thanks.'

'While you're down there, ask Rusty, she's the one with the red and brown bob, if she'll come up and wash this customer's hair.' Melanie pointed at a woman, seated near her, who was trying to separate the strands of her untidy shock of black hair.

Downstairs it was fairly quiet. Paul was cutting an old man's fade. Nicole and Rusty were chatting. Sian walked over and gave Melanie's message to Rusty. Then she found Lisa in the washroom, measuring some powder into a plastic dosing ball. Lisa glanced up then shut the door of the washing-machine with a clang.

'What do you want?' Lisa asked.

'I wanted to talk to you. Hell, I'm sorry, Lisa, about spilling your business but you hurt my feelings.'

'Yeah and what? Is that it, 'cos my day ain't over yet.' Lisa brushed past Sian and walked across the room to a tall cupboard. She took out a broom, walked out into the hairdressing area and began sweeping up the hair on the floor. Sian followed her. 'Come on, Lisa. You know I didn't mean for Tiffany to find out about you and Leon and anyway, can we just forget it?'

'What do you want me to do? Get down on my

knees and pledge allegiance? You knows that's not my style, girlfriend.'

'So you're not screwing?'

'No.'

'Good, then come to the studio with me, Lisa, please,' said Sian quickly.

Lisa shook her head vigorously. 'Nah, me and that clown don't get on. But you go do your thing.'

'But Vince keeps asking for you. He says that as my manager you should be there. On Wednesday evening he kept saying to tell you to remember the deal. Tell her no show, no tape. He said it just like that.'

Lisa stopped sweeping. She frowned.

'Well, what's he going on about? What deal? And he asked for your mobile number, saying he needed to talk about business. Did he call you?'

Lisa nodded.

'What did he want to talk to you about? Was it about me? Did you do some deal?'

'You're killing me with questions,' Lisa snapped.

'Well, you gotta tell me what's going on, Lisa. This is my life on the line,' Sian said. 'Don't palm me off with any more excuses, it's important.'

Lisa sighed. 'Look, I'll come, OK?'

'Thanks, Lisa.' Sian hugged her. 'Things seem to run so much smoother when you're around. So shall I just hang around for an hour or so or go and come back?'

'Just sit down out of the way. Over there where the customers usually wait.' Lisa motioned towards a chair then continued to sweep up the hair scattered across the floor. Sian sat down and turned her attention to a woman who was having her afro hair hot-combed by Nicole.

Lisa came over and sat down in the chair beside Sian.

'How was the studio on Wednesday?'

'It was all right. Jules and Otis were great. We got a lot of work done. I must have been there for six solid hours. Vince was annoying. Every so often he came in to check on our progress but all he really wanted to talk about was you. Sireeta wasn't there, thank goodness. That would have finished me off.'

'She wasn't very friendly, was she?'

'You can say that again. Anyway, luckily I didn't have to work with Vince, just the other two.'

'I'm glad it's going well. The main tune is almost finished now, right?'

'Yep. I think today we're wrapping up, hopefully starting a new tune. Just as well really since I think I only have five hours left. Maybe not even that.'

'What will you do when the hours are up? Can you buy more time if you need it?'

'I don't know but I don't suppose I could afford the dollars. I was hoping Vince might take me on, like he has Sireeta and that singer whose tape we heard in the car but it doesn't seem like he's going to. He doesn't seem that interested in me. At least not as interested as he is in *you*.'

'What are you trying to say?'

'It's obvious that he likes you, Lisa. Don't pretend you don't see it.'

'Does it matter whether he does or not?'

'No, I guess not, 'cept I'm the one caught in the middle if anything goes wrong.'

'Well, until then, you've got the right end of the stick. You don't know how awful it is to go in there and have him ogling you.'

'I know, I'm not jealous. Perhaps he'll still give me some contacts. So, how's things going with Leon? Showing his horns yet?'

'Leon is not the problem. It's attitudes like yours and my mum's that are the problem.'

'What's your mum saying?'

'Makin' up bare arguments in the house every day about me being out late every night and not coming home.'

'You stay out all night?'

'Oh, not you too. I'm not a teenager any more in case you forgot my party in September. Just 'cos you're acting like a nun doesn't mean everyone else has to.'

'I'd rather be single than take someone else's man.'

'Oh, don't start. Look, there's Myrtle. Let me ask if I can step.' Lisa stood up and crossed the room to talk to Myrtle. She came back smiling. 'Myrtle told me I could slip out now so let's go quick before she changes her mind,' said Lisa, taking off her apron. 'Let me just put this in the staff room and get my things.' On her return Lisa smoothed back her hair with some of the hair oil on the worktop.

They went upstairs.

'Bye, Mel. I'll see you on Monday.'

'Bye, Lisa. Have a good weekend, girl. Say hello to ice-man for me.'

'Sure will,' Lisa called back laughing.

'Who's ice-man?' asked Sian suspiciously as they reached the doors. 'A new man?'

'The same one, sorry to disappoint you.'

'I bought some nice talcum powder for my mum, it's her birthday today,' said Sian as they walked away from Cutting Edge.

'Time flies, man. Just the other day it was my birthday party in September, now November's almost over. Let's see.' Sian opened her shoulder bag and handed Lisa the box. 'Oooh, very nice. Not very imaginative though.'

'Well, I don't really try to be different, I just get people what they expect and want,' said Sian, putting the box back in her shoulder bag.

'So are you going to do anything special?'

'I'll cook and then we'll cut the cake I made with Buelah last night, but apart from that, no. Mum's working late anyway. She keeps working on Saturdays because of the overtime.'

'Your mother works damn hard.'

'Yeah, it's really tough being a single mum. I try and help but Sportsworld wages are so rubbish that it's difficult.'

'Tell me about it. Thank God Mum has Woody. Plumbers can charge almost anything they want.'

'Maybe we should become plumbers,' said Sian with a giggle.

'Yeah. Think how many houses we would flood,' agreed Lisa.

They were still laughing as they walked into Finsbury Park tube station.

*

'Hi, girls.' Vince, sitting at the receptionist's desk, looked up from a letter as they arrived. He was wearing a black shirt, black leather trousers and black baseball cap. Jules and Otis were in their usual positions. Jules was hunched in front of a PC. Otis was on the floor, trying to wire up a keyboard to the speakers. As Sian and Lisa walked into the studio they said hello.

'So, Lees,' Vince called out, without looking up from his mail. 'Have you been thinking about my, uh, "proposition"?'

Lisa cleared her throat. 'Yeah.'

'And?'

'I'm still thinking.' She avoided Sian's questioning look. Vince stood up and walked into the studio. He sat down on the sofa and held out two cards to Lisa, then patted the empty space next to him.

'What are those?' asked Lisa.

'Four-Play afterparty tickets to the mid-January Showcase. See how I look after you girls? I want you girls to come down and chill with me. Meet the boys. Do you know who's gonna be there? Jigga and Pearce, two producers from LockedDown records. Yeah, you're right to be impressed. Those guys are large, huge, all the way from the States.' Vince emphasized their importance by holding his arms aloft.

'You've gotta look wicked, trust me. Ghetto lick. Smart and sexy with attitude.' He leered at Lisa. 'I know you've got attitude.'

'So who's going to be there?' interrupted Sian.

'Didn't you hear anything I just said? These are the playaz, like me, they can make or break you. Come and sit down, Lees.'

'So you're well in with them then?' asked Lisa with just a hint of sarcasm. She glanced at Sian, shrugged her shoulders then walked across and sat on the sofa.

'I've known Pearce ever since he was that high and we maintained that brotherhood as he became more successful. I'm one of the big boys. Stick with me and you'll be sorted.' Vince pinched Lisa on the cheek. She giggled, then checked herself.

Lisa took the invitations from Vince and passed them to Sian who put them in her shoulder bag.

'So are we going to start work now or what?' demanded Sian.

'Yeah, you're right. We wrapped up that last track this morning. I did it in my own time because it was taking so long. There was no point messing with it any longer. You can still record your harmonies, if you've thought them out. That won't take more than ten minutes and you can do it later. But I want to start the second track now. You have written it, haven't you?'

'Yes and I've been practising. I think I've got it just about right.'

'Cool. Well, go into the voice room and give us an a cappella version or two first to show me what you've done and then we'll work on some accompanying music.'

Sian went into the voice room. She took up the headphones and put them on.

'OK, Jules, over to you,' Vince said. 'You and Otis are in charge. I'm going to chat right here with Lees. It's all business of course.' Vince tentatively put his arm around Lisa as Jules began working with Sian to adjust the headset volume.

'What's that for?' asked Lisa suspiciously.

'I think you're gonna accept my offer.'

'Vince, I'm not gonna pretend that I like you. Basically, I don't know you and I don't wanna sing or be no star but I don't mind going to a couple of parties with you if you can give Sian her break, though hell knows why me. Why not Sireeta?'

'Sireeta's old meat. And you're prettier. I've just fallen for you in a big way. I wanna do things for you, doll. I wanna take care of you. I think I'm in love,' Vince said with a childish giggle.

'Well, I'm only doing it 'cos me an' Sian are close,' Lisa hissed. Vince snickered. He put one stumpy finger underneath Lisa's pale chin and raised her eyes to meet his.

'Would Sian do the same for you?'

Vince stood up, just as Sian finished her second a cappella run-through and walked over to the computer. He looked through the stack of cassettes on top of the tape deck. 'OK, Sian, come in here,' Vince said into the microphone beckoning towards Sian. She took off the headset and re-entered the studio. 'That was perfect, Sian, you've been working hard. Now we're going to find a drum pattern and a couple of samples, nothing too complicated. After talking things over with Lisa here, I've got some good news. I've decided to give you extra studio time to produce and polish your two tracks and to produce you a really good demo tape all on my own time.'

'Really?' Sian's face lit up. 'Why?'

'You're so talented. I'd never do anything like this for someone unless I thought they were really special.

I'm gonna make you into a star. We're going all the way, doll.'

Sian walked across to the sofa and sat down beside Lisa who squeezed her hand.

'OK, Sian. We've got a lot of work to do before anyone can go home tonight. I want you to listen to the breaks we got on this computer file and tell me which ones you like.' Vince winked at Lisa. 'I think I've got an idea of what turns you on.'

chapter
thirteen

Later that Saturday evening, Lisa turned into Matthews Park Road. No light was visible through the curtains of the terraced house where Leon lived but his red Lotus was in front of the house, sparkling like a crown jewel between the old Fords and rusty Astras. Lisa walked through the small front garden full of weeds, bits of cardboard and scattered rubbish blown in from the street, and pressed the doorbell. A light was switched on and she could hear someone running down the stairs. Then the door opened.

'You're late,' Leon growled. Lisa grinned as he pulled her into the hallway and shut the door. She snaked her arms up around his neck and kissed him on his stubbly cheek.

'Mmm, you smell nice,' she said, breaking away and removing her long leather coat. Leon took the coat and hung it on the banister.

'Yeah, I knew you'd be coming round so I made an effort. I don't always stink of sweat and socks, y'know?'

'Is that so?' enquired Lisa smirking.

Leon chuckled. 'Instead of being feisty, why don't you come over here and give me a real kiss.' Leon caught Lisa's wrists and drew her towards him.

'A real kiss, huh?' said Lisa softly, looking up into Leon's charcoal eyes as he sank his hands into her dark hair. 'Sure you can handle that?'

'Try me.'

They kissed again, a heat-seeking kiss that lingered like sweet perfume. Finally Leon released her, smiling. 'Not bad for round one. D'you want a drink?'

Lisa nodded then followed Leon into the large kitchen at the back of the house. He bent down and opened the refrigerator.

'It's so clean,' she said admiringly, running a finger over the sparkling cooker and pristine worktops.

'It's always clean, Lisa,' Leon said, frowning, as he took a carton of orange juice out of the fridge.

'Orange juice OK?' he asked.

'Don't you have coke or something fizzy?'

'I'm training, I have to cut back on that shit. You shouldn't drink that stuff anyway, you'll get fat and spotty. Here.' He poured some orange juice into a glass and handed it to her. She pouted. Leon smiled. 'Just drink it like a good girl.'

Lisa took the glass and sipped the orange juice, grimacing. 'I don't really like orange.'

'Drink a bit and then tell me how come you're so late,' said Leon.

'Well, I didn't worry about the time because I knew you had a match today and I thought you'd go celebrating with your friends afterwards.'

'That's all you think we do, isn't it? Play a game and

then go to the pub. It's hard work being a footballer, it's not like being a hairdresser. You just do a couple of people's hair and then go home, put your feet up. One game is like a ten-mile run, non-stop. I could have got mud in my eye, dirt in my mouth and the rain could be licking me all over but I can't sit down and have a chat when I get tired.'

'It's quite hard work at Cutting Edge actually.'

'Pull the other one! How hard can it be? Everyone having a chat, listening to music, watching the videos, playing with someone's hair. You call that work?'

'OK, so how did the match go?'

'Stupid. Nil-nil. It was a *stupid* game. No energy, no one wanting to make any space or take any chances.'

'Were talent scouts there?'

'A couple. But I don't think they'll have noticed me. I didn't get the ball much. I didn't have any space to score. Their main men were marking me too well. I tried to get away.' Leon dipped and wove his way past imaginary tacklers as he moved backwards and forwards across the kitchen linoleum. 'I did my Sol Campbell, my Rio Ferdinand, my Ronaldo back kick, then I dribbled forward fast as I could.' He pretended to dribble forward and caught Lisa in a hug. They laughed together and began making their way out of the kitchen. 'But it didn't work. Next time though. Next time I'll score. You just wait, Lisa. This time next year I'll be signed to a Premier League team and then you won't keep me waiting all evening while you're out with other guys.' They made their way upstairs.

'Come on, Leon. You know I was at the studio with Sian.'

'Yeah, Sian and who else? The slick-talking nigga that's calling you on your mobile, telling you to go to the studio like you're his woman.'

'I didn't give Vince my number, Sian did. You know that,' snapped Lisa, sitting down on the bed. A silver table lamp cast a warm but dim glow over the ebony-wood bed.

'For all I know you probably give him one every time you go down there.'

Lisa picked up Leon's mobile phone from the bed-side table and hurled it at him.

'Oi, you wanna stop them ways there!' laughed Leon as he caught his mobile phone. 'You know it's jus' jokes.' Lisa kissed her teeth. Leon laughed again as he walked over to the wardrobe rail that held his clothes. He took a wool Armani jacket off a hanger. 'I know you'd never cheat on me, babes. You're my number one.'

'Are you off somewhere?' Lisa asked, suddenly suspicious.

'Yeah. I've gotta go and sort out some business.'

'But you told me to come and spend the evening with you.'

'Babes, don't nag. I'm always spending time with you.'

'You're always going off with your friends. Don't you wanna spend some time with your girl?' Lisa pleaded.

'Yeah, I do. But I waited for you all fuckin' night and where was you? With that Vince guy.' Leon zipped up his jacket. 'I'll be back soon, watch some TV.'

'Maybe I should just go home.'

'No don't do that. I'll be back soon, it's just something came up. You know how it is.' He flashed Lisa a quick grin as he stood in the doorway.

'Hurry up.' Lisa kicked off her shoes and propped herself up against the dark headboard. She picked up the television remote control and switched on the wide screen television. There wasn't much on. A Vincent Price horror film she had seen and random comedy that didn't make her laugh. She looked around the room. Leon's abode was like a showroom crossed with a half-way house. There were plenty of worldly goods, like his futuristic silver hi-fi but none of those things which turn a house into a home, items of sentimental value, like her worn-out teddy bear or Sian's taffeta basket. Lisa got up, walked over to the curtains, checked the street was clear and then returned to one of the bed-side tables. She opened the top drawer. It was empty except for packets of condoms, a cigarette lighter and a packet of Rizla. In the next drawer there was an old Christmas card. Lisa opened it. Inside was a big heart. 'To my darling Leon' was scrawled in spidery black handwriting and at the bottom, 'from Tiffany. I love you so much.'

Lisa read the card again. 'No wonder she still won't talk to me,' she muttered with a sigh. She carefully replaced the card then looked in the bottom drawer which was empty apart from a few keys and coins. She didn't bother investigating the other bedside table as she knew the three drawers just contained socks.

Lisa crossed to the cupboard on which the silver hi-fi rested and opened the doors. Inside she found football magazines, car documents and a white plastic bag. Lisa carried the white bag to the bed. She took out a photo album. 'At last some photos,' she said triumphantly. The photographs were old. A middle-aged woman sitting at a table. Some teenage kids on a sofa. A raggle-taggle bunch of kids with bad haircuts making rude gestures at the camera. A small girl of about eight. Other photographs seemed to be of Leon's footballing friends, all leg muscles and ballsy smiles. There was a picture of Leon with his arm around Tiffany. Him, dirty in his football gear, holding a cup in the air. Tiffany, in leggings and wearing his sports jacket holding onto him. They made a handsome couple. Lisa leaned back on the pillows. She had lost a good friend there and wondered if he was worth it. Was he even faithful? Where was he now? Lisa sighed and closed her eyes. She was woken by the sound of skidding tyres and the roar of a car engine. Lisa sat up, still dazed with sleep, then sprang up in alarm. She shoved the photo album back into its plastic bag and returned it to the cupboard. She checked all the drawers she had opened were shut and then threw herself back onto the bed just as the door flew open and Leon strode in. He walked over to the hi-fi and put a CD in.

'You took a long time,' Lisa snapped.

'Yeah, we were just talking,' Leon said. He chuckled.

'Who's "we"?'

'We. My friends, innit. Just lost track of the time.'

'I wasn't put on this earth to wait on you, y'know.'

'C'mon, babes, don't nag. You sound like an old woman.'

Maintaining an easy humour he took off his jacket

and hung it on a hanger. Lisa watched as he unbuttoned his blue shirt, took it off and hung it up on another hanger. He sat down on the bed to take off his boots and socks. He left his socks on the floor but placed his boots at the far end of a long row of shoes and trainers. The muscles in his chest rippled as he stretched, then he unbuttoned his jeans and dragged them off. Before Lisa could respond he sat down beside her and using the weight of his honey-coloured body eased her down onto the bed. 'Ahh, you feel so good, babes. What have I done to deserve you, huh?' he whispered, tickling her cheek with his stubble.

'I want to go home,' Lisa said, trying to wriggle out of his embrace. 'I'm not in the mood.'

'Why? What's the problem? You know how much I wanna make love to you, babes,' he said, nuzzling her neck. 'You'll be in the mood after I kiss you and touch you everywhere.' He slid his large hands underneath her jumper.

'Just get off me. I wanna go home. You leave me waiting for ages and then you think everything's fine again, the minute you come back?' Leon sat up and Lisa got off the bed. 'I mean, what kind of girl do you think I am? Do you know how many guys are just dying to take me out?'

'I know, babes. I'm sorry. C'mon, I'll make it up to you.' Leon got up and put his arms around her, trying to draw her back towards the bed but she pushed him away. 'What the hell is wrong with you?' Leon said as he backed off, confused and irritated.

'I just don't feel like it any more,' said Lisa, avoiding his gaze.

'There must be another reason.'

'Well, next time try staying, huh?'

'It must be more than that. You gettin' it from someone else? Maybe you had it from Vince today already,' said Leon petulantly.

'Oh, screw you, Leon. I'm not Tiffany, so don't ever take me for granted and stop harassing me. When I'm ready to fuck someone else, I'll sure as hell let you know,' Lisa shouted.

'All right, come on then,' Leon yelled back. He pulled his jeans on and angrily shoved his feet into some trainers not bothering with socks. He put on his wool jacket without a shirt. 'Same old story, isn't it, Lisa. Playing fucking games so that I'll fuckin' do what you want as usual. Let's go.'

Lisa sat in silence as Leon grumbled angrily as he turned the car around. He narrowly missed a beat-up Datsun parked opposite.

'You're being dangerous,' shouted Lisa in alarm, punching Leon's arm with a fist.

'Well, I'm a dangerous muthafucka and that's how the fuck I live so if you don't like it call a cab, or better still,' he paused as he turned into Romford Road at high speed, 'why don't we just call it a day, Lisa? I can't cope with these games you play. It's not like I treat you like a slut, is it? I've never treated a woman as good as I treat you and all I get out of it is headache. That's the trouble with black girls, man. You fuckin' take, take, take and all you give back is headache.'

Lisa sat silently watching shops, houses and other cars flash past. 'The only reason you wanna finish is because you can't get the bloody sex,' she said quietly.

'Your my woman and I'm your man. We're supposed to have sex. That's the whole fuckin' point!'

'Well, if that's all we had going then it's just as well.'

'You're almost home now, Lisa. Leyton Rise is just a minute away. You better be sure that you wanna end it 'cos when you step out of this car and walk away that's gonna be it.'

'Yeah, well maybe I'm better off with a guy who takes time out to be with me.'

'Takes time out to be with you? You're going on like I left you at my house all fuckin' night! You were late! I only left you there for an hour before I—'

'Look out!'

'Jeezus!'

An elderly drunk had suddenly stepped into the road causing Leon to swerve into the path of an oncoming car. The screeching of brakes and harsh blasts of car horns ripped through the cold night.

'That dumb fuck!' exclaimed Leon, opening his car door and jumping out. He ran across to the other car and banged on the bonnet. 'What the fuck were you doing? You nearly fucking killed us,' he shouted. He stopped banging the bonnet and started to kick the side of the car. 'Get out the car, you coward,' he snarled. 'I'll teach you how to drive. I'll bang the lessons into your fuckin' head.'

Lisa undid her seatbelt and opened her door. She got out of the car, crossed the road and began walking towards Leyton Rise. Leon turned. 'Oi, Lisa, come back . . . Lisa . . . Lisa,' he yelled, but she just kept walking.

*

When Lisa reached the eighth floor, Woody was on the landing smoking a cigarette and looking down at the road where the two cars had nearly crashed.

'That guy is gonna kill you one day, Lisa,' he remarked quietly.

'Actually, Woody, the way things are going I'm more likely to end up killing him, so don't worry,' she said with forced brightness as she kissed him on the cheek then walked through the front door into the flat.

'Don't worry?' There was an indignant noise from the kitchen and her mother came into the hallway. She was wearing a pink bathrobe, had rollers in her hair and a cigarette in her right hand. 'First you just disappear and don't tell me you were wiv Sian 'cos I called 'er. Now you come back at one in the mornin' drivin' at breakneck speed with some guy we've never seen before. Who is that man?'

'His name is Leon.'

'Ain't that Tiffany's boyfriend?'

'No, he's my boyfriend and one day you'll meet him. I'm twenty now, Mum. You and Woody can't tell me what to do for ever,' replied Lisa crossly.

'Shut your trap, you'll wake Liam,' hissed June. 'This is my 'ouse, young lady and I won't 'ave you treating it like some kind of slut hotel. You know I don't mind where you go just so long as you let someone know.'

'Well, maybe I'll just move out, then you wouldn't have a chance to know,' muttered Lisa, heading up the stairs.

'Suppose I was to tell your father what you were up to? Huh?'

'Go ahead, ring him up. He didn't even sign my bloody birth certificate so why should he care? I'll bet you don't even have his phone number,' she said, slamming her bedroom door.

Woody stubbed his cigarette out and walked into the house, shaking his head. He shut the front door and went into the kitchen. June gratefully accepted the security of Woody's embrace. 'What'm I gonna do, Woody? She doesn't talk to me any more, she tells lies. I can't tell 'er not to do somethin', she just screams at me. I can't take it any more and you see the kind of men she dates. All the roughest ones, the ones with fast cars and ready cash. That's no way for my Lisa to live.'

'Don't worry, she'll come around,' he said comfortingly.

'She'd better,' said June grimly. She took a long drag of her cigarette then exhaled slowly. 'It was 'ard being a single mum. *I* didn't 'ave a life, but Lisa does. She's beautiful an' smart. She's got a bright future and I'll be damned if I'm gonna stand by and watch her fuck it up.'

Lisa hung up her coat and began undressing. Her mobile rang.

'Hi, just saw your light come on. You didn't tell me you were going out.'

'Sian, you could have covered for me.'

'And said what? You didn't tell me you were going to see Leon, or was it someone else?' Sian huffed sulkily.

'Yeah, whatever. It's no big thing. Anyway, I'm really tired so—'

'What's going on with you and Vince?'

'Huh?'

'You and Vince. If it hadn't been for Jules and Otis I wouldn't have got anything done because he spends all his time flirting with you. So why the sudden attraction? He wasn't all over you for nothing.'

'That's up to him, ain't nothing to do with me,' Lisa pointed out.

'Well, you weren't exactly giving him the elbow, were you? Personally, Lisa, I think you should have more respect for yourself,' said Sian with a sniff.

'Let me tell *you* something, Miss High and Mighty, when I keep Vince sweet, you reap the rewards, when I pretend that I'm digging his lines he goes the extra mile for you but since you're so fucking concerned there ain't jack going on between me and Vince,' said Lisa.

There was a pause.

'Oh, well, I was just checkin', before you start blowing up on me. Calm down.'

'Goodnight, Sian.' Lisa switched off her mobile with a relieved sigh.

chapter
fourteen

'C'mon, Lisa. It's only about one o'clock. Sian's not gonna be here for a while yet, Jackie's not in the office today. I gave her the day off to go Christmas shopping. She wanted to get to the shops before the stampede starts. Otis and Jules ain't gonna come in till later. We've got an important client doing a session this evening, so why are you so uptight?'

'It feels funny, coming to the studio without Sian.'

'Well, it shouldn't. You're here to listen to her demo tape. You're her manager, aren't you? You're supposed to call the shots.'

'True. So you just wanted to listen to the tape and then talk to me, right? Well what do you want to talk about?'

Vince picked up the remote control and pointed it at the hi-fi. 'Let's listen to the tape first.' Sian's voice blasted out from the speakers on either side of the hi-fi.

'She sounds great,' Lisa exclaimed. 'So it's all finished. I don't believe it.'

'Yeah, she's a talented lady and really dedicated.

Never turned up late, always did extra work at home. Both tracks are wicked.'

'Are these all copies?' Lisa asked, indicating a pile of cassette tapes stacked on the coffee table.

'Uh huh. A dozen or so copies. The boys did a real good job. I think she sounds on point. The cassettes are all labelled and ready to give away. Treat me right and we can run off a whole lot more. Do you want a drink?'

Lisa shrugged. 'Sure, why not?'

Vince stood up, walked over to the small refrigerator in the corner of the chill-out room and bent down.

'We've got everything in here. What d'you fancy? Vodka? Hooch?'

'Coke.'

'I'm having rum and Coke. Don't you want some rum too?'

'No thanks, just the Coke.'

'Come on, it's nearly Christmas.'

'Just Coke, Vince. I see you go in for this Christmas thing in a big way. Tree in reception, all these cards everywhere.'

'Well, Jackie is into it, she did the tree yesterday. We always get lots of cards. Lord knows why as I never send any. But I like the parties and the good vibes,' Vince explained as he busied himself getting their drinks organized.

'Yeah, I know what you mean.' Lisa leaned forward, stretched across and quickly picked up two of the cassettes. She slipped them into her bag, then sat back on the sofa.

Vince came back to the sofa with two glasses.

'There you go.' He sat down and casually began

stroking her leg. Lisa moved away. 'C'mon, Lees. I called you to the studio to discuss your music career. I've got big plans for you. I see you as the next Venus Brown or Ebony Love. A creamy-coloured songstress with a look that has people guessing where she's from and an attitude that's sassy and cute. It's all about image. I can't stress that word enough. You don't know how frustrating it is to have the voice without the face. I mean, yeah, if you can sing, that's good but it's just one tenth of the story. You have to *look* the part.'

'What you're trying to say is Sian doesn't?'

'She's all right but she's just your average nappy-headed black girl and that just doesn't fit in with the R'nB image. That's why so many black female singers have weaves and coloured contact lenses. See, you don't need any of that, it's all natural. You could get a record deal just like how you look now.'

'Yeah, I know but we're supposed to be looking out for Sian. I mean what was the point of the competition?'

'I'll be honest. Sian had the best combination of looks and voice at that event and I have worked with her in good faith. Out of the studio time she won, she has managed to get a very decent demo tape that you or she can take to anybody and play it and be taken seriously. I'll also provide her with some contacts, introductions like at the Four-Play afterparty, that sort of thing. But really, Lisa, I wanted us to work together. Ever since you came into the studio I've seen me and you as the dream team.'

'What did you get from Sireeta?'

'Huh?'

'Well, you've made it clear you don't do favours for nothing yet she's one of your singers. How's that?'

'This isn't about Sireeta. This is about you, Lisa. However, since you mention it, Sireeta's got sense. She understands that you don't get something for nothing and she's done quite well out of it. Lisa, I would like for us to have a closer relationship. We had a deal.'

Lisa grimaced as Vince traced a finger along her neck and shoulders. She shifted on the sofa.

'Yeah, I'm a bit uncomfortable too,' said Vince. 'Oh, Lisa, I'm gonna make it happen for you, babydoll. You just watch. I'm a big man. Anything you want I'll give it to you.' Lisa stared at the ceiling as Vince pressed her against the arm of the sofa.

'The deal was a couple of parties, that's it. That's it, Vince. You're all over me, man.'

'Just one little kiss. I just wanna hold you, touch your hair.'

'If Sian or one of the others comes, this is gonna look so awful. I'm getting out of here,' Lisa hissed, pushing Vince away and standing up.

'Hey, Sian won't get in without my buzzing her in. Anyway after the Four-Play afterparty, when you see how much people I know, you're gonna beg *me* to make love to you, y'know,' Vince chortled.

Lisa straightened her leggings and adjusted her sweater. 'Don't count on it,' she muttered, with a worried glance at her watch. 'Look, Vince, I'm outta here. I came, we talked, I've done my part. I didn't tell Sian I was coming so I really don't want her to find me here. Can I take a tape?'

'Sure. Don't sweat it. I won't tell Sian you were here. I'll call you tonight,' said Vince as Lisa put on her coat. He followed Lisa out into the reception area.

'I wish you wouldn't call me in the evenings. I have a boyfriend and he doesn't like it.'

'You don't need him or Sian. You only need me. Just drop them. You'll make new friends.'

'Forget you, man. I don't betray my friends.' Lisa began making her way down the stairs.

'You're a fool. Life is a bitch and then you—'

'Die, yes I know that. But if I did sell Sian out, what's in it for me? I don't wanna end up like Sireeta.'

Lisa stopped in the small hallway and turned round to hear Vince's answer.

'Lisa, you haven't been listening. I'm here for you.' Vince began descending the stairs. 'I'm gonna make things happen for you. You just tell me what, when and where and I'll do it.' Reaching Lisa, he pressed her against the wall, trying to kiss her again. Lisa, in edging out from his embrace, leaned against the front door which flew open. Lisa and Vince stumbled out into the street holding onto each other for support. They nearly knocked Sian over.

'Lisa? What?' Sian looked from one to the other.

'Oh shit,' said Lisa, looking at the ground.

'What are you doing here, Lisa? You didn't say you were going to be here today when we spoke last night,' said Sian. Vince, an unsympathetic smirk creeping over his face, was the first to recover.

'Well, you had to find out sooner or later, Sian. Friendship isn't like rocks, y'know. It don't last.' He tried to slip his arm around Lisa's waist.

'There's nothing going on, Sian, I swear,' said Lisa, trying to smooth down her hair.

Lisa stepped forward but stopped when Sian quickly moved away.

Vince took Lisa's momentary hesitation as an opportunity to put his arm around her shoulders.

'It's all starting to clear now,' said Sian. 'You and Vince. Damn, I should have guessed earlier, Lisa. How long have you two been screwing each other?'

'Vince, tell her the truth,' pleaded Lisa.

Vince put his hands in his pockets and grinned. 'Well, Sian, the truth is, Lisa's going to be the star, but I'm sure we can fix you up with some backing work.'

'It's all lies, Sian,' said Lisa at once.

'Tiffany was right about you,' Sian said coldly, then turned and walked swiftly away down Eden Mews.

'Vince, why did you do that?' said Lisa angrily.

'Aw, c'mon, baby, it's the best thing. I'm clearing the air so we can get to work on us.'

'Us?' Lisa glared at Vince. 'I was only there so that you would do something for Sian. You must be out of your tiny mind!' Lisa shook her head. She began walking away.

'Yeah, walk away,' shouted Vince. 'You ain't shit. You think your looks gonna get you anywhere? Without me you'll never be on a music video, you'll be fuckin' up people's hair until you're fuckin' fifty, and Sian will never get into another studio in her life.'

Lisa stopped, turned around and walked back. 'You just don't get it, Vince,' she said. 'Sian doesn't need you. She's so talented she'll get where she's going with or without your precious help. And as for me, I don't wanna be made into something I'm not. I can't sing and I'm just not the sort of person who's ever gonna be famous. A lot of girls would jump at your offer but not me and there's nothing you can do about it.' Then Lisa turned and hurried after Sian.

Vince stared after Lisa's departing figure until she turned the corner. Then he walked back into the studio hallway and slammed the door behind him.

Lisa walked into the bus shelter where Sian sat. Sian kissed her teeth contemptuously and turned her head. Lisa stood opposite Sian.

'Sian, hey, don't go out like that.'

'Lisa, just get your train and leave me alone. Right now I'm calm so don't come upsetting me.'

'But don't you wanna know wh—' began Lisa, sitting down on an empty seat.

'I know all I need to know so why don't you go back to your man and we'll just call it a day. I'm not ready for no arguments.' A bus edged towards them.

'All right,' replied Lisa heatedly. 'Just call it a day. You don't even listen to what your best friend has to say before you go believing that, that idiot. Whose word do you trust more? His or mine? Well, I'm glad. I'm glad to know what you think of me, I'm glad to know that you can let how many years go in five minutes for the first Negro that feeds you scandal, but I ain't in the hearsay business, so maybe all this,' she held out her hands, 'maybe all this is the way it should be.'

The bus pulled up and people got out. Lisa remained in her seat, looking down at the pavement. After the bus drove away, she looked up. Sian was standing in front of her.

'Look me in the eye and tell me you haven't lied to me, Lisa.'

'Yeah, I lied.' Lisa began to wind a strand of hair around her index finger.

'Who would have guessed it, man? You screwed that ugly loser. You of all people. What did you get out of it? Is Vince going to make you into a superstar now?' Sian enquired bitterly.

'First of all, of course I didn't screw the creep, it wasn't like that and furthermore you shouldn't be asking me what I got. Look to yourself, Sian. What did you get?'

Sian thought about this.

'Why do you think Vince wanted us in the studio so much?' Lisa continued. 'Why do you think he was willing to hand out invites to parties and give you extra studio time? You can sing, Sian. I don't care what Vince says, you can really sing but that wasn't the reason.'

'I can't believe you're telling me this. How could you ever think that I would go to Vince's studio knowing that I was only there 'cos you was selling your butt.' Sian turned away then turned back in disbelief. 'That's the craziest thing, Lisa.'

'For the last time, I wasn't selling my butt. Think what you like, Sian. I felt guilty about the argument we had the other day after Vince had dropped us off at the Rise. I wanted to show myself that your career was important to me. Vince had made out like if I was nice to him, he would give you extra studio time, contacts and stuff. It was a deal. I was to go out with him once or twice and it didn't seem like much for you to get your music sorted out. We both got something, you got your demo tape and I felt like I'd helped you, like managers are supposed to do,' she said, smiling wryly. 'So when he called yesterday and said I should come see him at the studio on my half day I didn't tell you because I thought he just wanted to talk about going to some party.'

'You can come better than that, Lisa. Anyway, now it's over, we've both got nothing so what was the point?'

'Oh, there's a point. Sian, don't underestimate me, at least you got your demo tape. I listened to it, it sounds really good and—'

'Oh, shut up. Vince has got my demo tape.'

'Will you listen for one minute, Sian, *I* got copies. With what we got, we don't need Vince any more. I got a plan,' said Lisa with a slow wicked smile.

'Oh yeah?' Sian kissed her teeth dismissively and gave Lisa a long hard stare. 'And with your track record what makes you think I'm gonna trust any plan you dream up?'

chapter
fifteen

At Lisa's home a row was flaring.

'Liam, come upstairs and brush your hair. Lisa, you are comin' wiv' us to visit your gran. You are *not* spending Christmas Eve with that man!'

Lisa applied more lipstick, ignoring June who was ironing Woody's shirt in the upstairs hallway. She placed the lipstick case in her handbag. June slammed the iron back in its holder. Liam came running up the stairs.

'Mum, I'm twenty years old,' said Lisa. 'I daresay that if I wanna spend Christmas Eve with my boyfriend it's up to me.'

'But we always spend Christmas Eve at June's mum's,' said Woody, standing in the doorway of her bedroom. 'She'll be upset if you don't make the effort.'

'Woody, I can't go for the rest of my life. Gran'll understand if I can't make it this year. I'll make it next year.' Lisa walked over to Woody. She stood on her toes and kissed him on the cheek. 'I'd get that shirt on quick. Your thermal ain't the prettiest sight in the world,' Lisa said grinning.

'Don't you think your gran's more important than some guy you've only bin seein' for five bloody minutes,' shouted June. 'Woody, here's your shirt.' She passed Woody his shirt, rested the iron on the floor and began folding up the iron board.

'Mum, I can't find my shoes,' whined Liam, coming out of his room.

'Liam, careful of the iron. Now I didn't ask you to find your shoes!' shouted June. 'I said brush your hair. You're seven now. It's time you started listening to what people tell you.' Liam's face folded and he began to cry. June sighed and put a hand to her head. 'OK, OK, I'm sorry, darlin'.' She bent down and hugged him. 'Mummy didn't mean to shout at you, little man. Don't worry about your shoes, I'll find them. Now be a good boy and get your brush so Daddy can do your hair, like Mummy told you.' She wiped away Liam's tears and kissed him on the forehead before nudging him softly in the direction of his room.

'See what she's doin' to this family,' June said bitterly. 'It's supposed to be Christmas. We're supposed to love and cherish each other but no, Lisa has to go windin' me up, that selfish cow.' She walked across to Liam's bedroom.

Woody buttoned up his shirt in silence.

'Try and convince Mum for me please, Woody. Things can't always remain the same.'

'I'll have a go,' Woody said wearily as he turned away. 'But you can see what you've started ain't gonna be too easy to finish.'

As Lisa put her jacket on Woody and June started arguing.

'No, Woody, no, no, no and what does she look like?' exclaimed June, leaving Liam's room to see Lisa walking downstairs wearing a short red dress underneath her jacket.

'You're not goin' out on Christmas Eve looking like the slapper of the century when you should be visitin' your bloody grandmother!' June shouted from the top of the stairs.

'Jus' cool, June. There's no need for that sort of talk. Liam's already upset and it's Christmas,' Woody said, stepping forward and putting his arms around June.

'Mum, I'm still gonna be here for Christmas dinner. It's not like I'm not doing any family stuff. I'll still see Gran at some point. Leon doesn't have no parents, no brothers or sisters. I'm all he's got and I'm spending Christmas Eve with my baby. Try and understand,' Lisa said as she opened the front door.

'My baby?' echoed June. 'I thought he was Tiffany's baby a couple of months ago and before her he was someone else's baby.' But Lisa was gone.

'I can understand though,' said Woody gently.

'Woody, it ain't even a question of understanding. That Leon is dangerous. You know how close me and Tiff's mum are. She told me what he done to 'er and I don't want 'im doin' it to my Lisa, *my* baby.'

'This is a nice surprise,' remarked Lisa, looking around. They were sitting in a Chinese restaurant in Bayswater. 'I didn't think you had it in you,' she added with a smile.

Leon sat back in his chair, smirking. 'What, you think I'm like those cheap bres you're used to dating?

Nah, this is Christmas Eve, babes, so I've gotta make it special. And you look special tonight in that dress and your hair up like that.'

Lisa smiled. He sat back in his chair and glanced nonchalantly around the busy restaurant. 'So what have you been up to, babes, since I last saw you? Hope you've been behavin' yourself, not seeing any more of Vince.'

'Just working, Leon. It's been really crazy in Cutting Edge these last days before Christmas. You know I haven't been to the studio for a couple of weeks. You?'

'Some away games but training mostly. It's a bitch going out on that pitch at ten in the morning. The cold stabs you all over and it's dangerous 'cos your muscles can seize up, you can slip in the mud or on icy grass and your hamstring can get pulled like that.' He snapped his fingers. 'Then you're out for weeks. It happened to Reg a while back and he's already missed three weeks. You wouldn't believe how quick management forget about you unless you're a foreigner. Matt was saying the other day that he reckons nearly half the squad are foreigners. If it wasn't for all those Euro bastards takin' over, I'm sure I'd have been picked for better team by now.' He frowned and drummed his fingers on the table.

'I hope you take care.'

'Sometimes I think about it and it worries me, what with me being so close to my big break. But don't worry, babes, it might happen to other guys but not me,' he reassured her. 'This is Leon, don't forget. Master of the Universe. Yeah, that's the spirit, mate.' The waiter arrived with the duck starter. Leon turned back to Lisa. 'Now have you had this before?'

Lisa shook her head.

'OK,' said Leon. 'First you take one of those pancakes, babes. You put on some of that red sauce, add some duck, sprinkle on some of that veggie stuff then roll it up like a spliff. Watch me. Yeah, that's it. Now don't tell me you haven't been to the studio. Why would Vince keep calling if there wasn't a reason?'

'I can't stop him calling me. I told you Sian gave him my mobile digits.'

'Next time he calls your phone, I'm gonna take it, drive down to that studio and smash that phone into his ear,' Leon said as he finished rolling a pancake and stuffed it into his mouth.

'Well, don't worry 'cos he hasn't called for a few days. And you don't need to look so smug. If I wanted to talk to Vince, I would, regardless of what you think.'

There was a pause as Leon finished eating his pancake.

'You don't seem to get it, Lisa. You're going out with *me* now. When Tiffany was my girl, you didn't see her out at every little Leyton dance or on the street or telling me about a studio. But you now, you think life is a fashion show. I bet you wore that dress to the studio for Vince to look at. I bet you let him put his hands on your legs and I bet you bent over just like that so he could look down the top.'

'Fuck off! Stop trying to make out like I had something going on with Vince. Why do you always have to make me feel cheap? And I'm not trying to replace Tiffany either. I'm better than Tiffany 'cos I don't take your shit and say yes sir, no sir, three bags full sir, and you're gonna find yourself back with Tiffany very soon if you keep— stop laughing! It's not funny. Just stop it!'

Leon kept laughing. 'You know, Lisa,' he said through his laughter, waggling a finger at her. 'You sure are funny, but keep chuckin' it and I'll knock you into next week, babes.'

Lisa wiped her mouth. She stood up, grabbing her jacket and handbag.

'Sit down, what do you think you're doing now?'

'I'm not gonna be treated like Tiffany, Leon. I left my family to spend Christmas Eve with you because you don't have any family so don't act like you're doing me any favours, OK.'

Leon stood up. He stretched across and held Lisa's arm, the smile had gone from his face.

'All right, Lisa, sit down. I'm sorry, I didn't mean it.'

Lisa sighed and sat down.

'Here, have another glass of wine. We'll make a toast.' He filled her glass with white wine.

'I've had too much wine already and so have you.'

'I can't get drunk, I'm already high on life, babes. But you look sexy when you're drunk. You don't give so much lip and you get this wild light in your eyes that just says come and get me.' They smiled at each other.

'You talk shit sometimes,' said Lisa with an affectionate grin as they touched glasses.

They walked quickly to the car and got in as the odd flake of snow began to fall. On the drive back, Leon grew quieter and quieter.

'S'gonna be a white Christmas, baby,' said Lisa softly as they drove through the empty city streets.

'Hmmm.'

'So what are you gonna do tomorrow? I hope you're not just gonna sit at home on your jays.'

'Whatever.'

'Whatever? What do you mean by that? It's Christmas. I don't wanna sit over my turkey worrying about you,' she said with a nervous laugh. Leon didn't answer and they continued their journey in silence.

'What's wrong, Leon?' asked Lisa anxiously.

'Nothing. Don't worry about it.'

They continued driving.

'Well, there must be something wrong, Leon. Is it something I've done?'

Leon shook his head. 'No, babes. I just always get like this around Christmas, these moods that I can't shake off. Up one minute, down the next. It'll pass soon.'

'I don't want it to pass, Leon, if it's gonna come back. We should talk about this.'

'Talking about it doesn't help, it just makes it worse, makes it grow, makes it harder to think normally.'

'Pull over,' ordered Lisa. Leon slowed then stopped the car by the side of the road. He sat silently, looking down, then groaned.

'You wouldn't know what it's like, Lisa. You've got your cushy little family, your cushy little life. You can't understand.'

'My life isn't cushy, Leon, and you're right, maybe I don't know, but I'm here, isn't that the important thing?'

Leon reached across and hugged Lisa tightly.

'Leon, honey, why are you crying?'

Eventually Leon released her.

'Lisa, you know my past. I never knew my mother or father, never had no family, no real family. To all the foster families that took me, I was just the runt of someone else's litter passing through. None of them loved me. Back then, I was the kid that used to get beat up every day 'cos I was small, 'cos I was black, 'cos all I wanted was someone who'd love me. Christmas was the worst. I hated it 'cos it reminded me that I was the runt no one wanted. I still hate it, all that Santa Claus stuff. When I was younger I used to dream about kickin' the shit out of him, kickin' Father Christmas to death so everyone else could have a fuckin' great Christmas just like me,' he said bitterly.

'I love you.'

'I thought I could leave all that behind when I started football. Football was my ticket to somewhere, Lisa. Football made me big and strong and it made me money. If the boys that used to kick me around in the children's home could see me now, they'd cheer. They'd admire me and respect me and they'd call me a mate but that wouldn't change shit. It don't make no difference how much money you have if you ain't got no one in this life. There's no one out there for me. That's why I do mad shit sometimes. I get these moods, like I wanna fight the world for no reason.'

'You weren't alone. Tiffany loved you.'

'Maybe. Tiffany's white though. She's got a family. How could she understand what I was going through? All she could think about was that she was dating some footballer with a big black dick and a kriss ride. She didn't know the real me. Inside I'm still small like a kid. I'm still skinny and afraid and alone.' Leon turned and gripped Lisa's shoulders tightly. 'Are you gonna be there for me, babes? Stick by me, hold my hand, take care of me?' Leon was sobbing again. 'I know I'm jealous and sometimes I do get mad but the way I feel about you, Lisa, I never felt like that about anyone. You gotta tell me now if it's gonna be you and me for ever 'cos if it ain't I've got to let you go before I really start to care.'

chapter
sixteen

'**Sian, get** up, get up, GET UP!'

'Buelah, if you're not gone by the time I open my eyes, I am going to thump you harder than you've ever been thumped in your life.' Sian slowly opened her eyes to see Buelah looking down at her warily.

She beamed when she realized Sian wasn't going to hit her. 'How can you sleep, Sian? It's Christmas today!' She jumped on to the bed. 'You betta not shout, you betta not cry, you betta watch out I'm telling you why,' she sang, bouncing up and down. 'Santa Claus is coming to town! Santa Claus is coming—'

'Shut up, Buelah, and stop bouncing, the bed feels like it's going to tip over and I feel seasick. I wanna go back to sleep.'

'Oh good, you wake,' said Bernadette, coming into the bedroom. 'Happy Chris'mas, girls.' Buelah got off the bed and hugged Bernadette. Sian groaned and pulled a pillow over her head. 'Ah sleep you a' sleep, Sian? Get up! Out of bed now. Me bath an' cook up a nice Christmas breakfast already but now is housework time.'

'We tidied up at the weekend,' Sian said into the pillow.

'After breakfas' there is hoov'ring to do. I want to see not even one speck of dust 'pon de carpet, Buelah, and Sian, when you finish wipe down de doors and polish up ev'ry t'ing, then you come inna de kitchen and start peel up de Brussels sprouts. I want everyt'ing nice and tidy for when me sister get here.' Bernadette started to turn away. 'And if you come down when de breakfas' is col', you will eat it col'.'

Bernadette left the room and slowly walked downstairs.

'Come on, Sian, I'm starving.' Buelah tugged at the duvet. 'The sooner we get the work done, the sooner we can open our presents.' She paused for a moment then turned and hurried after Bernadette.

Buelah and Bernadette were halfway through breakfast when Sian staggered into the kitchen. Her hair was tangled and she had a miserable expression on her face. Buelah and Bernadette giggled.

'What are you lot so smart about? Where's my brekkie?' Sian demanded.

Bernadette stood up, put some oven gloves on and took Sian's plate out of the oven.

'Be careful, the plate hot,' she warned, putting it down on the mat in front of Sian. 'Don't forget to say grace,' she added quickly as Sian picked up her knife and fork.

'Sorry,' said Sian, pausing and closing her eyes for a few seconds. 'There. Oh Mum, what time did you have to wake up to fry these dumplings?' She took a bite. 'They're delicious.'

Bernadette smiled. She nudged Buelah. 'See how she a brighten up once she get food in her belly. There's more plantain in the oven but if you wan' more bacon you gwine cook it yourself.'

'No, this is more than enough for me. Gosh I'm tired. Yesterday was so busy, I don't think I've worked harder at the shop. You'd have been really surprised by the amount of people that were in there spending loot like this was the last Christmas ever, buying up all cack stuff like tennis balls. Who'd want tennis balls for Christmas?'

'Well, I wouldn't mind some new trainers,' said Buelah. 'I can feel the floor through mine.'

'I'll get you some trainers in the January sales, Buelah. Anyway, Alan said we had a record day. The shop took more money than on any other day of the year. He was really pleased although he still made me and Deris stay and help him clean up. It was really unfair. He let Marianne go early 'cos she said she had a train to catch. Then I went and had a drink with Deris in a nearby wine bar. Deris invited me so I couldn't say no.' She yawned. 'I could sleep all day, Christmas or no Christmas.'

'It's been busy at de hospital as well. I t'ink people always get sick dis time of year 'cos dem get wear out. Still good for me. I get more money to work Boxing Day and New Year's Eve.'

'That means we won't have to visit Mrs Dega on Boxing Day like we usually do,' said Buelah hopefully, with a sidelong glance at Sian.

'Not dis year. She is very upset about it but I explain about de bills and Hortense understand how it go,' said

Bernadette, rising from the table. 'Buelah, when you finish eat, bath. Sian, when you done finish eat, wash up de plate den hoover de living room. I going put de turkey in the oven now.'

'Yes, Mum,' chorused the two girls.

'Oh, Sian,' said Buelah with a heartfelt sigh. 'Don't you just love Christmas?'

After much hoovering and cleaning the doorbell rang.

'That'll be Cherry and Slick. I'll go and get de door. Keep on with de sprouts, Sian,' Bernadette said as she hurried into the hall and opened the door.

'Cherry, you make it here a jus' de right time. How de weather?' she asked before shutting the door behind them. 'Lord, it mus' be well col'.'

'Ev'ry day seem col' in dis country but it smell pretty in here.'

'Well de turkey in de oven. Sian jus' doing de sprouts. Slick, rude bwoy, come and give you auntie a kiss nuh.'

Slick hugged Bernadette.

'So where me present deh?' Bernadette joked with a chuckle.

'Moms has all the presents, Aunt Bernie, you gon' have to take it up wit' her,' said Slick, smiling. He walked into the kitchen and hugged Sian. Buelah came running in.

'Hi, Slick.'

'Buelah! Damn, those braids look like they gonna take off for the moon the way they're sticking up.' Buelah stuck out her tongue and walked back into the living room.

'Don't fuss, homegirl,' said Slick following her. 'Your hair looks good. I'm jus' playin'.'

Cherry took her coat off and hung it on the banister. Then she carried her bags into the kitchen and put them on the kitchen table. She kissed Sian.

'I brought a few things. There's fruits, mostly, a Christmas pudding I got up Oxford Street. Some chocolate, and two bottles of wine.'

'Thanks. I appreciate everyt'ing. On hospital wages is difficult to afford those little things. Usually, I jus' make my own t'ings. Buelah and I made mince pies last night. Homemade ones always taste nicer than de cardboard shop ones anyway. I see you got your hair done. It look really good. Where did you go?'

Cherry bent her head down so Bernadette could pat it. 'Well, I know it's a bomb to pay but I went to the hairdressers on Leyton High Road. They wrapped my hair up nice. I just thought I'd get it done in case I go somewhere.'

'Hmm, so you have boyfriend now to be going disco with?'

Cherry laughed sheepishly. 'Bernadette, if you just took a bit more care with your appearance and stop wearing those dowdy clothes you would have so many more callers.'

'The kind of man *I* want, no fancy hair and fancy skirt will find for me,' retorted Bernadette tartly.

'Yes, Bernie, I know all about your church men, all jheri curl and bad breath and want sit down eat curried goat all day.'

'Hmph. Well there's no sin in dat!'

'There's no fun in it either. Lord knows these past

few years you carryin' on like you got more religion than Mother Teresa, but I remember a time when you would curl up your hair, put on a short skirt and dance the night away with a fine brother, sin or no sin.'

Bernadette looked embarrassed. Sian laughed. She rinsed off the sprouts and threw the peelings into the bin. 'Well, that's the sprouts done. I'm just going to put a dress on and do my hair. I won't be long,' Sian said.

'Don't worry. You been a good help. De turkey won't be ready for a while. When you cleaned up, you look after Slick.'

'OK, see you guys in a while. Don't drink all the wine before dinner,' she joked.

'I just got so many things on my mind. Slick is causing me so much trouble,' Cherry said once Sian had left the room.

'Well, he a young man, what you expect?'

'It's not right, Bernie. He don't work, he don't learn nothing. His dad send him some money so he can just be lazy. If it wasn't for me I don't even t'ink him would wash.' They chuckled.

'Well, why don't you send him back to his father in America?'

'Dan? Dan is not a good role model for Slick. Never at work and at night, out with his friends, playing cards or whatever. And Slick, with those damn gangster friends he got, I had to get him out of New York before he got shot.'

'Really, it that bad?'

'It that bad, honey, and you know, if I tell you, it must be true. Mind your finger with that knife, Bernie. It's just that, it don't seem to be working out for him here either. If I could just find a man, then everything would settle down.'

'But that not too easy, Cherry. Still, come to church. I know that you like your parties and your tight-fitting clothes and your alcohol, but there are some good men there.'

Cherry laughed.

'What you trying to say? That I'm mutton dressed up as lamb? Well, maybe I am but I might take you up on that invitation, Bernie. I might just.'

Bernadette crossed to the sink and squeezed out a dishcloth. She wiped down the worktops. 'Well, I t'ank God for my two turning out as good as they have. It wasn't easy to raise Sian and Buelah either.'

'Oh, come on, Bernie. They're girls. How hard could it be? Do you think if I had a girl I would be having all this aggro now? Slick's a big eighteen-year-old. I can't tell him nothing. I can't slap him, even his father can't discipline him and I can't throw him out or he'll go really bad. You can't tell me Sian or Buelah are such a headache.'

'Well, as a mum you jus' try you best and hope nuttin' go wrong. Sian used to be so good and quiet. She would stay home, go church three times a week. Always used to sing at service in de choir, and *sing*?' Bernadette clapped her hands. 'You never heard any-body sing like she. Evr'y Sunday. It doesn't matter what kind of music you give her, she learn it one time and sing it straight back to you like an angel singing de Father praise. It was like de Lord breathe 'pon her, like Him touch her voice with Him finger. But time pass and she grow up, start looking at man. Start t'inking about money. Dis one stupid bwoy Stephan came into her life. Next t'ing, she leave church.'

'Jus' like dat?'

'Jus' like dat,' Bernadette declared, slapping her hand down on the worktop. 'Say she not going back. Don't believe in it any more. Now she win dis competition and she say she going be a singer.' She sighed wearily. 'But touch wood, at least Sian don't bring back no baby yet.'

'What about Buelah?'

Bernadette brightened. 'Buelah doin' very well at school. She get plenty A grade and love her church, boy, does Buelah love her church, you see. Cyan never sing like Sian but it no matter to Buelah. She gonna be de smart one. De one to take care of her mummy.'

'Don't you think you go a bit heavy with this church business? Why don't you jus' leave them to find it when they're ready?'

'Hmm, has Slick found it yet?' asked Bernadette shortly.

'No, but at least me never drag him to any altar,' said Cherry heatedly.

'Well, maybe you *should* have drag him!' said Bernadette just as heatedly. 'You should have drag him to altar mornin', noon and night from him old enough to walk. If it cold, if it wet outside, if it dark and you 'fraid fe get rob, you *still* drag him. Den maybe now you wouldn't have all dis problem on your head.'

'Yes, it easy to be wise after the bird fly out him nest,' replied Cherry stiffly. 'Now is you goin' boil those sprouts or just leave them to dry out on the side there?'

'Slick, you're there watching my MTV video with no shame while I've been working my butt off in the kitchen,' Sian said as she entered the living room.

'Yep, I knows how women loves they work, so I jus' leaves 'em to it. Anyway you look too sweet and pretty in that little dress to have been in the kitchen.'

'I just went upstairs, had a bath and changed my clothes. But I'm glad you appreciate the effort.'

'Yeah, you look very nice just like all these decorations on the tree.' Slick stood up and walked over to the Christmas tree. 'Any of them edible?' he asked, peering at the decorations.

Sian swatted him with a cushion then pushed him out the way. She bent down and took up a small rectangular package and threw it at Slick. 'You can amuse yourself with this, big boy. Christmas present from me and Buelah.'

'For me, aw Sian, you're too good, cuz.' Slick ripped open the packaging unceremoniously. 'Pete Beton, aftershave. Thanks, man. This is da bomb.'

'Ssh, I can't hear what they're saying.' Buelah turned up the volume.

'Slick, turn de tele down,' Cherry called from the kitchen a few minutes later. 'I cyan here a word we saying.'

'Oh, I don't mind,' said Bernadette, smiling. 'They enjoying themself, we enjoying ourself, so what the problem?' Bernadette was slicing cucumbers for the

166

salad. 'We always have good Christmas. The more noise the better. I hate quiet Christmas.'

'I'm much better than those buffoons on the TV, man. "Joking Aside"? They *are* the joke,' said Slick derisively.

'S'true. They're so ugly too. I only taped them because I never heard this song before.'

'My style is really coming together, Sian. All I need is a break.'

'Is that a hint?'

'Oh c'mon, Sian.' Slick got up from the sofa, kicking a ball of wrapping paper out of the way. He walked to the window and lifted the net curtain, looking out over the deserted road below. 'You got the contacts. You're my blood, and you know I'm good.' He turned to face her. 'Well, ain't I the shit?'

'Yes, OK, except that right now it doesn't look as if I have any contacts left. About a couple of weeks ago me and Lisa had one big fight at the studio.'

'Hey, you never told me about this.'

'I haven't spoken to you in a while and I didn't really feel like talking about it. The studio time I won at the competition had run out but the producer guy was still helping me to get my demo tape finished. I thought he was being kind, but it turned out he was only helping me out because Lisa was being "nice" to him.'

'What kind of nice?' asked Buelah.

Sian glanced at Buelah uncertainly. 'It doesn't matter. Basically we had to kick him to the kerb. So I've got a demo tape but not much else. Lisa says she has a plan, but until that materializes, we're out in the cold.'

'Damn, couldn't Lisa have kept up being "nice", just till you got a record deal?'

'Slick!'

'Nah, jus' jokes. But damn, so what kind of plan does she have?'

'Ain't that the sixty-four thousand dollar question,' Sian said glumly.

chapter
seventeen

The minicab moved slowly along the wet streets of central London.

'It's started raining again,' muttered Sian as she peered through the misty window of the car. 'It's been raining all week for cryin' out loud, you'd think it would stop sometime.' She turned to face Lisa who was singing along softly to the car radio. 'Man, I can't believe I let you talk me into this. I should've stayed at home.'

'Stayed at home and done what? Thought about your brilliant singing career and what could have been? Thought about the rest of your life selling trainers?' Lisa kissed her teeth. 'Girl, it may be raining and we may be on a long t'ing but we got one more chance and it's right here in these invitations.' She waved them in front of Sian. 'Lighten up, girl,' she said, rubbing her friend's arm. 'Everything's gonna come right, I can feel it.'

Sian shrugged and turned back to the window.

Lisa leaned forward towards the driver. 'Excuse me, but that looks like it over there on the left. Follow those cars going through the iron gates,' she said, indicating with her hand. The cab joined a queue of cars. Just inside the gates two burly men in leather trenchcoats stepped forward. One waved the cab to a stop and approached the car. The driver wound down his window.

'Let's see your tickets,' said the security guard, bending down and looking into the car. Lisa passed the invitations to the driver who handed them to the security guard.

'I'm just dropping these ladies off,' explained the driver as the bouncer examined the invitations. The guard nodded as he passed the invitations back through the window to the driver. 'OK, carry straight on. There's another security check further down,' he said as he straightened up.

'God, there's another one?' exclaimed Lisa. She kissed her teeth as she sat back in her seat. 'Are we ever gonna get there?'

As the minicab approached the second security check, Sian tugged Lisa's sleeve nervously. 'OK, Lisa, let's run through this once more.'

'Stop worrying, Sian. It's gonna go smooth like clockwork, you'll see. We'll go in. Mingle. Talk to as many people as possible. I know it goes without saying but ignore Vince and Sireeta as they might start trouble.'

The driver handed the invitations out of the window for a second time. When the invitations were returned he passed them back to Lisa. As he drove forward Lisa turned to Sian. 'Mission number one, find the guys from LockedDown.'

'Have you still got the demo tape?'

Lisa felt inside her satin drawstring bag, then nodded.

'Is it labelled properly?'

'Trust me, I'm still your manager, innit?'

Sian managed a small smile.

'Look. It's here, it's labelled with your name and telephone number and it's ready to go. Don't worry, we'll find them if it takes all night.'

Sian nodded.

'Now remember,' added Lisa. 'Just be cool and ignore Four-Play no matter how kriss they be looking. We wanna be taken seriously.'

'How do I look?' Sian asked, putting a hand to the base of her hair. 'Pins still holding it all up?'

'I should hope so, I put enough in. Don't worry, the curls haven't dropped and there are no stray hairs, you look kriss.'

'This looks like it, ladies,' said the driver, coming to a stop in front of a large modern building. 'The Dome. That'll be twenty pounds, please.'

'Oh, come on,' Lisa protested. 'A score? I've been to Chelsea x amount of times and I've never paid more than fifteen pounds, innit, Sian?'

'Look, love, the fare from Leyton to this part of Chelsea is twenty pounds, end of story.'

Sian took a twenty-pound note from her purse and passed it to the driver. 'Come on, Lisa, I'm not in the mood to haggle. Hey, thanks for the journey,' she said to the driver. Sian opened the car door, got out and began walking up the steps towards the brightly lit entrance.

'Wait up,' called Lisa, getting out of the car and hurrying after Sian. 'Hold on, I can't walk fast in these sandals.'

'What's your fuckin' problem?' Lisa hissed as she caught up with Sian at the top of the stairs. 'I was just tryin' to save us a bit of wong. Sian, will you just *stop* and listen to me for one minute!'

Sian stopped and turned around.

'Sian, this is me, Lisa. Your best friend in the whole fuckin' world. If you're still pissed about the whole Vince thing then tell me about it, don't just walk away.'

'I just don't feel sure about this, Lisa. I mean the guys we're looking for are supposed to be Vince's longtime friends which means as soon as Vince sees us it's all over. He's never gonna let us talk to anyone important. I'm not like you, Lisa. I can't just bat my eyes at a problem and watch it melt away. To be honest, yeah, I am still pissed about the whole Vince thing. I think what you did was dumb but *this*, this is even dumber. All that's gonna happen is we're gonna get shamed up.'

'Since when did you take what Vince said as gospel truth?' snapped Lisa. 'According to Vince, everyone's his longtime friend. Yeah, I was stupid, but I'm making up for it now. Vince isn't calling the shots any more, Sian, we are. You and me. Hey, everyone deserves a second chance, don't they?'

'True. I suppose you're right,' said Sian quietly.

'What? I'm sorry, could you speak a bit louder? I could've sworn you said I was right.'

'Yes! OK, Lisa. You're right, you do deserve a

second chance. Let's go and do this.' Sian smiled at Lisa.

'Now you're talking my lingo,' said Lisa. She linked her arm through Sian's. 'Remember, we're Rise girls. We can do anything.'

The two girls walked across to the entrance.

'Evening, ladies, invitations, please.' The doorman took the invitations from Lisa. He studied them then handed the invitations back. 'That's fine,' he said with a warm smile. 'Enjoy your night.'

'Wow, it's huge,' exclaimed Lisa, looking around the large circular ballroom with its dome-shaped ceiling. 'And they have a casino!' She pointed towards a cluster of gaming tables that had already attracted a small crowd. 'This is my kinda place!'

'This might be your kinda place but we could barely afford our dresses never mind trying our luck at casino. You wanna get them thoughts out of your head.'

'True. The music's good though. D'you wanna dance?' Lisa said, looking at the darkened dance area in the middle of the ballroom. 'There are loads of people dancing there already and some of those guys look well kriss.'

'I'll settle for a drink for now,' said Sian, walking towards the nearby bar. Lisa made a face but followed her. The two girls squeezed through the crowd of bodies thronging the bar. One of the bar staff walked over. 'Can I get a Southern Comfort and Coke, please?' asked Sian. Lisa laughed.

'You'd better watch out, girl, 'cos you knows I'm gonna get drunk and then where will you be?'

173

'That's always a worry, Lisa, but I need a kick of something if I'm gonna see tonight through.'

'I'll have the same as my friend, please,' said Lisa to the barman. She looked through her bag to find some change, taking out the invitations and her keys so she could look better. 'Damn, I know I've got some money in here somewhere.'

The barman serving them laughed. 'I see you've got VIP invites, ladies. Well there's a free bar in the VIP lounge.' He nodded in the direction of some heavy gold velvet curtains which fell either side of a doorway blocked by two large bouncers in dark suits.

'Wicked,' said Lisa as she handed over the money and put everything back in her bag. 'Are Four-Play in there?' she asked, smiling broadly at the barman as he passed her the drinks.

'Nah, they won't be here until at least one.' The barman checked his watch. 'It's only eleven-thirty. They're still performing, most likely. Enjoy your drinks, ladies.' He smiled and moved along the bar to serve another customer.

Lisa downed her drink quickly. 'Well, we might as well go into the VIP lounge now if they've got a free bar. I could do with a couple more drinks and we can always come back out and dance later.' They made their way out of the bar area and crossed towards the gold-curtained entrance.

'Invitations, please,' said one of the bouncers in front of the entrance. After he checked them he parted the curtain and opened the door. The girls were through.

'Jus' be cool, girl,' whispered Lisa to Sian as a waiter in a crisp white shirt greeted them.

'Would you like some champagne, ladies?' the waiter asked, presenting his tray with a flourish.

'Thanks,' said Lisa and Sian in unison as they each took a fluted glass. They giggled as the waiter moved away.

'And stop staring,' Lisa added nudging. 'If your eyes get any bigger they're gonna drop onto the carpet. Come on, let's sit down.'

Lisa steered Sian towards a small round table and pulled out a cushioned chair for her to sit down on. Then she pulled out another chair and sat down herself.

'It's sooo nice in here,' Sian exclaimed softly. 'And I can see *famous* people.' She watched as a lady in a red chiffon jacket, over a red mini dress and red high-heeled shoes got up from a crowded table and crossed the room to greet a middle-aged white man at the bar. 'Don't look now, Lisa, but that's Kellie from Eternal who's just walked over to the bar.'

'Look at you with your star-struck self. Me and Tiffany used to see celebs all the time at the parties we went to.' Lisa cast an indifferent eye around the other tables in the room. 'I can see about five footballers in here.'

'Where? How do you know what they look like?'

'Oh, Leon forces me to watch football all the time so by now I know who almost everyone is.' She sipped her champagne. 'They're sitting right at the other end of the room at the table on the left. Jan Bierkon for one. Next to him, Leo Black and Dave Mitchell.'

Sian squinted in the direction of the footballers. 'I'm surprised Leon let you come at all. You didn't come to one rave over the New Year. I mean what's that all about?'

'OK, so he gets a little jealous when I wanna go out. He'd rather I didn't do it. I guess all men get like that when they really love their girl.'

'But you never used to take it before, Lisa. You used to stand up for yourself.'

'He just makes such a big deal, you know. Every little thing sets him off and then it's a big argument. At the end of the day if it causes such a fuss then I'd just as soon not go anywhere and keep my man sweet.'

'You know who you're starting to sound like, don't you?'

'Look, he let me come tonight so he can't be all bad, can he? Leo Black is scoping me out,' Lisa murmured as she smiled flirtatiously across the room. 'Leo is definitely giving me the eye.'

'And you call me star-struck,' said Sian grumpily. She tried to see the man Lisa was smiling at but she couldn't even find the table where the footballers were supposed to be sitting. As Sian looked from table to table her gaze rested on a pretty fair-skinned girl wearing a pink lycra dress. Her black hair was slicked back into a ponytail and leopard-print earrings dangled from her ears. Beside her sat a man in a silver suit with a silver shirt and silver tie. The man turned his bald head slightly to look around the room. As he did so he caught Sian's gaze and his eyebrows met in annoyance. He slammed down his glass so hard the champagne sloshed up and out of the glass.

'Sorry to break up the eye contact between you and Mr Black, Lisa, but Vince is looking right this way and, boy, does he look pissed.'

The two girls watched as Vince pushed back his chair, stood up and marched over.

'What kind of stunt is this?' he demanded.

'Negro, puhleeze, that's no way to talk to your protégé,' said Lisa sweetly.

'Just answer the fucking question,' he said heatedly.

'You gave us those invitations so we have every right to come,' said Sian quietly. Vince laughed. Sian and Lisa looked at each other uncertainly.

'Actually it's clear as fucking day. You're looking for some producer to give him your two-bit demo tape,' he said sarcastically. 'Ghetto girls be getting bright. Well, let me tell you something. Producers don't like it when they go to parties to enjoy themselves and groupies fling themselves at them to get record deals.' Vince leaned close to Lisa's head. 'It won't work this time, babydoll,' he sneered.

'It won't need to,' replied Lisa coolly. 'If those guys are as big as you say, they'll recognize real talent.'

'Real talent?' Vince said loudly and sneeringly. The room hushed. Vince fiddled with his tie and waited until the attention had left him. Then he bent down again. 'There are a hundred girls like you, Sian. Light-skinned ones with long hair, all waiting in line for the big time. I gave you a chance and you blew it, so go back to Sportsworld, you haven't got a prayer,' he hissed. Turning, he strode back to his table and sat down. Lisa bit her lip as she watched Sireeta pat Vince on the shoulder.

'I should run over there and pour this champagne

over his bloody head,' said Lisa, gripping her glass purposefully. Sian took the glass out of her hand.

'Lisa, jus' cool. You'll only get us turfed out. That's exactly what he wants. Remember what you said, it's all or nothing.'

Pink spots danced angrily in Lisa's cheeks. 'I hate him. If it wasn't for you I would have dashed that champagne all over the punk.'

'Come, let's go to the ladies' and cool out. I need the loo anyhow.' The girls walked across to the ladies'. Sian disappeared into a cubicle while Lisa paced up and down the marble floor.

'Who the hell does he think he is? Sian, I can't believe you're so calm. You should be the angry one. Didn't you hear what he said? The way he talked to us, like we were nothing?'

There was the sound of flushing and Sian came out of the cubicle. She rinsed her hands in a marble basin, then walked over to Lisa and slung an arm around her shoulder. 'I don't get angry, I get even,' Sian said. 'Now who taught me that?' They looked at each other in the mirrors opposite for a few moments then burst out laughing. 'And I think you should cut your hair,' Sian continued, running her fingers through Lisa's hair. 'It's getting too long,' she said matter of factly.

'Yeah?'

'Yeah. You're starting to look white.' They laughed again.

'I dunno. Mum says I should cut it too. I'll do something in summer when it's really gonna make my neck sweat.' Lisa rested her head on Sian's shoulder. 'What would I do without you, girl?'

'My, my, this is cosy.' Sireeta stood in the doorway for a moment, then walked over to the basins. She took out her lipstick then bent over towards the mirrors to apply it. Sian and Lisa looked at each other. Sireeta smacked her lips together and put her lipstick back in her velvet leopard-print purse. She turned around and faced them, her hands resting on the edge of the basin behind her. 'That was quite a scene back there.' She smiled, a smug, gloating smile. 'You're lucky you're still in here. I thought you'd get thrown out for sure.'

'No one wants to know what you thought,' said Lisa hotly.

'Oh, Lisa. Yes, you do look pretty tonight. Very smart, but you see no one else will be going fool over you like Vince. These producer guys you're after have got girls prettier than you driving their limos.'

'Is that how come you're still with Vince, then?'

Sireeta's eyes narrowed and she curled her lip. 'Well, you got nothing. No producer.' Sireeta looked at Lisa scornfully. 'A so-called manager who doesn't know anything about the industry you're dealing with, no studio time, no record deal.' She snapped her fingers with the light catching on her bright pink fake nails. 'Oh yeah, Sian. You think you can come along with your little voice and your two-bit singing competition and be a star overnight? Who the fuck are you? You don't know jack, that's why you ain't got jack. I've been backing singers for years and I still haven't got a single released. It doesn't happen just like that. You want my advice?'

'No, I don't want advice from anyone who opens her legs to the first guy who tells her he's gonna make her into a star. You do realize you're just keeping Vince's bed warm, don't you?' Sian replied heatedly.

Sireeta started forward but stopped short.

'Listen. You take your big ideas and your fake manager and go back to your council flats and deadbeat friends. There ain't no more room for wannabes in this business.'

Sireeta paused at the door, turned and pursed her lips together, then sashayed out. Lisa and Sian followed her back into the VIP lounge where it was now hot and crowded. The seats at all the tables were occupied. Four-Play had arrived and were seated at a large round table. Lisa and Sian sighed. The pair that were handsome, Don and Devonia, were looking supreme. The pair that were ugly didn't look too bad either, looking immaculate in leather Guess jackets and thick gold chains. They lounged in their chairs, talking to their entourage of bodyguards, other celebrities and friends. When Lisa and Sian walked past they looked up in interest. For a moment Sian wished she had the jet black hair and startling blue eyes that could command attention like that. The girls walked over to the bar.

'Did you see any hot-shot producer?' asked Lisa.

Sian shook her head. 'It's hard to see. There's so many people over there.'

'Hmm,' muttered Lisa glumly, resting her arm on the bar counter. 'There must be a way. I refuse to give that damn bitch the satisfaction of knowing we didn't even find the guys.'

'Yeah, but man, they all look like hot-shot producers to me. Mind you, now if we was to start talking to Four-Play . . .'

'Mmm.'

'Or their bodyguards.'

'I bet they'd soon tell us, but only if we stepped to them with—'

'The right lyrics.'

'My girl *is* getting bright tonight,' said Lisa, the twinkle back in her eye. They walked back to the bodyguards and split up. Lisa tried to slip through the net of big beefy men in long basketball sweaters and chunky gold chaps or leather jackets.

'Hey, Shortie! Whey you think you going?'

'Hey, I just wanna say hello to Big J. I mean, like,' Lisa flashed a smile, 'these guys come all the way to England and they can't chat to no England girls?'

'Are those eyes real? They look ill! Yo, Dwayne, come look at this girl's eyes, they look butter!'

Lisa gritted her teeth. Another smile. 'So how about letting me through, huh?'

'No can do, Shortie. See, if I was to let you through there, I'd get into trouble.'

'With who?'

'With my boys' manager, he don't play. That muthafucka carry on ill when he gets angry.'

'Which one's he?'

'Hey! Hold it right there!' The bodyguard hurried after another girl who had tried to make a run for it.

Lisa held her breath and calmly walked through the gap in the line-up of heavies. She smiled warmly down at Big J. 'Hi, I'm Lisa and I just love your work,' she said coyly. The singer smiled.

'Yeah?' His voice was deep. 'Take a seat,' he said, offering his lap.

Lisa perched on his knee.

'So what do you do, Lisa? Let me guess, you're a singer, right?'

'Actually no, I'm a hairdresser.'

'I thought you were gonna say singer. I've spoken to nuthin' but singers all night, man. Seem like every fool wanna be a star. My head all messed up wid "I'm workin' on my single. I would like to work with you." So you're a hairdresser, huh? Would you like to get your hands on my hair?'

'I would, but won't your producer mind me takin' your time away from your music?'

'Jigga?' Big J looked across to a nearby table littered with glasses and bottles of alcohol where two men sat looking disinterestedly at the crowd. 'Nah, he's cool. So whey you goin' now?' Lisa got up off Big J's knee and brushed off the hand that crept up her dress as she stood up.

'C'mon, Lisa, I'm looking for honies to take back to the hotel for the *after* afterparty,' he sniggered. 'So what you sayin', cutie?'

'Well, what kind of party is it?' said Lisa, scanning the crowd for Sian.

'Well, baby, it's gonna be live. If you're ready to have fun, I'll show you how the East Side play.'

'Gee, thanks, but it doesn't sound like my sort of rave,' she said and squeezed back through the barrier of human torsos. She gave Sian the time-out signal and they regrouped at the bar.

'Two Southern Comforts with Coke,' demanded Lisa. 'Fast, and with lots of Southern Comfort.'

'You look done, Lisa. What you got?'

'I got a headache, I got no voice left and I got stepped on by the punk in the Chicago Bulls T-shirt. But I also got a name and a face and an idea of what to do next.' She chuckled triumphantly.

Sian took a swig from her glass while Lisa filled her in. Lisa pointed out the two men at the table behind the band. One was tall with broad shoulders, the other of average height and skinny. 'Nice suits, huh,' said Lisa appreciatively, 'and they look fine, or what is that word they're all using?'

'Butter?'

'Yeah, that's it, they look butter, especially the tall one.' Lisa picked up her glass and drained it. Then she smiled deviously.

'He ain't all that,' said Sian. 'So stop whatever you're thinking. How do we get to him and what do I say when we do?'

chapter
eighteen

The two men were tired and bored. The larger man watched as his friend drowned his sorrows with a cocktail of white overproof rum sprinkled with Coke.

'Man, you're gonna drown in that shit if you don't watch yourself.'

'You just wish you could, Pearce.' Jigga waved the glass under Pearce's nose, provocatively. 'Smells good, huh? Good strong shit. There ain't nuthin' like good ol' fashioned spirits.'

Pearce smiled good-humouredly and looked across the room.

'This isn't New York, Jigga. You're gonna start scaring people if you don't stop shoving that Appleton down your gut.'

Jigga downed the drink, grimaced as the fire hit the back of his throat, then exhaled. 'Aahh, yeah! That was good.' He slapped the table. 'Have a drink too, Pearce.' Jigga quickly poured two shots of rum. 'Come on, I remember when you used to throw them away quicker than me. Here. One for you,' he slid the glass across the table to Pearce, 'one for me.' Jigga downed his glass quickly. He stared at Pearce for a few moments then shrugged, reached across the table and, picking up Pearce's glass, downed that drink also. Jigga leaned forward and wagged an inebriated finger with mock sobriety. 'You know your trouble? You fell in love and you got screwed.'

'Whereas you'd let some poor girl fall in love with you and then you'd screw her.'

Jigga paused, contemplated the rationality of what Pearce had said, then guffawed and chucked Pearce on his shoulder. 'Yeah, that's my way, nigga, that's my way.' There was an awkward pause.

'The concert was butter tho',' Jigga continued after a few moments.

'It was cool, Jigga. It wasn't great. Big J was high, Don was sloppy in remembering the lyrics. Lil' K and Devonia did all the work, but hell, nobody noticed. The girls went crazy. They'll be back for more next year. You made your money and delivered on your promises and when Four-Play are forgotten like last year's sneakers, your name will still be guaranteeing cheques, so it was cool.'

'What's next?'

'Well, I can't follow your drunken ass around for ever. I gotta do something about my own life,' Pearce said. He sighed and sank his head into cupped palms.

Jigga looked at Pearce, truly confused. Estella was hot. There was no denying that, but that in itself wasn't a reason to get depressed. There were so many pretty women, like the two over by the bar watching them and the best thing about having a pretty woman was that you could trade her in for a similar model when the juice turned sour.

The manager of the group got up. 'OK, boys, we gotta go walk around the dancefloor for ten minutes. You can dance, play casino, lay down and go to sleep on the floor if you want.' The boys guffawed as they shifted. 'Just make the shorties happy.'

As the entourage wound its way out of the VIP room along with many of the other people present, Pearce looked at Jigga. 'Don't you wanna go? You might meet some girls.'

'Nope.' Jigga poured some more rum into his glass and downed it. 'Brrr. No, man, I can't figure out English girls. They play too many games, blow hot and cold. I haven't got time for games so I'll just wait until I get back to NYC, then it's *on*.' Pearce and Jigga chuckled together.

'When you get back to New York you won't have no time for women. You've got Tameka's album coming out. Four-Play will be touring the States. It's gonna be "Jigga" all over again.'

'Yeah, and you?'

'I'm not sure but I've been thinking about making a complete change for sometime. You guys move on to Germany soon. Well, I think I may stay here, rent a flat, check out the music scene, see which way the wind is blowing.'

'What about your family?'

'Oh, I'll have to go home eventually, sign the papers and sort out the business. I'm sure it ain't gonna be pretty. But they don't need me right now. The way things are, we could all use some space.'

Jigga stared blankly at Pearce. He held up his hand for silence. 'Let me get this straight. You're not coming home? You're gonna stay here in England?'

Pearce nodded. Jigga leaned forward.

'And do what?'

'I see myself as manager of several as yet undiscovered artists. Singers, songwriters, rappers.'

'Take a look around this room.' Jigga made a sweeping gesture around the crowded room. 'Tell me exactly who you're trying to emulate 'cos all I can see right now are wannabes and small-timers. Every single one of 'em.' He leaned forward again. 'Come on, Pearce, you know better than that. There's no money in England!'

'There's just less money, Jigga. Besides, I'm looking for more personal work that doesn't need too much investment. Your kind of big bucks producing outfit doesn't suit me any more. I've been there and got the fuckin' T-shirt. It'd be hard for me to get another label going now. Everyone in the LA recording industry knows about my drink problem. Here people know me as a successful producer. They don't know too much about the alcohol business.'

'You can't reinvent yourself in this industry,' said Jigga rolling his eyes at Pearce. 'What you gon' call yourself anyway – The Artist Formerly Known As Drunk?' He laughed loudly and slapped the table.

Pearce smiled. 'At the end of the day I'm English, this is my home. America's made me, but it nearly destroyed me too.'

Jigga contemplated this. 'But that's the American way. You don't have to make this drastic change, Pearce.

You can make it again in the US, be bigger even. But all you'll get from England is pocket change. I guarantee it!'

'You can guarantee nothing. Look at you, you can't even see straight.'

Jigga fumbled around in his pocket and withdrew a small white business card. He read it aloud. 'Boilerhouse Records.' He waved it in front of Pearce. 'This *was* your label, wasn't it? Oh, I can read just fine.' He put it on the table and pushed it towards Pearce. Pearce watched the card making its way past puddles of rum and cigarette ash, to rest directly in front of him.

'Those were the days, huh?' said Jigga. 'Lil' English boy made good. One of *Ebony*'s ten most eligible bachelors. Remember Pearce and Estella? The black wedding of the year?'

'Not quite true, Jigga. That was quarterback Jay White and model Casey Clark.' Pearce managed the ghost of a smile.

'You could get it all back, Pearce, without this reinvention shit. Come back to New York with me. I could help you out. You don't have to go back to LA. There's so much raw talent in NYC. We could go on more of our notorious talent-spotting trips like back in the ol' days. Remember Queen's 1989?'

'You only went there to find the singers who had the largest breasts, man,' Pearce reminded him.

'And we can do it again, homie! Just you and me.'

Pearce knew Jigga was trying to help his longtime friend. A boy alone in a strange land had met a boy who was also alone in his own land and together they had made a way from nothing. They were like brothers. For a split second Jigga's enthusiasm ignited something inside Pearce. The old Pearce would have reached over and grabbed the bottle of rum from Jigga's shaky fingers. The old Pearce would have finished two in one night. But the new Pearce wasn't on that vibe any more. What had folded had folded and Pearce was now seeking something else, something very far away from where he had been.

'The fat lady sang long ago, Jigga. It's over.'

'You don't even know what you're looking for. You're just hung up on Estella. That's what this is all about.' Jigga pointed a finger at Pearce menacingly. 'She's screwed you up so bad she don't even have to be on the same continent as you.'

Pearce squeezed his eyes closed to shut out the memories.

'Um, excuse me.'

Pearce opened his eyes. The girl in front of him was tall and slender, her skin colour a cross between stained wood and golden honey. He found himself looking up and smiling. She smiled back.

'Yeah, what can we do for you ladies?' Jigga demanded sharply, his eyes narrowing.

'Well, my name's Sian and I'm a, er, singer. I'm looking for a producer.'

'So?'

Sian shifted her weight from one foot to the other, embarrassed. Lisa stepped forward, taking Sian's demo tape out of her bag and smiling warmly. Pearce watched as Jigga sat up slightly in his seat.

'Look, here's Sian's demo tape. We were hoping you could listen to it.' She held out the tape confidently. Jigga took the tape.

'And your name is?'

'Lisa, I'm Sian's,' Sian nudged Lisa and shook her head, 'friend.'

Jigga gave the cassette a cursory glance and passed it to Pearce who opened it and read the writing on the cassette cover.

'So what's wrong with English producers? Someone must have done this tape,' said Jigga coolly.

'Yeah, Vince Havering from CREAM.'

'Who?'

'Vince. He said he knows you,' said Lisa with a sidelong glance at Sian.

Pearce looked at Jigga quizzically. 'Never heard of him,' he said, laughing.

'Well, we had a bust-up and we knew you'd be here so we thought—'

'Well, you thought wrong,' said Jigga testily. 'This is a party. I'm not here to do business. I'm here to relax, drink some rum and talk to my boy here.' He leered at Lisa. 'If you like, you girls can pull up a chair and we can all get high together but we ain't listening to no tape.' Pearce saw Sian bite her lip.

'What my friend here is trying to say, ladies,' interrupted Pearce as he put a restraining hand on Jigga's shoulder, 'is that we'll take this tape and give it our full attention.' He smiled broadly at Lisa and Sian. 'And we'll call you. *I'll* definitely call you to let you know what I think.'

'It's my own work. I backed myself and helped

create the track too. If you don't like it, you only have to take it out the tape deck and—'

'Yep, OK, whatever.'

'My name and telephone number are on the cassette cover.'

'Cool.' The tape disappeared into one of Pearce's pockets. 'Like I said, one of us'll be in touch.'

As the girls walked away, Jigga sniggered.

'What did I tell you, Pearce?' Jigga said, his eyes following Lisa's hemline. 'Small-timers and wannabes. Welcome home.'

The trees glistened and sparkled as the limousine flashed past. Turning away from the desolate and deserted sidewalks Pearce took out his mobile phone, flicked the mouthpiece down, and dialled.

'Hello.'

'Hi, Estella?' Pearce could hear splashing, kids shouting, a Puerto Rican band on the radio. Pearce closed his eyes and inhaled.

'Pearce, how is England?'

'Unchanged.'

'And the tour?'

'It's gone well but it has finished for me. The boys are off to Germany in a day or two. How are you?'

'Fine. Why wouldn't I be?'

'You running daycare now? How many kids are in the pool?'

Estella laughed. 'Shanna's here with her school friends Rosa and Jose.' There was a pause.

'Well, let me speak to her.'

Estella hollered and Shanna came on the phone.

'Hi, Poppy.'

'How's my shortie?'

'Fine. I swimmin' wit' Rosa an' Jose.'

'Who else is there?'

'Al. He's always here, Poppy.' Pearce heard Estella curse then hiss for Shanna to say goodbye. 'I gotta go now, Poppy, I love you.'

'I love you too, shortie an' I'm gonna bring you back somethin' special, 'kay?' There was a splash and cries of laughter as Shanna jumped back into the pool.

'Pearce, that was low, asking Shanna when you could've asked me.'

'Fine. Who the fuck is Al?'

'Well, hell.' The pool sounds grew fainter, Estella was heading towards the house. 'Look at the alcoholic talkin' now? You didn't worry what I was up to when you'd disappear for days at a time, no phone call, no message to say where you were, with who or what you were doing. But now in the eleventh hour of our divorce you wanna start *this* bullshit? Give me a fuckin' break.'

'Maybe it's all too much to handle in one go,' said Pearce quietly.

'Yeah, well, I wasn't the one who drank our marriage away.'

There was an awkward pause and Pearce knew the only reason why Estella didn't hang up was because she wanted to keep the house, Shanna and a third of his savings.

'Look, Pearce, is everything OK?' Her voice was soft and Pearce wondered if he judged her too harshly.

'I might be away for a while. I've got a few business ideas I wanna sound out. You've got my mobile number if you need to get hold of me. Otherwise I'll be in touch.'

'Take care of yourself over there.'

Pearce coughed. He didn't mind the cold. He enjoyed English weather. No two days were the same and the chill let you know you were alive. There was a time when he'd thought LA was his city. LA meant endless summer, glamour and excitement. LA meant Estella and the pool and Shanna. Shanna and the best of times. His head sank back against the cool leather headrest. He closed his eyes. His thoughts drifted over the evening's events. He had been quietly impressed. Most people scampered off sheepishly when Jigga snubbed them, but those girls had heart, reminding him of that stick-'em-up sexiness he still loved about Estella. Pearce wanted a drink now to help him forget the regret that chased him through his bad dreams. But alcohol was not an option; six months of drowning his sorrows in drink had already burned many bridges for him in LA's music industry. He reached in front of him and switched on the television. The only thing that seemed to be on was a slushy black and white affair, French, subtitled, and Pearce did not have his glasses. He switched it off and turned his attention to the state-of-the-art radio and cassette player. He fiddled around with the tuning button. There was random drum and bass, house and dizzy pop music but nothing that he wanted to listen to while he was being driven through a rainy night with a heavy heart and a troubled spirit. He paused for a moment, then reached in his pocket and drew out the tape, slotted it in and sat back. Pearce knew about real talent; he'd been at enough open-mike nights and listened to enough artists to know the difference between a pretty voice and one that lifted your spirits like Florida sunshine, between a good song and one that lingered in your dreams night after night. When the rewind button click-stopped, he pressed play for the second time. As the first notes of the track introduced a subtle snare, he picked up his mobile and dialled.

'Yo, Jigga.'

'Whassup, P?'

'Remember the girl at the party?'

'What girl? Oh yeah, the one with the tape. So what?'

'I think I've found what I was looking for.'

chapter
nineteen

Pearce saw Sian enter the bar and look around uncertainly. He stood up and crossed the polished marble floor to meet her.

'Your timing's perfect,' he said, smiling. 'Let's go and sit down. Follow me.' He ushered Sian towards his corner table. 'Did you find the hotel OK?'

'Well, actually I cheated. I got the central line straight from Leyton to Notting Hill Gate and then took a cab. I didn't want to get lost.'

'Smart thinking.' Pearce chuckled.

'It's posh in here, isn't it?' Sian said, looking across to the marble bar. Pearce smiled.

'I'll get some drinks, what would you like?'

'Just a Coke for me, please.'

Pearce walked over to the bar. He came back with two tall glasses. 'There.' He sat down. 'So you got the time off work OK? I remember you telling me your boss wasn't very accommodating.'

'Well, I worked this morning, so I only took a half

day which he can't complain about too much.' Sian laughed.

'What's so funny?' asked Pearce smiling.

'Three months ago I was just a girl in a sports shop thinking about my bills and how I was gonna pay them,' said Sian. 'Now I'm sitting here in this top-dollar bar. I still can't believe you even listened to my demo tape. We only met a month ago yet here we are and you're being so nice.'

'Yeah, things move fast in this business. Sometimes it's all good, sometimes nothing goes right. One moment you have a deal, dollars and lots of friends, next moment you're yesterday's news and no one, and I mean no one, is interested. And another thing. People aren't "nice" in this business, Sian. Including me. That said, you have a very special talent as I explained on the phone.' He paused and sipped his orange juice. 'You wanted a record deal and I think I may have arranged one for you.'

'Really?' said Sian excitedly.

'Don't get too excited, Sian,' said Pearce. 'A record deal is good, no question, but it's not the be-all and end-all. Last week I went to Planet and spoke to an A&R man there. He loved the track. He also confirmed that his superiors liked the tape and are keen to do a deal. Naturally they want to meet you, find out what you're about and hear you sing in person. But without raising your expectations too high, if you sound even half as good as you do on that demo tape, you got yourself a record deal.'

Sian blinked. 'OK. And what do you get out of this?'

'Well, as I explained on the phone, Sian, I'd be your manager so I would get twenty per cent of everything you make. You've just seen what you get out of having me as your manager. I don't sit down on the job. I get results. Can you live with that?'

'Suits me. Man, wait till I tell Lisa. She's never gonna believe it.'

'Lisa's the friend from the party?'

'Yeah. She'll be so pleased. We've been trying to get somewhere for so long.'

Pearce held up his hand. 'Hey, this ain't gonna be no fun and games, Sian. The next few months, hell, the next year, is gonna be real busy. You'll have to re-record "Moments In Time" and record enough new songs for an album. There'll be unpaid personal appearances in nightclubs and when your first single breaks, endless promotion. Then hopefully, if the single does well, your album will come out and then a tour of some kind. You will have to work hard, really, really hard.'

'Well, it will beat a twelve-hour shift at Sports-world.'

'Yeah,' conceded Pearce. 'I kinda suppose it will. But look, don't give up your day job just yet. We still don't have the paperwork in front of us and even when that is sorted it will take a while for the money to come through.'

'Money? How much?'

'It's very difficult to say now. But most first-time artists signing to an established record company like Planet would expect to receive somewhere between fifty and a hundred thousand pounds for their first recording contract.'

'A hundred thousand! You're joking!'

'Hold on. You'll probably be nearer the fifty grand end and you won't get it all at once. And anyway you will have to spend a lot of it on producing the songs for your album and any kind of video that you make. Unless you're planning to write all the material yourself.' Pearce laughed. 'Come on, don't look so serious. I'll try and get them to rent an apartment for you so you can be close to the recording studio. You'll have quite a few thousand to live on and eventually there will be royalties but you should try and hang on to your job at Sports-world until it becomes real difficult.'

'I guess I just got carried away,' said Sian with a wry smile. 'A few months ago I told my boss where to stick the job and although I'm still working 'cos I need the money, I was hoping I could finally leave permanently.'

'It's tempting but don't burn no bridges till the money's in the bank. Like I said, Planet will be bringing people in to produce you and it can be expensive.'

'I know. Vince Havering, the guy who did my demo tape, used to charge at least one hundred pounds an hour to produce music in his studio and he's not famous.'

'OK, so you get the picture. In the US I know Jigga sometimes charges forty thousand dollars to produce a single song.'

'What?'

'Don't worry,' said Pearce with a smile. 'Planet won't be hiring him. I also wanted to ask you how much of the tape was this Vince Havering's work. You know, for copyright purposes.'

'Well, not that much really. I wrote most of the

lyrics and the harmonies. The basic melody is Vince's but the rest is Stevie Wonder.' Sian giggled.

'Good. Do you think you can materially change the melody?'

'No problem. I only included his tune to keep him sweet anyway.'

'Yeah, from everything you've told me about Vince Havering, I gather he really played you.'

Sian clinked her empty glass against Pearce's. 'You got that right.'

'Well, I guess that's basically all we needed to discuss today.' He checked his watch. 'It'll soon be time for me to start making endless overseas calls.'

'You have to call America?'

'I'm always calling America. If it's not one thing it's another. Plus I have to see a lawyer about a recording contract.' He grinned. 'Do you have any questions?'

'Well, my mother says never look a gift horse in the mouth,' Sian said with a smile. 'Even so, I just wanted to know why me, Pearce? You're the big-shot producer all the way from LA. I'm a small-time unsigned artist. Why would you come all the way to London to manage little ol' me?'

'Fine. I guess you deserve a little honesty, Sian,' said Pearce uncomfortably. 'Although I've been very success-ful in America, I got into trouble too. I had alcohol problems and those led to business troubles and marital strife. I've sorted all those out but now I want a complete change of scenery. I don't want to produce any more, deal with boys like Four-Play who don't care about anything except the money and how many women they can cram into their hotel rooms on tour nights.

I'm looking to develop some meaningful relationships with artists who are genuinely talented. Hopefully you're the first. Sure, everyone loves money, but I'd like the music to be a big part of my motivation. You're the first person I've met who seems to fit the profile. You need a break and quite frankly so do I.' Pearce looked at Sian solemnly. 'What do you say?'

'Let's do it,' said Sian, stretching her small hand across the table to shake Pearce's.

'Deal?'

'Deal.' They both laughed.

'Lisa, it's me, Sian. Where are you?'

'Hi, Sian. I just got home from Cutting Edge. Shitty day and as soon as I walked through the bloody door Mum started stressing me out. Leon this, Leon that. The sooner I move out of this shithole the better. You been to see Pearce already?'

'Yeah. It didn't take long. Guess what?'

'D'you think you could speed it up, Sian? I'm busy.'

'I got a record deal.'

'That's great. I'll call you tomorrow and you can tell me what happened.'

'Well, I thought we could go out and celebrate, Lisa. I just have to tell someone about it.'

'Sorry, girl. No can do. I'm going out with Leon tonight and I need to get ready. He's picking me up in less than an hour.'

'Oh, come on, Lisa. Just tell him you'll meet him tomorrow. You and me could go out for a drink. I'll pay. I know you are meant to be going somewhere but you know how important this is. Can't you see Leon tomorrow?'

'Girl, you know as well as I do that Leon won't have it and my life being the way it is, the last thing I need is to start arguing with my man as well. I'll meet you tomorrow and then we'll do something, promise.'

'All right. Well, tomorrow then.'

'Yeah, see ya.'

Sian hung up the pay phone and checked the coin return for change. Then she walked slowly towards the ticket window at Notting Hill Gate tube station.

'Buelah, are you home?' called Sian as she let herself into the flat. There was no answer. Sian checked the kitchen, living room and then went upstairs. She found Buelah on her bed curled up over a textbook with a school friend.

'Buelah, guess what?' Sian said, walking into the bedroom.

'Sssh,' said Buelah, irritated. 'Me and Melissa have to finish this exercise by tomorrow and it's really difficult.'

'Yeah, but I was gonna tell you about my record deal.'

Buelah and Melissa looked up from the textbook. 'Tell me a bit later?' suggested Buelah. 'Melissa's got to go home soon and we really need to finish this.'

'OK, OK, fine,' muttered Sian, leaving the room.

Sian went into her own room and dropped her shoulder bag on the floor. She took off her coat and shoes and sat down on the bed. She heard the front door open.

'Sian, Buelah. I'm home,' called Bernadette.

Sian stood up and hurried downstairs. She found Bernadette in the kitchen putting some tins in a cupboard.

'Mum, it's a good thing you're back,' Sian said, standing in the doorway.

'That Mr Singh's prices. They keep goin' up an' up,' said Bernadette, closing the cupboard door. She turned around. 'You know Convention comin' up?'

'Yeah but—'

'Well, I was wond'ring if you would please come to church with me dis Sunday coming, maybe even sing somet'ing.' Bernadette smiled eagerly.

'I don't think so, Mum. I just found out today I've got a record deal. Isn't that great?'

Bernadette's eyes narrowed. 'What great about dat? And if it so great unno should run down to church and t'ank God for making it so.'

'Why would I want to go to *church*?' asked Sian, walking into the kitchen. 'I've got much better things to do with my time now than sing before a group of smelly Leyton people.' She laughed, raising her arms and twirling. 'I'm gonna be a star.'

Bernadette stiffened. She walked over to the sink and rolled up her sleeves. Then she turned on the hot water tap. Steam rose in spiralling columns.

'I was only joking. Aren't you pleased for me?' asked Sian, smiling.

Bernadette turned around. 'I'll be pleased when you in church a Sunday 'stead of running up and down street talking about singing dis and singing dat. It's singing de Fader praise what you should be doin' instead of singing sin and talking blasphemy,' she said.

'Oh, I'm not listening to this,' said Sian angrily, spinning around and walking out of the kitchen. She crossed into the living room and threw herself down on the sofa. She picked the phone up off the floor and, after a slight hesitation, dialled Stephan's number.

'Sexy speaking,' came the smooth greeting.

'Hi, it's Sian.'

'Sian, I was meaning to call you. I saw you in *The Voice* the other day, looking all kriss in your white dress. I really wanted to congratulate you on winning that competition. But after our last conversation, I figured you wouldn't appreciate it.'

'Well, you can congratulate me now. I've just got a record deal with Planet Records.'

'Really. See, I always knew you were special, Sian.'

'Is that so?'

'Yeah. I, er, know I haven't always shown it but deep down I felt that leaving you was the biggest mistake I ever made.'

'That's surprising coming from you.'

'Look, hang on a minute, Sian. Let me switch off the TV. We've got some catching up to do.'

chapter
twenty

'This it?' asked Lisa, peering out of the car window as the cab driver pulled off the road and into a small parking lot. 'This looks more like a church!' she said doubtfully.

'Nah, it just looks like a church. It's been converted into a huge recording studio, trust me. The record company has a contract with my cab firm so I do drops and pick-ups here all the time. See the hall on the side?' The driver pointed across the parking lot. 'Go right up to the double doors and press the buzzer. Someone'll let you in.'

'All right, I'll take your word for it. Thanks,' said Lisa, getting out of the cab. She slammed the door behind her and hurried towards the double doors. She pressed the buzzer and waited, rubbing her hands together vigorously to keep them warm.

'Hello? Who's this?'

'It's Lisa,' she said into the intercom. 'I'm here to see Sian Wallace.'

'Wait a minute,' ordered a crackly voice. 'All right, someone'll let you in.'

'Hurry up,' muttered Lisa watching her breath form white, cloudy vapour that melted away into the March night. 'It's so cold.'

After a while Sian opened the door.

'Oh, Lisa, come in quick, it's freezing,' she said breathlessly. Lisa walked into a brightly lit reception area and Sian shut the door behind her.

'Sorry I took so long, this place is enormous.'

'Another ten seconds and I would've got frostbite.' Lisa touched Sian's face as proof. Sian jerked backwards.

'God, your hands are like ice. Well, don't worry, they'll soon defrost. It's almost too warm in here.' Sian led the way down a carpeted hallway. 'It feels like ages since we last spoke.'

'It's only been a couple of weeks but what do you expect when you're always here at the recording studio?'

'Well, I've tried calling you but your mobes is off twenty-four-seven. Why is that?'

'I'm probably at Leon's. I have to keep my phone off when I'm at his just in case a guy rings. He gets so mad when that happens.'

'You're always at Leon's,' grumbled Sian. 'That must make your mum happy.'

'Tell me about it. Mum really hates Leon. Every time I come home late I get a headache. It's Leon this and Leon that. I've got round to thinking I may as well just move out.'

'You can't move in with Leon.'

'Why not?'

'I don't know, you just can't. We need to talk about this, Lisa. Please don't do anything stupid.'

'This place is big, innit?' said Lisa. She looked

around at the framed photographs on the wall. 'You could've fitted Vince's whole outfit right here in the corridor.'

Sian laughed.

'They've got five studios in here so several singers can be recording at any one time. I still get lost in here.'

'I recognize her,' said Lisa, pointing to a photograph. She moved closer. 'That's – oh, what's her name?'

'Deneka.'

'Yeah. She was on *Top of the Pops* last week. Leon's got her album. Have you met any of these singers yet?'

'No, I'd only meet them if they were recording at the same time as me one day or if I went to a party and they were there.'

'You get to go to parties!'

'Chill, Lisa. I haven't been invited to any yet. When I get an invite, you'll be the first to know.'

'I should hope so too,' said Lisa as they turned a corner. 'Wow, you can even play pool,' she exclaimed as they passed a billiard table in the hallway.

'Yeah, forget Vince's chill-out room,' said Sian. 'They've got everything here. Come on, I'll show you one of the studios.' Sian ushered Lisa towards a wooden door. Lisa followed Sian into a large recording studio. Sian flicked all the light switches on.

The studio was a mini-auditorium set on three levels with all the equipment facing the voice room, a glass-fronted performance area. Lisa walked up the steps and sat down on a seat on the first level.

'There's room for a whole orchestra down there,'

she exclaimed, pointing at the glass-fronted performance area.

'That's money for you. You can do anything if you've got the wong, Lisa.'

'Where is everyone then?'

'We're having a break right now. People are scattered around. I'm re-recording "Moments in Time" so there are sound technicians here, doing the same sort of thing that Otis and Jules did but we're using another, smaller studio.' Lisa nodded. 'There are two girls here as backing singers. Mel and Nicole. You'll meet them, they're fun. There are a few people in the other studios but I think they're just doing maintenance 'cos no one else is recording today as far as I know. Let's go and meet Mel and Nicole. Pearce is here, obviously and, er, Stephan is here too,' said Sian, glancing at Lisa.

Lisa stopped. 'You're joking? Sian, I told you it was wrong to call him and tell him about your deal. Now you'll never get rid of him.'

'Oh, he's changed. He's not like he was before,' Sian said, switching off the lights as they left the studio. 'Anyway he was really keen to come down to the studio.'

'You don't say!' Lisa grumbled as they continued along the hallway. 'Sian, you don't know what men are like at all.'

'Oh, shut up! He's treating me good so far. Come on, they're in here,' said Sian, pushing open an oak-panelled door.

They walked into a large room with two sofas in the centre set opposite a widescreen television. At the back of the room there was a keyboard and a Subbutio table.

'Lisa, how nice to see you again,' said Stephan sarcastically, grinning from his spread-eagled position on one of the sofas. Lisa noted his neat fade and Hugo Boss sweater. She had to admit he was extremely handsome.

Two black girls were stretched out on the other sofa watching MTV. One was slim and pretty with braids, the other had a long weave. They smiled at Sian and Lisa.

'Nicole, Mel, this is my friend Lisa,' said Sian, walking towards the sofas.

'Hi,' said Nicole. 'We've heard a lot about you.'

'Good things I hope,' said Lisa, ignoring Stephan and crossing the room to sit down on the sofa beside the girls. They laughed. 'What are you watching?' she asked.

'Yo MTV Raps,' said Mel, brushing some loose braids back from her face. 'We're on a late lunchbreak, so right now it's all about watchin' some cable, eating some food and making a few calls at Planet's expense.' She nudged Nicole and they giggled.

'Food sounds good to me,' said Lisa. 'I've been at work all day. I'm starved.'

Mel passed Lisa a Chinese menu. 'We ordered just before you came in. Gerry, a studio assistant, is waiting for some guys working in the upstairs studio to decide what they want then he's going to phone up the restaurant and order everything, so just choose something now before he comes back down.'

Lisa took the menu and ran a finger down it. The phone rang. Stephan answered it. 'It's some woman for you, Sian.'

Sian took the phone while Nicole turned down the television's volume with the remote control. Mel wandered over to the kitchen area in the far corner. She opened the fridge and took out a bottle of Coca-Cola. 'Anybody for Coke?'

'Yes, please,' said Lisa.

'And me while you're there,' seconded Stephan.

Mel took three glasses out of the cupboard.

'So what do you do, Lisa?' asked Nicole, as Mel poured the drinks.

'I'm a hairdresser at the Cutting Edge hair salon in Finsbury Park. Do you know it?'

'No, but then I'm from New Cross so I'm not really up them sides a lot. You enjoy it?'

'Pay could be better, but yeah, it's what I've always wanted to do.'

'That's a lot like this job but the other way round. The pay is good but singing work isn't regular. I have to temp when I don't get enough work. I'm not a superstar like Sian here,' said Nicole.

'I heard that,' said Sian as she put down the phone. 'Listen, I don't know what you're talking about but I still have my job at Sportsworld so don't try it. You got more money than me.'

Gerry, a young man with spiky brown hair, entered the room. 'I'm gonna phone in the Chinese now.' He checked his notepad. 'So that's egg-fried rice and sweet and sour chicken for you, Sian. Mixed vegetables and noodles and beef for you, Stephan. Mel and Nicole, you're gonna share a serving of special fried rice and barbecued ribs?'

The backing singers nodded.

'Gerry, this is my friend, Lisa. Lisa, what do you want?' said Sian, pointing to Lisa.

'Hi, Gerry. I'll have a special fried rice with sweet and sour pork, please.'

'No problem. OK food in fifteen, everyone,' said Gerry, leaving the room.

'Who's paying for all this?' asked Lisa, impressed.

'Planet,' said Nicole. 'So don't worry about it. They pay for everything, food, taxis, telephone. It's all taken care of.'

'Hey, don't watch that,' interrupted Mel, walking towards them. She handed out the drinks and sat back down beside Lisa. 'I've been in this business long enough to know they claw it all back. Sorry, Sian, but this is probably all on you at the end of the day.' Everyone laughed.

The door opened and Pearce walked in.

'Hey, Lisa,' he said, smiling warmly as he walked up to the group. 'How you keepin'?'

'Safe. You?'

'Oh, it's all good, Lisa. It's all good. Haven't seen you since the Four-Play party.'

'Well, I'm still working and spending a lot of time with my man. I don't think Sian needs me any more now she's got a hot-shot manager like yourself and a record deal.'

Pearce smiled. 'Yeah, Sian told me how you'd pretend to be her manager.'

'I didn't pretend,' said Lisa. 'I did everything that you so-called managers do and more.'

'C'mon, Lisa,' said Sian, smiling. 'It was mostly a joke.'

'Well, it's the truth, so when you go around tellin' people I *pretended* to be your manager remember that without me there would've been no kriss demo tape, you wouldn't have thought of going to any afterparty and you wouldn't have dared to talk to Pearce so don't tell me about any pretence jus' 'cos I don't have a suit and an American accent. I *was* your damn manager.'

Mel and Nicole looked from Sian to Lisa. Stephan smirked at Lisa.

'Whoa, Sian didn't put it quite like that,' said Pearce, holding up his hands. 'She gave you your dues. Honest.'

'Fine,' said Lisa shortly.

'Look, Lisa, you know what I meant. I just meant that you weren't a real full-time manager like Pearce is. I wasn't tryin' to be nasty,' explained Sian.

'Yeah whatever,' said Lisa with a dismissive wave. 'Forget it, Sian. It's a minor.'

The door opened again and a tall, lanky white man walked into the room holding a tangle of cables. 'OK, Nicole and Mel, follow me. We've gotta do that chorus again.'

Mel and Nicole groaned as they rose from the sofa.

'What about our Chinese?' asked Nicole.

'You can eat it in the studio when it comes. We all have homes to go to and we're pushed for time,' the man explained as they left the room.

Pearce sat down at the keyboard and began to play. Stephan and Sian talked in low tones while they watched the television. Lisa sat for a few minutes watching them, then stood up and walked over to where Pearce was sitting.

'What are you playing?' she asked softly, standing beside him.

'This is the new melody for "Moments in Time". You wouldn't have heard it before. The producer only came up with it yesterday. I can't stop playing it. You feel it?'

'Yeah. It's more original than Vince's although I really liked his too.'

'How would you describe it?'

Lisa chewed her tongue and thought. 'Well, it sounds beautiful but at the same time it's so sad. It makes you think about the best and the worst of times.'

Pearce smiled and nodded. 'That's what I thought too.'

'I've never really understood this whole music thing. I mean, it must be so hard to pull a song out of thin air.'

'Well, I myself am not writing anything here, I'm strictly management, but Sian makes the whole process seem easy. She always seems to know where she wants to take a track.'

'You've done a lot for Sian. You must think I'm a real bitch for getting mad back there.'

Pearce looked over to the sofa where Sian now sat on Stephan's lap, whispering something in his ear. Lisa followed his gaze. 'Friendship ain't easy, Lisa. You gotta take the rough with the smooth. When one of you has it smooth the other might have it rough but you need to hang on to your friendship. Friendship is as good as it gets in this life. My friend Jigga, you met him at the afterparty, taught me that.'

Lisa shuddered. 'I didn't think he was too friendly.'

'He's a little scandalous,' admitted Pearce. 'But he's the best thing that ever happened to me. And that's the way he thinks of me.'

'So what's managing Sian like for you?' Lisa asked with a wry smile. 'She work you as hard as she worked me?'

Pearce laughed. 'I will not be drawn on that one. I think we both found what we were looking for in each other. I'll leave it at that.'

Sian looked over at them and grinned before disentangling herself from Stephan and wandering over.

'So you like the melody, Lisa? You think it fits?'

'Yeah, it's good. Sing it with the words.'

Sian sang softly, playing around with the lyrics, adding ad-libs here and there and although it was still far from finished, Lisa liked the refrain, 'You'll never ever know'.

The buzzer went.

'Oh, that'll be Gerry with the Chinese,' said Sian. 'Someone else'll let him in. You know, I can't believe you're serious about moving in with Leon?'

'I don't know what to do any more, Sian,' began Lisa. 'What do you think I should do?'

'Well, basically I—'

'Sian, you said you were only gonna be a minute,' called Stephan. He sat up and grinned at them over the back of the sofa. 'It's getting lonely here on my own.'

'Don't worry, Stephan, I'm just coming. We'll talk later, Lisa.' Sian hurried back to the sofa and sat down next to Stephan.

Lisa and Pearce looked at each other. They smiled.

'Some people only come back on the scene when the going gets good,' said Lisa acidly.

'Then they'll soon be gone again,' Pearce pointed out.

'Not soon enough for me,' muttered Lisa as she turned to help Gerry who had just come in, carrying several bags of Chinese takeaway.

Various people came in and began taking containers and cutlery before disappearing back to their parts of the building. The phone rang again. Stephan picked it up. It was for Sian.

'I bet every stupid punk wants to know you now you've got a deal,' said Lisa when Sian had finished on the phone. She stared at Stephan pointedly.

'Sian's not worried.' He smiled back. 'She's got her man here to get rid of them, ain't that right, Sian?'

Sian smiled and carried on eating.

'Where was he before you had the record deal, Sian?' asked Lisa, throwing Stephan a sour look. Stephan and Sian laughed together. Lisa picked up her food and went back over to hang out in Pearce's corner.

'Can you sing at all, Lisa?'

'Not a note. It's kind of shameful, innit? I mean, most people can at least sing a little, but not me, star.'

'Everybody can sing, y'know, but people express themselves in different ways.'

'Well try hitting pebbles off a wall and you get my voice.'

'Even pebbles hitting a wall is a kind of music,' said Pearce with a smile.

Mel re-entered the room. 'Hi, I'm back,' she said gaily.

'Gosh, you girls finished already?' asked Stephan.

'Just me. Nicole's still going strong. Sian, they need you in the studio to hear our vocals and record some more with Nicole.'

As Sian left the room, Mel flopped down on the sofa next to Stephan. 'I'm done for today,' she said with a yawn. 'I'm gonna call myself a cab and head home.' She bent down, picked up the telephone and called the cab company. She put the phone back on the floor and sat back in the sofa.

'So you live in Kilburn? Own place?' asked Stephan.

'Yeah. It's Housing Trust so it's well cheap. The area's not so hot but it suits me for now.'

'I like girls with their own yard,' said Stephan smiling. He lowered his voice. 'I find it very sexy.'

Mel giggled and pushed back her straying braids. 'What's so sexy about it?'

'Home cooking, quiet nights curled up on the sofa watching videos. Sharing the shower, sex all night.' He traced a finger down Mel's arm.

She brushed him off and laughed. 'I thought you were with Sian.'

Stephan glanced over to where Lisa and Pearce were talking. He put a finger to his lips. 'What if I said we have a fairly open relationship?'

'Oh, is that why you're whispering? Because you have an *open* relationship? Don't make me laugh. Look, Stephan. I come to the studio, do what I gotta do and then go home – alone. I don't cause no trouble and I sure don't mess with anyone else's man.' The buzzer went and Mel stood up. 'That'll be my ride. See you around, Casanova.' She blew Stephan a kiss and walked quickly out of the room. Stephan smiled after her.

As Mel left, Lisa joined Stephan on the sofa and began watching television. The phone rang. Stephan answered the phone then passed it to Lisa. It was Buelah.

'Sian's recording at the moment, B. Whassup?' asked Lisa.

'She's always recording.' Buelah sounded like she was crying. 'I just wanted to talk to her but she's always busy. That stupid Stephan never passes her my messages.'

Lisa sighed. 'Tell me about it, but what's wrong, B?'

'I just had a big argument with Mum and I want Sian to talk to her. But Sian's busy. She's always busy.' Buelah hung up.

Lisa walked over to the large Subbutio table and fiddled around while Stephan phoned reception and asked them to call a taxi to take him home.

'Wanna game?' asked Stephan, walking over. 'My ride's gonna be a few minutes.'

'Why not? I'll beat you anyhow,' said Lisa. They started to play.

'So when was the big reunion with you an' Sian?' asked Lisa.

Stephan laughed, never taking his eyes off the ball. 'We never broke up, man, we just had a break.' The ball went through Lisa's first line of defence but was blocked by the second.

'You've got front telling me about a break. Who do you think had to pick up the pieces when you dumped her to go out with the neighbourhood slusher?' The ball skidded to a halt at the feet of Stephan's goalkeeper.

'That was then, wasn't it? This is now.'

'Yeah, when Sian's got something you want.'

Stephan laughed again and said nothing, adjusting his lines of attack in preparation for his onslaught.

'Why don't you admit that you only wanted to know after she told you about her record deal?'

'You must be well jealous of Sian,' said Stephan, looking at Lisa with a crooked half-smile. 'She's famous, she's got fat pockets, she's got garms, look at you in your faded Dalston stretch jeans. But don't worry, we'll invite you to parties when we buy our kriss yard up west.'

The ball was past Lisa's first line of defence.

'I saw the way you were looking at Mel. I swear to God, if you hurt Sian again, you'll have me to answer to,' Lisa warned.

'I've had worse threats from Buelah,' Stephan sneered and with a deft flick of his hand, scored effortlessly. 'Anyway, you can talk. Everyone in Leyton is talking about how you took Tiffany's man.'

'I didn't take him. Leon chose me. Anyway, she can't still be mad about that. Look how long ago it was.'

'Well, I guess when you love someone you can't let go that easily. But you wouldn't know about that, would you, Lisa? You're a player, just like me.' He smiled engagingly at Lisa. 'Well, with my looks how could I *not* be? We should get together sometime and pool our talents.'

The buzzer went and Stephan grabbed his coat.

'That'll be my ride. Later on, Lisa,' he said, leaving the room.

'Speng,' muttered Lisa, leaning on the Subbutio table with her head in her hands.

'What's a "speng"?' asked Pearce, with a grin. 'I've been away from these streets too long.'

'A speng is a fool,' Lisa said, walking over.

Lisa pulled a chair over and sat back to front on it, resting her chin on the back. 'So, Pearce. If you were such a big producer as everyone who knows you seems to think, why would you come all the way over here to manage Sian? I mean she's talented but hardly Lauren Hill.'

Pearce observed Lisa, her eyes laughingly demanding an answer. 'What do you have against Stephan?' he asked. It was a trick he always used with Estella. Answer a question with a question.

Lisa's face fell. 'He's a creep. I just hate him so much. I mean, he went out with Sian for about five months and she was just so crazy about him. He was her first proper boyfriend.' Lisa began scratching a groove into the wooden chair. 'He brought something good out in her. She was confident and outgoing, but when he dumped her she switched. Became depressed. Stopped going to church, stopped thinking about guys. It's like she just stopped living! He didn't give a damn about her, it was obvious he was never gonna get back with her. Then all of a sudden, after he realizes Sian might get somewhere, he starts answering her telephone calls and bam, she's hooked again. She's my friend and that but she's heading for a fall.'

'So is your relationship so great that you can judge?'

Lisa was quiet for a moment. 'Me and Leon, that's my man, we have our problems but I've never been as crazy as Sian is over someone. Before it came to that I would leave him, just go. I'm sure I would.'

'You ever been in love?'

Lisa frowned. 'Love's something I try to avoid. Lately it's been getting kinda difficult but love fucks up your life. I'm gonna get by on good ol' fashioned lust. Lust is something you can really hold on to.' They laughed together.

'Don't worry, Lisa, one day Sian will realize Stephan's no good and he'll find someone else to hang out with. That's always the way.'

'Great. Sian will go through it all over again.'

'Then you'll just have to be there.' Pearce was serious again. 'That's the way friendship works. You just have to be there to pick up the pieces. I'm sure she'd be there for you.'

Lisa shrugged.

The buzzer went and a few minutes later the door opened and three middle-aged white men entered the room.

'Pearce,' one shouted, as they strode over to him.

'Just thought we'd pop by and say well done for getting that deal with Planet,' another explained. 'Everyone's talking about her. They're saying she might be the biggest soul act to break in the UK this year.'

There was much patting on the back and producer banter going back and forth. Lisa walked over to the phone and called reception. 'Hi, any taxis available?'

'Sure, I can get one here in a couple of minutes. Where do you want to go?'

'Leyton, please.'

'No problem.'

'Thanks.' Lisa put down the phone and picked up her coat. She stole out unnoticed.

chapter
twenty one

Pearce pushed the recline button on his seat and leaned back. He nodded to the speed garage playing on the coach stereo and watched the fields roll by as the tour bus glided smoothly along the motorway. There was a white flash and then a faint whizz close to his face. He looked to his left.

'Hey, Carlton, I know you gotta get your story but I'm just chilling here. If you're looking for the main story it's sitting right over there.' He thumbed backwards in the direction of Sian's seat.

Carlton sat down next to Pearce and unhooked his camera. He took out his Dictaphone, ignoring Pearce's irritated sigh.

'It's like this, Pearce,' he explained, pressing the record button. '*Pulse* magazine just weren't that interested in Sian Wallace, the singer from nowhere. They've already reviewed her single and decided that it's good, a little too commercial perhaps but still a great song. What's really got them excited is you. Pearce, the one-time LA hit-maker, the South London bwoy made good, the comeback king.'

'Comeback king,' echoed Pearce bemused. 'Where do you guys find your sound bites?'

'I'm gonna be honest here.' Carlton tugged at his goatee. 'The story is *you* and Sian, not Sian alone or even Sian and you. Sian is to you what the house hit "Joi de Vivre" was to Ed Gelotti, a second chance to prove himself.'

'It ain't even like that. I'm just here on this tour as Sian's acting manager. She is not my protégé. I wasn't looking for work. I came over here with Jigga of LockedDown Records on a tour of his group Four-Play. That's how I met Sian and when she gave me her demo. I thought she was so talented that it would be an honour to work with her. I didn't create her. She already was this amazing person bef—'

'I see. Are you planning to start your own British Street Sound label as was suggested by *Badmouth* magazine?'

'There will be no label, there will be no new recording empire. Look, you're here to blend into the background. You're doing a fly-on-the-wall-style feature on a bus tour for Sian Wallace, so just sit back and observe. Don't keep plugging me for scoops. There's nothing to tell that I haven't already told everyone else.'

Carlton grinned, undeterred, but switched off his Dictaphone. He pushed his chair back as well and snoozed.

'This is a warehouse-type club. Large capacity. Lighting is stark and stroby. So I want the act to be warehousey and funky, not too pretty, with the emphasis on sexy rather than glamorous. Straight down the line.' The stylist paused to make sure the choreographer and the camera-crew were keeping pace. They nodded.

'I've got blue boiler suits for the dancers and a red one for Sian.'

'Boiler suits?' demanded the choreographer. 'How are they supposed to dance in those?'

'They come up on stage with boiler suits on and goggle glasses on their heads. Once the lights come up the girls jump out of the boiler suits.'

'As you do.'

The stylist looked sternly at the choreographer who smiled and gestured her to carry on.

'The girls will be wearing hot pants and bra tops underneath. Juan and Nick will only unzip their boiler suits half-way down so their torsos are bare and dance like that. Then it's over to you, Zoe, for the dancing. As for Peter and Adam, just remember that we're looking for strong, dramatic images, not fancy footwork. You don't want the camera to be undermined by the lighting.'

'OK, Caitlin, no need to tell me my job. I'm the cameraman so I'll deal with it. There's going to be a rehearsal, right?'

'There has to be, so I can see how much space I have for my dancers,' insisted Zoe.

'I'm afraid that's something you're going to have to ask Sharon. I don't know anything about that. I just do outfits and make-up.'

Their three heads turned in the direction of Sharon, the personal assistant assigned to Pearce to smooth things over. She was talking animatedly to Sian so it was a few minutes before she noticed them trying to get her attention.

'What's up?' she asked, holding onto the seat headrests for support as she walked down the aisle towards them.

'We were just wondering what the schedule is like and if there'll be time for a rehearsal?' explained Zoe.

'I'll make an announcement in a moment so that everyone is clear on what's going on,' Sharon said. She went back to her seat to pick up her clipboard then flicked through the pages until she reached the right one. She ran a hand through her long brown hair then walked unsteadily to the front of the coach. She had a quick word with the driver and the music was switched off.

'OK, OK, can I have everyone's attention, please?'

The dancers stopped chattering and looked up expectantly. Pearce opened his eyes.

'We should arrive in Manchester at five p.m. That's about an hour and a half away. First of all we'll put our things down. Once we're sorted we go straight to the Hyperion club for a rehearsal. May I suggest that we all go to the rehearsal so we know where everyone else is at and there are no misunderstandings. Once we're set, we're heading back to the hotel to eat. Sian then has a live radio show with Manchester-based DJ Tick, so I'm going over to the radio station with her. I suggest Juan, Nick, Jada and Billie take this time out to perfect their routines.'

Juan held up his arms as if to say 'what routine?', sending the other dancers into fits of giggles.

'We hit the club at about twelve a.m. and will be onstage at about one a.m. There will be two bus trips, one for those who want to head back to the hotel straight away and a later one for those who wish to stay and party. While I don't want to stop anyone having fun, Lord knows these things are stressful enough, I must impress on everyone that we leave at ten in the morning immediately after breakfast to head for Bristol where we do it all over again. After Bristol you have Sunday to rest but on Monday we have an early start at *Good Morning* Midland television, then finally it's home.'

'Thanks for the lecture, Mum,' whispered Jada, nudging Billie. They broke into stifled giggles.

'Are there any questions?' Sharon asked.

'When do we get paid?' yelled Juan.

Sharon grinned. 'As you all know, we collect the money before the performance and dole it out after-wards – Juan. Your salaries are all guaranteed but should you have any doubts about the security of your pay-check, feel free to stop the coach and hitchhike back to London.' Everyone cheered. 'Well, if that's all, enjoy the rest of the coach ride.' She walked slowly back to her seat.

'God, that was stressful,' she said as she leaned back beside Sian.

'Not as bad as it's going to be for me.'

'Oh pshaw, you'll be OK. You've done this a few times now in London, haven't you?'

'Yeah but it's my first on-the-road gig.'

'Relax. Look, get some sleep. You'll be working the hardest of anyone over the next couple of days so stop worrying and sleep.'

'Yeah but—'

'Sleep!'

Sian grinned, then turned onto her side and drifted off.

Hyperion was Manchester's biggest, a huge warehouse-style club which held mainly house raves. Every month it featured the hottest swing tunes and a personal appearance by one of Rn'B's newest acts. This evening there was a special Rn'B night hosted by Radio 1 Rn'B DJ Johnny Zoo.

They were met at the front door by the caretaker who led them into the club.

'This way to the stage.'

They followed the caretaker to the far end of the dancefloor where there was a slightly raised stage with large Colosseum-style pillars at each side.

'OK, all the dancers on the stage, including you, Sian,' Zoe shouted, clapping her hands.

'I'll go and get some drinks,' Sharon said, walking off.

When Sharon returned some twenty minutes later, Sian's track was pounding from two giant speakers either side of the stage. The four dancers and Sian were on the stage, sweating as they followed Zoe's quickfire directions. As soon as they saw Sharon laden with drinks, they scrambled to the edge of the stage.

'OK, OK, here you go. I've got water, Coke, juice.'

'Hurry up, people,' said Zoe. 'We're getting there but we still have a fair way to go.'

The dancers grumbled but they downed their drinks

then hurried to centre stage. Sharon walked over and sat down on a bench next to Pearce. They watched the dancers run through the routine a couple more times.

'How's it going?'

He nodded. 'Looks good. They are almost there.' Pearce rubbed the back of his neck. 'Man, I'm whacked. That coach journey was something else.'

'Hey, you're talking to me? I'm up and down the country all the time with these acts.'

'Yeah, I can tell you've had a lot of experience. You're really handling this tour but what gets me is that you've got so much more damn energy than the rest of us.'

Sharon laughed. 'Remember you said that when Sian's ready to do a world tour and you need a road manager.'

'No doubt,' said Pearce seriously. 'What are the ticket sales like for tonight?'

'I checked with the promoters. They said it's a sell-out.'

'Right then, it's money upfront, no problem.'

'For a change.' They laughed.

'Put it there, lady.' Pearce gave Sharon a high-five. 'You know how it is in this business.' He stood up and walked over to the stage. 'Zoe, how are we doing?'

'We're there. Sian's fine. The routine's not difficult. The dancers know what they're doing. A tweak here, a nip there.'

'Can you do that in the hotel?'

'Sure.'

''Cos we're going to have to get back and eat now so Sian can get to her radio show in time.'

'OK,' said Zoe. She turned back towards the dancers. 'You did well. Just remember your steps, Jada, and we'll swim through this.' Sharon motioned for them to come off the stage.

As they left the club, Sharon walked over to Caitlin. 'Did you get any ideas for hair and make-up?'

'Well, it's got to be neat, obviously. Neat, gelled back, restrained, workman-like, to go with the boiler suits. Make-up will be shiny and futuristic. What do you think?'

'Sounds great. Now while you lot have dinner I'm going to call Johnny Zoo and check that our routine is going to work with his programme, then I've got to call the promoters and remind them that it's money upfront,' said Sharon as she walked ahead.

They ate in the hotel restaurant. The dancers chattered away gaily. Zoe, Caitlin and the cameramen talked in low tones. Pearce nudged Sian.

'You're just pushing your food from side to side.'

'I guess it's nerves. I can't eat like this.'

'Things'll be fine.'

'I know that, deep down. I've done this before but that doesn't change the way I feel.'

Pearce patted Sian's hand.

'It'll be a runaway success just like your listening party. Everyone loved the single there. This'll be no different.'

'I hope so.'

'So, how's Lisa?'

'Well, I think she must be OK.'

'That means you don't know?'

'Well, it's been busy. Me with my work. Because of this boyfriend she's got her mobile is turned off most of the time so it's difficult to get through to her.'

'Aha, the infamous Leon.'

'It's like she's obsessed. Last time we spoke she was thinking of moving in with him, for Chrissakes. For all I know she has by now. We haven't talked properly for ages.'

'Yeah, she only came to the studio that one time. What's up with that?'

'To be honest it's just as well. Her and Stephan are at each other's throats all the time. It creates so much tension and I'm not sure I can handle that just now.' Sian sighed. 'I don't know if this is the place to mention it, Pearce, but you know I gave up my job at Sportsworld last week and the dollars are running a bit low. Any sign of the money from Planet?'

'Yeah, I'll be able to give you a cheque in a couple of weeks. The accountant suggested waiting until the start of the new tax year before handing over any money. You've left Sportsworld? I thought you'd gone part time.'

'They wouldn't let me switch to part time. Anyway, the last couple of months have been almost impossible what with trying to combine everything. It was one thing doing the recording and working but now all these interviews and gigs are adding to the workload. I couldn't have coped at Sportsworld a day longer.'

'I understand. I'm working on that new flat for you then your travelling time should be cut down as well.'

Sharon walked into the restaurant. 'Everyone OK?' She stopped beside Sian's chair. 'Sian, can I steal you?

We should really go to the radio station now, so you can come back, have a rest and then get to the club in time.'

'What's the frequency? I'll listen to it,' said Pearce.

'Ninety-two point five FM. Juice FM,' said Sharon.

'Right. You better knock 'em dead, Sian. I'll be listening.'

The light drizzle rained down on the partygoers. The queue stretched back along Hyperion Avenue past factories and warehouses. Bouncers patrolled the queue in hooded black jackets. The coach stopped in the road right outside the club entrance.

'Please hurry,' called Sharon. 'We're holding up traffic here and don't forget your special passes. The coach will be back here at two o'clock sharp for those ready to go home then.'

They got off the coach and hurried through the rain towards the entrance. One of the bouncers led them through the club towards the VIP area. As they followed him through the swing doors Sian covered her ears to protect herself from the throbbing bass. It was dark and hot. She could make out a small group of people on the stage dancing while the mass of people just in front of the stage surged and swayed to the music. To one side there were a few people in the raised DJ box which was well lit.

'Are my ladies in da house? Ladies, if you're in da house and you look fine, make some noise,' hollered a DJ into the microphone. A roar rose from the crowd. He grinned. 'Yeah, that's how we like it. Johnny Zoo and the Hit Squad keepin' you rockin' till six in da morning.' He put on the next record then wiped his forehead. It was hot in the DJ box. 'Don't forget we've got Sian Wallace tonight. Sian will be in da house singing her debut single, "Moments". Get your drinks now. 'Cos when she comes on you won't be going anywhere, 'cos after that I'm gonna rock this joint so hard girls won't be walking straight tomorrow.'

As the track drew to a close, one of the other men in the DJ box tapped Johnny Zoo on the shoulder and pointed to the VIP area where Sharon and the performers were waiting. He nodded and signalled ten minutes with his hands. Then Johnny Zoo grabbed the microphone again.

'People, you got ten minutes to get those drinks. We got Sian singing at Hyperion in ten minutes so the stage needs to be cleared right now. Yo, if it gets any hotter someone's gonna *explode* up here! Hey, if Zoo said it, then you *know* it's gonna happen.'

Ten minutes later strobe lights laced the stage in red and green light and Sian's backing CD began to play. The dancers stood on the stage in their blue boiler suits and boots, hands behind their backs, heads hung down. Sian was in the middle in her red boiler suit. Peter and Adam were in the crowd, videoing the performance, along with Carlton and Pearce who wanted to get the crowd's reaction. The rest of the crew were watching from the VIP room beside the stage.

As the dancers and Sian skipped out of their boiler suits the crowd broke into wolf-whistles. Then Sian began to sing. Pearce nodded. Everything had worked out. He'd done some nightmare gigs, but this one was fine. He turned and saw Carlton making his way through the jostling crowd towards him.

'Great routine,' Carlton shouted over the din of Sian's track.

'So what do you think, Carlton? You still think she's my vehicle?'

'She's her own vehicle, man. The crowd ate it up,' Carlton said. Then he moved off through the crowd towards the other side of the stage.

Pearce smiled. He knew that when Sian ran off stage asking him how it had all gone, he could tell her honestly that the pay was there, the performance was spot on and it had been a runaway hit. He couldn't remember being as happy in a long time.

chapter
twenty two

'Don't look so sad, Tiffany, something else will come along,' the red-haired girl said. She took a sip of her vodka and lime and set her glass back down on the black marble bar counter. 'You usually get all the best modelling jobs, this time it's me, but next time it'll be you again.'

'Easy for you to say,' said Tiffany as she fumbled with her cigarette lighter. 'You got the damn job. That catalogue assignment would've paid my mortgage for the rest of the bloody year.' Eventually she managed to light her cigarette and put the lighter back in her jacket pocket.

'Look, we came here to have a drink and celebrate me getting the contract, not moan 'cos you didn't get it. They only wanted one person. At least it was one of us that got it rather than someone from a different agency, so lighten the fuck up!'

Tiffany drew deeply on her cigarette. She smiled briefly, then her shoulders sagged. 'I know you're right, Sam, it's just that my life has just been one big nosedive for the last six months. First my boyfriend cheated on me with my best friend, then he ran off with her,' she said, tracing her hand along the edge of the bar.

'Oh, that's gotta hurt,' said Samantha, waving a hand to deflect Tiffany's cigarette smoke.

'I thought I'd get over it but I still feel so angry,' said Tiffany, ignoring Samantha's irritation. 'To top it all I'm missing out on important assignments to a girl who hasn't been modelling five minutes.' She looked up. 'God, here I am telling you my whole life story and you probably don't care.'

'Come on, Tiffany. I haven't known you long, fair enough, and I don't know anything about this guy but I do care. I just don't understand. At the casting you were so confident and cheerful. Now you're acting like it's the end of the world. You're slim and gorgeous. There'll be other jobs and I'm sure you'll find a great guy. Men love models. Now drink up. We've got celebrating to do.' She swirled her drink and then took a sip while Tiffany puffed on her cigarette in melancholy silence.

After a few moments Samantha touched Tiffany's wrist gently and pointed her in the direction of a handsome young black man standing on the other side of the bar.

'I haven't seen anyone else here who looks *that* good,' she said softly, smiling as she caught his eye. Tiffany looked across the bar. She caught her breath. The man acknowledged her with a brief nod and a slight smile, then he looked at Samantha and his smile broadened. Tiffany looked away.

'Is he famous?' Samantha continued. 'Do you think he has a nice car?'

Tiffany's eyes narrowed. 'Stay away from him, Sam. I know him and he's trouble.'

'How do you know him?'

'I know him through friends.'

'Do you know him well?' asked Samantha. 'Does he have a girlfriend?'

'Not very well. Look, I just know him!' Tiffany said shortly. She drummed her fingers restlessly on the bar, willing herself not to look and see him smirking at Samantha.

'Well, he clearly likes redheads,' said Samantha, running a hand through her curly hair. 'And he definitely loves me.'

'Stop staring at him,' snapped Tiffany. 'You'll only make yourself look easy.'

Samantha giggled but eventually turned away from the handsome man. She tapped her foot to the loud house music as she watched the young, trendy, after-work crowd gradually filling up the busy wine bar which was now heavy with cigarette smoke. She unbuttoned her jacket and rearranged her loose-fitting satin vest. 'If I could get with him,' mused Samantha, turning back to stare at the young black man sipping an orange juice, 'it would be the perfect end to a perfect day. First I get the modelling job of my dreams, then I get the man of my dreams.'

'He isn't all that,' said Tiffany with a snort.

'I disagree. Maybe it's just me. I have a thing for black guys and he looks like he has a great body.'

Samantha giggled again. 'You ever been with a black guy, Tiffany?' she asked then sipped her drink.

'Yeah. It didn't leave any lasting impression.'

'He might be a footballer,' said Samantha, ignoring Tiffany. 'Footballers always hang out in this bar and the guy he's talking to looks like he might be a footballer too. Which footballers do they look like, Tiffany?'

'Why do you care? I didn't see him looking at you,' said Tiffany irritably. She stubbed her cigarette out in an ashtray then picked up her drink and drained it.

'Oh, come on, Tiffany, he was practically undressing me with his eyes.'

'Do you wonder why? Everyone can see your breasts when you lean forward like that.'

'You mean like this?' said Samantha, leaning forward deliberately so that her vest fell slightly open, exposing her cleavage. Tiffany raised her eyebrows as Samantha shook with laughter. 'Come on, Tiffany, it's just a joke. No one even noticed. Let's have another drink.'

Tiffany looked at her watch. 'Sam, you've had enough already. And it's getting on. Don't you wanna go home?'

Samantha looked across the bar and made eye contact again. 'No, I'm gonna stay and try my luck with hotstuff over there. Stay,' she urged. 'He has a friend.'

'No, I have to get going.'

Tiffany got down from her stool. She straightened her jacket. 'I need to get my sleep in case I get another casting call.'

'Oh, but I wanted you to introduce me,' said Samantha disappointed. 'You know him and I don't even know his name.'

'We're not exactly friends, Sam. The last thing I want to do is talk to him.'

'Fine, just go then. I'm staying,' said Samantha stubbornly.

Tiffany looked at Samantha. 'What, you're gonna stay here on your own?'

'It's only just gone eight. I'll be fine, Tiffany. I'm not drunk, yet.' She giggled. 'I think I'll just stay here for a bit and have another vodka and lime. I'm in the mood to talk to tall, dark, handsome strangers.' Samantha waved across the bar and flashed an inviting smile. 'Perhaps if I wave my empty glass at him he'll buy me my next drink.'

Tiffany hesitated. 'Samantha, there's something I should tell you.'

'I know what you're gonna say,' said Samantha, rolling her eyes. 'A gorgeous guy like him probably has a girlfriend already. Don't tell me, I bet she's beautiful and he loves her to death and never ever cheats on her.' Samantha played with her glass. 'Well? Go on then, try and put me off.'

Tiffany thought for a minute.

'Hello, earth to Tiffany? The lights are on but no one's home,' joked Samantha, prodding Tiffany. Tiffany's thoughtful expression was replaced by a bitter gleam in her eyes.

'Well, I have to get going, but actually I've changed my mind. I think you should stay,' she said with a bright smile. 'Don't get the wrong idea, he's not the kind of guy who calls the next morning but, apart from that, there's nothing wrong with him. And I'm sure it won't take too long for him to start chatting you up, Sam.

He's a guy who takes what's offered regardless of who he's going out with.' She shot a bitter glance in the direction of Samantha's admirer. 'You'll have as much luck as the next girl.'

'Well, that's a quick change of heart,' said Samantha surprised. 'One minute you're dragging me out the bar, next you're cheering me on.'

'I just realized that some opportunities are too sweet to be missed,' said Tiffany, laughing. 'So go for it, and remember to call me tomorrow and give me a complete run-down.' She patted Samantha on the shoulder then walked quickly out of the bar.

Lisa stood outside Leon's house, confused. She looked at her watch. It was already nine o'clock. 'Damn, I'm gonna be late,' she muttered. She looked up and down the street for the red Lotus but couldn't see it. 'Where the fuck can he be so early in the morning?'

She pressed the bell one more time then turned and hurried back the way she had come.

The phone rang. Leon tried to ignore it but it just kept ringing so he felt for it on the floor beside the bed.

'This better be good,' he growled sleepily.

'Leon, where are you?'

'Huh!' Leon sat bolt upright. 'Who's this?'

'What do you mean who's this? It's Lisa of course.'

'Lisa, I can hardly hear you, where are you?'

'I'm at Cutting Edge of course, it's Saturday. I've been trying to call you all morning. You haven't been answering your phone.'

'Yeah, course. I was asleep.'

'Asleep *where*?'

Leon paused. He rubbed his eyes. 'Look, Lisa. Can I call you later? I was still sleeping when you called and – damn!' Leon felt a stirring in the sheets next to him. He got out of bed and padded naked out of the bedroom. 'Christ, it sounds like a madhouse at your end.'

'You can't call me, Leon, remember? I left my mobile at your house the other night. So we agreed that I would come round to yours this morning before work to pick it up but you weren't there. So where did you spend the night?'

''Course I was at home, you just didn't ring the bell enough times. You know what I'm like, Lisa, when I've come home late. I'm out like a light.'

'You never told me you were goin' out.'

'So now you're my jailer, are you?' Leon sighed. 'If you must know it was a night out with the boys. I had an orange juice or two, nothin' heavy, but still, I'm not gonna wake up for a fuckin' doorbell at what time was it?'

'About nine.'

'Yeah, nine. Too damn early to be wakin' up on a Saturday unless there's a game.'

'Well, where was your car then? I sure didn't see it.'

'You know how hard my road is to find a parking space,' explained Leon, shivering from the cold as he paced the passage. 'I parked in another road. Look, babes, let's talk about this another time, please. It's too early. I'm not thinking straight.'

'So you've been at home all the time?'

''Course, babes, where else would I be, huh?'

Lisa hesitated. 'All right, Leon. Well, you know my mobile's my life so I'll come round and get it this evening.'

'Sure, whatever, babes. Now get back to work like a good girl.'

'Bye, Leon,' said Lisa doubtfully as she hung up the phone.

Later that evening Lisa entered her block in Leyton Rise. She hit the button calling the lift. The steel chains slowly ground into action. There was an ominous thud as the lift stopped mid-floor before groaning as it descended the last few inches. Inside the lift, the light flickered crazily. Lisa wondered if she would be left in darkness as the lift slowly ground its way up eight floors. Eventually the doors opened and she walked slowly along the landing. She opened the front door and walked into the living room. She sank down onto the cream leather sofa. June was sitting in an armchair watching television, holding a cup of tea.

'Hi, Mum. God, I'm so tired,' said Lisa.

June put her cup of tea down on the glass coffee table.

'Tough day at work, love?'

'Yeah. Woody on a late job?'

'No. He got off early so he came home and took Liam to the barber's. Liam was on 'is way to a proper little afro.'

They laughed.

'Sian called for you again,' continued June. She picked up the television remote control and turned down the volume. 'She's bin calling for about a week now. Ain't you gonna call her back?'

'I would if I had a phone but I left my mobile at Leon's.'

June frowned. 'Always Leon. Maybe if you didn't see that boy so much your life wouldn't be such a mess.'

'Yeah, whatever,' said Lisa, looking at the television. 'If it wasn't Leon, it'd be some other boy and you'd be sayin' the same thing.'

'Anyway, I'm glad you're back. I need you to babysit Liam for me this evening.'

'Oh, you've gotta be havin' a laugh, Mum! I've been at work for nearly twelve hours. I am so tired I could cry. You tryin' to kill me or what?'

'It's just for a couple of hours. Me an' Woody 'ave been invited round to a friend's 'ouse for drinks.'

'So can't you take him with you? He won't get in the way.'

'It'll be too late.'

'Oh shit, I can't anyway. I've got to go and pick up my phone, innit?'

'What?'

Lisa sighed. 'Mum, I just told you Leon's got my phone. What am I supposed to do? Just let him keep it for ever?'

'And what time are you gonna come back – bloody two in the mornin' as usual?'

'Oh, don't start, Mum. I've had a crap day.'

'That's not my problem. My problem is when you come creepin' in this 'ouse at two in the mornin' like some kind of tart. My problem is that your so-called man likes to hit girls. My problem is that he drives too fast and,' June's voice rose to a shout, 'I'll tell you what my bloody problem is, madam. My problem is that he's got you wrapped around his little finger and he'll ruin your life.'

'That's enough,' Lisa shouted back, jumping up from her chair. 'I'm not sittin' here while you cuss my man. He doesn't sit down an' cuss you all day.'

'I'd like to see 'im try,' said June, laughing bitterly. 'I'd like to see 'im bloody try it.'

'I don't even know my own fuckin' dad but I don't tell you about him. I don't ask you how you could've had a baby for a guy who didn't even wanna know you.'

June stood up. 'Don't you dare talk to me like that!'

'Well, it's the fuckin' truth,' spat Lisa.

June leaped forward and slapped Lisa's face. Lisa ran out of the living room.

'He didn't wanna know 'cos he was a bastard, just like your Leon,' June called after Lisa. 'Yeah, walk away. In fact why don't you walk right out of this bloody 'ouse? I'm tired of you comin' in 'ere and treatin' everyone like dirt. I'm sick and tired of the arguments. My life's bin 'ard enough and I'm not gonna 'ave *you* givin' me a stomach ulcer so why don't you just GET OUT!' She slammed the living-room door just as Lisa slammed her own bedroom door.

Lisa sat down on the bed and wiped away her angry tears. She put her head in her hands and stared miserably at the wall. Maybe she should go. She was sick of the fighting. Sick of being told what to do, sick of being caught between her mum and Leon all the goddamn time. She began taking some underwear out of her chest of drawers. She put it in a large shoulder bag. She opened her wardrobe and took out a couple of jumpers and a pair of jeans. She folded them up and packed them neatly into her bag. Mid-way she paused. What the hell was she thinking of? Maybe she should talk to Sian first. Sian would know the right thing to do. But since Sian had signed to Planet Records, she had been in her own world, wrapped up in her music career. She called less. They hardly saw each other. It had all started when Stephan came back on the scene. It was as if the oneness they shared was ebbing away. Nah, this time she was on her own and *she* had to decide what was right. Lisa began packing again more vigorously. Anyway, the way things were, they couldn't get much worse.

'Yeah, I wanna see you again too . . . You miss me already, huh? Well, we're gonna have to do somethin' about that. One second, I've got call waiting.' Leon pressed a switch. 'Hello? . . . Oh, Lisa, you all right? . . . Yeah, I'm at home. Where are you? . . . Stratford bus station? . . . Sure I'll come pick you up . . . Calm down, I'm leaving the house right now, babes. Be there in two seconds.' Leon pressed the switch again. 'Yeah, that you, Samantha? . . . Something urgent's come up. It's business, babes . . . No, I don't know when I can see you . . . No, *I'll* call you . . . Yeah, I'll be in touch. Promise.'

Lisa breathed a sigh of relief as the red Lotus careered around the corner and came to a smooth stop in front of the bus station. She got up from her seat at the bus stop and walked over to the car. She opened the door and passed Leon a bag which he pushed into the small space behind the passenger seat. Lisa gave Leon a grateful kiss as she sat down.

'What was all that palava on the phone back there?' said Leon, glancing in his rear-view mirror as he drove off.

'I'm havin' so much drama at home,' said Lisa, shaking her head. She opened the shoulder bag on her knees and took out a tissue. She blew her nose. 'And now I've caught a cold. Shit, can my life get any worse?'

'Your mum needs to loosen up,' said Leon, laughing. 'You're a big girl now. She needs to get off your case.'

'I just don't know what to do any more, Leon. It's making me so unhappy,' said Lisa wretchedly. 'I'm done talking to her. I've tried and tried and I've just got nowhere.'

'I suppose it's about me again.'

'Yeah. I don't know what Tiffany's mum's been telling her but she just won't accept it.'

'Don't worry about that, Lisa. I'm your man. I'll tell you what's what. All these other people are just trying to break us up. 'Course Tiff's gonna be tellin' her mum shit. She's jealous, babes. Everyone knows that.'

'I know but—'

'Forget them, Lisa. As long as you trust me, you don't need to be listenin' to no one else.' Leon patted her knee comfortingly. 'So what's with the big bag? You been shopping, babes?'

'No, I'm moving out, or maybe I should say I'm moving in.'

'You what?' Leon looked from Lisa to the road and then to Lisa again. 'Movin' in where? Not with me?'

Lisa burst into tears.

Leon parked outside his house, then he jumped out and slammed his door shut. Lisa opened her door, got out and hauled her bags onto the pavement. Leon remote-locked the doors, then stormed up the path and into the house. Lisa hurried after him.

'What's the big problem with me moving in all of a sudden?' Lisa asked as she pushed the front door shut. She dropped her bags in the passage then followed Leon up the stairs. 'You're the one who's been saying "it's me and you, babes".'

'I know, babes, but *movin' in* is a whole different thing,' shouted Leon. 'That's like getting fuckin' married.' Leon strode into the bedroom and crossed to the hi-fi. He began fiddling with the CD player.

'If I'm your bona-fide girlfriend and you're faithful to me, why wouldn't you want me to be with you twenty-four-seven?'

'Don't try and pull them ones on me. We've only been going out for a few months!'

'What's that got to do with anything? Do you think that unless we're married we don't have to be faithful to each other? Maybe this morning you weren't really at home, maybe you were in someone else's bed.'

Leon sat down on the bed and began unlacing his trainers. 'Now what are you going on about? You know how busy I am, babes. I just don't have the time for a live-in woman right now. I'm always training, I need my space. This is a real important time. Next season is make or break for me.'

'Well, it's an important time for me too, Leon,' shouted Lisa. 'I'm in trouble and I'm asking you to help me out. But don't worry, there's other places for me to go.' She turned and walked towards the door. Leon was off the bed and across the room in a flash. He grabbed her arm and led her back to the bed.

'Sit down. What do you mean there's other places for you to go?' he demanded. 'Just what kind of games are you playing?'

'This isn't a game, Leon,' said Lisa quietly, sitting down. 'This is real life. This is my life.'

Leon sat down on the bed next to Lisa. 'Damn, I can't take this shit. It gives me a headache,' he said, scratching his head. 'But I don't wanna hear any more about "other places".' He put an arm around Lisa's shoulders. 'You're staying with me, babes, where I can keep an eye on you.'

Lisa rested her head on his shoulder. 'Thanks, Leon. I knew I could count on you,' she said with a sigh. 'I'm sure I've made the right decision.'

chapter
twenty three

'**So what's** it like living with Leon now?'

'I told you, it's the best thing,' said Lisa as she turned sideways and studied the red velvet halter-neck dress in the mirrors. 'I don't get shouted at all day for no reason. I've got my man right there. All I have to do is cook dinner and keep the place tidy.'

'You? Cook? I don't believe it,' said Sian with a smile as she watched Lisa's reflection.

'Hey, you don't know about me and my cooking,' joked Lisa.

'And why did you only return my calls *after* you moved in with him?'

'Because I didn't have my mobile with me. Hey, the last time we saw each other was weeks ago what with you being off every weekend doing gigs and getting ready for your single to be released.'

'I'm sorry, Lisa. For a while I was working at Sportsworld and doing all that recording. Then when I stopped working at Sportsworld the promotion started. What with all these interviews and stuff I never seem to have a minute to myself. You know the flex, Lisa. I'm an unknown artist and this is my first single. I haven't even finished recording my album yet.'

'So when does your single come out?'

'Three weeks,' said Sian excitedly.

'And then I suppose you'll be famous and won't have any time for me at all.'

'Hey, stop trying to change the subject. How long have you been living with Leon now?'

'Since the end of May. Two weeks or so now.'

'I hope you're being treated right.'

'Yeah, Leon treats me just fine. He does like his dinner to be cooked on time, but then no more than Woody. And of course I can't really be out and about like before 'cos he gets jealous if I don't tell him where I'm going first and what time I'll be back. But when we're ready, we can go all night long. No creeping home at three in the morning.' She laughed.

'Sounds to me like you got a better deal at home,' remarked Sian. She unzipped the black dress she was trying on and slipped it over her head. 'Meals, your own room and the freedom to come and go as you please.'

'It's all right for you,' grumbled Lisa. 'Now you've got a flat, you don't even have to live with your mum.'

'I've only had it for a week or so and it's not permanent. I'll probably have to go back home at some point. Anyway, don't try and twist things around to get yourself off the hook. I didn't move out to be with a man. I mean what kind of foolishness is that?' She held up the black dress in her hands. 'I'm gonna get this one, what do you think?'

'Apart from the fact that it's black, I love it.'

'Right, that's me out of the way then.' Sian put the dress back on the hanger and began putting her clothes back on. 'And if he's jealous how come he's letting you out tonight with me, Pearce and Jigga?'

Lisa smiled wickedly. 'He left for a pre-season training camp this morning so I've got tonight to party and Saturday to sleep. He's not back till Sunday.' She twirled before the wall-size mirrors. 'Party, party, party!'

'Isn't it a little early to be training for the *new* season?' asked Sian.

'Who cares? The main thing is that I can rave with Leon being none the wiser.'

'Great, so now you have to sneak around in order to have some fun. You're only twenty, for Chrissakes.'

'Well look, I'm here, aren't I?' said Lisa, undoing the dress. 'I didn't wanna come but I'm here so just give it a rest.'

'Yeah, 'cos you get a free dress out of it.'

'I *deserve* a fuckin' free dress if I'm gonna have to sit next to Jigga all evening. Girl, I should be getting ten free dresses for that!'

'Oh, c'mon, Jigga won't be here long and Pearce especially asked us to take him out. Somewhere we'd go on the regs, like Ezekiels or Swingers.'

'Yeah and I bet if Pearce asked you to take Jigga to the moon you'd go. In fact don't even answer that, I don't wanna know.' Lisa stopped moving around and stared at her reflection. 'So what do you think?'

'It's too loud and too short – perfect,' said Sian, putting the various dresses she had tried back on hangers.

'Change and let's go home. I need to wash my hair. It's gonna take hours and ten o'clock isn't as far away as you wanna think.'

'And if Jigga tries anything, I'm gonna slap him square in his fat face.' Lisa said as she began getting changed.

'He'd probably like that,' said Sian with a chuckle. Lisa kissed her teeth. 'Anyway, we won't be out all night. The crew are coming to see my new flat tomorrow so I'll need my sleep. I know I'm just renting but it's been really exciting moving out of Leyton Rise and I want them all to come and look at it. Then we're going shopping. Please come.'

'Yeah, why not? It's not like I'm working tomorrow. Who's coming?'

'Vanya, Ebela and Tiffany.'

'Hmm, actually you'd better leave me out.'

'Oh, come on, Lisa. This is stupid. You can't ignore her for ever.'

'Watch me,' said Lisa as she began to dress.

'Limo transport there and back. All clothing expenses pre-paid. The best champers all night. I personally have no complaints,' said Sian as they joined the end of a long queue leading to the pay desk.

Lisa rolled her eyes. 'Can you stop selling this night out to me? I've already taken the bait. I've got my free dress and I'm coming, so 'llow it now, Sian.'

Sian handed over the fifties Pearce had given her at the till. Their dresses were wrapped in tissue paper and put in bags, then they made their way out of the store.

'When we walk into Swingers with these kriss

dresses on, the other girls are just gonna die,' said Lisa, giggling, as they found themselves back on bustling Oxford Street. They walked down towards Bond Street tube station where they fought their way onto a tube crammed with sweaty homebound shoppers.

'So, do you trust Leon?' asked Sian, tightening her grip on a hand rail as the train shuddered through the tunnel.

'Do you trust Stephan? And yeah, I do trust Leon,' said Lisa, smiling. 'Why shouldn't I? He *is* my man.'

'I mean do you think he's always been faithful?'

'Yeah,' said Lisa stiffly. 'We share the same yard. I'd know if he was playing me.'

'Still, you can't guarantee it. Men will find a way.'

'Well, why don't you tell me about it? You know better than me.'

Sian ignored Lisa. The tube thundered into Oxford Circus station and even more people tried to squeeze into the hot, crowded carriage. The girls were wedged back into a corner.

'I know Stephan is no angel, but right now I'm not worried about him. I just don't wanna see you getting hurt.'

'What do you mean hurt?' asked Lisa crossly. 'Quit the mind games, Sian. If you're trying to say something just say it! I'm not gonna bite your head off.'

'Well, someone told me that they saw him at a bar up west one Friday quite recent, chatting up some white girl.'

'What?'

'Yeah,' said Sian, finally receiving Lisa's undivided

attention. 'Some white girl, at a bar up west. Apparently she was on her own, he walked up to her and chatted her up then they went off together.'

'*Whatever*,' exclaimed Lisa with a derisive laugh. She shook her head. 'It won't work, Sian. Leon's been home every night since I moved in. No question.'

'And how long has that been? Two weeks? This probably happened before you moved in with Leon. It was a Friday or Saturday about two or three weeks ago, the person said. Tell me what day you moved in and then you'll know for sure.'

'No, *you* tell *me* who the hell this person is first. What the hell are they doing in my business?'

Sian looked away. 'I can't tell you, Lisa, and I'm only bringing it up 'cos I care about you.'

'If there's one thing I hate, it's people talking about me and not even telling the fuckin' truth.'

Two middle-aged women glanced in their direction but quickly looked away when they met Lisa's stormy eyes.

'Yeah,' said Sian soothingly. 'You're right. It probably is a lie. Let's just drop it.'

'No, you're the one who brought it up. Who's the person? Only person I know who'd care and who goes to bars up west is that bitch Tiffany.'

Sian didn't say anything.

'It's her, isn't it? For *Chrissakes*, Sian, that girl would say anything to break us up.'

'She probably is lying,' said Sian quickly. 'I mean, if you were already living at Leon's on that Saturday, then you would know if he spent the night at someone else's house.'

'I keep telling you, Sian, I'm not in the hearsay business. Unless someone comes to me and shows me solid proof, I'm gonna stick with my man.'

'OK,' said Sian. 'Look, I'm getting off in a couple of stops. The car will pick me up at nine. We should reach your yard around nine thirty. Plenty of time to get to Pearce's hotel by ten. If the night ends early, you could come back and see my place afterwards. Maybe sleep over.'

'Won't Stephan be there?' asked Lisa doubtfully.

'No,' said Sian. 'He's gone to visit his mother in Birmingham for the weekend. It's her birthday.'

'Oh yeah?' said Lisa with a grin.

Lisa got off the tube at Stratford. Once outside the station she dialled Leon's mobile number. The answerphone came on and she frowned as she listened to Leon's recorded message. Lisa walked slowly along Romford Road thinking hard. Saturday two weeks ago was the day she moved in. She wasn't going to give Sian the satisfaction of knowing that she had called Leon on his mobile that very morning and, getting no reply, had then turned up at his house and knocked vainly on the front door for half an hour. In a conversation later that day, Leon, flustered and sounding unnaturally nervous, had wanted to get off the phone as quickly as possible. After a day or two of uncertainty she had forced the possibility of him cheating on her out of her mind.

Lisa hurried along Matthews Park Road and let herself into the house. She took off her coat and dropped her shopping bag on the floor. She sat down on the bottom stair and rested her chin on her knees.

Her mind ran back over the events of the previous afternoon. She'd asked Leon about the training camp, where it was, if the whole team was going and he'd mumbled something about a coach picking them all up from the club and taking them to the camp in Essex. Had there been a bag? Yeah, she was sure she'd seen him throw his faded leather sports bag into the Lotus. Then she'd stood by the car asking him if he had remembered everything. Trainers, tracksuit, T-shirts, clean underwear? 'Yes, Mum,' he'd replied playfully, raising his eyebrows and smiling. He'd reached out and hugged her. 'I'd better get going or the boys'll leave me behind. See you on Sunday. Behave yourself, babes,' he had said before kissing her quickly, jumping into the car and driving off.

Lisa stood up and ran up the stairs. She marched into the bedroom and stood in front of his clothes rack, her hands planted on her hips.

'Well, Leon, let's see if you're really the Casanova that everyone thinks you are,' she said grimly.

Sian was beginning to wish she had stayed at home. The four of them were sitting on two sofas. They faced each other across a low table, watching the surging dancefloor in front of them. Jigga seemed to be in the party mood as he lifted a fresh bottle of champagne out of the ice bucket and refilled all the glasses on the table. Everyone else wished they were someplace else. Lisa, who was sitting next to Jigga, seemed hell-bent on drinking herself into a coma. Pearce, to Sian's right, looked spectacular in a pin-striped velvet suit with an extravagant silk shirt underneath but he was in a very ugly mood. Sian nudged him.

'Pearce, you look as though you wanna kill somebody. Tell me what's up.'

'Just me and my problems, Sian. Don't worry about it. You girls can go and dance if you like, don't let me spoil your night.'

'I don't understand why you're so down, I mean, you should be glad. I managed to get Lisa and Jigga sitting next to each other without a fight.'

Pearce didn't laugh. 'Guess I should be glad, but right now I got bigger strife.'

'Go on.'

'Well, my daughter is five today.'

'Shanna?'

'I only got one,' he said morosely.

'And you miss her?'

'Yeah, that too, but her damn mother wouldn't even let me speak to her.'

'Why she want to do something like that?'

'It was my fault. I started an argument about this new guy she's seeing and she started screaming about how I'm hiding out in London when I should be taking care of things in LA. Then she just hung the fuck up.'

'What does she mean?'

'Money, Sian. She wants money, cash, greenbacks, you name it she wants that too, but then that's Estella all over. You give her the sun, moon and stars, she'll want Jupiter too. I gave her the fucking best years of my life but now she wants to drain me like a blister.'

'Why does she want you back in LA?'

''Cos Estella's getting worried now. She's realized things are working out here and that I might not be coming back. If I'm here she can't bleed me so hard. She thought I would rebuild the business in LA and that she'd get half of it. My new plans have really pissed her off.'

'Sounds like she really hates you.'

Pearce laughed. 'Hate me? Guess I should feel sorry for Estella. All she wanted was a man who'd keep house and bring home the chips. When it all went wrong, she must have felt so cheated.' He stared grimly at the bubbling, enticing liquor. He raised his glass and drained it. As he put down the empty glass on the table his hand shook.

'Shit,' he said. 'I'm getting out of here before I finish the bottle and then several more.'

'But this was all your idea, Pearce. You can't just leave. Where are you going?'

'For some fresh air, Sian. To think. I'll be back in a while. Enjoy yourselves,' he said as he strode off. Jigga stood up and hurried after Pearce.

Lisa was hunched over her third or fourth glass of champagne. There was an aura of inebriated melancholy about her. A cigarette Jigga had given her hung limply between her index and middle finger. Heavy hip hop blasted from huge black speakers all around them and the seething dancefloor of Swingers was packed with bodies. Women, in tight miniskirts and low-cut tops, danced close to men in open shirts and tight pants. The ultra-violet light picked out a group of girls in white dresses on the dancefloor, each doing the same move. Dip and twist, dip and twist, then back in the other direction, dip and twist once again. On a stage at the back of the dancefloor the more exhibitionist partygoers were dancing in spotlights. The DJs were leaping around in a box set high above the crowd and with microphones in their hands they egged on the dancers on the stage.

'Lisa, how can you just sit here when everyone is enjoying themselves?'

Lisa didn't even acknowledge the question. She raised the cigarette to her mouth and took a long drag.

'Not you as well.'

'The thing I don't get,' said Lisa softly, 'is one day you can feel like you're on top of the world, like nothing can touch you, but the next day life comes down on you like a ton of bricks.'

'What's that supposed to mean?'

'Well, I thought I knew men. Thought I had them pinned down and sussed out but I was wrong.'

'Oh, is this to do with our conversation on the tube?'

'You're the one with the sense,' Lisa said, a slur creeping into her voice. 'I'm the one that plays with fire. Well, now I've been burned good and proper.'

'I thought Leon was treating you OK.'

'He isn't at any training camp,' said Lisa dully.

'Come on, Lisa, I thought you were sure he went.'

'Obviously I wasn't so damn bright after all. He wasn't home that Saturday either. I went round to his house that morning – banged on the fuckin' door for half an hour. Then today, on the way home I was thinking about what you said so when I got home I went upstairs and looked in his things and all his sports stuff is still there, his trainers and tracksuit. He didn't take any of it. But he took his watch, his gold and one of his Armani jackets. No way he'd be taking any of that stuff to no training camp. So basically the bastard's playing me just like he played Tiffany.'

'Lisa—'

'Now I see where you're coming from, Sian. Men, huh. It's either screw or get screwed, but you gotta treat 'em mean no matter what. Treat 'em mean, keep 'em keen.' She managed a grim smile. 'That's what men do to us, innit? Treat us like the bitches we are to keep us sniffing around for more.'

'What are you gonna do now?'

'We used to have fun, Sian. Didn't matter where we were, didn't matter what we were doing, we used to catch joke twenty-four-seven. We never had no men to tell us what to do and who to do it with. It's a fuckin' shame.'

'Well, at least you found out before you got in any deeper. You can be out of there and back home before he gets back.'

'Back home?' Lisa raised her chin. 'I'm not going home with my tail between my legs. I'm gonna sit right here and show Leon. I'm gonna make him pay for this.'

'Be better than him, Lisa. Don't sink to his level.'

Lisa laughed. 'I'm not like you, Sian. You've always wanted to be somebody, move out of Leyton Rise, get away and get a new life. I don't ask for much from life. I don't have a brilliant singing career. Don't even have much of a hairdressing career. I had the job I wanted, had the man I wanted. I didn't even ask for love. Never believed in love till now,' said Lisa, her voice growing quieter. 'But I must be in love, 'cos it hurts so much.'

'I'm sure he loves you too,' said Sian, reaching across the low table and touching Lisa's arm reassuringly. Lisa turned away.

'The only person *he* ever loved was Leon,' she said bitterly, looking over at the dancefloor. 'But don't worry. I'll get him back somehow. I'll think of a way to screw him like he's screwed me.'

They watched as Jigga came walking towards them. He sat down on a sofa. 'Hey, you girls look *depressed*,' he exclaimed, reaching for the bottle of champagne.

'Men problems,' said Sian, holding her glass out for him to refill it. 'Don't worry about it. Is Pearce OK?'

'Yeah. He's having women problems.' Sian and Jigga laughed. 'Everybody having too many damn problems, it seems to me. That's why I came prepared,' he said as he reached into a trouser pocket and pulled out a small plastic container. He twisted the top off and tipped several pills on to the table. Lisa and Sian looked at each other. 'Come on, girls, don't stare at me like you never seen this before.'

'What is it?' asked Sian suspiciously.

'It's ecstasy. Normally it'd be a line of coke but I couldn't risk making a line of coke in a club I don't know. A friend of mine told me this was just as good. Just pop one in your mouth and kick it back with some Moet. In ten seconds you'll be straight Jiggy – like me.' Jigga chuckled as he filled his glass with champagne. It fizzed pleasantly. Then he popped a pill in his mouth, picked up his glass and drained it. 'Aah, that hit the spot. So who's next?' he said, grinning at Sian and Lisa.

'Not for us,' said Sian firmly. 'We don't mess around with drugs.'

'Good girls, huh?' said Jigga. 'Good girls don't have any fun.'

'I'll try one,' said Lisa suddenly. She leaned forward. 'God knows I could do with some fun,' she said, holding out her hand.

'Lisa, don't,' said Sian. 'You don't know what's in that pill and you've had enough champagne anyway!'

'Don't listen to her, Lisa. We're here to have fun, not sit around looking at the walls.'

'Yeah,' said Lisa, nodding. 'I need cheering up.'

Jigga passed Lisa a pill which she held gingerly.

'Put it in your mouth,' urged Jigga as he handed her a glass of champagne.

'You should take one as well. You need to have some fun too,' Lisa said excitedly to Sian as she raised her pill to her mouth.

Sian stood up. 'I'm not staying here to watch this,' she said angrily. 'Lisa, if you put that in your mouth, I'm going home.'

'Oh, 'llow it, Sian,' said Lisa. 'There's nothing to it. It's just a little pill.' She popped it in her mouth and washed it down with the champagne.

'That's my girl,' said Jigga as he reached for the champagne bottle and refilled Lisa's glass. He handed Lisa her glass and lifted up his own. 'I propose a toast,' he said, 'to fun.' Lisa clinked her glass against his.

'To fun,' she said, giggling.

Sian swept off. She was soon lost in the crowd.

Lisa watched her go, then quickly drank some more champagne. She hiccuped then giggled nervously. 'I guess I'm not a good girl,' she said. Jigga laughed and leaned forward to pat her knee.

'You're as good as you wanna be,' he replied. 'Why should the bad people have all the fun?'

'Yeah,' agreed Lisa. She sat back on the sofa. 'The bad people do have all the fun. And then the good people get all the pain.' She felt light-headed. The music seemed so loud. 'Do you wanna dance?'

'Sure,' said Jigga, standing up and holding out a hand. Lisa took his hand and stood up. 'But I warn you,' he added, 'I'm the Dancehall King of NYC.' Lisa giggled as she followed Jigga onto the dancefloor. They found a space and began dancing to the energetic reggae beat. Lisa laughed as she jerked her body in time to the music. The strobe lights were making her feel dizzy but this was *fun*. She smiled flirtatiously at Jigga and ran her hands through her long hair as she moved her hips provocatively. Jigga watched her as he danced. Lisa laughed. He was a good dancer. The next song had a slow tempo. Jigga moved closer to Lisa and took her in his arms.

'What does an average Joe like me gotta do to get a beautiful young lady such as yourself?' Jigga asked with a grin.

'Well, you've got me for this song, enjoy it while you can.'

'But then you're gonna go home to your man, like a good girl again, instead of having fun with me.'

Lisa giggled into Jigga's ear. 'I feel dizzy,' she said. 'The room is spinning.'

'That's what happens when you have fun, shortie. Does your man teach you how to have fun?'

'No,' she said. 'Not like this. Right now I feel like dancing all fuckin' night.'

'Well, I've got some tunes back at the hotel. This club's gonna close soon but you could always come back with me and then we can dance all night.'

Lisa smiled dreamily. 'But I'm a good girl.'

'And good girls don't have any fun,' Jigga reminded her.

'No,' agreed Lisa, 'only the bad people.' They laughed together. She put a hand to her head. Everything was a blur. 'Where we going now?' she asked as Jigga gently led her off the dancefloor. He looked back and grinned.

'We're gonna have some more fun, of course, and dance all night long.'

Sian joined the end of a queue of scantily clad young women in the white-tiled ladies' room. Other women jostled each other for space at the mirrors as they fussed with make-up purses and hairbrushes.

'Why is it that these places never have enough loos?' a short, overly made-up woman with a large afro asked Sian. Sian shrugged her shoulders, shivering slightly as the queue shuffled along. Eventually Sian re-emerged into the hot crowded disco.

Other people now filled the two sofas where they had been sitting so Sian squeezed her way onto the crowded dancefloor. She couldn't see Jigga and Lisa anywhere. Finally she pushed her way out into the hallway. She walked up to one of the bouncers on the door.

'I'm looking for my friends,' she explained.

'Everyone's looking for friends,' replied a bouncer with a raspy laugh. 'What did these friends of yours look like?'

'A big guy in a shiny grey suit and a mixed-race girl in a red dress.'

'The dress was really short and she had long hair, right?' asked another bouncer.

Sian nodded.

'Yeah,' said the one with the raspy laugh, turning towards his colleague. 'You remember. They drove off in that limousine.'

'A nice big white one,' his colleague added. They nodded together. 'Now that's a car. That's a car.'

chapter
twenty four

Sian raised her head, moaned and let it sink back onto the soft pillow for a few more minutes. Eventually she sat up. The phone rang. She grabbed it, hoping it might be Pearce or Lisa returning her messages.

'Hello? Hi, Tiffany. No, don't come yet, I'm not dressed or anything. An hour? *Puhleeze*, I'm still in bed! Yeah, at least an hour and a half. Bye.'

Tiffany, Vanya and Ebela burst into Sian's tiny flat like a small hurricane, re-arranging chairs, flicking through television channels, opening and shutting cupboards, peering into her wardrobe, upsetting her stack of CDs.

'Ebela, it took me ages to put those CDs in order!'

'Don't worry, I'll put everything back. Uh, uh, how did you manage to get hold of Redman's new album before everybody else?'

'Well, I asked my manager, Pearce, and he got his friend Jigga to bring it over from New York.'

'Sly bitch. So you couldn't even bring me in on that one,' said Ebela, shaking her head reproachfully.

'Oh yeah, like when you went to Lagos and came back dripping in gold, where was my chain?'

Ebela cleared her throat. 'Well, ahem, OK, you got me there, girlfriend, but I'm just a poor student. You're the big pop star. How did you get Planet Records to get you this flat anyway?'

'Well, Pearce told them I needed my own place so I could get to the studio and interviews more easily. Somewhere quiet where I could concentrate on my songwriting. They came through for me. It's just rented so I have to be very careful with it.' Sian frowned as Tiffany fiddled with one of the lamps. 'I haven't got all of my stuff here yet. I'm going to move in properly when I've got some time.'

'What's this?' asked Vanya, picking up Sian's TalentSearch trophy from the mantelpiece.

'Oh, that's what I won at the competition last year. It's a miniature microphone stand,' said Sian.

'Yeah, our girl's come a long way since then from the TalentSearch Competition to *Top of the Pops*,' said Vanya.

'From Leyton Rise to Islington heights,' said Tiffany. They all laughed.

'But Islington is so far from Leyton,' said Ebela. 'That fifty-six bus ride is no joke.'

'Well, don't worry about it, 'cos none of you are coming to stay.'

'Rah! Is that she's going on?' said Ebela, looking at Vanya and laughing.

'I've just told you I have to be careful of the place. Pearce said if the record company get it into their heads that the place is being used for wild parties then they'll just take it back.'

'What, so not even Lisa or Stephan can stay?'

'Well, Lisa's staying with her man so she'd never stay here and I haven't seen Stephan for a few days. I've been doing so much promotional stuff and this weekend he's visiting his mum. It's tough luck. Just as I get some free time he's off somewhere. Still, just as well. Too many girls are after him down these sides,' Sian said jokingly.

'Well, you know he's a ladies' man better than anyone else,' said Ebela uncomfortably.

'As long as he stays true to me, I don't care how many girls are after him,' said Sian. 'But anyway, he hasn't stayed. Last night I was alone just like all the rest.'

'Don't expect me to have any sympathy, I'm hungry,' complained Vanya, walking into the tiny kitchen. 'Don't you have a packet of crisps or something? I don't know why I keep eating like this. I hope I'm not pregnant.'

'No, it's just greed, remember that word?' said Tiffany, following Vanya.

'Oh well, at least I won't look like you, Tiffany, all bones and horse teeth.'

Tiffany thumped Vanya who fell onto the worktop, sending two mugs clattering over into the sink.

'Watch her now. Vanya is going on like she wanna mash up Sian's place, already,' said Tiffany, placing the blame squarely on Vanya with a sassy grin.

'That's right,' said Sian, hurrying into the kitchen with Ebela. They all burst out laughing.

'Man, I've missed you guys,' said Sian, leaning back against the refrigerator.

'We've missed you too,' said Vanya. 'You and Lisa both.'

'Yeah, since Lisa moved out of Leyton Rise no one's clapped eyes on her,' said Ebela.

'I can't believe she's still with Leon after everything Tiffany saw,' exclaimed Vanya. 'Tell us what happened again, Tiffany.'

'It's just like I said before,' said Tiffany innocently. 'I was in a bar with my friend and we saw Leon chatting up some pretty girl, with reddish blonde hair. He bought her a couple of drinks then they left the bar with his arm around her waist.'

'Didn't he see you?' asked Ebela. Tiffany shook her head.

'Nope and I didn't want him to either.'

'You must have felt so bad,' added Ebela. 'Why is Lisa still with him?'

'I've tried telling her,' said Sian. 'But it's like he's got some hold over her. She just won't cut her losses and run. Lisa's been acting very strange recently. When I try and talk to her about it we just end up arguing. If this is what going out with Leon does to people, you were well out of it, Tiffany.'

'Yeah, I'm over him,' said Tiffany, smiling brightly. 'Right now I've got so much going for me, Leon's the last thing on my mind. I've got a top-dollar modelling assignment coming up in Cuba and I'm really looking forward to it.'

'Ooh, you're going to Cuba?' said Sian.

'Yeah, I got the assignment last week. I was feeling a bit depressed so I was well pleased to get this job. It's a photo shoot for a travel company's brochure for next summer.'

'What do you have to do?'

'Sit by the pool, look good and get paid for it.'

'It's not fair,' said Sian. 'Watch you in your white boob tube with your stomach ring. Looking good is effortless for you.'

Tiffany smiled. 'You don't look too bad yourself, Sian. I like your new hairstyle.'

Sian combed her fingers through her shoulder-length bob. 'It's a weave,' she confessed. 'I have to do a lot of photo shoots at the moment and it's much easier than running to the hairdressers every minute.'

'You can't tell,' said Ebela admiringly.

'So are we going cruising or what?' asked Vanya. 'It's a perfect summer's day outside and we're in this flat – no offence, Sian – when we could be outside in the sun. I listened to the weather forecast and they said it was gonna be about twenty-five degrees today, well hot for June. You're in your little denim shorts, Tiffany's got her white boob tube on, I've got my Moschino vest and Ebela's wearing her new sandals. We should be out there, in Tiff's convert, showing ourselves off.'

'Where are we going?' asked Sian as they headed for the door.

'Everywhere. But me and Ebela are leaving you guys in Wood Green. We've got to find a birthday present for my man,' said Vanya.

'Yeah, and I thought you and I could go down to that bar in Brixton. This summer it's *the* place to be seen and I know the barman so I think I can wangle us a couple of freebies,' said Tiffany to Sian.

They walked into the corridor and waited while Sian locked the door. 'Sounds great,' said Sian, turning around. 'Let's go.'

They got into Tiffany's green convertible Golf that sparkled like an emerald in the bright sunlight.

Tiffany started the car, turned into Essex Road and drove up towards Dalston.

'Why are we going to Dalston?' asked Sian. 'There are no good shops there.'

'Just to *go*,' explained Ebela. 'None of us have been up that way for a while, so we're just gonna breeze through on our way to Wood Green.'

At Kingsland High Street they joined a long queue of traffic leading up to Stoke Newington.

'Great cruise, guys,' said Sian as they got stuck behind a bus that belched filthy petrol fumes.

'Come on, Sian. It's Saturday, everywhere is gonna be chokka like this. Man, look how many people are in the pattie shop,' Vanya said. 'Stop here, Tiffany. I must have a pattie before I die of hunger.' Tiffany pulled over to the side of the road. 'Does anyone else want one?'

Ebela nodded. She took some money out of her purse and passed it to Vanya who got out of the car and hurried over to the shop.

'Get the new issue. The truth from Louis Farrakan.' A tall young man in a smart suit and red bow-tie walked across to the car. 'Would you young ladies like to buy a copy of the *Final Call*? It's only one pound and profits go to a local Saturday school.'

Sian and Ebela smiled but shook their heads. The

tall young man nodded at them before heading along the road.

'Damn, he must be so hot,' said Tiffany.

'I don't believe in all that stuff,' said Ebela.

'I don't know what I believe any more,' said Sian. 'I find my own church confusing enough.'

'If I thought the man had looked good, I would've bought his paper,' said Tiffany, laughing. 'Who cares what it's about?'

Sian rolled her eyebrows. 'Tiffany, you're an airhead.'

'Yeah,' agreed Ebela. 'Don't you think about important issues?'

'Life is already stressful, why make it more compli-cated by trying to solve the problems that have no answers?' replied Tiffany airily.

A young woman with a pushchair stopped by the car. 'Hi, Sian, I haven't seen you around for ages.'

'Oh, hi, Ceelie,' said Sian who waved at the pretty little girl kicking her legs in the pushchair. 'How are you?' she asked.

'Fine. Thought I'd come up Dalston and get some clothes for Sahi.'

'How is she?'

Ceelie bent down and patted her child's head. 'She's fine. Getting feisty.'

'Every week Buelah tells me something new about Sahi.'

'Oh, all Buelah talks about at church is you,' said Ceelie with a little laugh. ' "My sister has the best voice in the whole world, my sister's gonna be on *Top of the Pops*, my sister's famous." '

The other girls in the car tittered.

'That Buelah,' said Sian, a little embarrassed. 'And how is everyone at church?'

'Same people, same ways. Pastor Brown still picks his nose when he thinks no one's watching. Mum still gets the spirit every week. Everyone misses you. Last week your mother asked the church to say a prayer for you.'

'You're kidding.'

'"For she need help, Fader, more den ever, at dis uncertain time."' They laughed. Vanya walked over and got back in the car. She passed Ebela her pattie. 'Anyway, I'd better get this one home before she needs changing,' said Ceelie.

'Yeah, we better get going too. It was good to see you though, Ceelie. Take care.'

Tiffany put her foot on the gas and the girls drove up through Stoke Newington and down to Seven Sisters and Wood Green where Vanya and Ebela jumped out, before heading towards the West End. With Tiffany doing the driving, Sian was able to sit back and look up at a sky so blue that the only trouble spots on the horizon were deep in her thoughts.

'Turn up the music, Tiffany, and stop talking on your phone. Lord, Mercury didn't know what they were doing when they gave you free weekend calls.'

'Well, that's their lookout.' Tiffany put the phone back on the dashboard in time to wave to a group of boys walking down the road. 'They gave me a phone, now I'm gonna rinse it.'

Sian smiled. Tiffany and Lisa were so alike, pretty, fun-loving and warm-blooded, but Lisa was the real thing and Tiffany was the diet version.

'Omigod, that guy was the cream.' The car swerved crazily as Tiffany glanced at a group of young men walking along the road.

'Calm down, girlfriend, fe dis here body waan fe get home in one piece!' yelled Sian.

They stopped at some lights. A black Vitara jeep playing loud garage pulled alongside. A man leaned out of the windows. 'Excuse me, ladies,' he said, smiling, 'but don't I know you from somewhere? You both look really familiar.'

Sian and Tiffany looked at each other and grinned.

'We'll leave you to think about it,' hollered Sian as the Golf sped off, leaving all other cars way back.

They reached Brixton later that afternoon and drove up Coldharbour Lane towards the popular bar that spilled outside onto a patio set with small garden tables and chairs.

'It's a complete roadblock,' said Tiffany. 'Now where are we going to park?'

'I've never seen so many nice cars in one place,' said Sian as Tiffany tried to find a parking space.

'Forget the cars, what about the drivers?' said Tiffany with a dreamy sigh, already trying to catch the eye of the driver of a red convertible.

'Do you wanna drink?' asked Tiffany, turning off the engine. 'I know one of the men who works in there and he usually serves me for free.'

'Yeah, why not? It's free and you get an opportunity to show off your legs. I'll have a Southern Comfort and Coke.' Tiffany stuck out her tongue then opened the door. Sian watched the male reaction as Tiffany got out of the car. Then her phone rang.

'Yo, Sian, I just got your message.'

Pearce pushed his way through the crowd.

'Dammit, Pearce. You've taken ages,' said Sian crossly.

Pearce held up his hands in a gesture of apology. 'Sorry, I had the bright idea of jumping into a taxi. Thought it'd be quick. My mistake. Next time I'll just take the tube.' He looked around. 'This is some hang-out.'

Tiffany looked from Pearce's Polo shirt to his silver watch. She nudged Sian.

'Pearce, this is my friend Tiffany. Tiffany, this is my manager, Pearce,' said Sian, smiling.

Pearce held out his hand, Tiffany shook it, smiling prettily. 'C'mon and sit down, Pearce,' she said, gesturing towards the chair next to hers.

Pearce looked towards the bar. 'I was thinking of buying a drink first. What do you think my chances are of getting served inside of half an hour?'

Tiffany stood up. 'Let me get it. I know the barman so I get free drinks. Just tell me what you want.'

'Thanks. I'll just have an orange juice if they have it.'

'Not even a beer?' asked Tiffany. Sian glared at her. 'OK, fine – one orange juice coming up,' said Tiffany, walking away towards the bar.

'I think I have an admirer,' said Pearce, smiling after Tiffany. 'And she's fly too.'

'Stop grinning, Pearce. I mean, you seem to think this is all some damn joke.'

'Sian, I'm here. Tell me.'

Sian told Pearce what had happened after he had left the club. When Sian finished, Pearce looked serious.

'Damn,' Pearce said thoughtfully. 'That's deep, but it takes two, y'know.'

'He deliberately got her drunk and then gave her that E. I used to think you two were decent but now I'm not sure.'

'I'm not Jigga's keeper.'

'I even had to go home on my own.'

'I'm sorry Jigga took the limo and I apologize for that. But he left me stranded too. When I got back from my walk you had all gone. Anyway, have you spoken to Lisa?'

'She's not answering her phone,' said Sian. 'Have you spoken to Jigga?'

'No. I called him around midday but he wasn't taking any calls.'

'So he hasn't told you anything?'

'Naw, but then maybe there isn't anything to tell. Oh, come on, Sian. Don't you think you're being a little naive? People can get it together in the most unlikely of circumstances.'

'Lisa is my friend, Pearce. My very best friend, so I know the difference between Lisa getting it together and Lisa being taken for a ride.' She glanced up and saw Tiffany walking towards them.

'Well, what do you want me to do?' asked Pearce as Tiffany reached them.

'Do what you have to do, Pearce. It's on you. I'm

going to the loo.' Sian stood up and strode off towards the bar just as Tiffany sat down.

'One orange juice to order,' said Tiffany with a surprised giggle. 'What's up with Sian?'

'Hey, you tell me,' said Pearce, taking a long sip of the juice. 'If Jigga and Lisa wanna kick it with each other there's not a damn thing I or anyone else can do about it.'

'Yeah,' said Tiffany cool as a cucumber. 'I agree.'

'She been dragging you through it as well?'

'It's all we've been talking about all day,' said Tiffany, wide-eyed.

'And the thing is, Sian doesn't even know for sure if anything happened, but she's running off like that. Well, let her run,' snapped Pearce testily. 'Like I said, sex is a fact of life. Jigga may not be love's young dream but it's not unthinkable that Lisa might find him attractive after a couple of glasses of champagne.'

'She might have been drunk then?'

'That's Sian's story. Drunk and doped up on ecstasy but hell – until we can get hold of one of them, how can we really know what really happened last night?'

'So they could still be together?'

'Who knows,' said Pearce gloomily.

'Hmm, yeah, well, we'd better change the subject or Sian'll just get even more vexed,' said Tiffany. 'The weather for instance,' she said smiling warmly. 'It's been a perfect day.'

chapter
twenty five

'**Slick, will** you get your butt out of the fridge! Cherry sent you over here to help, not stuff your face.'

'Aw, Mom sent me 'cos she know she woan have to cook a big Sunday dinner for me when I gets home.' He emerged from the refrigerator with a yoghurt. 'Gimme a spoon!'

'Boys are getting too greedy nowadays,' agreed Vanya, throwing Slick a spoon. 'And wash it out when you're finished.'

'You just red-eye 'cos you wanna eat too but you know you need to be on a diet.'

'Hey, just watch it or that yoghurt gwaan end up on those new Air Max of yours.'

'Yo, back off,' said Slick, using his spoon as a microphone and waving his arms in rapping gestures. ' – 'cos I got the skills and you knows that I'm ill enough to make you smoke Phills. Ain't no other nigga filled, with a rhyming to kill. I spills thrills to all the chicken heads who try and throw their drill on this li'l Jamerican drawing crowds like Canevil and yes I'm Evil too, like all them yout's from Cypress Hill, so Vanya better chill, and go eat another meal, I look like a million dollars, hit you like ecstacy pills. And when a honey wants me still I go all lyrical. I make all the honeys feel, like I wuz Johnny Gill. Whenever—'

'Jus' cool,' interrupted Sian. 'We all know you've got the lyrics and you can rap. Hurry up and finish that and then come upstairs and help me with my keyboard. There's more stuff than you'd think.'

'Yeah, I don't even know if it's all gonna fit in my Fiesta,' said Vanya.

'We'll just have to have a go. I'm not taking absolutely everything. The flat is furnished, so I'll leave the old television and my desk. There's just a few clothes and shoes. My keyboard obviously. Some books and photos.'

'So does Buelah get your room?' asked Vanya with a grin.

'No. I'm keeping my room here, just in case I have to move back. The flat is only temporary. They can take it away from me at any time.'

Slick finished his yogurt and passed Vanya the spoon. She made a face but washed and dried it and put it in the cutlery tray.

'OK, Sian, I'm ready. Let's go.'

They trouped upstairs.

'It looks so unlived in already,' Sian said wistfully, looking at the neatly made bed.

'Mmm. This estate isn't gonna be the same without you,' said Vanya.

'Hey, don't worry, baby. You've still got me,' said Slick.

Vanya smiled at him. 'Yeah, true, you feisty wretch.'

'For a while anyway.' Slick sighed. 'Things are startin' to get a little hot round here for me as well.'

'What do you mean?' asked Vanya.

Slick put a finger to his lips. 'Don't worry.'

'He thinks he's too bad, that's the problem,' said Sian unsympathetically.

'Aw, come on,' appealed Slick.

'No. Aunt Cherry's always complaining about the company you keep.'

Slick snorted. 'I love my mum but she don't know nothing. Listen, you got a box for this keyboard or what, 'cos I got other things I need to get done today.'

Sian rolled her eyes at Vanya as she fetched the box from the hall cupboard.

Vanya was busy taking down ornaments, photos and pictures from the wall and mantelpiece.

'Omigod, you was such a pretty baby,' exclaimed Vanya.

'That was Buelah,' said Sian, looking over Vanya's shoulder.

'Well, yeah, I was a bit surprised,' Vanya joked. She put the photograph in a box then took another off the wall.

'Come and look at this one, Skinny. I know that ugly thing in the corner is you, is this, Lisa?'

Sian put down a stack of books to look. The two little girls in the picture were doing handstands against the wall, so their grinning faces were upside-down, Lisa's pigtails hanging down while Sian's afro puffs stubbornly defied gravity.

'Actually, it's really sweet,' said Vanya, walking over to show it to Slick who was folding up the keyboard.

'Yup,' agreed Sian shortly. She returned to her stack of books.

'When did you last see Lisa?' Vanya asked.

'When did anybody last see Lisa?' responded Sian.

'I see her all the time, being driven around in Leon's fancy car,' said Slick.

'That's because you're always walking the streets,' remarked Vanya dryly.

'Yeah, since she moved in with Leon no one's seen her. Does she ever come home?' asked Sian.

'Not really,' admitted Vanya. 'Mostly just passing through for mail and stuff.'

'Sian, don't you talk ever?' Slick asked. 'I mean, come on, you two were like the Cagney and Lacey of Leyton Rise.'

Sian shrugged. 'Last time I saw Lisa was the day before we all went for that drive in Tiffany's car.'

'That was a gorgeous day,' said Vanya sighing. 'It seems so long ago.'

'Well, it was a long time ago,' said Sian. 'We're well into July now, so at least three weeks.'

'You haven't spoken to Lisa for three weeks?' said Slick.

'Not properly. She's well cold when I call her and she never calls me so I've kinda just left her to it. I guess life isn't running so smoothly for her.'

'Well, you should help her out,' said Slick. 'I mean you got the dough and she's your best friend.'

'Why does everyone think that I'm bathing in it,

just because I've got a record out? Trust me, I've hardly seen air as yet!'

'Shit, OK, calm down,' said Vanya, laughing. 'We believe you, Sian.'

'Anyway, money isn't her problem. Her man's the problem. And before you say anything, I know Stephan isn't much better.'

'Well, as long as you know,' said Slick.

'I'm not stupid. I've heard rumours. One of my backing singers actually confessed to me the other day that he made a pass at her a while back.'

'Oh yeah?' said Vanya with a chuckle. 'I saw him down SW1 on Friday, chirpsing as usual. But he looked kriss tho', in some swank Moschino suit.'

'I bought him that suit,' said Sian crossly.

'Well, he putting it to good use,' suggested Slick.

'Slick's got a point,' said Vanya with a giggle.

'So that's why he didn't come to the studio Friday. Said he was helping his brother move house.' Sian kissed her teeth. 'Forget him. God, we worked so late that day. It's like I never see daylight any more.'

The front door banged shut and they heard Bernadette and Buelah returning from church, Buelah chattering happily as she took off her shoes and then the creak of her first step on the stairs. Buelah paused when she reached the landing, watching them through the open doorway.

'Hey, Buelah. You gonna help me pack my things?' Sian called out. But Buelah ran into her room and slammed the door.

'What's up with B?' asked Slick as he taped the keyboard box shut.

'I don't know. I'll go and see if she's OK,' said Sian, putting down a book she had been flicking through. She walked out of her room and tapped on Buelah's door.

'Go away,' said a muffled voice.

Sian pushed open the door. Buelah was stretched on her bed, her face buried in a pillow.

'Hi, Buelah,' Sian said, taking a few tentative steps into the room.

'Go away,' said Buelah again.

Sian walked across to the bed and sat down. 'Come on now, B,' she said. 'What is this foolishness?'

Buelah turned over. 'It's not foolishness!' she said sullenly. 'You don't know anything, Sian.'

'Did something happen at church?'

'No. Church was fine.'

'Well, did you have a row with Mum?'

'NO!'

'Oh. Then I guess I'm the problem.'

Buelah began to cry. 'I don't want you to go.'

'I'm staying right here,' said Sian.

'No, I mean I don't want you to move out.'

Sian sighed. 'Well, I wasn't going to live here for ever, Buelah.'

'I want things to go back to the way they were when you used to come to church with me and Mum. I want us all to eat dinner together and I want Lisa to come round again like she used to. Mum's always at work and I keep having to go to Mrs Dega's yard for my dinner. I *hate* it there.'

'Things can't stay the same, Buelah. Sometimes I wish I could spend more time with you guys as well but I can't turn the clock back.'

'But we never see you and I can't talk to Mum about everything.'

'I've got to move forward with my life and that means moving out.'

'Then I *hate* you!' spat Buelah. She jumped off the bed and ran out of the room and down the stairs. Sian heard the bang of the living-room door. She sat there for a while, remembering how it used to be before she won the singing competition, how she'd come home from Sportsworld and they'd sit at the kitchen table around a steaming dish of ackee and saltfish with dumplings and boiled potatoes. Buelah would chatter excitedly about school, Mum would talk about church and Sian would moan about her crap job selling trainers. She smiled. She remembered how Lisa would come bursting into her room to tell her about some amazing new guy she'd met or some party she was just dying to go to. Lisa, Sian and the white-hot bond between the two of them had slowly cooled until now it seemed they barely knew each other.

'You OK, Sian?' asked Vanya softly, putting her head around the door. Sian smiled up at her.

'Sure. I'm fine – well, sort of.' She stood up. 'Come on, let's get that room sorted out.'

The weeds and the debris were gone from the small front garden at 11 Matthews Park Road. Pretty net curtains hung in the windows. Sian glanced nervously around as she walked up the path. She hesitated before pressing the bell.

After a few minutes, the door opened. Lisa stared at Sian in surprise.

'Hi, Sian, long time no see,' she said coolly. 'Come in.' Lisa led the way along the hallway into the kitchen where she had been preparing dinner. A small chicken lay in an oven tray on the table, some spice containers nearby and potatoes on the side ready for peeling.

'Is Leon around?' asked Sian quietly. Lisa shook her head.

'No, he's out. Off kicking a ball around with some mates. You're quite safe.'

There was an awkward silence. Lisa moved towards the table and continued seasoning the chicken.

'So, what's been happening?' she asked with a forced brightness. She wore faded denim shorts and one of Leon's old team-shirts that swamped her like a sheet. Her hair was roughly twisted up and held by a scrunchie.

'Oh, you know, the usual,' said Sian. 'I spent most of today moving to my new flat. Vanya and Slick came around to help me. We finished a while ago.'

'Yeah?'

'And, I figured, it being a Sunday evening you might be around.'

'Seen.'

'I tried to call you on your mobile, but it was off.'

'Well, I didn't really wanna talk to anyone. So how's Vanya?'

'She's still studying for the social work. The rest of the crew are doing OK too. Ebela did really well in her exams. Slick's having a few problems with his mum, but then that's Slick for you. Problems just seem to follow that boy around. Who else? Oh yeah, I saw Tiffany the other day.'

'So? Tell the bitch I said hi.'

'I think you two should sort out your differences. You were good friends.'

Lisa ignored Sian.

'She's going away on Tuesday on a modelling assignment in Cuba.'

'Am I supposed to be happy for her?'

'No, I guess you wouldn't really care.'

Lisa folded the edges of the foil paper over the chicken and put it in the oven. She crossed over to the sink, picked up a potato and began to peel it.

'That chicken looks good,' said Sian, watching Lisa.

'Thanks. Leon is a bit fussy when it comes to food.'

'How is he?'

'Just fine,' she said defensively.

'Oh yeah, how is his football going?'

'Well, the season's over and it went quite well. He is supposed to be signing a new contract for next season with Crystal Palace.'

'That's great, man. He must be excited.'

Lisa smiled wryly. 'Well, I don't know. It was all going smoothly but then at the last minute Palace said they weren't sure and needed some extra time to make their decision.' She hesitated. 'They say he has a problem with temper management. He's a bit stressed out by the delay. That's why I'm trying to keep everything here going right, the least thing can start an argument at the moment.'

'So why haven't you called me since the night we went out together?'

'Well, it didn't exactly end well, did it?' said Lisa crossly.

'Up till now, I don't even know how it ended.'

'Look, you're not the only one. I had enough glasses of champagne and a couple of those pills.'

'How do you feel about that?'

Lisa slapped the potato peeler down and spun around. 'How do you think it feels?' she said fiercely. 'I didn't even wanna go to that bloody club in the first place!'

'Oh, so now it's my fault? I *told* you not to take anything from Jigga. Blatant. You didn't listen.'

'So you just left me in the club on my own with that creep. Some friend.'

'You left *me* in the club! I only went to the ladies'. By the time I got back you were both gone.'

'Yeah, well, whatever. It's done now. What's the point dragging them things up again? The important thing is that you haven't been telling everyone.'

'Of course not. No one knows.'

''Cos the last thing I need right now is Leon finding out.' Lisa picked up the potato peeler again and resumed her peeling.

'Did you ever ask him about the training camp?'

'I know he didn't go so what would be the point making up bare arguments after I went and did what I did? As far as I'm concerned, he's home with me now and that's what's important, so I'll just let sleeping dogs lie.'

'If Leon's so important then why'd you do it?'

Lisa glanced at Sian.

'I don't know,' she said dully. 'To get him back I guess. It's done with, it's no big deal.'

'So why have you been avoiding everyone then if it was no big deal?' asked Sian.

'Maybe I just feel like doing my own thing at the

moment,' said Lisa. 'Isn't that what you're doing at the moment with your singing?'

'I've missed you,' said Sian. 'Today when we were taking the photos down in my bedroom, I started thinking about the way things used to be between us, Lisa, how tight we used to be and now you don't return my calls. You don't come round and visit me at my new place.'

'And what about you?' Lisa said as she peeled a potato. 'All the times when you are doing your recording or when you travel around and sing, I am having problems. You don't care. Everything is your singing this, singing that. Since you got this record deal it's all you can think about.'

'But you are always welcome to come down to the studio.'

'Yeah but when I get there, there's all these fake people hanging around, like Stephan, and it just makes me feel ill the way they act and the way you fall for it.'

'Maybe you're a teeny-weeny bit red-eye. I used to be jealous of you. It does happen, Lisa. But that's not the reason to break up a friendship.'

'But you don't really want me as a friend. You chose them over me.'

'I just felt as though you and Stephan were at each other's throats all the time,' said Sian.

'The difference between me and hangers-on like Stephan is that they see you as this person who's earning wong and taking them places. But I look at you and I see all the things you used to be. You used to be a friend I could share my problems with and tell my dreams. Laughing at the same jokes, looking out for each other, putting each other first. That's what you used to be, Sian, and now it's gone.'

The front door opened and Leon walked in lugging a huge sports bag over his back. He dropped the bag in the hallway and sauntered towards the kitchen.

'You all right, Sian?' he said gruffly, looking from Sian to Lisa. He crossed the room and gave Lisa a kiss on the lips. 'Everything all right, babes?'

'Yeah. I'm just getting dinner ready. Sian came round for a chat. Thought you'd still be playing ball.'

'It's baking outside. The weather's freaked. Yesterday it was cool, perfect weather for football but today it was sunny and hot so the park's full of fuckin' kids and people sunbathin'.' Lisa and Sian giggled. 'There was no way we could get a decent game.' He opened the refrigerator and took out a carton of orange juice. Lisa got him a glass from a cupboard.

'So how you doing, Sian?' Leon said as he poured orange juice into the glass.

'OK. My single's out and it's going quite well.'

'Yeah, I hear it on the radio every now and then.' He pulled a chair out from underneath the table and sat down. 'Babes, I can't wait for them potatoes. Can't you do me sandwich or something? I'm starving.'

'Sure,' said Lisa. She opened the bread-bin and took out a loaf of bread.

'So what were you and Lisa talking about before I came in?' There was a brief silence.

'Oh, Sian was just inviting me to some party,' said Lisa, quickly shooting Sian a look as she went to the fridge.

'What party is this? I don't think I like your parties,' said Leon. He grinned at Sian. 'I can't have my Lisa out misbehaving.'

'Don't worry, I'm not going,' said Lisa.

'Everyone needs to have fun,' said Sian lightheartedly. Lisa glared at her.

'Lisa's got me if she needs to have fun. If she goes elsewhere she knows what's coming to her.'

'Oh Leon,' grumbled Lisa as she sliced some tomatoes for the sandwich.

'What's coming to her?' asked Sian, smiling.

'Can we talk about something else?' said Lisa loudly. She passed Leon a plate with his sandwich.

'See, she knows.' Leon grinned broadly at Lisa. 'Innit, babes?'

Lisa kissed her teeth and turned away. Leon reached out and grabbed her arm, pulling her towards him. 'Innit, babes?' he said again.

'Yeah, Leon,' Lisa said quickly. He let her go and she smiled at Sian, embarrassed.

'I'd better be off now,' said Sian uncomfortably.

'Yeah. Nice seeing you again Sian,' said Leon, picking up his sandwich. 'Drop by anytime.'

Lisa walked Sian to the door.

'See what you caused?' Lisa hissed when they were out of Leon's earshot.

'There's something not right about him, Lisa,' said Sian quietly as she opened the front door. 'Temper management is an understatement.' She stepped out onto the doorstep.

'Why did you go saying all that stuff about everyone needing to have fun? I told you he's going through a difficult period. Why'd you have to set him off?'

'Well, maybe I'm starting to look out for you again, Lisa,' said Sian grimly. 'And right now I don't like what I see.'

chapter
twenty six

Lisa's head lolled against the car window. She was curled up asleep. The mobile rang. Leon answered it.

'Yeah.'

'Hi, baby. I see you still answer the phone rudely.'

'Yeah. What do *you* want?'

'To talk to you.'

'Oh yeah? Since when?'

'I've been away for a while. Modelling again. I went to Cuba.'

'Had a good time, did you?'

'There's no need to be sarky. I'm not sore about Samantha. You're a free man.' She giggled. 'Is Lisa around?'

'Yeah, she's sitting next to me asleep. We're heading home after a night up west. You wanna speak to her? I could wake her up if you want.'

'Very funny. Just checking that she can't hear what I'm saying.'

'Well, make it quick.'

'Do you remember what *we* used to get up to in the car?'

'Yeah.' Leon chuckled, then checked himself as Lisa stirred. He reassumed his businesslike tone. 'So what's this all about then? I'm tired too. I wanna shoot home so I can get some shut-eye.'

'Dinner at my place, tomorrow?'

'It's difficult.'

'Lunch.'

'Hold up, I'm thinking.'

'I've got some interesting news for you.'

'Yeah? What kind of news?'

'Believe me, this is something you don't wanna miss.'

'Just lunch then?'

'Yeah. I've been doing the place up and now it's finished. You get the grand tour, some lunch and then you get your surprise.'

'Oh yeah?'

'One o'clock, then. For good food, good wine, and old times, 'cos they were good, weren't they, Leon?'

'No,' said Leon. 'They were bloody great, babes.'

As Leon put the phone back on the dashboard, Lisa shifted and opened her eyes.

'Who was that?' she said with a long yawn.

'Darren.'

Her eyes narrowed. 'But you said "babes". I could have sworn I heard you say "babes".'

'C'mon, Lisa,' said Leon with a grin. 'You must have been dreaming.'

*

Lisa woke up to the ringing of the alarm. The early morning sunlight crept through the grey blinds casting stripes of shadow over the room. Leon's arm was under her neck and one of his legs crossed one of hers. His lips quivered slightly as a snore rattled through him. His sleepy eyes flickered open briefly at the noise of the alarm then closed again. Lisa eased her trapped hair from under his arm and sat up. She stood up, put on Leon's oversize bathrobe and padded to the bathroom.

'I'm gone, Leon,' she said half an hour later as she slipped her arms into her black denim jacket. She was wearing a Cutting Edge T-shirt and her hair was gelled back into a bushy ponytail. Leon rubbed his eyes.

'Oh shit, it's so early.'

'What are you up today? Are you going to sort out the contract?'

'What's the fuckin' point?'

'Well, training for the new season's gonna start soon, Leon. It's been a couple of weeks now since you've heard anything. Maybe they're losing interest.'

'They'll sign the contract, don't worry. It's a done deal.'

'You should call someone at Palace and explain the misunderstanding with that coach.'

'Those fuckers know they're onto a good thing. They'll see sense. Anyway I don't have time for lots of phone calls, I've got something on.'

'Oh?'

'Just something to sort out, y'know. Give me a kiss then,' Leon demanded gruffly. Lisa bent down over the bed and kissed him. He waved her away, grinning. 'Go on now and make sure you behave yourself, babes.'

Leon stood swinging his car keys on the threshold of Tiffany's Highbury flat. He took in the glistening white paint, the ruffled curtains and pretty plants in the small front garden. He turned and studied the new dark green Golf parked in front of the house. As the door began to open he instinctively straightened his Armani jacket.

'Don't worry, honey, I like the ragamuffin look.'

Leon smiled. Tiffany was wearing a pair of denim shorts and a white cropped top. As she kissed him on the cheek Leon had to check himself.

'You smell nice.'

'I know.' Tiffany smiled and drew him inside, shutting the door after him. She led him along a freshly painted hallway and through an open door into her living room. She helped him off with his jacket and draped it over the back of one of the easy chairs in the living room. 'C'mon, honey, I'll show you around,' she said, taking his hand and pulling him down the hallway. 'Kitchen.' It was slimline, crisp, neat and sparkling, like Tiffany.

'Bathroom.'

'The modelling must be going well.'

'Yes, you could say that.' Tiffany gave a little giggle. 'Bedroom.'

Leon walked in. A large double bed with satin peach sheets. Leon turned to see Tiffany watching him from the doorway, one foot sliding up and down her leg. Leon grinned knowingly and walked past her, out of the room.

'So, where's the lunch, Tiffany? I'm hungry.'

Tiffany went into the kitchen. She took a small bowl of salad and a bottle of champagne out of the refrigerator. 'Take them in with you,' she said as she passed the salad bowl and bottle to Leon. 'Be careful of the cork as you open the bottle.' She put on oven gloves and took some lasagne out of the oven, putting the dish on a tray and carrying it into the living room. Leon had opened the bottle and was pouring champagne into the wine glasses on the already laid table. After putting down the tray, Tiffany served the lasagne.

Leon tucked in.

Tiffany sat down and shared out the salad onto side plates.

'This is good. What is it?'

'Lasagne.'

'Yeah, I like it. Now tell me about this modelling thing you did.'

'It went really well. I got to lie on a perfect white beach for most of the time in a bikini.'

'Yeah, you look tanned.'

'It was good money too. Pays the rent on this place.'

'It's a nice flat,' admitted Leon. 'Beats Leyton Rise, any day.' They laughed.

'Yeah. Looks like all us Rise girls are getting out, one way or the other,' said Tiffany with a rueful smile. 'That place is so quiet now without our crew running things like back in the days.'

'Back in the days you were just a skinny girl with long legs and big knockers,' said Leon, chuckling.

'That never stopped you though.'

'When I see something I want, I take it. You were the prettiest girl on the block so it was a given that you'd be with me,' he said proudly.

'Anyway, a little birdie told me you're about to sign with Palace.'

Leon grinned. 'Yeah.'

'Except that they say you have a problem with, what was it now? *Temper management*?'

'Who told you that?' Leon said crossly. 'What's Lisa telling people my business for?'

'Maybe she's worried about you.'

'Worried about what? It's a minor. Watch. I'll sign for Palace for this season and I'll sign for an even better team next season.'

'You don't need to convince *me*,' said Tiffany smiling. 'I'm not your woman any more.'

Leon stared at her sullenly as he drained his glass of champagne.

'Actually what I really wanna know is how things are going with Samantha?'

'What would *you* wanna know that for? Do you have to know all my business?'

Tiffany smiled. 'I already know you spent a weekend with her a few weeks ago. She told me.'

'Wondering what she's got that you ain't?' asked Leon, taking the bottle and refilling his glass.

'Just wanna know whether the interest is real or whether it's just one of your flings.'

'At the end of the day, it's me and Lisa. But a guy's got to have some fun in this world. You wouldn't expect your man to eat beef for dinner every day for the rest of

294

his life. I'm like that with women. I love Lisa but I need variety.'

Tiffany laughed as she drank some more champagne. 'Like I said, you don't need to convince me. I'm not your woman, but I think that maybe you're just playing yourself.'

'What's that supposed to mean?'

'I'll tell you a little later. Eat up, honey.'

Leon eyed Tiffany with suspicion then gave his pasta his full attention.

When they had finished eating, Tiffany cleared the table and put the dishes in the dishwasher. While she did so, Leon flipped through her CD collection, chose a CD and put it in the hi-fi. Then Tiffany brought their glasses and the bottle of champagne over to the sofa and they talked and joked about old times.

'Have some more champagne,' urged Tiffany as she leaned on Leon. She undid the top few buttons of his shirt and slipped her fingers inside. 'Season's over.'

'No, I can't, babes,' said Leon, removing her hand. He redid the buttons. 'You know I'm driving.'

'Well, you can stay here till you've recovered. I've got another bottle in the fridge.' She began fiddling with Leon's buttons again.

'You've had enough, anyway, Tiffany.' Leon glanced at his watch casually. 'Tell me the surprise then, babes. I'm thinking about making a move.'

'Gotta run home to wifey?' said Tiffany mockingly.

Leon smiled. 'You never had any news, did you, Tiffany? This was just an excuse to try your charms on me again.'

Tiffany smiled as she sat up and stretched out her arms. She yawned then curl back up beside him. She traced a finger down his arm. 'Leon, why do think that you're the hottest thing since sliced bread? Don't you think that I might have found another guy by now?'

'Once a woman's had me, she'd find it difficult to go elsewhere.'

'Oh, so you don't think your girlfriend could ever cheat on you?'

Leon frowned. ''Course not. You should know.'

'How do you know I never cheated on you?'

'You'd have been too bloody scared.' He laughed. 'You knew what you'd get if you cheated on me, Tiffany. Even now if I ever found out you'd been sleeping around while we were together, you'd know about it. Blatant.'

Tiffany hesitated. 'What would you do if Lisa cheated on you?'

Leon smiled. 'My Lisa'd never do anything like that. She's a good girl.'

'So what was I?'

'You were just scared.' Leon laughed. 'Let's face it, Tiffany, you had put it about before I came along. You're just like Samantha. You're crazy about black guys. You just can't say no.'

'I loved you,' said Tiffany indignantly.

'So does Samantha, in her own little way. Nah, you never loved me the way Lisa loves me. She cooks for me, she's got my back, always there when I need her. She's loyal to *me*. You were just loyal to the dick.' He laughed even louder.

'Well, that's more than can be said for Lisa.'

'What's that supposed to mean?' said Leon, still grinning.

'Let's just say that when the cat's away playing, the mouse is also away playing,' said Tiffany. She stroked his chest. Leon's smile faded.

'Don't fuck about, Tiffany,' he snapped, brushing her off. He sat up. 'If you're trying to say something then just come out with it.'

'When you were at your training camp with Samantha, Lisa was also away at camp.'

'Don't bother.'

'See when you thought you were being really clever, you were just playing yourself. Lisa wasn't fooled.'

'OK, let's say Lisa did go out behind my back. I still trust her. She behaves herself.'

'Why would you think she'd be any better than you?'

'She's my woman, for Chrissakes! Lisa would never cheat on me.' Leon put his head in his hands. 'I'd go mad if I ever thought she'd do that to me.'

'She went out with Sian but she got drunk and left with one of Sian's producer friends. I went to Sian's flat the next morning and she hadn't seen Lisa since the night before. Then a bit later her manager complained to me that Sian had been giving him a hard time because of the way his friend and Lisa were behaving.'

Leon stood up. 'All right, that's enough. I'm not gonna sit here and let my ex tell me what my girlfriend's doing. That's insane.'

'I don't see why you care,' said Tiffany, looking at him unsympathetically. 'You were getting it on with Samantha.'

'Shut up, you bitch,' said Leon angrily, grabbing his

jacket. He jabbed his finger at her. 'Don't say another word.'

'Well, you know, honey. Don't listen to what I say. All you have to do is ask Lisa,' said Tiffany quietly, watching Leon as he pulled his jacket on.

'I'm not asking her jack-shit. Like I'm gonna believe some drunk bitch over my bona-fide. If you're not making up shit about me, you're spreading shit about Lisa. "Interesting news"? I was a fool to come here. You need help, Tiffany.' He strode out of the flat and slammed the front door. Tiffany curled back up on the sofa. For a minute or two her expression was blank but then she smiled.

'Ooh, my, my, my, come look at Lisa's man, tho'.' The hairdressing staff ran to the window.

'But look how he kriss tho'.'

'Look 'pon the car dere. Lisa, him 'ave a friend?'

'My, but see how my girl keep it quiet.'

'Lord 'ave mercy, and him 'ave the body, yes?'

'If it wasn't for this rain, I would just run out to that car and Lisa could find herself a new man.'

'You lots ain't got no shame. Eyeing my boy like he's some kind of joke t'ing.'

Everyone laughed.

'See ya, people,' said Lisa, hurrying past the unattended reception desk. She walked over to the car and got in.

'Hi, babes. You never see you turn superstar now,' said Lisa, gaily putting on a Jamaican accent. She took off her jacket. 'Thanks for picking me up. The rain is terrible, but I suppose after all the hot weather it'll clear the air.' The thunderous drops were hitting the roof ominously, like a drum roll. Leon swung the car around and headed up the Seven Sisters Road. Lisa opened the glove compartment and rifled through the tapes. She picked one and slotted it into the car stereo and sat back humming. Leon glanced at her out of the corner of his eye. Lisa caught him looking at her and smiled. He returned his eyes to the road ahead. They reached Stamford Hill and headed down towards Clapton.

'How was your day, babes?'

Leon shrugged.

'Did you talk to anyone at Palace?'

'I told you, I'm not arse-lickin' anyone.'

'It's not arse-lickin' to show that you care.'

Leon ignored her.

'Work was fun today,' said Lisa, changing the subject. 'We were just catching pure joke. There's this Turkish woman, Mrs Fulani, who owns the clothes shop next door and she always comes in for her black rinse, everybody knows it. But Nadine has only been in England for a few weeks. She's Mr Nelson's niece from Jamaica and he gave her some work. Anyway, she couldn't understand Mrs Fulani's accent and thought she wanted a blonde rinse. When Mrs Fulani saw her hair, you wanna hear one piece of renk cussin'. It was so funny . . . Well, I guess you had to be there.' They stopped at a red light.

'You know when I went to the pre-season training camp?'

Lisa nodded.

'You never told me what you got up to that weekend?'

'Oh, well, it was quiet. I had a nice rest from you,' Lisa said, smiling.

'You didn't leave the house at all?'

'Er, yeah, I met up with Sian on Friday. But it was during the day. We went shopping up west.'

'No party? Come on, Lisa. If you went out, just tell me. It's a long time ago, now.' Leon watched Lisa hesitate.

'There was no party. I had work the next day.'

'But I remember you saying that you didn't have to go into work that Saturday.'

Lisa looked uncomfortable. 'Oh well, I can't remember. It was a long time ago like you said. Maybe I slept.'

'All day?'

Lisa rubbed her forehead. 'No, I guess not *all* day. Hey, I don't remember, OK?' The lights changed and Lisa was able to breathe freely for a few minutes.

'So what did you buy at the shops?'

'Huh?'

'What did you buy?' asked Leon a little more sharply.

'Just a dress,' said Lisa without thinking. She instantly regretted it.

'What kind of dress?'

Lisa looked out of her side window and cursed silently.

'Just a dress.'

'A party dress?'

'No – maybe. It's a nice dress, that's all.'

'Why would you buy a nice dress if you're not going anywhere?' Leon asked, a dangerous gleam in his eye.

'Well, Sian was buying some clothes so I just thought I'd buy something too. You know what I'm like with clothes, Leon.'

'So you haven't worn it yet?'

Lisa thought of the dress, washed and ironed, hanging conspicuously on Leon's clothes rack.

'No,' she said. She had no choice. Thankfully, Leon didn't ask any more questions. He focused on the road ahead, his face impassive.

Back at the house, Lisa hung up her jacket and then went upstairs to take a shower. Afterwards, she put on a pair of shorts and a T-shirt and went downstairs to the kitchen. Leon was sitting at the kitchen table, hunched over a carton of orange juice. He drank straight from the carton. His eyes followed her as she filled a pot with water and put it on the stove, then reached up and took down a packet of rice from one of the cupboards. She opened a drawer and removed a sieve. She measured two cups of rice into the sieve then rinsed it over the sink. She tipped the soaked rice into the heated water then put the sieve in the sink.

'You're all the fuckin' same,' muttered Leon gloomily.

Lisa had bent down to take some chicken breasts out of the refrigerator. She glanced back over her shoulder but said nothing.

'You're all fuckin' slags,' repeated Leon.

Lisa slammed the refrigerator door and straightened up. She turned around. 'What did you say?'

'I said you're all the same,' said Leon coldly. 'Slags, every one of you.' He hurled the carton at Lisa. A fan of orange juice sprayed out into the air as the carton sailed into her chest. She looked down at her stained clothes in shock.

Leon stood up, sending his chair clattering to the floor.

'Guess who I saw today?' he said grimly. Lisa stared at him blankly. 'Tiffany, that's who.'

'Oh yeah?'

'Yeah. And you weren't home on that Friday night, you were out partying with Sian and her music friends.'

Lisa was silent.

'And you had quite a weekend in some other geezer's bed.'

'What makes you so sure?' said Lisa uncertainly.

Leon reached her in a split second. He grabbed hold of her wrist. 'This is how I know,' he said, dragging her out of the kitchen. He forced her up the stairs and into the bedroom. He found the red dress on the clothing rack and pulled it out. Lisa caught her breath.

'I found this while you were in the shower,' shouted Leon, pushing it into her arms. 'This is the new dress, isn't it? This is the dress you wore to the party.'

Lisa didn't say anything.

'Answer me,' yelled Leon. He grabbed her by the shoulders and shook her furiously. 'Answer me.'

Lisa burst into tears.

'And what happened at that party?'

Lisa opened her mouth but no sound came out. Leon shook her like a rag doll.

'What happened?'

'I don't know,' Lisa said finally, trying to get away. Leon's fist caught the side of her head and sent her spinning backwards onto the bed.

He snatched the dress up off the floor. It ripped easily in his hands. 'What do you mean, you don't know, you lyin' bitch?' He threw the pieces of the dress at Lisa. They floated down on top of her. 'Of course you know.'

'I don't remember,' she sobbed. 'He gave me some pills. And after that I don't remember.' She sat up and watched as Leon began wrenching her clothes off his clothes rack.

'Why the fuck did you do it?' he raged as he threw them around the room. 'Why?'

'I did it to get back at you,' Lisa shouted. 'You weren't at any training weekend,' she said fiercely. 'You were away fucking some girl with red hair. Everyone knows. And where were you the night before I moved in? You weren't at home. You must have been with *her*. *You're* the fuckin' liar.' Lisa got up from the bed and ran towards Leon. 'You're the liar,' she sobbed, pummelling him with her fists. 'You're the one that's been fuckin' *lyin'* from day one.' He grabbed her wrists and shoved her back against the wall. She crumpled in a dazed heap on the floor.

'I asked you, Lisa. I asked if it was gonna be me and you. Or don't you remember that either? When I went with Samantha it was just sex. That's *all* it was. You still came first. I thought you was worth ten of them white slags. I thought you were clean and decent. I thought you was fuckin' loyal.' Instinctively he kicked her. Leon looked at her contemptuously as she flinched away. 'Just a damn fuckin' slag like all the others,' he said as he kicked her again. He turned and walked out of the room.

chapter
twenty seven

Leon sat on the stairs re-reading the letter. So they didn't want to sign him after all. Bastards. He crumpled the letter into a tight ball and hurled it away. His mobile rang. He fished it out of his pocket.

'Yeah?'

'Hi, Leon. It's Sam.'

'Yeah, what do you want?'

'Well, I haven't heard from you in a while and thought I'd call to see if everything was all right.'

'Yeah, right as rain,' said Leon sardonically. There was a pause.

'Oh, is this not a good moment?'

'No.'

'Fine. I'll call you another time then?'

'You do that,' said Leon as he switched off his phone. It was women like that who had ruined his life. He couldn't imagine telling Samantha how he felt about being rejected by Crystal Palace. Girls like her didn't wanna know about that. All they wanted to know about was the car you drove and the size of your dick. He could've told Lisa. Lisa would have understood. Lisa would've made everything all right. Leon sighed as he stood up and walked slowly up the stairs. He took off his jacket and hung it on the clothes rack. Damn, there was so much space on it now without Lisa's clothes.

Leon sat down on the bed and put his head in his hands. They'd been a team, him and Lisa. If only he could've controlled his damn temper. If only he hadn't let Tiffany wind him up. He lay back on the duvet, looking up at the ceiling. He would go and find her. Lisa would forgive him. She loved him. Of course Lisa would forgive him. He would *make* her forgive him.

Lisa wiped her nose with a fresh tissue. Sian stroked her head gently.

'I guess I was stupid for thinking that I was right and the rest of the world was wrong.'

'You weren't the only one to make that mistake.'

'That's what hurts. I'm not even special.'

'How's your eye?' asked Sian.

Lisa put a finger tip to her bruised eye. 'Well, I hope it heals in time for your concert,' she said with a grimace. 'Otherwise you knows I ain't going.'

Sian smiled. 'It better heal 'cos I really need you to be there.'

There was a knock. June stuck her head around the door and looked into the bedroom. 'Everything OK?' she asked. 'Lisa, love, do you need anything?'

Lisa smiled at her mother. 'No, Mum, I'm cool. Don't worry.'

June nodded and shut the door behind her. They listened to her walking downstairs.

'I just appeared on the front doorstep with my clothes, you know,' said Lisa, her eyes filling up again. 'She never even said "I told you so". She took me in her arms and said, "Don't worry Lisa, you're home now."'

'That might have had something to do with your black eye,' Sian pointed out. 'A few days ago it must have looked terrible.'

'I still miss him though,' said Lisa wistfully.

'Well, it's early days yet,' said Sian. 'When I finally stopped kidding myself and dumped Stephan, I missed him too.'

'But you don't know what it's like. Sometimes I wake up and miss him being there beside me and having him to talk to. We were a team.'

'Some teammate!'

'I know. You don't need to tell me. I've still got the bruises to remind me. It's only been a week. Like you said, it's early days but I'll get there.'

'How the hell did he find out?' said Sian, shaking her head in disbelief.

'He mentioned Tiffany's name. She must be involved. Maybe she told him herself.'

Sian pondered this. 'But I didn't tell anyone what happened. Not a soul, except Pearce.'

'Somehow she figured it out. Maybe some friends of hers were at Swingers. I dunno,' said Lisa. She sighed. 'If it *was* Tiffany then I guess she really got me back and then some.'

'Trust Tiffany to sniff out a secret,' said Sian.

'Forget Tiffany,' said Lisa. 'What happened with Stephan?'

'Oh, *Stephan*,' said Sian with a wry smile. 'How long have you got?'

'Just hit me with it. On second thoughts don't. I think I've been hit quite enough.' They met each other's eyes. Lisa smiled. 'Go on, girl. What's your drama?'

'Well, I knew that he had made moves on Mel, the backup singer with braids.'

Lisa nodded.

'He did it a couple of times. She mentioned it to me.'

'That must have taken some guts.'

'Well, I think he was getting on her nerves. Apparently a couple of weeks ago he went round to her place in Kilburn late one night, drunk.'

'What did he do?'

'Mel's a smart girl. She can see trouble coming a mile away, not like us. She didn't let him in but he still created a palava outside her block. The next morning, I wasn't around so Mel told Pearce. Pearce then had words with Stephan. I think Stephan must have assumed Pearce would tell me—'

'Damn right.'

'But he didn't. Not one word.'

'So go on.'

'Stephan went round to my flat, took one of my credit cards and went on a buying spree.'

'No!'

Sian nodded. Lisa groaned.

'Why on earth did you give him the keys to your pad?'

Sian shrugged. 'I gave him the keys to my heart.'

'So what did he buy? No, let me guess. Garms.'

'Bare garms, then a top-dollar stereo, some jewellery. You name it, he has it at my expense.'

'Shit! How much did he spend?'

'About three ks.'

'What!' Lisa sat up. 'Girl, are you crazy? Tell me you didn't let him get away with that.'

'Stephan's hiding out somewhere. I could find him if I really wanted to but Pearce already got hold of Stephan on his mobile and told him he could keep the things but from now on Stephan should leave me and the backing singers alone, that if he ever tried to contact me again we'd put the Bill onto him.'

'The Bill? And what would they do? Give him a brush down and send him on his merry way! No, you need to get Slick to go get him with a couple of his bres. They would sort him out good and proper.'

'I was mad at first but then after what happened to you I knew that the best thing would be to walk away. I mean what's worse, losing three grand or being beaten up?'

Lisa's eyes dropped. Sian took Lisa's hand.

'Hey, Lisa, I wanna thank you for having my back from day one. You had Stephan pinned down and sussed out from day one. It's my fault I didn't listen.'

Lisa's voice was sad. 'Stephan was the only mistake you ever made. I've gone through my whole life fucking up.'

'No you haven't, Lisa. Take a look around you. You could've ended up like Ceelie, or look at Slick. This is the Rise Estate, don't forget. It could be so much worse. You could be working at Sportsworld.' Sian nudged

Lisa. Lisa looked up. She met Sian's twinkling eyes and began to smile. Soon they were giggling.

Lisa's mobile rang. She saw Leon's name illuminated on the screen and rejected the call.

'How often does that happen?' asked Sian, concerned.

'Once or twice a day.' Lisa lay down on the bed. 'It's such an effort not talking to him, 'cos I want to, very much, in spite of what he's done to me. Deep down I want to hear him say all the right things. I want to be convinced that he's not a bad person, that the feelings I have for him aren't wrong.' She began to cry softly. 'Why did he hit me, Sian? Why did he hurt me like that?'

'You're not the problem, Lisa,' said Sian, rubbing her friend's arm. 'He is. You deserve better. Just remember that, each time he phones. You deserve better than him.'

There was another ringing sound. This time it was Sian's phone.

'Hello? . . . Hi, Greg, um, I'm a little tied up. Can I call you back a little later? . . . Thanks. Bye.'

'Who's Greg?' asked Lisa, wiping her eyes.

'He's the chief organizer of the Teen Music Awards concert. I think he wants to give me my rehearsal times. I couldn't believe it when they asked me to take part, considering I'm so new on the block. Pearce keeps saying how it's a really good opportunity for me.'

'How did you manage to get in on it?'

'It was a bit of luck. Some other group had to drop out and Pearce and Planet Records had to pull a lot of strings to get me on instead. The rehearsals start in a few days and look like they're gonna eat up all of the next couple of weeks.'

'Singing in front of all those people? That's insane.'

'Well, I've sung at so many clubs by now and in front of some quite large audiences that it's no big deal. I'm actually looking forward to it.'

'Imagine,' said Lisa. 'A *Rise* girl on the telly. That's when you know you've made it. I'd give anything to see Vince's face when he realizes it's really you, Sian Wallace, on that television screen.' She sighed. 'You're so lucky. All your dreams are coming true.'

'Getting out of Sportsworld was my dream, Lisa. The rest is just icing on the cake.'

'Come on, you dreamt about getting out of Leyton Rise and having a designer wardrobe and going on kriss holidays.'

'And growing up to look like Barbie and marrying a prince and having identical sextuplets.' They laughed. 'None of that stuff was important, it was all just icing. The cake was important and that was getting the hell out of Sportsworld.'

'I wouldn't mind getting the hell out of Leyton Rise,' said Lisa. 'I used to enjoy being a Rise girl. Now I find it so depressing.'

'Well, why don't you move in with me once the Teen Music Awards concert is over?'

'You're not serious.'

'Why not? You wanna get out of Leyton Rise. I've got a flat all to myself.'

Lisa nodded. 'Yeah, why not?' She looked around her bedroom. 'Get me out of this place for a bit. What are you going to wear to the concert?'

'A black dress, naturally.' Sian smiled. 'I saw a kriss one in Donna Karen. Pearce said he'd pick it up for me.'

'Not even a splash of colour?'

'I'm singing a quiet song so I guess a quiet colour should do the trick. Anyway, who needs colour when they've got you?'

Lisa smiled. 'So now the million dollar question, what's going on between you and Pearce?'

'What would make you think anything was going on?' asked Sian coyly.

'You've always liked him and I think he likes you. Now Stephan's out of the picture, maybe something could happen there.'

'I'll give you three reasons why it won't,' said Sian, standing up. 'He's still married, has loads of women after him and isn't interested in me.' She took her jacket off the back of the chair.

'Oh, don't go,' begged Lisa. 'We've got so much catching up to do.'

'I have to, Lisa,' said Sian as she slipped her jacket on. 'August is turning out to be the busiest month of my whole life. Recording and promoting and more recording. It's driving me insane. I don't have any free time.'

'Get the violins out. Come on, Sian, you've been in magazines and on the radio. In two weeks you're going to be on television in front of millions of people. After this, you'll be a superstar.'

'Well, I won't be on television unless I go home and call Greg to sort out my rehearsal times.'

'When's the concert again?'

'Tuesday the first of September, so make sure you're not working late that day.'

'If I'm back at work by then. There's no way I can work with my face like this,' said Lisa gloomily. She stood up to hug Sian.

'Don't worry about that, Lisa. In a few days the bruising will disappear and you'll be kriss again. Now you can always call me on my mobes and if I'm not answering leave a message.'

'Looking out for me, huh?' said Lisa, smiling. 'What would I do without you, huh?'

'You're a Rise Girl,' said Sian. 'You'd do just fine.'

Lisa walked Sian to the front door and they said goodbye, then she walked back upstairs to her room. She sat down on her bed dejectedly. Sian had gone on to such good things and Lisa had come home worse off than when she'd left. She lay down tired and depressed, gradually drifting off.

A few hours later the phone rang again. Lisa willed herself not to answer it, but she couldn't help herself.

'What do you want, Leon?' she asked in a subdued tone. 'Why do you keep calling me?'

''Cos I care about you, Lisa. I miss you so much. I want you to come home.'

'I'm not coming back.'

'I'm sorry, Lisa. You know I'm sorry. Please give me another chance.'

'No, Leon. It's over.'

'You can't do me like that, Lisa. I don't care any more about you going off with that guy. We can sort this out if you'll just give me a chance to prove it to you.'

'I'm going now.'

'Well, I'll call you later and we'll talk.'

'Bye, Leon.'

Lisa turned off her phone and bit her lip to stop the tears. She knew she was doing the right thing but inside she felt desolate.

chapter
twenty eight

June stood in the doorway and watched the ringlets bounce downwards as Lisa removed each of her heated curlers.

'That's a pretty style,' said June admiringly.

'Yeah, I got the idea at Cutting Edge a while back,' said Lisa. She dropped the rollers into a drawer and fluffed out her hair. 'If you like, I could do it to your hair as well. It would look nice with your perm 'cos it makes your own curls more defined.'

''Cept I'd be all dressed up wiv nowhere to go,' said June. 'You know Woody, 'is idea of a night out is a pint down the Leyton Arms.' They laughed.

'You can't still see the bruise, can you?' said Lisa. June crossed the room and took a closer look at Lisa's bad eye.

'Not if you don't point everyone to it.'

'Is it blatant?' asked Lisa anxiously.

'You can't expect it to disappear completely in three weeks but it's gone down a lot. It ain't purple any more, there's just a faint puffiness and a wincy shadow, like you 'ad a late night and you know you've 'ad enough of those in the past to not care about that. Come on,' reassured June as Lisa pulsed the area around her eye doubtfully. 'You look gorgeous.'

'You think so? I don't usually wear black.' Lisa smoothed down her dress. 'I feel a bit dorkish.'

'Believe me, love, black is definitely you. It really brings out the colour of your eyes. I'm jealous. Looking at you makes me wish I was twenty-five again and blonde instead of grey.'

'Mum, you know you're still as blonde as you ever were.'

'Yeah, but now I 'ave Clairol to thank for my good looks, not Muvver Nature.'

'It's good to be back, Mum.' Lisa smiled. A real smile. June went pink with pleasure as Lisa threw her arms around her. 'You've been so kind to me.'

When Lisa released her June had tears in her eyes. 'You're my baby, Lisa. You always were and always will be.' She kissed Lisa on the forehead. 'You're going to 'ave a great life, Lisa. Good things are gonna start 'appenin'. You'll see.' She walked to the doorway. 'Hurry up,' she said glancing over her shoulder. 'You don't wanna be late for Sian.' She gently shut the door behind her.

Lisa studied her reflection. It looked like the same fun-loving girl, the same mass of jet-black hair, the same olive skin, the same mischievous blue eyes. But Lisa didn't know for sure who that girl was any more. Being that girl had almost destroyed her. It was hard to come home to Leyton Rise and be the same happy-go-lucky Lisa. Leon had changed her and the change lingered over her like a dark cloud. As if on cue, her mobile rang.

Pearce sat beside Sian, talking superfast into his mobile phone. As the limousine approached the enclosure, she watched the fans, pointing, fighting each other for viewing space and screaming while the photographers were clicking away before knowing who was going to step out of the car. The rain ran in rivulets off the photographers' hooded anoraks. Pearce eventually clicked the flip-top back into place.

'How are you feeling?' he asked. 'And please don't say, like the weather.'

'Nervous.'

'Uh uh. Now remember what I said. Stars don't have nerves. Nerves are when you're going to do an exam or take your driving test. This is *excitement* because you're going to go out there and enjoy every minute.'

'Sorry, *excitement*. I just hope Lisa makes it. I mean, you know she's the biggest no-show in history.'

'C'mon. You gotta have faith. It's the biggest night of your life. She'll be here.'

The chauffeur got out of the car and hurried around to open the door for them. Sian followed Pearce past the security guards in through a backstage entrance. People hurried past, some carrying clothes, others heaving sound equipment towards the stage. They were met by Greg who showed them to Sian's dressing room where a make-up artist was waiting.

'You're nice and early,' said Mikki, a diminutive Chinese woman in her early thirties who was wearing a heavy-duty handy-man's belt around her waist filled with

316

eyeliners and blushers, brushes and other tricks of her trade. 'That's always good. Now let's take a look at you.' She walked up to Sian and pulled a strand of her hair. 'Clean hair. You're making my job so easy. Take a seat. I'll be back in a minute, I have to check on BoyZone.' She left the dressing room.

'Are these for me?' Sian crossed over to the dressing table where there was a bouquet of exotic flowers. 'They smell so good and they're from you,' she said excitedly as she read the little card. '"Good luck, Sian, love, Pearce." That's sweet.' She walked back and gave Pearce a hug.

'You deserve it. You do the singing. Your voice is selling the records.'

'So it's all just business, huh?'

Pearce smiled.

'Do you think it's more than that?' he teased.

The door opened. Mikki walked back in with a huge make-up bag.

'Hi, I'm not really here yet, I have to dash to the loo.' She left the room again.

Sian laughed nervously. She looked away. 'Maybe I do think it is something more. Maybe you do too.'

Pearce looked down at the floor for a moment and when he looked back at Sian his eyes were serious. 'I'm a man with problems,' he said with a sad smile. 'You don't need to share them, Sian. Believe me.'

'Lisa. Lisa, are you there?'

'What do you want, Leon?'

'I wanna talk to you, babes. That's all, I just wanna talk.'

'I've got nothing to say,' said Lisa coldly. 'And stop calling me. It's over.'

'Don't say that, Lisa. It's not over, how many times do I have to say it? It's *not* over.'

'Goodbye, Leon.'

'I really need to see you, Lisa. I can't take this shit any more.'

'See me?'

'Yeah, I'm outside.'

Lisa walked over to the window and parted the curtains. Through the rain, Leon's red Lotus gleamed obstinately on the tarmac of the car park. She cursed.

'What the fuck are you doing outside?'

'Shall I come up?'

'Are you crazy?' Lisa thought of June and Woody curled up on the sofa downstairs and Liam stretched out on the rug playing his Nintendo Gameboy. 'Mum will call the police.'

'Well, I need to see you, Lisa,' said Leon stubbornly. 'I'm not leaving. I don't care about jail. My life's all fucked up anyhow.'

Lisa hesitated.

'All right, I'll come down in about five minutes.' She put her phone in her handbag. She squeezed some serum into her hands and ran it through her hair. Then she put on her leather jacket and went downstairs.

'You off now, love?' asked June, raising her head from the sofa as Lisa put her head around the door. 'Let's see you then.'

Lisa walked into the room and twirled.

'Very nice,' Woody said approvingly. 'Hey, Liam, your sister's a knock-out tonight.'

Liam put his Gameboy down and stood up. He ran over to Lisa and hugged her. She bent down and kissed him on the cheek.

'I'll see you later, little man,' she said, patting his head.

'If it's still raining I could run you down to the station in the van,' offered Woody.

'Thanks, Woody, but I've, er, already called myself a cab,' said Lisa quickly. 'It's waiting downstairs.'

'You better get goin' then, love,' said June, resting her head against Woody's shoulder again.

'Yeah, I'll see you guys.' Lisa closed the living-room door reluctantly.

She shut the front door behind her and took out her umbrella. It was still raining hard. She looked over the balcony as she walked along the landing. He was still waiting for her. Lisa felt a twinge of fear. She remembered how he'd kicked her viciously before calmly walking out of the room. She hesitated for a moment then continued slowly towards the lift. She would only be in the car for a few minutes and she could get out any time she wanted.

She left the block and hurried across to the car. Leon leaned over the passenger seat and pushed the door open for her. She got in quickly.

'Thanks for coming, Lisa.'

'Just get out of here,' said Lisa, with a nervous glance up at the eighth floor. 'I don't want anyone to see us.'

Leon obeyed, slowly turning the car around and pulling out of Leyton Rise.

*

'No fuss, please, Mikki. A very simple style. A chignon or a bob.'

'OK, well, how about a ringlet at each side, or a bob of feathery curls or even a long hair piece? That would look really dramatic,' suggested Mikki enthusiastically. 'C'mon, this is your big night.'

'What do you think, Pearce?' Sian asked his reflection in the mirror. 'The feathery bob? Or the ringlets?'

'The bob. Pretty but not busy. Your image is simple and the lights out there must be so hot the ringlets would droop after the first few minutes.'

There was another knock at the door and a stagehand wearing a headset with a mouthpiece and carrying a clipboard and another bouquet of flowers walked into the room.

'Flowers from your mother and someone called Buelah,' said the stagehand.

'They were out front?' asked Pearce, taking the flowers from the man. The stagehand nodded and left the room, shutting the door behind him. Pearce put the flowers on a chair.

'Wow, who's the star tonight?' said Mikki, smiling.

Sian laughed. 'I'm glad they're here nice and early. I wish Lisa was here too. Do you think she's OK?'

'I'm sure she's fine,' said Pearce reassuringly.

'Can you hold your ears back a second? I need to do some curls here,' said Mikki.

'I wonder if she's left yet,' said Sian as she held back her ears out of the way of the hot curling tong.

'You got her number?' asked Pearce.

'I know it off by heart.'

'OK, wait.' Pearce took his phone out of the pocket. 'Shoot.'

Sian told him the number. He tried to dial it.

'Hell, it doesn't seem like I can get reception in here. I'm gonna go upstairs and try calling from there. I've got to talk to Greg anyway to find out how things are going. See you later. The hair's looking very sexy by the way.'

Sian smiled after Pearce as he left the room.

'I saw that look,' said Mikki with a knowing smile. 'And it wasn't just for the compliment.'

As soon as Lisa got into the car she smelt the alcohol. She put her seat belt on.

'Where are you off to?' asked Leon as they drove towards Leyton Station.

'Sian's singing in a big concert up at Wembley Arena. Just drop me off at Leyton tube station.'

'You look really pretty,' said Leon.

'No thanks to you,' she said curtly. 'You look awful. You need a shave.' Leon stroked his bristly chin. 'And you smell of drink.'

'Yeah, Palace decided not to sign me after all,' said Leon. 'That really shook me. Made me think about how fucked up my life is. I messed up big time, with football and you. But now I can change, Lisa. With you by my side I'd work on my temper. But I can't do it without you.'

'Well, you'll just have to try,' said Lisa.

'What's it gonna take? Tell me what I have to do to earn your respect again.'

'Leave me alone and stop calling me. You can park anywhere here.'

Leon drove past Leyton tube station. 'I'll give you a lift to Wembley,' he said matter of factly.

'I didn't ask you to drop me to Wembley,' said Lisa crossly. 'I said Leyton tube station.'

'I just want a little more time with you, Lisa. For the first time in ages I've got you to myself, without other people getting in the way. That's the way it used to be, before everyone started interfering.'

'There's things you did quite well without any interfering from anyone else.'

'It's the interfering that's destroying us,' continued Leon. 'It should've been just you and me from the start but you always, *always* let them get in the way.' He jabbed an accusing finger at her. 'I know you love me, Lisa. You can front, but in spite of everything you still love me. I bet you haven't stopped thinking about me since the day you left.'

Lisa remembered leaving. After he had left her crumpled in the bedroom she had grabbed her phone and what clothes she could, stuffing them into a carrier bag. She'd thrown her jacket on and run downstairs. He'd come into the hallway. When he'd seen her, frozen to the spot, unable to move, he'd laughed.

'Running home to Mum?' he had asked mockingly. 'Or maybe you're running to your one-night stand. You'll be back. When he realizes what kind of a slut you are, you'll be back for more.' He'd advanced towards her and, grabbing her arm, had thrust her out through the front door, slamming it behind her.

'Have you found someone else yet?' he asked.

'You're drunk,' she said, peering out of the window.

'Yeah, maybe I am a little,' he admitted. 'But it helps me forget about the mess I've made of everything.'

Lisa's mobile rang. Leon watched her pause uncomfortably then reluctantly take the phone out of her bag.

'Hello?'

'Hi, Lisa, it's Pearce.'

'Hi.'

'Just checkin' that you're on your way and everything's cool.'

'Yeah, I'm on my way. I'm in a – a cab and I've just reached the North Circular so I shouldn't be too long now.'

'You sound a little stressed. Are you sure that things are fine?'

'Yeah. Don't worry. I'll get there.'

'Great. I'll let Sian know.' He hung up and Lisa put her phone back in her bag. There was silence for a few moments.

'So, you're off to see your fancy man,' said Leon. His tone had changed, it was meaner. 'I suppose that's the guy you've been fucking behind my back.'

Lisa sighed. 'It was only Pearce,' she said. 'Sian's manager.'

'Yeah, you would say that. You'd say anything, but you would have told him you were with your man if you weren't fuckin' him.'

'You're not my man.'

'Wanna bet?'

'This was a big mistake,' she said. 'Drop me off here and I'll catch a cab or something.'

'You know it's never gonna be over between us, Lisa,' said Leon. 'You're *my* woman.' He gave a little laugh. 'Might as well call us married.'

'You're driving too fast,' she said, a little afraid. 'It's dangerous.'

'Well, I'm a dangerous muthafucka, babes, and that's how the fuck I live.' Leon laughed as he stamped on the accelerator sending the red Lotus shooting forward into the neon-lit night.

Alone, Sian looked at herself in the mirror set with lights. Each one like a promise. She twirled in her stretchy black dress with cross-over straps. Three hundred and sixty-four days of this year they might call her skinny but tonight she was willowy, with curves. Tonight she was beautiful.

'Sian, we need you in the wings now.'

Sian left her dressing-room and walked down the corridor towards the stage. On the way she passed other singers who patted her on the back and mouthed words of encouragement. When she reached the wings, Pearce was waiting. Her took her hand and raised it to his lips.

'I'm assuming I'm not ruining any make-up here,' he said smiling. 'I must say you look very fine in that dress, Sian.'

'No Lisa?'

'She's out front,' lied Pearce.

'Really?'

'Yeah, just now, I asked around and she's at the front, waiting to hear you do everybody proud and when you come offstage she'll be back here with your mom and your sister. Now are you nervous?' he asked quietly.

'No, stars don't get nervous, Pearce. I'm *excited*,' replied Sian with a smile. A lady with a headset motioned for Sian to follow her. Sian left Pearce and walked into a darkened area directly behind the stage. Her knees were shaking but she was looking forward to going on stage because she knew that when she stepped into that pool of light, everything else would just melt away. As the first notes rang out, self-doubts and distractions would disappear. It would simply be Sian doing what she loved best . . .

As her last note ebbed away, Sian looked over the screaming audience, breathless. She held out her arms to the thunderous applause that surrounded her. Never before had any spotlights seemed so bright, the darkness before her so friendly or any applause so loud. It was her finest hour and she savoured each floodlit moment like it was her last.

'Let me out.'

'No! We're gonna meet your one-night stand together. I wanna know what's so great about him that you have to go sneakin' around behind my back and, believe me, I'm gonna find out if I have to open up his head to do it.'

'Why are you doing this? Why can't you just leave me be?'

'I've got no choice, Lisa. I love you. You don't seem to understand that.'

'Don't fuckin' tell me about love, you bastard,' she

spat. 'I found out more about love from my so-called one-night stand than you.'

She gasped as his fist caught her square in the mouth. They reached the red light and he slowed down. She quickly unlocked her seat belt and turned to open the door. But Leon decided to keep going. He didn't see the lorry and when he finally did see it, it was too late.

'It wasn't my fault,' the lorry driver said repeatedly. He looked at the blood on his hand, shocked. 'It wasn't my fault.' He barely registered the policewoman kneeling beside him as he sat on the pavement propped up against a brick wall, holding a blood-soaked rag to his head. He looked up at a sky that seemed full of sirens and screaming. He'd been on his way home from a delivery job. He was keen to get home to see his wife. It was their wedding anniversary. He'd been driving along cursing the traffic and the shit weather and thinking of the slap-up meal awaiting him when he finally got to Ponder's End but he'd been careful. He hadn't speeded. He'd waited for the lights at the cross-roads like everyone else. The lights had turned orange and he'd stepped up the gas, green and he'd let go of the brake. But then a red sports car had come streaking out from nowhere. He'd braked, of course he'd braked, but it was a big lorry and a wet road. The car had spun out of control and . . . he looked at the blood on his hand. 'It wasn't my fault.'

'Driving too fast they were,' the middle-aged woman was saying loudly to the young-looking police-man. 'And arguing, as they slowed for the red light. A woman and a man. We could see them screaming at each other. And he might have slapped her, I couldn't see clearly. There was a struggle. She opened her door a little as if she were going to jump out, but then the car shot forward in spite of the red lights. Like a bullet it was. A lorry was coming from the left. It slowed down but the driver had lost control of the car. It spun right into the lorry's path. Awful it was. Really awful. Yes, that's Mrs Bennet. With a double "n". Me and my husband were in the car behind. Saw everything I did, in slow motion just like in the movies. It was awful.'

chapter
twenty nine

The two small girls stood clapping on the eighth-floor balcony of the Leyton Rise estate. One girl's hair was neatly cornrowed and she wore a navy duffel coat, the other wore pink Barbie earmuffs over her bushy hair that jiggled as she sang.

'My name is Lisa Peters, I'm a pretty girl. When I grow older gonna rule the world.' She gyrated her hips repeatedly. 'Lisa, Lisa, oh no! Lisa, Lisa, oh no!'

The two girls giggled.

'Now it's your turn, Sian, it's your turn,' prompted Lisa. 'Think of something.'

The girl with cornrows hesitated. 'I can't think of anything,' she wailed.

'Oh, I know, I know,' said Lisa excitedly. She whispered hastily into her friend's ear. Then the girl with cornrowed hair smiled and nodded. They began clapping again.

'My name's Sian Wallace, I sing heavenly. Gonna be a star just like Whitney.' She gyrated her hips as she sang. 'Sian, Sian, ooh ahh! Sian, Sian, ooh ahh!'

*

The rain lashed down as the mourners made their way into the cemetery.

'It was Whitney Houston,' muttered Sian as she looked out of the car window. 'Not Mariah Carey.'

'Did you say something, Sian?' asked Pearce as he turned left following a long line of cars. The hearse, eight or nine cars ahead, was making its slow journey through the cemetery gates. Sian shook her head. As the graveyard loomed up ahead, Sian could only see tombstones, grey and hard. And hopeless, she thought as they passed through the tall wrought-iron gates. If this was death, then it was grey and hard and hopeless.

Pearce reached out and squeezed Sian's hand. 'How you doing?'

Sian tried to smile but couldn't. She looked out over the graveyard. 'It's a shame that you didn't know Lisa like I did. When you met her she was having a lot of problems but my Lisa, she was so much fun, so alive, so colourful. Not like today.'

Pearce looked out through the windscreen at the angry clouds.

'It's an awful day,' he agreed.

'It's like summer went away and took everything beautiful with it.'

'It can't take your memories,' said Pearce. 'And that's no consolation,' he added hastily. 'But it's true.'

'Who wants memories?' said Sian bitterly, but she retreated to hers all the same.

Pearce parked the car. They got out and followed the other mourners to the graveside. The rain had relented but sticky mud clung resolutely to boots and shoes as they gathered about the open pit. Sian could feel cold water seeping into her black shoes as her feet sank in the mud. She glanced across to June, her blonde hair damp and clinging to her head. She was bent down beside Liam, tightening the laces on his smart boots.

'You OK, little man?' June asked softly.

'I don't want my sister to die,' he said, wiping his eyes.

'She's gone to heaven, Liam,' said June gently. 'Woody told you about heaven, 'member?'

'I don't want her to go to heaven,' he sobbed. 'I want Lisa to come home with us. I don't want her to die.' He threw his arms around his mother's neck and wept.

'I know, love. I know,' said June, her own tears spilling over as she held him tight.

After a few moments, she gently detached the arms knotted around her neck. She kissed the little boy on the forehead before straightening up. Woody put his arms protectively around the two of them, forming a dismal triangle.

The vicar stepped forward. He looked at June sympathetically before addressing the small crowd. A short prayer followed. Sian bowed her head.

'And yea though I walk through the shadow of the valley of death I shall fear no evil . . .'

Any minute now, Lisa will come out from behind that tree, Sian imagined. She'll come out and she'll say, 'Uh-uh, don't say you really believed I was dead? Skinny, you'll never learn but I ain't in the hearsay business, girl.'

Sian remembered finishing her song and running backstage. Her forehead perspiring from the heat of the stage lights, a triumphant glow in her eyes, she had launched herself on Pearce. He'd removed her hands from around him but gripped them in his own. He'd looked so sad, so dismayed.

'C'mon, Pearce, cheer up!' she'd said playfully. 'Wasn't I the best?'

Pearce had waved a hand and all the others had silently melted away like hot air on a cold night. Something to do with Estella again, she'd imagined with a touch of irritation. She prepared herself to say something suitably consoling. Instead, it was her shoulders which had sagged. She'd sunk to the floor, suddenly feeling so tired. Tired and sick as her world came crashing down around her.

And the rest is history, Sian thought bitterly as the other mourners began to sing, their broken voices rising in a reedy lament. She couldn't sing. The printed words on the hymn sheet didn't begin to describe how she felt. The sombre chorus could never match the utter desolation in her heart.

'You used to be the friend I could share my problems with and tell my dreams. Laughing at the same jokes, looking out for each other, putting each other first. That's what *you* used to be, Lisa, and now it's gone,' Sian murmured.

Sian began to cry softly. They could have got it back. She could have been that friend again. Everybody deserved a second chance. Lisa had said so herself.

As if to compound the injustice of it all, slowly but surely, it began to rain once more.

But that was not the worst. The lowering of the coffin into the muddy pit was not the worst, nor the flowers being thrown in afterwards. The worst was not the vicar's final sentence, 'Ashes to ashes, dust to dust, now may she be laid to rest.' Nor even the soft thud as each shovel full of slimy mud hit the coffin six feet below. The worst was the moment June began to weep loudly, as only a mother knows how, with each dispirited, wordless cry piercing the hearts of everyone gathered there.

Sian sat numbly in the car as Pearce fiddled with the car heater. She didn't see the point. What heat could warm the chill in her heart? What warmth could rid her of the sound of June's grief? Some of the cars had begun the slow descent out of the cemetery. While they waited for the other cars to move off, there was a tap at the window. Sian and Pearce looked up. It was Tiffany.

'She's got a cheek,' Sian muttered, ignoring Tiffany who stood in the rain tapping on the car window.

'Maybe she needs a lift,' said Pearce.

'Well, then she can walk,' replied Sian stonily.

'Oh, don't be so silly,' said Pearce, pressing the automatic button on the driver's panel. The window slid down. Tiffany, pale and nervous, bent down to talk to Sian.

'I just wanted to say how sorry I am, Sian,' she began. 'You two were the closest.'

'Don't bother, Tiffany,' Sian interrupted. 'I know you told me about Leon cheating just to get back at Lisa and I bet you told Leon about Lisa cheating to stir things up, so save it.'

Tiffany burst into tears. 'I'm sorry,' she sobbed. 'I was so confused. I never thought Leon would hurt Lisa.'

'Leon was sick,' said Sian icily. 'And you're fuckin' twisted as well to turn up here like you're anybody's friend.'

'It's my loss too.'

'It was your *fault*, that's what it was. Now they're both dead. I hope you can live with yourself.' Sian stabbed the automatic window button until the window was closed, then she looked away. Pearce reluctantly started the car and drove off, watching Tiffany in the rearview mirror as she stood in the pouring rain, crying.

He turned right out of the cemetery and along Romford Road, back towards Leyton Rise.

'Don't you think you were a bit harsh back there?'

'What do you mean?' asked Sian irritated.

'Come off it, Sian. Tiffany did some stirring, no question, but with something as big as this can you honestly say it's anybody's fault?'

'You weren't Lisa's friend, Pearce, so don't expect to understand.'

'Whoa, don't bite *my* head off! I'm just saying. It was a car crash, Sian. Leon was drunk. Yeah, he may have forced Lisa to get into the car but maybe she chose to get in. Either way, I'm sure Leon didn't intend to kill both of them. Are you really gonna let that poor girl think she's responsible for two deaths when you know in your heart of hearts that it was really an accident?'

Sian pointedly ignored Pearce and the rest of the drive was conducted in silence.

'I don't think I'll go to the church hall,' said Pearce as he drove up into the Leyton Rise car park. He stopped the car. 'You probably want your space. Besides, I didn't really know Lisa and I'd feel like an intruder.'

'That's right,' said Sian coldly. 'You didn't know Lisa.' She ignored the hurt in his eyes as she got out of the car, slammed the door and walked away quickly. It was only when she heard the car driving off that she paused and regretted her harsh words.

Buelah and Bernadette were in the kitchen getting food ready to take around to the church hall where most of the mourners had gone. Sian kicked off her mud-encrusted shoes by the door, then walked upstairs, and into her old room. She sat down on the bed, looking at her hands. After a few moments Buelah came in. Buelah sat on the bed beside Sian and gave her a small hug. Sian wanted to return it but couldn't.

Buelah began to cry.

'Oh, shut up or get out,' groaned Sian. She covered her ears with her hands. Nevertheless the sound of Buelah's continued sniffing and blubbering was still audible. Sian stood up, strode to the door and threw it open. 'I mean if anyone should be crying for Lisa, it should me, me, got that? I was her bloody best friend.'

Buelah got up without protest but just before leaving the room, she said softly through her tears, 'I'm not crying for Lisa, Sian. I'm crying for you.'

Sian shut the door after Buelah then leaned against it. She peeled off her waterlogged coat and sneezed violently. She hung the coat over the back of a chair and took off her soggy tights. Then she lay on her bed, trying to blank out the sound of June's agonized cries.

The doorbell rang. There was the sound of people talking downstairs. A few minutes later there was a knock at the door. The door opened and Slick walked in. He mumbled a hello and sat down on the bed. Sian, lying on the bed, ignored him. He sat still for a few minutes but then set about making a spliff. He took a packet of Rizla papers out of his pocket and a small clear plastic sachet of marijuana. He drew a paper out and carefully creased it along the middle. Then he lined the crease with the marijuana and rolled up the paper between his fingers.

'If you light that, you'd better get out of my room.'

'What? You think Bernadette's gonna notice li' ol' me up here smoking this joint?' He got up and opened a window. 'Anyway, I'm bad, everybody know that. Nuthin' anyone can do about it neither.'

'You can smell it a mile off and, like I said, you light it and you're out.'

'Oh, Sian, you so good,' he teased. 'I'm sure you got a halo up on your head somewhere. I bet if Lisa was here, she'd say "Go ahead, Slick, but be sure to save me some."'

There was a short silence. 'Yeah, I suppose she would,' said Sian softly. She eased herself up into a sitting position and hugged her knees. 'I remember one time, it was winter, proper cold. I was brassic. Just left school, no job and I had no coat. Mum didn't have any money at all. I didn't know what the hell I was going to do. Lisa had already bought a new coat that Woody had given her the money for. Well, we were down Wood Green looking at all the leather jackets I couldn't afford. Lisa kept saying, "This one's cheap, Sian." Or, "Well, what about that one?" I kept shaking my head. I just didn't have the wong. In the end I said, "Let's just splurt, Lisa. There's nothing here," but Lisa said, "No, watch this, Skinny. I'll get you your coat." She took off her own coat and handed it to me. I was like, "Lisa, don't do this," but she walked into another shop and started trying on jackets. And dammit if she didn't just button one up and walked right out of the shop, bold as brass.' Sian laughed. 'We ran halfway down the street, before we ran out of breath. She took off the jacket and handed it to me. "You got your winter coat now, Sian," she said, laughing. I couldn't believe it, told her to take it back, but she said, "We're best friends, Sian, and best friends look out for each other. Now are you gonna take this coat or did I just do all that for nothing?"'

'So you took it?'

''Course. I didn't need a winter coat after that,' said Sian with a rueful grin.

'They didn't catch you or nothing?'

'I don't know what kind of charm she worked but by the time they must have figured it out we were on the two-thirty bus on our way back to Leyton.'

'I miss her, man. None of us guys knew Leon was that crazy. Plus he was the big footballer. Everyone respected him, no one would have stepped to Leon to tell him about the way he treats his woman. I feel bad, like I should have done something. Lisa was always smiling, she was nice.'

'She wasn't nice, she was crazy. Lisa was the craziest person that ever lived.' Sian wiped the sudden tears from her eyes.

'You OK, cuz?'

'No, yes – I dunno. I've never really cried and laughed at the same time before.'

'First time for everything. Aw, c'mon on over here.' Slick cradled Sian in his arms.

'Oh, why did she have to go? Why does it all have to end like this?' she sobbed. Slick didn't say anything. He just let it happen. For half an hour Sian cried into Slick's shirt. When her tears dried up she cried dry tears.

'Man, my shirt's been used and abused,' Slick observed finally. Sian smiled ruefully. 'So now you've kinda set your feelings free, I hear you're going to Jamaica?'

'Yeah, Mum suggested it and I've already booked the ticket for early next week. Monday morning.'

'Yeah, Bernadette mentioned something. So you're sure?'

'I need to get away. I'm not ready to get on with my life.'

'What about your singing?'

'I know but—'

'And Pearce. I know you two got something flaky going on there between you.'

'I thought so too, but now I'm not so sure. Anyway, just now I was so mean to him, I think it'd be safe to say that he won't be ringing back.'

'Hmm, I'm sure he'd understand anything right now, what with Lisa being your best friend.'

'Oh, what's the point? I seem to mess everything up. I messed up with Stephan, messed up with Lisa. What's the point starting something else so I can mess it up again?'

'If it's gonna happen, then it's gonna happen,' said Slick matter of factly. 'Messing up ain't got nuthin' to do with it s'far as I can see.'

'Enough about me, Slick. What are your plans? I see you're still slinging weed on the side.'

'You know how it go, Sian. Things is getting rough for me with Mom, though. She knows about it now and she's mad as hell.'

'Oh, come on, Slick. What do you expect? Aunt Cherry's been through hell and back for you. She just wants to see you straight and out of trouble.'

'Well, she had the wrong son. When I was in Brooklyn, that's what I learned how to do. I can't change overnight. Maybe she should have sent me to stay with you guys instead of my pops. At least then I'd know how to sing.' They laughed.

'Now you're cheered up can I get a little relief?'

Sian nodded grudgingly. Slick lit the end of his roll-up with his cigarette lighter and soon the room was filled with the pungent smell of the burning weed.

'And my mom's yo, constant in my ear every minute, every day. "What you good for, Slick?" and "I's gonna tell your father to come get you" and "Slick, I don't want police at my door." So I'm thinking of leaving. Might even be gone by the time you get back from Jamaica.'

'If you leave where will you go?'

'Damn, I don't know. I'd go to NYC, to Brooklyn where all my homies be at. Bring the ruckus! You know how it go.'

'I'll miss you, Slick. You've been a real cousin to me, lately.'

'Aw shoot. That's pretty. That's nice.' They rested there a few minutes longer before Sian got up.

'I'm just going to go check on Buelah. You be all right?'

'Yeah. I'm just gon' sit here and, er, enjoy this.'

Sian left the room and Slick sat staring into his own smoke, thinking about Lisa and how everyone had his or her time. When his time came around, he wondered what he'd have to show for it.

Sian knocked on Buelah's door softly. Then she opened the door and walked in. Buelah was reading a book.

'I'm sorry, B. I didn't mean to shout at you.'

'Yeah, whatever.' Buelah turned the page.

'I'm going away.'

'Huh?' Buelah looked up. 'For how long?'

'I dunno, Buelah. But I have to get away. Being here is killing me.'

'You're selfish, that's what you are, Sian Wallace. Mum needs you here, I need you. Why do you always have to go further and further away?'

'I have to be—'

'Oh, Sian, don't go,' Buelah begged. 'Please stay. We all miss Lisa, not just you.'

Sian was silent. Buelah got off her bed and ran downstairs.

Bernadette was covering a tray of roasted fish with clingfilm.

'Mum, Sian's going away.'

'I know,' said Bernadette calmly. She opened the refrigerator and took out a large bottle of coke.

'Mum, don't you care?' Buelah pulled at her arm. 'She's leaving us. She's so-so mean.' Buelah burst into tears.

Bernadette turned around and hugged Buelah. 'You wanna know what I t'ink? I t'ink it's de best t'ing fe everyone. Surely you can see dat everyt'ing here would remind Sian of Lisa. Right now she feeling well guilty. Every time she look out of her bedroom window, every face, every voice in the street feel like a pointed finger sayin' you wasn't dere for you best friend. You was only lookin' out fe you'self. If it carries on, Sian might get real depressed.'

'But—'

'Come on, Buelah. She not like you. You talk to me or God if you have a problem, you full of life, you a good little girl. Sian was never so close to me and she only really had Lisa to talk to. She's always been too serious about life and keep her problems bottle up. I'm worried about her.'

'But when would she be back and why can't I go too?'

'Buelah, don't be silly. You gonna pay for you'self? Me cyan afford to pay for you. Sian gonna go to Jamaica and stay wid me parents. They so old they couldn't cope with both of you. As to how long, who knows? How long is a piece of string?'

They looked up to see Sian in the doorway. Buelah gave Sian a dirty look and shoved past her angrily.

'I thought she'd calmed down,' sighed Sian, looking after her.

Bernadette kissed her teeth in exasperation and struck the surface of the sideboard.

'Sian, is times like dis I feel like give you a clap roun' de ear hole. You can't see what is troub'ling Buelah. You is so damn blind when it is as clear as daylight to me. How you so stupid? Sit down.' They sat down at the small kitchen table.

'You and Lisa were so close, right from de start

340

when I met June in de toddler class and we realized we live so close. We share de babysitting. June was on her own then and I was with your fader so I used to help her out when she went to work. You kids hit it off right from the start. I think because Lisa was so pretty and lively, she kinda ate up all your attention, so when Buelah came along, it was like you already had a sister.'

'I love B more than anything!'

'But look at it from her point of view. You told Lisa all your deepest secrets. You shut Buelah out of your room. How many places did you ever take Buelah when Lisa didn't come too?'

Sian looked down.

'Buelah was always jealous of Lisa and the closeness you shared. I guess with Lisa dead she hoped that there was opportunity for her to take away some of de pain by becoming as much of a friend to you as Lisa was.'

'That's horrible.'

'No. It's beautiful. Buelah could have been glad Lisa was gone but she wasn't. She's always been too sweet and kind for any of dat. She offered you de hand of friendship and you bite it off by telling her you leaving.'

'I thought you were on my side!'

'I am, honey. I t'ink you should go away, but not for de reasons you t'ink. I know, Sian. You want to run, to escape. You feel guilty and responsible. You shouldn't feel like dat, dear. You've done nothing wrong. You a good girl dat just got lost somewhere on de road. I don't want you to run away. I want you to go to Jamaica.' Bernadette patted Sian's hand. 'Find your four corners. You've lost dem, Sian, confused by you fancy friends and you new life. De devil been working his brain on you but he won't win. Find out where you been and where you is going. Who you have loved and where you heart is now.'

Sian sat silently looking down at her hands.

'Now come on, Sian. I must tek' this food I make over de church hall. You coming?'

Sian shook her head. 'Not right now,' she said. 'I'd like to spend sometime remembering Lisa on my own first.'

'Yes, dear. Come over when you good and ready.' Bernadette walked out of the kitchen and Sian heard the heavy creaks as her mother climbed the stairs. She stood up and went to the kitchen window. She parted the net curtain and looked out. There was Lisa's block. The landing where they used to play. There was Mr Singh's shop where they would meet Vanya, Ebela and Tiffany and talk about who was dating who on the Rise Estate and alongside the shop, the wall where the boys would sit wearing designer caps with the labels hanging out and smoke. Nothing had changed. It was the same world. Everything was where it should be. Sian let the curtain drop. Everything except Lisa. Lisa was gone for ever.

chapter
thirty

Sian took her phone card out of its plastic wrapping as she waited in the departure lounge for a free payphone. She looked nervously at the large clock. She didn't have much time before her flight left. Finally the man using the phone finished his call and walked away. Sian took the receiver off its hook and quickly dialled Pearce's number.

'Hello.'

'Hi, Pearce, it's Sian.'

'Hey, how are you? I was getting a little worried.'

'I'm fine. I just wanted to say sorry about the other day. It really meant a lot to me, you being there.'

'Look, I understand. I'm just glad to hear from you. I figured you'd need some space.'

A loudspeaker announced the imminent departure of Sian's flight.

'Where are you?'

'I'm at the airport, Pearce.'

Pearce gave a low whistle.

'I'm going to Jamaica for a while. I'll be staying with my grandparents. I need to get out of here.'

'So this is when you tell me – at the airport?'

'Come on, Pearce, it's no big deal. The single's had its run. There are only a couple of minor interviews left and no recording for a while. I'm just supposed to be writing some new songs. And as for the follow-up single—'

'Fuck the follow-up single. I'm talking about *you*. What are you running away from, Sian?'

'Everything.'

'Me included?'

'Maybe.'

'We should have talked about this.'

'What's the point of talking? Some things don't need to be said. Just remember, Pearce, you're not the only one with problems.'

Sian hung up and hurried towards the boarding gate.

Sian felt tired and disorientated as she left the plane at Kingston airport. All the people rushing around, talking loudly, some laughing, some shouting confused her. She felt dizzy. By the time Sian found her large suitcase all the porters were busy. She slowly made her way towards the exit. Sian stood outside the Arrivals doors and scanned the sea of faces.

'Lawd, God, Shawn. Shawn!' Sian turned in the direction of the shouts and saw her grandmother waving vigorously. She was standing next to her grandfather. With difficulty, Sian made her way across the crowded hallway. Her grandfather took the suitcase while her grandmother showered her with kisses and hugs.

They eventually reached an old beige Toyota in the

airport car park. Sian relaxed in the back seat, unable to shake off the dizzy feeling, answering as best she could her grandmother's quick-fire questions. Had Buelah grown much? Were they all still going to church? Was Sian still singing in the church choir? Had Bernadette met a nice man yet? How was Aunt Cherry coping with Slick? How was Sian's music going? Sian almost laughed out loud. They were treating her like a child. She closed her eyes and inhaled the warm damp evening air.

The drive through Kingston's chaotic city centre was slow. Crowds of workers still lined the dusty roads waiting for buses or taxis to take them home. After leaving Kingston it was a long drive, up lonely roads with little light except for the car headlights. As her grandmother's questions ceased, Sian was left to her own thoughts and the cloud of misery that had temporarily lifted now enveloped her in its entirety.

Sian rubbed her eyes. It was so bright. She lay there looking up at the white ceiling, not quite sure of where she was at first. She thought back to the funeral. The grey skies and the plethora of black hats and black coats. But now, Sian sat up, all was light. She could hear insects chirruping. The sunshine darted in through the chinks in the wooden shutters. She got out of bed. There were sounds outside but no one appeared to be in the bungalow. She walked through the living room to the kitchen where the door was wide open and descended the stone steps into the back yard. The ground was hot underneath her bare feet. The sun blazed down. Her grandfather's feet protruded from the underbelly of a blue Datsun. Her grandmother shouted words of encouragement as she sat by the cellar door, peeling cacao beans onto a large square plastic sheet. When she saw Sian, she grinned toothlessly.

'Ahhh, she ah wake up now.'

'Yes. What's Grandad doing?'

'Him fixing dat ol' piece of tin can car fe one of him wutless friends,' her grandmother raised her voice, 'when he should be building a new garden fence!'

'What are you doing, Gran?'

'Making choc'lit, dahling.'

'Why?'

'To drink. Why else?'

'Oh.'

'You feel better, dear?'

'Yeah, I guess. I had a good sleep.'

'Me know you had a good sleep. Unno sleep for two whole days.' Her grandparents laughed together. In the heat their aged cacklings sounded like dry twigs splitting in an open fire. Her grandmother stood up, brushing the empty shells off her skirt. 'We t'ought you was sick. Runnin' a fever an' all.'

'I didn't feel too good when I got here.'

'We even call de doctor,' called her grandfather from underneath the car.

'De doctor say is a bad chill you catch. De doctor leave de antibiotics an' say you jus' sleep it out.'

'I don't remember any of this.' Sian stretched out her arms and yawned. 'I can smell the sea,' she said.

'Well, if you turn lef' an' walk down to de bottom of de hill you find de beach.'

'Ooh, a beach,' said Sian. 'That sounds good.'

'If you turn right an' keep goin' you come to the

Hi-Lo shopping mall and furder up, de libry, de movie and de market and den, uuh Dulcie,' Sleeper said, rolling out from underneath the car. He stood up, a short round man with Bernadette's ebony complexion and quiet eyes. He wiped his oily hands on his blue overall. 'What else can de poor chile do roun' here?'

'Don't bodder to get Shawn t'ings fe do, for me nuh want her to get into no trouble,' warned Dulcie with a disapproving look at Sleeper's grimy clothes. 'And tek dat shirt off before you step inna de house.'

'Well, don't worry about me,' Sian said. 'I'll just go down the hill and look around on my own.'

'I'll take you, Shawn, once you better,' said Dulcie. 'But now I'd better make you some breakfas' while de choc'lit dry out.'

Sian walked up to Dulcie and bent down. 'You cut your hair. It used to be so long.'

'Of course. Is too hot for any of dat out here,' she said with a girlish laugh and a dismissive wave with her wrinkled hand. 'But look at you, Shawn. Out here in your shift fe' all de worl' to see! Go in and bade before de water finish.'

The bungalow was light and carpeted. Large ceiling fans whirred quietly creating a faint breeze that wafted from room to room. Sian bathed and then went into her bedroom to dress.

'Did de water cut out?' asked Dulcie as she put a plate of just-fried dumplings, plantain and bacon in front of Sian.

'No. It was fine. I'm not going to finish all this, Gran.'

'Jus' eat what you can. You look as dough you could put on a couple pounds.'

347

'I'm not skinny, Gran,' said Sian. 'I'm willowy.'

Dulcie snorted. 'Me never see willowy, but me see plenty cockroach with more body dan you,' she said, chuckling as she left the kitchen.

Sian examined her arms self-consciously before she tucked into her breakfast.

'Well, Sian, you been here for near a week and not moved from dis verandah,' said Dulcie, coming out onto the porch. She walked down onto the lawn in her straw hat and flat brown Jesus sandals and squinted up at the sunny sky. 'You feel like a walk down de Hi-Lo?'

'Oh yes, Gran. I'm feeling a lot better,' Sian said, getting up from the chair. 'I'd love to look around. Let's go.'

Dulcie grinned at Sian. 'Well, you not goin' out barefoot.' She pointed to Sian's feet and giggled. 'Go put some sandals on.'

When Sian returned to the porch. Dulcie checked inside her little wheeled trolley for her handbag and then they began to walk down the hill towards the Hi-Lo.

Suddenly Sian was startled by a dog barking ferociously from behind the confines of a high steel fence. The house the dog was protecting had just been built. Its cream walls loomed high with a colonnade on the ground floor and a bay-shaped first-floor balcony that jutted out over the main entrance.

'That's Bernadette's dream house,' said Sian with a sigh. 'She wants a first-floor verandah just like that one where she can watch the sun set over de Caribbean.'

'Yes, I've heard is English people who buy it. Property changing hand so fast these days in Jamaica. Prices are going t'ru de roof. Before you look roun' the price gon up an extra fifty t'ousand dollars.'

They carried on down the stony path, past leafy hedges and sweet-scented flowers. A small furry creature shot out from one side of the path and plunged into some wild bushes on the other side.

'What was that? There aren't any monkeys in Jamaica.'

'No, it just a mongoose,' said Dulcie with a laugh. 'Look at you, so fast to chase it and it nuttin' more dan a flying rat.'

'Well, I've never seen anything that looked like that before,' explained Sian, as they stood to one side to let a car pass.

'That's de beauty of it. No noisy car, no crowd of people in de street. Jus' sunshine and de odd church convention,' Dulcie said smiling.

'Oh, church conventions. Gee, get the party hats out. I've been to enough church conventions to last me a lifetime.'

Dulcie chuckled good-naturedly. 'Don't let Sleeper hear you talk like dat. Sometimes I'd rather stay at home meself but dat man love him convention.'

They carried on walking.

'So how your bad cousin, Slick?'

'What do you mean bad? Slick is lovely.'

'Slick!' Dulcie snorted. 'Now what kind of name is dat? His mudder give him a perfickly good name. Hernist, but no, him must find a way to twis' it up. His name shouldn't even be Slick, it should be Slack. That bwoy so lazy and good-fe'-nuttin'. All him do is smoke weed and drink brew all day. Me never see him wid a job more than say t'ree weeks.'

'There's nothing wrong with Slick. He just needs to try a little harder. He's not bad.'

'He a weed-seller!'

'Maybe so, but he's still kind and crazy and fun. I wouldn't change him for anyone else. Slick has been there for me.'

Dulcie kissed her teeth. 'You young people always stick togedder.'

The following evening as the sun was turning pink and gold Sian sat down on the rocking chair on the front verandah. She watched a group of girls burst out of one of the houses opposite and erupt onto the quiet street. They began playing tag, chasing each other up and down the road in their neat brown and yellow pinafores, screaming with laughter. It brought back bittersweet memories and Sian turned away to see her grandfather watching her from the doorway in his dusty jeans.

'Hi, Grandad,' she said, managing a smile. 'You checking up on me?'

He looked faintly embarrassed.

'No. Me never check. Me jus' interest in what you doin'.'

'Just watching the world go by.'

'I'm sorry. You must want to go here, go dere and jus' me and Dulcie aroun' too ole and sceered to do anyt'ing you young people would wan' do. We jus' go ah church and maybe visit a few people. That's it.'

'I said don't worry,' Sian said easily.

Her grandfather's forehead still had a deep crease of

concern. 'If you like we could walk down to de beach,' he offered.

'Oh, I don't know. How's your back?'

'Nuttin' wrong wid' me back,' he said defensively.

'I remember Granny telling Mum that—'

'Is jus' Dulcie wid' her foolishness. My back is like a rock. Next t'ing she'll be telling people that me dead!'

Sian laughed. 'OK then, I'd love to go.'

Her grandfather led the way out of the front garden and down a road that wound its way to the beach at the bottom of the hill. It was fringed with tall trees so Sian couldn't see the beach until they were almost upon it.

'Wow, it's so beautiful,' she exclaimed as they reached the bottom of the hill. The white sand stretched out before them, met by the blue waves that gently lapped the shore. Sian kicked off her sandals and picked them up in her hands as they walked along the beach slowly. 'Why aren't there more people here?'

'Well dis not really a tourist area an' school holidays done finish so de locals would only come down on weekends.'

'Oh, I'm coming every day from now on,' said Sian with a sigh. 'I can't believe it's right at the bottom of your road.'

'Tell me what Buelah gettin' up to dese days,' said Sleeper. 'I haven seen dat lickle pick'ny in how long?'

Sian linked her arm through her grandfather's. 'Well, she's almost twelve now. She's started secondary school. She's very smart and is already taking care of Mum, better than I did.'

'You've done very well.' Sleeper squeezed Sian's arm. 'Buy your mam furniture for de house – you t'ink

351

we never know about how well you're doing with your singing. Bernadette tell us all about it. We so proud ah you.'

'It's just things, Grandad. Lots of times when I could've been there for her, for Mum, I was doing my own thing, wrapped up in my own life. But Buelah is always there, always there for everyone. Sometimes I think I let us down. All of us. Especially my friend Lisa. I could've made a difference. I know I could – but . . .' Her voice trailed off and she blinked away the tears that suddenly welled up.

Sleeper took off his cap, wiped his sweaty forehead then fitted the cap firmly back on. He thought for a moment.

'Look, how would you like it if I took you into town tomorrow? We could have a talk.'

'Only if you're sure your back won't give out. I'd never forgive myself.'

'Hey, me back fine. Tough like tree trunk,' said Sleeper indignantly. Sian threw her arms around his neck.

'I love you, Grandad. You're the best.'

He hugged her back. 'So are you, Sian. You de best. De best granddaughter anyone could want!'

chapter
thirty one

The next day, Sleeper drove with Sian up the narrow road leading towards the nearby town. Some ten minutes later he parked the Toyota in the Hi-Lo car park. They walked into the local newsagents and Sleeper bought the day's paper. Then they went into the hardware store where Sleeper bought a measuring tape.

'What's that for?' asked Sian.

'Oh, Dulcie's new fence. She not gonna let me forget 'bout dat long as she have breat' in her body.'

They got back in the car and drove further into town. Eventually they stopped outside a bar with a blue corrugated-iron roof and coloured bulbs strung along the front.

'Feel like a drink?' asked Sleeper with a wink.

'Yeah,' said Sian, looking over at the painted wooden sign hanging from the roof that read 'Joe's Yard'. 'It's been so hot today I couldn't say no to a cold drink. But Dulcie won't like it.'

'We keep it a secret.' Sleeper smiled sheepishly. 'Jus'

you an' me, Sian. Keep it outta dat ol' woman ear an' we home free.'

They laughed and got out of the car.

Inside, several old men were sitting around the wooden bar, intently watching a cricket match on an old television on a wall stand above the bar.

'Well, if it nuh me ol' frien', Sleeper,' said the wizened barman looking up in surprise. The other men turned around and stared inquisitively at Sian. Sleeper nodded to the men in greeting as he walked up to the bar.

'Hello, Joe,' said Sleeper, grinning. 'How you keepin'?'

The barman held out his hand and Sleeper slapped it.

'Not as good as you,' said Joe with a nod in Sian's direction. He laughed. 'Me jus' cool, man. Joe's Yard still standin'.'

'It lookin' better wid' de lights on the roof outside. And de air conditioning a good idea,' said Sleeper, looking up at the whirring fan. 'It used to get hot like de devil backyard in here.' He leaned on the counter and sighed. 'Lawd. It's been too long. Me never taste a whisky in months.'

Joe nodded. 'So Dulcie finally let you gwaan free?' They chuckled.

'Not quite,' said Sleeper, pulling Sian forward. 'Here me excuse. Me beautiful granddaughter Shawn come all de way from Englan' jus' to have a drink wid her crusty ol' grandad.'

'Yes, she sure is beautiful,' said Joe, offering Sian his

hand. She shook it, smiling shyly. 'And what can I get de beautiful lady from foreign?'

'Hmm.' Sian looked at the array of bottles lined up on the wall behind the bar. 'I'll have a Southern Comfort and Coke, please,' said Sian.

'Right,' said Joe. 'One Southern Comfort and one Jack Daniels for you, Sleeper, just like in de ol' days?'

Sleeper nodded. 'Make it a big one. Dis drink haffe last me till me granddaughter next visit.'

Joe guffawed loudly as Sleeper pointed Sian to a small table away from the bar. Sian sat down as Sleeper paid for the drinks and brought them over.

'So what you gonna do now, Sian?' asked Sleeper after thirstily sampling his large whisky.

'I dunno, Grandad,' Sian replied. 'Maybe I'll just stay here for ever.'

'No, Sian. It is not a joking t'ing. You have a bright future waiting you. You is a singer, you have a sister and mum dat loves you. Is all right for me and Dulcie to spend our days on de verandah watching de worl' go by. We ol' and brock-down. We not goin' anywhere.'

Sian sighed heavily. 'I don't feel like I have anywhere to go either.'

'Look, Sian. Me an' Dulcie love having you here. It so nice to have someone young and pretty in de house again. I jus' don't want you to lose what you have.'

'What is it that I have that's so wonderful? My singing?'

'Dat too, but I don't mean money or career. When Bernie was about your age, I sit her down. I tell her, "Chile, dere's t'ings more important den money or career. Dere's de people dat you love an' de people dat love you."'

'Yeah, the four corners talk,' said Sian. 'I've heard it.'

'Well, dese *are* de best t'ings in life, Sian,' insisted Sleeper. 'And you not gonna find dem lyin' on de beach.'

'Well, my best friend's dead,' said Sian miserably. 'My sister hates me. The man I have feelings for doesn't want to know. If those are the best things in my life, I might as well be dead too 'cos it feels like nothing good is ever going to happen again.'

Sleeper took another sip of whisky before answering.

'Bad t'ings happen but dat is part of life,' he said. 'You t'ink Bernie never see bad t'ings? You t'ink Cherry never see bad t'ings? Come to dat, you t'ink a crusty ol' fool man like me never see bad t'ings? I seen more bad t'ings den anyone, but in dis life when you get beat down you get up. You t'ank God an' you start again. It nuh matter what Him tek' away. It nuh matter if when you get up you don't have a dollar in your han' or a frien' in de worl'. T'ank God for de breat' in your body an' de sun in de sky and start again.'

Sian was quiet for a long time, looking into her glass. Eventually she leaned across the small wooden table and kissed Sleeper on the cheek, tears in her eyes.

'I know you mean well, Grandad.'

Sleeper smiled kindly. 'All me sayin', Sian, is doan waste you life here. Decide what you gotta do, then do it.'

*

When they got back to the house, Dulcie was in the kitchen by the cooker, slowly stirring a bubbling swirl of sliced onions, diced red peppers, saltfish and small yellow puffs of ackee. She looked at Sleeper disapprovingly. He raised his eyebrows at Sian, then sat down at the kitchen and began reading his paper.

Dulcie banged the spoon down on the worktop and turned around.

'Sleeper, why did I jus' get a telephone call from Sister Margaret telling me she see you in Joe's bar when she pass by town today?'

'Me nuh know,' muttered Sleeper uncomfortably. He hiccuped loudly and covered his mouth quickly.

'Then *me* will tell you why I jus' get dat telephone call. Is because you *was* dere!'

'Now why would you be listenin' to an ol' dryhead busybody woman like Sister Margaret?'

'Sister Margaret is not an ol' dryhead busybody woman. Sister Margaret is de Pastor wife!'

'Well, she dryhead sameway,' said Sleeper. 'And busybody,' he added with a chuckle. Dulcie left the cooker. She circled the kitchen table slowly, coming to a stop just behind Sleeper's chair. He scratched his neck uncomfortably.

'You *drunk*, Sleeper,' said Dulcie angrily. 'I can smell you breat' a mile away.' She returned to the cooker grumbling. 'Sick man like you, drinking yourself inna de grave.'

'Oh, stop you noise, woman,' said Sleeper good-naturedly.

'Who you tellin' stop? I gwine tell you exactly what

I t'ink of you an' you drunk self. I gwine tell you mornin', noon an' night. Drinking. In front of de Pastor wife too!' She threw her hands up in the air. 'Lawd have mercy.'

Dulcie crossed the room and opened the cupboard door. She screamed. 'Ah, watch dat big cockroach, sitting inside de cupboard, jus' waiting to rush out.' She reached for one of Sleeper's shoes and began chasing it.

Sian and Sleeper laughed.

'Yes, laugh after me, Sleeper,' snapped Dulcie as she finally caught and squashed the cockroach. 'But me not gonna end up in Kingston hospital with de flies to feed 'pon my back.'

'Jus' cool, Dulcie,' said Sleeper. 'If you had unno way, me couldn't even leave de house. Anyway, today I buy de measuring tape fe' de garden fence. Me gonna mek a start on it in de morning.'

'Don't try fe' sweeten me wid measurin' tape,' said Dulcie, putting her hands on her hips. 'Look how long me ask you to see about de garden fence. Nearly t'ree months now.'

'Well, me cyan jus' *build* a fence. Me needed to t'ink of a good plan.' Sleeper winked at Sian. 'It was a very *pretty* fence me wanted.'

Dulice still looked cross but she walked over to the kitchen table and sat down. 'What kind of pretty fence?' she demanded.

'A white picket fence,' said Sleeper, demonstrating with his hands. 'A pretty fence for me pretty wife.'

Dulcie snorted. 'Dat sound like drink talkin' to me.' She stood up and gave Sleeper a doubtful look. 'Drink and dyam foolishness,' she said again. But a smile crept across her face as she returned to the hissing saucepan and she hummed softly as she stirred.

Sleeper looked over at Sian and gave her the thumbs-up. Sian stood up laughing. She left the kitchen and made her way out onto the verandah. She sat down in the rocking chair and closed her eyes. The Southern Comfort, combined with the heat, had made her feel sleepy.

'Me can come play?' asked a soft sing-song voice from beyond the verandah. Sian opened her eyes and looked around but couldn't see anyone.

'I can't play with someone I can't see,' she called.

A halo of fuzz then two gleaming eyes appeared above the low brick wall at the edge of the verandah and finally a little girl scampered up the path leading to the verandah.

'You're a pretty girl,' said Sian, smiling as she stood up. 'What's your name?'

'My name is Lorella.'

'Oh, that's very pretty. My name is Sian.'

'You wanna play ball?' Lorella asked, producing a soft pink and yellow bouncing ball.

'Sure, come on in.'

Lorella walked onto the verandah. 'You English?'

'Yes. I'm staying with my grandad and grandma.'

'Whey your grandmudder?'

'Oh, she's inside.'

'My grandmudder give me ice-cream. Does yours?'

'Only if I'm very, very good,' said Sian laughing.

They played catch for a while, throwing the ball at each other until they became tired and Sian sat back down in the chair.

'Do you know any clap?' asked Lorella, sitting on Sian's lap.

'I do but it's an English one.'

'Oh please. Me wanna learn de English clap,' said Lorella excitedly. 'Teach me.'

'What do you know about English clap?' asked Sian with a grin. She ruffled Lorella's plaits.

'Oh, I know ev'ryt'ing 'bout Englan'. My cousin and antie live a Englan' and my mama go a Englan' ev'ry weekend,' Lorella informed Sian proudly.

'*Every* weekend?' said Sian, trying to keep a straight face. 'That's a lot of holidays.'

'Ev'ry weekend,' Lorella insisted. 'And she says when I's seven, I can go too.'

'All right then, stand up.'

Lorella clambered off Sian's lap. She stood on her short chubby legs. Sian scooted forward to the edge of the chair. They began clapping.

' "My name's Elizabeth Taylor, I'm a movie star. I've got a cute, cute figure and a sexy bra." Now wiggle your hips like this. "Elizabeth, Elizabeth, ooh ahh! Elizabeth, Elizabeth, ooh ahh!" '

Lorella clapped her hands and jumped around excitedly.

'Again, again.'

' "My name's Elizabeth Taylor, I'm a movie star." '
A blue ramshackle pick-up truck pulled up at the end of the street and a man got out.

' "I've got a cute, cute figure and a sexy bra." '

There was the sound of loud laughter, oddly familiar. Sian, distracted, glanced over her shoulder.

'"Elizabeth, Elizabeth, ooh ahh!"' In a great cloud of dust the van drove off.

'"Elizabeth, Elizabeth, ooh ahh!"' The man squinted at the house numbers as he carried a small suitcase down the street.

Sian slowly got to her feet. She shook off the little girl tugging at her shorts and ran out into the street. She stood on the hard sun-baked stone, staring as the man walked up to her and dropped his bag at her feet.

'Is that all you can do, Sian? I've nearly been kidnapped by some crazy cab driver at the airport. Ended up down in goodness knows where. Had to walk five miles in thirty-eight-degree sunshine before anyone would give me a ride and all just to tell you that I agree.'

Sian looked at him blankly.

'You're right,' he said with a smile. 'Everyone has their problems. What I guess I'm trying to say, Sian, is that you're the best thing in my life right now and I'd like to keep it that way, if that's all right with you.'

Sian looked up at the candy blue sky and laughed.

'I'm a recovering alcoholic,' Pearce continued. 'With a poisonous soon-to-be-ex-wife, looking to develop a meaningful relationship with a certain genuinely talented singer. You're the only person I've met who seems to fit the profile. Frankly I need a break.' Pearce looked at Sian with a twinkle in his eyes. 'What do you say?'

'Let's do it,' said Sian, stepping over the suitcase.

'Deal?'

'Deal.'